Prize Stories 1973:
THE O. HENRY AWARDS

Prize Stories 1973:

THE O. HENRY AWARDS

Edited and with an Introduction by

WILLIAM ABRAHAMS

Doubleday & Company, Inc., Garden City, New York
1973

ISBN: 0-385-06693-7
Library of Congress Catalog Card Number 21–9372
Copyright © 1973 by Doubleday & Company, Inc.
All Rights Reserved
Printed in the United States of America
First Edition

CONTENTS

PUBLISHER'S NOTE

This volume is the fifty-third in the O. Henry Memorial Award series.

In 1918, the Society of Arts and Sciences met to vote upon a monument to the master of the short story, O. Henry. They decided that this memorial should be in the form of two prizes for the best short stories published by American authors in American magazines during the year 1919. From this beginning, the memorial developed into an annual anthology of outstanding short stories by American authors published, with the exception of the years 1952 and 1953, by Doubleday & Company, Inc.

Blanche Colton Williams, one of the founders of the awards, was editor from 1919 to 1932; Harry Hansen from 1933 to 1940; Herschel Brickell from 1941 to 1951. The annual collection did not appear in 1952 and 1953, when the continuity of the series was interrupted by the death of Herschel Brickell, who had been the editor for ten years. Paul Engle was editor from 1954 to 1959 with Hanson Martin co-editor in the years 1954 to 1956; Mary Stegner in 1960; Richard Poirier from 1961 to 1966, with assistance from and co-editorship with William Abrahams from 1964 to 1966. William Abrahams became editor of the series in 1967.

Doubleday also publishes *First-Prize Stories from the O. Henry Memorial Awards* in editions which are brought up to date at intervals. In 1970 Doubleday also published under Mr. Abrahams's editorship, *Fifty Years of the American Short Story,* a collection of stories selected from the series.

The stories chosen for this volume were published in the period from the summer of 1971 to the summer of 1972. A list of the magazines consulted appears at the back of the book. The choice of stories and the selection of prize winners are exclusively the responsibility of the editor. Biographical material is based on information provided by the contributors.

INTRODUCTION

"Who reads short stories?" In a long, thoughtful, and heartening review of last year's collection in the *New Republic,* Stanley Kauffmann raised the question, and argued that "A case might be made that fiction in magazines is even less thoroughly read than poetry, and that's getting pretty low."

Such a case might indeed be made, and I fear it is being made use of by editors eager to reserve more space for informative articles and attractive artwork at the expense of fiction that "nobody reads anyway." But even presuming that editors were willing to crowd their pages with fiction, a reader who followed the practice of "sampling" or reading at random would have reason to grow discouraged. Most of the stories he would encounter would be no more likely to rise above the level of the merely pedestrian than do contemporary novels, or verse, or the so-called new "creative non-fiction." Yet some do; some rise even to the level of art; it is for those uncommon stories that one reads, and I would like to think that it is a selection of those that I have brought together here.

At the end of each year's O. Henry volume there is a list of magazines consulted. It includes any magazine that publishes stories, whatever its editorial bent or auspices, that sends copies to the editor. The list has tended, over the past decade, to run between eighty-five and a hundred each year. Of that number— ranging from the ephemeral to the long-established, from magazines claiming a readership in the millions to those making do with the happy few—more than a third have been represented in one or another of the O. Henry volumes. In the four most recent collections, there have been stories from *The Antioch Review, The Atlantic, Audience, The Carleton Miscellany, Epoch, Esquire, Four Quarters, Harper's, The Hudson Review, The Iowa Review, Kansas Quarterly, The Kenyon Review, McCall's, The*

Massachusetts Review, New American Review, The New Yorker, The North American Review, Playboy, The Paris Review, Partisan Review, Redbook, The Sewanee Review, The Southern Review, Transatlantic Review, Tri-Quarterly, The Virginia Quarterly Review, and *Vagabond.* An impressively varied group—but it would be misleading to argue from it, therefore, that good stories are in ample supply, and to be found everywhere. My own conclusion is quite opposite: that the good story is an uncommon occurrence, and one never knows where it may occur, which adds to the pleasure and difficulty of the quest.

For all the differences between them in subject matter and style, the eighteen stories in the present collection are alike in at least two particulars: none, I feel safe in saying, has been written to order, or to a formula, or with an eye on editorial taboos, restrictions and preferences; each expresses a vision of life and art that is personal to its author. And this is as true for writers as famous as Joyce Carol Oates, Bernard Malamud, and John Cheever (whose stories, even if unsigned, would be unmistakably theirs), as it is for writers as little known for the moment as Henry Bromell and Randall Reid, both of whom are represented here by their first published stories.

There is perhaps one other quality common to all these stories: an uninhibited acceptance by their authors of what has to be written. None conforms to stereotypes or textbook definitions of "the story," simply for fear of breaking "rules," or violating canons of "good taste." If rules are to be broken, or if the indecorous word be spoken, so be it. These authors, unsensationally and without the self-approbation and preening that in the past have distinguished (extinguished?) so much experimental writing are prepared to strike out in new directions—as in Mr. Reid's "Detritus," where the story, invisible at first, grows out of a loosely organized sequence of aphorisms and pensées by a latter-day Don Giovanni awaiting the arrival of the Commendatore—or to return to the most traditional forms and symbols, as in Mr. Malamud's "Talking Horse," another of his anthropomorphic fables to take its place beside "The Jew Bird," so comic in its immediate fanciful detail, so painful in its cumulative realistic burden, of a man in a horse—literally so!—desperate to break out of the prison of the flesh.

There is hardly one of these eighteen stories that mightn't have appeared with equal appropriateness in any number of other magazines than the one that in fact published it. Which is to say—and I think it is a point worth calling attention to—that the lines of distinction are being increasingly blurred, that it is increasingly difficult to define "a typical story" for any given magazine. Nor can one any longer identify, as one could until fairly recently, a writer with a particular magazine. In this respect, the publishing history of Joyce Carol Oates—whose emergence as a writer of short stories is one of the most remarkable events of the past literary decade—proves highly instructive. "The Dead," to which I have awarded First Prize this year, is the eleventh story by Miss Oates to be chosen for the O. Henry annual, beginning with "The Fine White Mist of Winter" in *Prize Stories 1963*. These eleven stories were first published in eleven different magazines, in a spectrum from *The Literary Review* to *McCall's*. Miss Oates's most recent collection, *Marriages and Infidelities,* contains twenty-four stories drawn from twenty-two different magazines. (Two of the stories were first published in *The Atlantic,* and two in *Shenandoah.*) While there may well be a recognizably "Oatesian" story, there is certainly no magazine that can be described as the one where one looks for a story by Joyce Carol Oates.

Admittedly, Miss Oates's publishing history has its special aspects; even so, I think it encouraging for serious writers of short stories in general. The cool attitude (when not downright hostile) of editors toward fiction, and the indifference toward it of a good part of the magazine reading audience, as Stanley Kauffmann suggests, means that writers are left pretty much to themselves, freed from any expectations and preconceptions but their own as they begin to write. It is true that the old-fashioned commodity producers, of the sort who crowded the pages of so many large-circulation magazines now defunct, would be having a hard time of it had they not shrewdly followed their some-time readers into the newer technologies. But the story in America at the present time, insofar as one may generalize, thrives in its apparent neglect, perhaps even because of it.

There is a further, exemplary aspect of Miss Oates's career upon which I should like to comment. It was as a writer of stories that she began her career in the early 1960s, and she has continued to write stories ever since, not as a diversion or spin-off from the writing of her novels, essays, poems and plays, but as a central concern in her work: a fortunate recognition that the shorter form is peculiarly suited to her. At their best, her stories reach a level of achievement that sets her impressively apart. There is a sense of tension, of nerves stretched to the breaking point, of "the pitch that is close to madness" in much of what she writes. Sustained too long, it would lose its emotional effectiveness and intellectual credibility. As it is, a story such as "The Dead," which tells with the utmost conviction of a young woman writer going gradually to pieces, is not only harrowing to read, but unfaltering in its control, written as close to the edge as possible without crossing over. Ilena, whose story it is, in her pill-sweetened descent from husband to lover to lover, even in the blankness of her final, incommunicable despair, is all too recognizably what she is—a casualty, not only of marriage, but of the decade that began in assassination and is ending in a seemingly never-ending war, whose strains and pressures find a counterpart in her own deterioration. She is the most deeply realized and truly felt of the characters Miss Oates has yet chosen to write about, or perhaps one should say, responding to the sense in her work of an irresistible compulsion, the characters who have chosen her to write about them.

I run the risk of having said more about "The Dead" than a prospective reader might want, and I will refrain from comment on the other stories in this year's collection. Part of the pleasure of reading (and rereading) one's contemporaries is in making discoveries of one's own.

Here then are eighteen American short stories. To avoid misunderstandings, I repeat a point I have made in the past: "Logically, and by custom, the First, Second, and Third Prize stories lead off the collection. Thereafter, the stories are arranged in an order that is meant to show them to best advantage . . . There is no question of relative rank or merit: none is intended and none should be inferred from a story's place in the table of contents."

WILLIAM ABRAHAMS

Prize Stories 1973:
THE O. HENRY AWARDS

Joyce Carol Oates has written many short stories, poems, and several novels, her most recent of which is *Wonderland*. In 1970 she won the National Book Award for Fiction with her novel *them*. She has recently published *The Edge of Impossibility*, a collection of critical essays, and *Marriages and Infidelities*, a volume of short stories. Miss Oates was born near Lockport, New York; she received her B.A. from Syracuse University and her M.A. from the University of Wisconsin. She is an Associate Professor of English at the University of Windsor in Windsor, Ontario.

THE DEAD

Useful in acute and chronic depression, where accompanied by anxiety, insomnia, agitation; psychoneurotic states manifested by tension, apprehension, fatigue. . . . They were small yellow capsules, very expensive. She took them along with other capsules, green-and-aqua, that did not cost quite so much but were weaker. *Caution against hazardous occupations requiring complete mental alertness.* What did that mean, "complete mental alertness?" Since the decline of her marriage, a few years ago, Ilena thought it wisest to avoid complete mental alertness. That was an overrated American virtue.

For the relief of anxiety and the relief of the apprehension of anxiety: small pink pills. *Advise against ingestion of alcohol.* But she was in the habit of drinking anyway, always before meeting strangers and often before meeting friends, sometimes on perfectly ordinary, lonely days when she expected to meet no one at all. She was fascinated by the possibility that some of these drugs could cause paradoxical reactions—fatigue and intense rage, increase and decrease in libido. She liked paradox. She wondered how the paradoxical reactions could take place in the same body, at the same time. Or did they alternate days? *For the relief of chronic insomnia:* small harmless white barbiturates. In the morning, hurrying out somewhere, she took a handful of mood-elevating pills, swallowed with some hot water right from the faucet, or coffee, to bring about a curious hollow-headed sensation, exactly as if her head were a kind of drum. Elevation! She felt the very air breathed into her lungs suffused with a peculiar dazzling joy, worth every risk.

Adverse reactions were possible: *confusion, ataxia, skin eruptions, edema, nausea, constipation, blood dyscrasias, jaundice, hepatic dysfunction, hallucinations, tremor, slurred speech, hyperexcitement. . . .* But anything was possible, after all!

A young internist said to her, "These tests show that you are normal," and her heart had fallen, her stomach had sunk, her very intestines yearned downward, stricken with gravity. Normal? Could that be? She had stared at him, unbelieving. "The symptoms you mention—the insomnia, for instance—have no organic basis that we can determine," he said.

Then why the trembling hands, why the glitter to the eyes, why, why the static in the head? She felt that she had been cheated. This was not worth sixty dollars, news like this. As soon as she left the doctor's office she went to a water fountain in the corridor and took a few capsules of whatever was in her coat pocket, loose in the pocket along with tiny pieces of lint and something that looked like the flaky skins of peanuts, though she did not remember having put peanuts in any of her pockets. She swallowed one, two, three green-and-aqua tranquillizers, and a fairly large white pill that she didn't recognize, found in the bottom of her purse with a few stray hairs and paper clips. This helped a little. "So I'm normal!" she said.

She had been living at that time in Buffalo, New York, teaching part-time at the university. Buffalo was a compromise between going to California, as her ex-husband begged, and going to New York, where she was probably headed. Her brain burned dryly, urging her both westward and eastward, so she spent a year in this dismal Midwestern city in upstate New York, all blighted elms and dingy skies and angry politicians. The city was in a turmoil of excitement; daily and nightly the city police prowled the university campus in search of troublesome students, and the troublesome students hid in the bushes alongside buildings, eager to plant their homemade time bombs and run; so the campus was not safe for ordinary students or ordinary people at all. Even the "normal," like Ilena, long wearied of political activism, were in danger.

She taught twice a week and the rest of the time avoided the university. She drove a 1965 Mercedes an uncle had willed her, an uncle rakish and remote and selfish, like Ilena herself, who had taken a kind of proud pity on her because of her failed marriage and her guilty listlessness about family ties. The uncle, a judge, had died in St. Louis; she had had to fly there to get the car. The trip back had taken her nearly a week, she had felt so unaccountably lazy and sullen. But, once back in Buffalo, driving her stodgy silver car, its conservative shape protecting her heavily, she felt safe from the noxious street fumes and the darting, excitable eyes of the police and the local Buffalo taxpayers—in spite of her own untidy hair and clothes.

The mood-elevating pills elevated her several feet off the ground and made her stammer rapidly into the near, dim faces of her students, speaking faster and faster in the hope that the class period would end sooner. But the tranquillizers dragged her down, massaged her girlish heart to a dreamy condition, fingered the nerve ends lovingly, soothingly, wanted only to assure her that all was well. In her inherited car she alternately drove too fast, made nervous by the speedier pills, or too slowly, causing warlike sounds from the rear, the honking of other drivers in American cars.

In the last two years Ilena had been moving around constantly: packing up the same clothes and items and unpacking them again, always eager, ready to be surprised, flying from one coast to the other to speak at universities or organizations interested in "literature," hopeful and adventurous as she was met at various windy airports by strangers. Newly divorced, she had felt virginal again, years younger, truly childlike and American. Beginning again. Al-

ways beginning. She had written two quiet novels, each politely
received and selling under one thousand copies, and then she had
written a novel based on an anecdote overheard by her at the
University of Michigan, in a girls' rest room in the library, about
a suicide club and the "systematic deaths of our most valuable
natural resource, our children"—as one national reviewer of the
novel said gravely. It was her weakest novel, but it was widely
acclaimed and landed her on the cover of a famous magazine,
since her *Death Dance* had also coincided with a sudden public
interest in the achievement of women in "male-dominated fields."
Six magazines came out with cover stories on the women's liber-
ation movement inside a three-month period; Ilena's photograph
had been exceptionally good. She found herself famous, and
fame made her mouth ironic and dry with a sleeplessness that was
worse than ever, in spite of her being "normal."

The pills came and went in cycles—the yellow capsules fa-
vored for a while, then dropped for the small pink pills, tranquillizers big enough to nearly knock her out taken with some gin
and lemon, late at night. These concoctions were sacred to her,
always kept secret. Her eyes grew large with the prospect of all
those "adverse reactions" that were threatened but somehow
never arrived. She was lucky, she thought. Maybe nothing adverse
would ever happen to her. She had been twenty-six years old at
the start of the breakup of her marriage; it was then that most of
the pills began, though she had always had a problem with insomnia. The only time she had truly passed out, her brain gone
absolutely black, was the winter day—very late in the afternoon
—when she had been in her office at a university in Detroit, with
a man whom she had loved at that time, and a key had been
thrust in the lock and the door opened—Ilena had screamed,
"No! Go away!" It had been only a cleaning lady, frightened off
without seeing anything, or so the man had assured Ilena. But
she had fainted. Her skin had gone wet and cold; it had taken the
terrified man half an hour to bring her back to normal again.
"Ilena, I love you, don't die," he had begged. Finally she was
calm enough to return to her own home, an apartment she shared
with her husband in the northwestern corner of the city; she went

home, fixed herself some gin and bitter lemon, and stood in the
kitchen drinking it while her husband yelled questions at her.
"Where were you? Why were you gone so long?" She had not
answered him. The drink was mixed up in her memory with the
intense relief of having escaped some humiliating danger, and
the intense terror of the new, immediate danger of her husband's
rage. Why was this man yelling at her? Whom had she married,
that he could yell at her so viciously? The drinking of that gin was
a celebration of her evil.

That was back in 1967; their marriage had ended with the
school year; her husband spent three weeks in a hospital half a
block from his mother's house in Oswego, New York, and Ilena
had not gone to see him, not once, being hard of heart, like stone,
and terrified of seeing him again. She feared his mother, too.
The marriage had been dwindling all during the Detroit years—
1965–1967—and they both left the city shortly before the riot,
which seemed to Ilena, in her usual poetic, hyperbolic, pill-sweetened state, a cataclysmic flowering of their own hatred. She had
thought herself good enough at hating, but her husband was
much better. "Die. Why don't you die. *Die*," he had whispered
hypnotically to her once, as she lay in bed weeping very early
one morning, before dawn, too weary to continue their battle.
Off and on she had spoken sentimentally about having children,
but Bryan was wise enough to dismiss that scornfully—"You
don't bring children into the world to fix up a rotten marriage,"
he said. She had not known it was rotten, exactly. She knew that
he was jealous of her. A mutual friend, a psychiatrist, had told
her gently that her having published two novels—unknown as
they were, and financial failures—was "unmanning" to Bryan,
who wanted to write but couldn't. Was that her fault? What
could she do? "You could fail at something yourself," she was
advised.

In the end she had fallen in love with another man. She had
set out to love someone in order to punish her husband, to revenge herself upon him; but the revenge was forgotten, she had
really fallen in love in spite of all her troubles . . . in love with

a man who turned out to be a disappointment himself, but another kind of disappointment.

Adverse reactions: *confusion, ataxia, skin eruptions, edema, nausea, constipation, blood dyscrasias, jaundice, hepatic dysfunction, hallucinations.* . . . Her eyes filmed over with brief ghostly uninspired hallucinations now and then, but she believed this had nothing to do with the barbiturates she took to sleep, or the amphetamines she took to speed herself up. It was love that wore her out. Love, and the air of Detroit, the gently wafting smoke from the manly smokestacks of factories. Love and smoke. The precise agitation of love in her body, what her lover and her husband did to her body; and the imprecise haze of the air, of her vision, filmed-over and hypnotized. She recalled having loved her husband very much at one time. Before their marriage in 1964. His name was Bryan Donohue, and as his wife she had been *Ilena Donohue,* legally; but a kind of maiden cunning had told her to publish her novels as *Ilena Williams,* chaste Ilena, the name musical with *l*'s. Her books were by that Ilena, while her nights of sleeplessness beside a sleeping, twitching, perspiring man were spent by the other Ilena. At that time she was not famous yet and not quite so nervous. A little insomnia, that wasn't so bad. Many people had insomnia. She feared sleep because she often dreamed of the assassination of Kennedy, which was run and rerun in her brain like old newsreels. Years after that November day she was still fresh with sorrow for him, scornful of her own sentimentality but unable to control it. How she had wept! Maybe she had been in love with Kennedy, a little. . . . So, sleeping brought him back to her not as a man: as a corpse. Therefore she feared sleep. She could lie awake beside a breathing, troubled corpse of her own, her partner in this puzzling marriage, and she rehearsed her final speech to him so many times that it became jaded and corny to her, out of date as a monologue in an Ibsen play.

"There is another man, of course," he said said flatly.

"No. No one."

"Yes, another man."

"No."

"Another man, I know, but I'm not interested. Don't tell me his name."

"There is no other man."

"Obviously there is. Probably a professor at that third-rate school of yours."

"No."

Of course, when she was in the company of the *other man,* it was Bryan who became "the other" to him and Ilena—remote and masculine and dangerous, powerful as a nightmare figure, with every right to embrace Ilena in the domestic quiet of their apartment. He had every right to make love to her, and Gordon did not. They were adulterers, Ilena and Gordon. They lost weight with their guilt, which was finely wrought in them as music, precious and subtle and prized, talked over endlessly. Ilena could see Gordon's love for her in his face. She loved that face, she loved to stroke it, stare at it, trying to imagine it as the face of a man married to another woman. . . . He was not so handsome as her own husband, perhaps. She didn't know. She only knew, bewildered and stunned, that his face was the center of the universe for her, and she could no more talk herself out of this whimsy than she could talk herself out of her sorrow for Kennedy.

Her husband, Bryan Donohue: tall, abrupt, self-centered, amusing, an instructor in radiology at Wayne Medical School, with an interest in jazz and a desire to write articles on science, science and sociology, jazz, jazz and sociology, anything. He was very verbal and he talked excellently, expertly. Ilena had always been proud of him in the presence of other people. He had a sharp, dissatisfied face, with very dark eyes. He dressed well and criticized Ilena when she let herself go, too rushed to bother with her appearance. In those days, disappointed by the low salary and the bad schedule she received as an instructor at a small university in Detroit, Ilena had arrived for early classes—she was given eight-o'clock classes every semester—with her hair barely combed, loose down to her shoulders, snarled and bestial from a night of insomnia, her stockings marred with snags or long disfiguring runs, her face glossy with the dry-mouthed euphoria of tranquillizers, so that, pious and sour, she led her classes in the prescribed ritual prayer—this was a Catholic university, and Ilena had been brought up as a Catholic—and felt freed, once the prayer was finished, of all restraint.

Bad as the eight-o'clock classes were, the late-afternoon classes (4:30–6:00) were worse: the ashes of the day, tired undergraduates who needed this course to fill out their schedules, high-school teachers—mainly nuns and "brothers"—who needed a few more credits for their Master's degrees, students who worked, tired unexplained strangers with rings around their eyes of fatigue and boredom and the degradation of many semesters as "special students." When she was fortunate enough to have one or two good students in these classes, Ilena charged around in excitement, wound up by the pills taken at noon with black coffee, eager to draw them out into a dialogue with her. They talked back and forth. They argued. The other students sat docile and perplexed, waiting for the class to end, glancing from Ilena to one of her articulate boys, back to Ilena again, taking notes only when Ilena seemed to be saying something important. What was so exciting about Conrad's *Heart of Darkness,* they wondered, that Mrs. Donohue could get this worked up?

Her copper-colored hair fell in a jumble about her face, and her skin sometimes took a radiant coppery beauty from the late afternoon sun as it sheered mistily through the campus trees, or from the excitement of a rare, good class, or from the thought of her love for Gordon, who would be waiting to see her after class. One of the boys in this late-afternoon class—Emmett Norlan— already wore his hair frizzy and long, though this was 1966 and a few years ahead of the style, and he himself was only a sophomore, a small precocious irritable argumentative boy with glasses. He was always charging up to Ilena after class, demanding that she explain herself—"You use words like 'emotions,' you bully us with your *emotions!*" he cried. "When I ask you a question in class, you distort it! You try to make everyone laugh at me! It's a womanly trick, a *female* trick, not worthy of you!" Emmett took everything seriously, as seriously as Ilena; he was always hanging around her office, in the doorway, refusing to come in and sit down because he was "in a hurry" and yet reluctant to go away, and Ilena could sense by a certain sullen alteration of his jaw that her lover was coming down the hall to her office. . . .

"See you," Emmett would say sourly, backing away.

Gordon was a professor in sociology, a decade or more older than Ilena, gentle and paternal; no match for her cunning. After a particularly ugly quarrel with her husband, one fall day, Ilena had looked upon this man and decided that he must become her lover. At the time she had not even known his name. *A lover. She would have a lover.* He was as tall as her own husband, with a married, uncomfortable look about his mouth—tense apologetic smiles, creases at the corners of his lips, bluish-purple veins on his forehead. A handsome man, but somehow a little gray. His complexion was both boyish and gray. He did not dress with the self-conscious care of her husband Bryan; his clothes were tweedy, not very new or very clean, baggy at the knees, smelling of tobacco and unaired closets. Ilena, determined to fall in love with him, had walked by his home near the university—an ordinary brick two-story house with white shutters. Her heart pounded with jealousy. She imagined his domestic life: a wife, four children, a Ford with a dented rear fender, a lawn that was balding, a street that was going bad—one handsome old Tudor home had already been converted into apartments for students, the sign of inevitable disaster. Meeting him, talking shyly with him, loving him at her finger tips was to be one of the gravest events in her life, for, pill-sweetened as she was, she had not seriously believed he might return her interest. He was Catholic. He was supposed to be happily married.

When it was over between them and she was teaching, for two quick, furtive semesters at the University of Buffalo, where most classes were canceled because of rioting and police harassment, Ilena thought back to her Detroit days and wondered how she had survived, even with the help of drugs and gin: the central nervous system could not take such abuse, not for long. She had written a novel out of her misery, her excitement, her guilt, typing ten or fifteen pages an evening until her head throbbed with pain that not even pills could ease. At times, lost in the story she was creating, she had felt an eerie longing to remain there permanently, to simply give up and go mad. *Adverse reactions: con-fusion, hallucinations, hyperexcitement.* . . . But she had not gone mad. She had kept on typing, working, and when she was finished it was possible to pick up, in her fingers, the essence of that shattering year: one slim book.

Death Dance. *The story of America's alienated youth* . . . *shocking revelations* . . . *suicide* . . . *drugs* . . . *waste* . . . *horror* . . . $5.98.

It had been at the top of the *New York Times* best-seller list for fifteen weeks.

Gordon had said to her, often, "I don't want to hurt you, Ilena. I'm afraid of ruining your life." She had assured him that her life was not that delicate. "I could go away if Bryan found out, alone. I could live alone," she had said lightly, airily, knowing by his grimness that he would not let her—surely he would not let her go? Gordon thought more about her husband than Ilena did, the "husband" he had met only once, at a large university reception, but with whom he now shared a woman. Two men, strangers, shared her body. Ilena wandered in a perpetual sodden daze, thinking of the . . . the madness of loving two men . . . the freakishness of it, which she could never really comprehend, could not assess, because everything in her recoiled from it: this could not be happening to her. Yet the fact of it was in her body, carried about in her body. She could not isolate it, could not comprehend it. Gazing at the girl students, at the nuns, she found herself thinking enviously that their lives were unsoiled and honest and open to any possibility, while hers had become fouled, complicated, criminal, snagged, somehow completed without her assent. She felt that she was going crazy.

Her teaching was either sluggish and uninspired, or hysterical. She was always wound up and ready to let go with a small speech on any subject—Vietnam, the oppression of blacks, religious hypocrisy, the censorship haggling over the student newspaper, any subject minor or massive—and while her few aggressive students appreciated this, the rest of her students were baffled and unenlightened. She sat in her darkened office, late in the afternoon, whispering to Gordon about her classes: "They aren't going well. I'm afraid. I'm not any good as a teacher. My hands shake when I come into the classroom . . . The sophomores are forced to take this course and they hate me, I know they hate me. . . ." Gordon stroked her hands, kissed her face, her uplifted face, and told her that he heard nothing but good reports about her teaching. He himself was a comfortable, moderately popular professor; he had been teaching for fifteen years. "You have some very enthusiastic students," he said. "Don't doubt yourself, Ilena, please; if you hear negative things it might be from other teachers who are jealous. . . ." Ilena pressed herself gratefully into this good man's embrace, hearing the echo of her mother's words of years ago, when Ilena would come home hurt from school for some minor girlish reason: "Don't mind them, they're just *jealous.*"

A world of jealous people, like her husband: therefore hateful, therefore dangerous. Out to destroy her. Therefore the pills, tiny round pills and large button-sized pills, and the multicolored capsules.

There were few places she and Gordon could meet. Sometimes they walked around the campus, sometimes they met for lunch downtown, but most of the time they simply sat in her office and talked. She told him everything about her life, reviewing all the snarls and joys she had reviewed, years before, with Bryan, noticing that she emphasized the same events and even used the same words to describe them. She told him everything, but she never mentioned the drugs. He would disapprove. Maybe he would be disgusted. Like many Catholic men of his social class, and of his generation, he would be frightened by weakness in women, though by his own admission he drank too much. If he commented on her dazed appearance, if he worried over her fatigue—"Does your husband do this to you? Put you in this state?"—she pretended not to understand. "What, do I look so awful? So ugly?" she would tease. That way she diverted his concern, she bullied him into loving her, because he was a man to whom female beauty was important—his own wife had been a beauty queen many years ago, at a teachers' college in Ohio. "No, you're beautiful. You're beautiful," he would whisper.

They teased each other to a state of anguish on those dark

winter afternoons, never really safe in Ilena's office—she shared
the office with a nun, who had an early teaching schedule but
who might conceivably turn up at any time, and there was always
the possibility of the cleaning lady or the janitor unlocking the
door with a master key—nightmarish possibility! Gordon kissed
her face, her body, she clasped her hands around him and gave
herself up to him musically, dreamily, like a rose of rot with only
a short while left to bloom, carrying the rot neatly hidden, deeply
hidden. She loved him so that her mind went blank even of the
euphoria of drugs or the stimulation of a good, exciting day of
teaching; she felt herself falling back into a blankness like a
white flawless wall, pure material, pure essence, a mysterious essence that was fleshly and spiritual at once. Over and over they
declared their love for each other, they promised it, vowed it,
repeated it in each other's grave accents, echoing and uncon-
sciously imitating each other, Ilena carrying home to her apartment her lover's gentleness, his paternal listening manner. Maybe
Bryan sensed Gordon's presence, his influence on her, long before the breakup. Maybe he could discern, with his scientist's
keen heatless eye, the shadow of another personality, powerful
and beloved, on the other side of his wife's consciousness.

Ilena vowed to Gordon, "I love you, only you," and she made
him believe that she and Bryan no longer slept in the same bed.
This was not true: she was so fearful of Bryan, of his guessing
her secret, that she imitated with her husband the affection she
gave to Gordon, in that way giving herself to two men, uniting
them in her body. *Two men. Uniting them in her body.* Her body
could not take all this. Her body threatened to break down. She
hid from Bryan, spending an hour or more in the bathtub, gazing
down through her lashes at her bluish, bruised body, wondering
how long this phase of her life could last—the taunting of her
sanity, the use of her rather delicate body by two normal men.
This is how a woman becomes prehistoric, she thought. *Prehistoric. Before all personalized, civilized history. Men make love to
her and she is reduced to protoplasm.*

She recalled her girlhood and her fear of men, her fear of
someday having to marry—for all her female relatives urged mar-

riage, marriage!—and now it seemed to her puzzling that the physical side of her life should be so trivial. It was not important, finally. She could have taken on any number of lovers, it was like shaking hands at a party, moving idly and absent-mindedly from one man to another; nothing serious about it at all. Why had she feared it so? And that was why the landscape of Detroit took on to her such neutral bleakness, its sidewalks and store windows and streets and trees, its spotted skies, its old people, its children —all unformed, unpersonalized, unhistoric. Everyone is proto-plasm, she thought, easing together and easing apart. Some touch and remain stuck together; others touch and part. . . . But, though she told herself this, she sometimes felt her head weighed down with a terrible depression and she knew she would have to die, would have to kill her consciousness. She could not live with two men.

She could not live with one man.

Heated, hysterical, she allowed Gordon to make love to her in that office. The two of them lay exhausted and stunned on the cold floor—unbelieving lovers. Had this really happened? She felt the back of her mind dissolve. Now she was committed to him, she had been degraded, if anyone still believed in degrada-tion; now something would happen, something must happen. She would divorce Bryan; he would divorce his wife. They must leave Detroit. They must marry. They must change their lives.

Nothing happened.

She sprang back to her feet, assisted by this man who seemed to love her so helplessly, her face framed by his large hands, her hair smoothed, corrected by his hands. She felt only a terrible chilly happiness, an elation that made no sense. And so she would put on her coat and run across the snowy, windswept campus to teach a class in freshman composition, her skin rosy, radiant, her body soiled and reeking beneath her clothes, every-thing secret and very lovely. Delirious and articulate, she lived out the winter. She thought, eying her students: *If they only knew*. . . . It was all very high, very nervous and close to hys-teria; Gordon loved her, undressed her and dressed her, retreated to his home where he undressed and bathed his smallest children,

and she carried his human heat with her everywhere on the coldest days, edgy from the pills of that noon and slightly hungover
from the barbiturates of the night before, feeling that she was
living her female life close to the limits, at the most extreme
boundaries of health and reason. Her love for him burned in-
ward, secretly, and she was dismayed to see how very soiled her
clothes were, sometimes as if mocking her. Was this love, was it
a stain like any other? But her love for him burned outward,
making her more confident of herself, so that she did not hesitate
to argue with her colleagues. She took part in a feeble anti-
Vietnam demonstration on campus, which was jeered at by most
of the students who bothered to watch, and which seemed to embarrass Gordon, who was not "political." She did not hesitate to
argue with hard-to-manage students during class, sensing herself
unladylike and impudent and reckless in their middle-class Catholic eyes, a *woman* who dared to say such things!—"I believe in
birth control, obviously, and in death control. Suicide must be
recognized as a natural human right." This, at a Catholic school;
she had thought herself daring in those days.

Emmett Norlan and his friends, scrawny, intense kids who were
probably taking drugs themselves, at least smoking marijuana,
clustered around Ilena and tried to draw her into their circle.
They complained that they could not talk to the other professors.
They complained about the "religious chauvinism" of the university, though Ilena asked them what they expected—it was a
Catholic school, wasn't it? "Most professors here are just closed
circuits, they don't create anything, they don't communicate anything," Emmett declared contemptuously. He was no taller than
Ilena herself, and she was a petite woman. He wore sloppy,
soiled clothes, and even on freezing days he tried to go without a
heavy coat; his perpetual grimy fatigue jacket became so familiar
to Ilena that she was to think of him, sharply and nostalgically,
whenever she saw such a jacket in the years to come. The boy's
face was surprisingly handsome, in spite of all the frizzy hair and
beard and the constant squinting and grimacing; but it was small
and boyish. He had to fight that boyishness by being tough. His
glasses were heavy, black-rimmed, and made marks on either

side of his nose—he often snatched them off and rubbed the bridge of his nose, squinting nearsightedly at Ilena, never faltering in his argument. Finally Ilena would say, "Emmett, I have to go home. Can't we talk about this some other time?"—wondering anxiously if Gordon had already left school. She was always backing away from even the students she liked, always edging away from her fellow teachers; she was always in a hurry, literally running from her office to a classroom or to the library, her head ducked against the wind and her eyes narrowed so that she need not see the faces of anyone she knew. In that university she was friendly with only a few people, among them the head of her department, a middle-aged priest with a degree from Harvard. He was neat, graying, gentlemanly, but a little corrupt in his academic standards: the Harvard years had been eclipsed long ago by the stern daily realities of Detroit.

The end for Ilena at this school came suddenly, in Father Hoffman's office.

Flushed with excitement, having spent an hour with Gordon in which they embraced and exchanged confidences—about his wife's sourness, her husband's iciness—Ilena had rushed to a committee that was to examine a Master's degree candidate in English. She had never sat on one of these committees before. The candidate was a monk, Brother Ronald, a pale, rather obese, pleasant man in his thirties. His lips were more womanish than Ilena's. The examination began with a question by a professor named O'Brien: "Please give us a brief outline of English literature." Brother Ronald began slowly, speaking in a gentle, faltering voice—this question was always asked by this particular professor, so the candidate had memorized an answer, perfectly—and O'Brien worked at lighting his pipe, nodding vaguely from time to time. Brother Ronald came to a kind of conclusion some fifteen minutes later, with the "twentieth century," mentioning the names of Joyce, Lawrence, and T. S. Eliot. "Very good," said O'Brien. The second examiner, Mr. Honig, asked nervously: "Will you describe tragedy and give us an example, please?" Brother Ronald frowned. After a moment he said, "There is *Hamlet* . . . and *Macbeth*. . . ." He seemed to panic then. He could think of nothing more to say. Honig, himself an obese good-natured little man of about fifty, with a Master's degree from a local university and no publications, smiled encouragingly at Brother Ronald; but Brother Ronald could only stammer, "Tragedy has a plot . . . a climax and a conclusion. . . . It has a moment of revelation . . . and comic relief. . . ." After several minutes of painful silence, during which the only sounds were of O'Brien's sucking at his pipe, Brother Ronald smiled shakily and said that he did not know any more about tragedy.

Now it was Ilena's turn. She was astonished. She kept glancing at O'Brien and Honig, trying to catch their eyes, but they did not appear to notice. Was it possible that this candidate was considered good enough for an advanced degree, was it possible that anyone would allow him to teach English anywhere? She could not believe it. She said, sitting up very straight, "Brother Ronald, please define the term 'Gothicism' for us." Silence. Brother Ronald stared at his hands. He tried to smile. "Then could you define the term 'heroic couplet' for us," Ilena said. Her heart pounded combatively. The monk gazed at her, sorrowful and soft, his eyes watery; he shook his head *no,* he didn't know. "Have you read any of Shakespeare's sonnets?" Ilena asked. Brother Ronald nodded gravely, *yes.* "Could you discuss one of them?" Ilena asked. Again, silence. Brother Ronald appeared to be thinking. Finally he said, "I guess I don't remember any of them. . . ." "Could you tell us what a sonnet is, then?" Ilena asked. "A short poem," said Brother Ronald uncertainly. "Could you give us an example of any sonnet?" said Ilena. He stared at his hands, which were now clasped together. They were pudgy and very clean. After a while Ilena saw that he could not think of a sonnet, so she said sharply, having become quite nervous herself, "Could you talk to us about any poem at all? One of your favorite poems?" He sat in silence for several seconds. Finally Ilena said, "Could you give us the *title* of a poem?"

A miserable half minute. But the examination was nearly over: Ilena saw the monk glance at his wrist watch.

"I've been teaching math at St. Rose's for the last five years . . ." Brother Ronald said softly. "It wasn't really my idea

to get a Master's degree in English . . . my order sent me
out. . . ."

"Don't you know any poems at all? Not even any titles?"
Ilena asked.

"Of course he does. We studied Browning last year, didn't we,
Brother Ronald?" O'Brien said. "You remember. You received a
B in the course. I was quite satisfied with your work. Couldn't
you tell us the title of a work of Browning's?"

Brother Ronald stared at his hands and smiled nervously.

"That's my last duchess up there on the wall. . . ." O'Brien
said coaxingly.

Brother Ronald was breathing deeply. After a few seconds he
said, in a voice so soft they could almost not hear it, *"My last
duchess? . . ."*

"Yes, that is a poem," Ilena said.

"Now it's my turn to ask another question," O'Brien said
briskly. He asked the monk a very long, conversational question
about the place of literature in education—did it have a place?
How would he teach a class of high-school sophomores a Shake-
spearean play, for instance?

The examination ended before Brother Ronald was able to answer.

They dismissed him. O'Brien, who was the chairman of the
examining committee, said without glancing at Ilena, "We will
give him a B."

"Yes, a B seems about right," the other professor said quickly.

Ilena, whose head was ringing with outrage and shame, put her
hand down flat on the table. "No," she said.

"What do you mean, no?"

"I won't pass him."

They stared at her. O'Brien said irritably, "Then I'll give him
an A, to balance out your C."

"But I'm not giving him a C. I'm not giving him anything.
How can he receive any other grade than F? I won't sign that
paper. I can't sign it," Ilena said.

"I'll give him an A also," the other professor said doubtfully.

"Then . . . then maybe he could still pass . . . if we averaged it out. . . ."

"But I won't sign the paper at all," Ilena said.

"You have to sign it."

"I won't sign it."

"It is one of your duties as a member of this examining board to give a grade and to sign your name."

"I won't sign it," Ilena said. She got shakily to her feet and walked out. In the corridor, ghostly and terrified, Brother Ronald hovered. Ilena passed by him in silence.

But the next morning she was summoned to Father Hoffman's office.

The story got out that she had been fired, but really she had had enough sense to resign—to write a quick resignation note on Father Hoffman's memo pad. They did not part friends. The following year, when her best-selling novel was published, Father Hoffman sent her a letter of congratulations on university stationery, charmingly worded: "I wish only the very best for you. We were wrong to lose you. Pity us." By then she had moved out of Detroit, her husband was in San Diego, she was living in a flat in Buffalo, near Delaware Avenue, afraid of being recognized when she went out to the drugstore or the supermarket. *Death Dance* had become a selection of the Book-of-the-Month Club; it had been sold for $150,000 to a movie producer famous for his plodding, "socially significant" films, and for the first time in her life Ilena was sleepless because of money—rabid jangling thoughts about money. She was ashamed of having done so well financially. She was terrified of her ability to survive all this noise, this publicity, this national good fortune. For, truly, *Death Dance* was not her best novel: a hectic narrative about college students and their preoccupation with sex and drugs and death, in a prose she had tried to make "poetic." Her more abrasive colleagues at the University of Buffalo cautioned her against believing the praise that was being heaped upon her, that she would destroy her small but unique talent if she took all this seriously, etc. Even her new lover, a critic, separated from his wife and several children, a fifty-year-old ex-child prodigy, warned her against success: "They want to make you believe you're a genius, so they can draw back and laugh at you. First they hypnotize you, then they destroy you. Believe nothing."

The flow of barbiturates and amphetamines gave her eyes a certain wild sheen, her copper hair a frantic wasteful curl, made her voice go shrill at the many Buffalo parties. She wondered if she did not have the talent, after all, for being a spectacle. Someone to stare at. The magazine cover had flattered her wonderfully: taken by a Greenwich Village photographer as dreamily hungover as Ilena herself, the two of them moving about in slow motion in his studio, adjusting her hair, her lips, her eyelashes, the tip of her chin, adjusting the light, altering the light, bringing out a fantastic ethereal glow in her eyes and cheeks and forehead that Ilena had never seen in herself. The cover had been in full color and Ilena had looked really beautiful, a pre-Raphaelite virgin. Below her photograph was a caption in high alarmed black letters: ARE AMERICAN WOMEN AVENGING CENTURIES OF OPPRESSION?

Revenge!

Death Dance was nominated for a National Book Award, but lost out to a long, tedious, naturalistic novel; someone at Buffalo who knew the judges told Ilena that this was just because the female member of the committee had been jealous of her. Ilena, whose head seemed to be swimming all the time now, and who did not dare to drive around in her Mercedes for fear of having an accident, accepted all opinions, listened desperately to everyone, pressed herself against her lover, and wept at the thought of her disintegrating brain.

This lover wanted to marry her, as soon as his divorce was final; his name was Lyle Myer. He was the author of twelve books of criticism and a columnist for a weekly left-wing magazine; a New Yorker, he had never lived outside New York until coming to Buffalo, which terrified him. He was afraid of being beaten up by militant students on campus, and he was afraid of being beaten up by the police. Hesitant, sweet, and as easily moved to sentimental tears as Ilena herself, he was always telephoning her or dropping in at her flat. Because he was, or had been, an alcoholic, Ilena felt it was safe to tell him about the pills she took. He seemed pleased by this confidence, this admission of her weakness, as if it bound her more hopelessly to him—just as his teen-aged daughter, whose snapshot Ilena had seen, was bound to be a perpetual daughter to him because of her acne and rounded shoulders, unable to escape his love. "Drugs are suicidal, yes, but if they forestall the actual act of suicide they are obviously beneficial," he told her.

With him, she felt nothing except a clumsy domestic affection: no physical love at all.

She was so tired most of the time that she did not even pretend to feel anything. With Gordon, in those hurried steep moments back in Detroit, the two of them always fearful of being discovered, her body had been keyed up to hysteria and love had made her delirious; with Bryan, near the end of their marriage, she had sometimes felt a tinge of love, a nagging doubtful rush that she often let fade away again, but with Lyle her body was dead, worn out, it could not respond to his most tender caresses. She felt how intellectualized she had become, her entire body passive and observant and cynical.

"Oh, I have to get my head straight. I have to get my head straight," Ilena wept.

Lyle undressed her gently, lovingly. She felt panic, seeing in his eyes that compassionate look that had meant Gordon was thinking of his children: how she had flinched from that look!

The end had come with Gordon just as abruptly as it had come with Father Hoffman, and only a week later. They had met by accident out on the street one day, Gordon with his wife and the two smallest children, Ilena in a trench coat, bareheaded, a leather purse with a frayed strap slung over her shoulder. "Hello, Ilena," Gordon said guiltily. He was really frightened. His wife, still a handsome woman, though looking older than her thirty-seven years, smiled stiffly at Ilena and let her gaze travel down to Ilena's watermarked boots. "How are you, Ilena?" Gordon said. His eyes grabbed at her, blue and intimidated. His wife, tugging at one of the little boys, turned a sour, ironic smile upon Ilena and said, "Are you one of my husband's students?" Ilena guessed that this was meant to insult Gordon, to make him feel old. But she explained politely that she was an instructor in the English Department, "but I'm leaving after this semester," and she noticed covertly that Gordon was not insulted, not irritated by his wife's nastiness, but only watchful, cautious, his smile strained with the fear that Ilena would give him away.

"In fact, I'm leaving in a few weeks," Ilena said.

His wife nodded stiffly, not bothering to show much regret. Gordon smiled nervously, apologetically. With relief, Ilena thought. He was smiling with relief because now he would be rid of her.

And so that had ended.

They met several times after this, but Ilena was now in a constant state of excitement or drowsiness; she was working out the beginning chapters of *Death Dance*—now living alone in the apartment, since her husband had moved out to a hotel. Her life was a confusion of days and nights, sleepless nights, headachey days, classes she taught in a dream and classes she failed to meet; she spent long periods in the bathtub while the hot water turned tepid and finally cold, her mind racing. She thought of her marriage and its failure. Marriage was the deepest, most mysterious, most profound exploration open to man: she had always believed that, and she believed it now. Because she had failed did not change that belief. This plunging into another's soul, this pressure of bodies together, so brutally intimate, was the closest one could come to a sacred adventure; she still believed that. But she had failed. So she forced herself to think of her work. She thought of the novel she was writing—about a "suicide club" that had apparently existed in Ann Arbor, Michigan—projecting her confusion and her misery into the heads of those late-adolescent girls, trying not to think of her own personal misery, the way love had soured in her life. Her husband. Gordon. Well, yes, men failed at being men; but maybe she had failed at being a woman. She had been unfaithful to two men at the same time. She deserved whatever she got.

Still, she found it difficult to resist swallowing a handful of sleeping pills. . . . Why not? Why not empty the whole container? There were moments when she looked at herself in the bathroom

mirror and raised one eyebrow flirtatiously. *How about it? . . .
Why not die? . . .* Only the empty apartment awaited her.

But she kept living because the novel obsessed her. She had to
write it. She had to solve its problems, had to finish it, send it away
from her completed. And, anyway, if she had taken sleeping pills
and did not wake up, Gordon or Bryan would probably discover
her before she had time to die. They often telephoned, and would
have been alarmed if she hadn't answered. Gordon called her
every evening, usually from a drugstore, always guiltily, so that
she began to take pity on his cowardice. Did he fear her commit-
ting suicide and leaving a note that would drag him in? Or did he
really love her? . . . Ilena kept assuring him that she was all right,
that she would be packing soon, yes, yes, she would always remember him with affection; no, she would probably not write to
him, it would be better not to write. They talked quickly, sadly.
Already the frantic hours of love-making in that office had become history, outlandish and improbable. Sometimes Ilena
thought, *My God, I really love this man,* but her voice kept on
with the usual conversation—what she had done that day, what
he had done, what the state of her relationship with Bryan was,
what his children were doing, the plans his wife had for that
summer.

So it had ended, feebly; she had not even seen him the last week
she was in Detroit.

Bryan called her too, impulsively. Sometimes to argue, sometimes to check plans, dates. He knew about the pills she took,
though not about their quantity, and if she failed to answer the
telephone for long he would have come over at once. Ilena would
have been revived, wakened by a stomach pump, an ultimate
masculine attack upon her body, sucking out her insides in great
gasping shuddering gulps. . . . So she took only a double dose
of sleeping pills before bed, along with the gin, and most of the
time she slept soundly enough, without dreams. The wonderful
thing about pills was that dreams were not possible. No dreams.
The death of dreams. What could be more lovely than a dreamless
sleep? . . .

In late April, Bryan had a collapse of some kind and was admitted to a local clinic; then he flew to his mother's, in Oswego. Ilena learned from a mutual friend at Wayne Medical School that Gordon had had a general nervous collapse, aggravated by a sudden malfunctioning of the liver brought on by malnutrition— he had been starving himself, evidently, to punish Ilena. But she worked on her novel, incorporating this latest catastrophe into the plot; she finished it in January of 1968, in Buffalo, where she was teaching a writing seminar; it was published in early 1969, and changed her life.

Lyle Myer pretended jealousy of her—all this acclaim, all this fuss! He insisted that she agree to marry him. He never mentioned, seemed deliberately to overlook, the embarrassing fact that she could love him only tepidly, that her mind was always elsewhere in their dry, fateful struggles, strung out with drugs or the memory of some other man, someone she half remembered, or the letters she had to answer from her agent and a dozen other people, so many people inviting her to give talks, to accept awards, to teach at their universities, to be interviewed by them, begging and demanding her time, her intense interest, like a hundred lovers tugging and pulling at her body, engaging it in a kind of love-making to which she could make only the feeblest of responses, her face locked now in a perpetual feminine smile. . . . With so much publicity and money, she felt an obligation to be feminine and gracious to everyone; when she was interviewed she spoke enthusiastically of the place of art in life, the place of beauty in this modern technological culture—she seemed to stress, on one national late-night television show, the tragedy of small trees stripped bare by vandals in city parks as much as the tragedy of the country's current foreign policy in Vietnam. At least it turned out that way. It was no wonder people could not take her seriously: one of the other writers at Buffalo, himself famous though more *avant-garde* than Ilena, shrugged her off as that girl who was always "licking her lips to make them glisten."

She did not sign on for another year at Buffalo, partly because of the political strife there and partly because she was restless, agitated, ready to move on. She sold the Mercedes and gave to

the Salvation Army the furniture and other possessions Bryan
had so cavalierly—indifferently—given her, and took an apartment in New York. She began writing stories that were to appear in
fashion magazines, Ilena's slick, graceful prose an easy comple-
ment to the dreamlike faces and bodies of models whose photographs appeared in those same magazines, everything muted and
slightly distorted as if by a drunken lens, the "very poetry of
hallucination"—as one reviewer had said of *Death Dance*. Lyle
flew down to see her nearly every weekend; on other weekends
he was with his "separated" family. She loved him, yes, and she
agreed to marry him, though she felt no hurry—in fact, she felt no
real interest in men at all, her body shrinking when it was touched
even accidentally, not out of fear but out of a kind of chaste boredom. So much, she had had so much of men, so much loving, so
much mauling, so much passion. . . .

What, she was only twenty-nine years old?

She noted, with a small pang of vanity, how surprised audiences
were when she rose to speak. *Ilena Williams looks so young!*
They could not see the fine vibrations of her knees and hands,
already viciously toned down by Librium. They could not see the
colorless glop she vomited up in motel bathrooms, or in rest
rooms down the hall from the auditorium in which she was
speaking—she was always "speaking," invited out all over the
country for fees ranging from $500 to a colossal $2000, speaking
on "current trends in literature" or "current mores in America"
or answering questions about her "writing habits" or reading sec-
tions from her latest work, a series of short stories in honor of
certain dead writers with whom she felt a kinship. "I don't exist
as an individual but only as a completion of a tradition, the end
of something, not the best part of it but only the end," she explained, wondering if she was telling the truth or if this was all
nonsense, "and I want to honor the dead by reimagining their
works, by reimagining their obsessions . . . in a way marrying
them, joining them as a woman joins a man . . . spiritually and
erotically. . . ." She spoke so softly, so hesitantly, that audiences
often could not hear her. Whereupon an energetic young man
sitting in the first row, or onstage with her, would spring to his

feet and adjust the microphone. "Is that better? Can you all hear now?" he would ask. Ilena saw the faces in the audience waver and blur and fade away, sheer protoplasm, and panic began in her stomach—what if she should vomit right in front of everyone? on this tidy little lectern propped up on dictionaries for her benefit? But she kept on talking. Sometimes she talked about the future of the short story, sometimes about the future of civilization—she heard the familiar, dead, deadened word *Vietnam* uttered often in her own voice, a word that had once meant something; she heard her voice echoing from the farthest corners of the auditorium as if from the corners of all those heads, her own head hollow as a drum, occasionally seeing herself at a distance—a woman with long but rather listless copper-red hair, thin cheeks, eyes that looked unnaturally enlarged. *Adverse reactions: confusion, edema, nausea, constipation, jaundice, hallucinations. . . .* Did that qualify as a legitimate hallucination, seeing herself from a distance, hearing herself from a distance? Did that qualify as a sign of madness?

During the fall and winter of 1969 and the spring of 1970 she traveled everywhere, giving talks, being met at airports by interested strangers, driven to neat disinfected motel rooms. She had time to write only a few stories, which had to be edited with care before they could be published. Her blood pounded barbarously, while her voice went on and on in that gentle precise way, her body withdrawing from any man's touch, demure with a dread that could not show through her clothes. She had been losing weight gradually for three years, and now she had the angular, light-boned, but very intense look of a precocious child. People wanted to protect her. Women mothered her, men were always taking her arm, helping her through doorways; the editor of a famous men's magazine took her to lunch and warned her of Lyle Myer's habit of marrying young, artistic women and then ruining them—after all, he had been married three times already, and the pattern was established. Wasn't it? When people were most gentle with her, Ilena thought of the tough days when she'd run across that wind-tortured campus in Detroit, her coat flapping about her, her body still dazzled by Gordon's love, damp and sweaty from him, and she had dared run into the classroom, five minutes late, had dared to take off her coat and begin the lesson. . . . The radiators in that old building had knocked as if they might explode; like colossal arteries, like her thudding arteries, overwhelmed with life.

In the fall of 1970 she was invited back to Detroit to give a talk before the local Phi Beta Kappa chapter; she accepted, and a few days later she received a letter from the new dean of the School of Arts—new since she had left—of her old university, inviting her to a reception in her honor, as their "most esteemed ex-staff member." It was all very diplomatic, very charming. She had escaped them, they had gotten rid of her, and now they could all meet together for a few hours. . . . Father Hoffman sent a note to her also, underscoring the dean's invitation, hoping that she was well and as attractive as ever. So she accepted.

Father Hoffman and another priest came to pick her up at the Sheraton Cadillac Hotel; she was startled to see that Father Hoffman had let his hair grow a little long, that he had noble, graying sideburns, and that the young priest with him was even shaggier. After the first awkward seconds—Father Hoffman forgot and called her "Mrs. Donohue"—they got along very well. Ilena was optimistic about the evening; her stomach seemed settled. As soon as they arrived at the dean's home she saw that Gordon was not there; she felt immensely relieved, though she had known he would not come, would not want to see her again . . . she felt immensely relieved and accepted a drink at once from Father Hoffman, who was behaving in an exceptionally gallant manner. "Ilena is looking better than ever," he said as people crowded around her, some of them with copies of her novel to sign, "better even than all her photographs. . . . But we don't want to tire her out, you know. We don't want to exhaust her." He kept refreshing her drink, like a lover or a husband. In the old days everyone at this place had ignored Ilena's novels, even the fact of her being a "writer," but now they were all smiles and congratulations—even the wives of her ex-colleagues, sturdy, dowdy women who had never seemed to like her. Ilena was too shaky to make any sarcastic observations about this to Father Hoffman, who might have appreciated them. He did say, "Times have changed, eh, Ilena?" and winked at her roguishly. "For one thing, you're not quite as excitable as you used to be. You were a very *young* woman around here." She could sense, beneath his gallantry, a barely disguised contempt for her—for all women— and this knowledge made her go cold. She mumbled something about fighting off the flu. Time to take a "cold tablet." She fished in her purse and came out with a large yellow capsule, a tranquillizer, and swallowed it down with a mouthful of Scotch.

Father Hoffman and Dr. O'Brien and a new, young assistant professor—a poet whose first book would be published next spring —talked to Ilena in a kind of chorus, telling her about all the changes in the university. It was much more "community-oriented" now. Its buildings—its "physical plant"—were to be open to the neighborhood on certain evenings and on Saturdays. The young poet, whose blond hair was very long and who wore a suede outfit and a black silk turtleneck shirt, kept interrupting the older men with brief explosions of mirth. "Christ, all this is a decade out of date—integration and all that crap—the NAACP and good old Martin Luther King and all that crap—the blacks don't want it and I agree with them one hundred percent! King is dead and so is Civil Rights—just another white middle-class week-night activity the blacks saw through long ago! I agree with them one hundred percent!" He seemed to be trying to make an impression on Ilena, not quite looking at her, but leaning toward her with his knees slightly bent, as if to exaggerate his youth. Ilena sipped at her drink, trying to hide the panic that was beginning. Yes, the NAACP was dead, all that was dead, but she didn't want to think about it—after all, it had been at a civil-rights rally that she and Bryan had met, years ago in Madison, Wisconsin. . . . "I haven't gotten around to reading your novel yet," the poet said, bringing his gaze sideways to Ilena.

Ilena excused herself and searched for a bathroom.

The dean's wife took her upstairs, kindly. Left alone, she waited to be sick, then lost interest in being sick; she had only to get through a few more hours of this and she would be safe. And Gordon wasn't there. She looked at herself in the mirror and should

have been pleased to see that she looked so pretty—not beautiful tonight but pretty, delicate—she had worked hard enough at it,
spending an hour in a hotel bathroom steaming her face and
patting astringent on it, hoping for the best. She dreaded the
cracks in her brain somehow working their way out to her skin.
What then, what then? . . . But beauty did no good for anyone;
it conferred no blessing upon the beautiful woman. Nervously,
Ilena opened the medicine cabinet and peered at the array of
things inside. She was interested mainly in prescription containers.
Here were some small green pills prescribed for the dean's wife,
for "tension." Tension, good! She took two of the pills. On another shelf there were some yellow capsules, perhaps the same as
her own, though slightly smaller; she checked, yes, hers were 5
mg. and these were only 2. So she didn't bother with them. But
she did discover an interesting white pill for "muscular tension,"
Dean Spriggs's prescription; she took one of these.

She descended the stairs, her hand firm on the bannister.

Before she could return safely to Father Hoffman, she was
waylaid by someone's wife—the apple-cheeked Mrs. Honig, a
very short woman with white hair who looked older than her
husband, who looked, in fact, like Mrs. Santa Claus, motherly
and dwarfed; Mrs. Honig asked her to sign a copy of *Death Dance*.
"We all think it's so wonderful, just so wonderful for you," she
said. Another woman joined them. Ilena had met her once, years
before, but she could not remember her name. Mr. Honig hurried
over. The conversation seemed to be about the tragedy of America—"All these young people dying in a senseless war," Mrs.
Honig said, shaking her white hair; Mr. Honig agreed mournfully. "Vietnam is a shameful tragedy," he said. The dean's wife
came by with a tray of cheese and crackers; everyone took something, even Ilena, though she doubted her ability to eat. She
doubted everything. It seemed to her that Mrs. Honig and these
other people were talking about Vietnam, and about drugs and
death—could this be true?—or was it another hallucination?
"Why, you know, a young man was killed here last spring, he
took part in a demonstration against the Cambodian business,"
Mrs. Honig said vaguely; "they say a policeman clubbed him to

death. . . ." "No, Ida, he had a concussion and died afterward," Mr. Honig said. He wiped his mouth of cracker crumbs and stared sadly at Ilena. "I think you knew him . . . Emmett Norlan?"

Emmett Norlan?

"You mean—Emmett is dead? He died? He died?" Ilena asked shrilly.

The blond poet came to join their group. He had known Emmett, yes, a brilliant young man, a martyr to the Cause—yes, yes—he knew everything. While Ilena stared into space he told them all about Emmett. *He* had been an intimate friend of Emmett's.

Ilena happened to be staring toward the front of the hall, and she saw Gordon enter. The dean's wife was showing him in. Flakes of snow had settled upon the shoulders of his old gray coat. Ilena started, seeing him so suddenly. She had forgotten all about him. She stared across the room in dismay, wondering at his appearance—he wore his hair longer, his sideburns were long and a little curly, he even had a small wiry brown beard— But he did not look youthful, he looked weary and drawn.

Now began half an hour of Ilena's awareness of him and his awareness of her. They had lived through events like this in the past, at other parties, meeting in other groups at the university; a dangerous, nervous sensation about their playing this game, not wanting to rush together. Ilena accepted a drink from a forty-year-old who looked zestful and adolescent, a priest who did not wear his Roman collar but, instead, a black nylon sweater and a medallion on a leather strap; Ilena's brain whirled at such surprises. What had happened? In the past there had been three categories: men, women, and priests. She had known how to conduct herself discreetly around these priests, who were masculine but undangerous; now she wasn't so sure. She kept thinking of Emmett dead. Had Emmett really been killed by the police? Little Emmett? She kept thinking of Gordon, aware of him circling her at a distance of some yards. She kept thinking of these people talking so casually of Vietnam, of drugs, of the death of little Emmett Norlan—these people—the very words they used turning flat and banal and safe in their mouths. "The waste of youth in this country is a tragedy," the priest with the sweater and the medallion said, shaking his head sadly.

Ilena eased away from them to stare at a Chagall lithograph, "Summer Night." Two lovers embraced, in repose; yet a nightmarish dream blossomed out of their heads, an intricate maze of dark depthless foliage, a lighted window, faces ghastly-white and perhaps a little grotesque. . . . Staring at these lovers, she sensed Gordon approaching her. She turned to him, wanting to be casual. But she was shaking. Gordon stared at her and she saw that old helplessness in his eyes—what, did he still love her? Wasn't she free of him yet? She began talking swiftly, nervously. "Tell me about Emmett. Tell me what happened." Gordon, who seemed heavier than she recalled, whose tired face disappointed her sharply, spoke as always in his gentle, rather paternal voice; she tried to listen. She tried to listen but she kept recalling that office, the two of them lying on the floor together, helpless in an embrace, so hasty, so reckless, grinding their bodies together in anguish. . . . They had been so close, so intimate, that their blood had flowed freely in each other's veins; on the coldest days they had gone about blood-warmed, love-warmed. Tears filled Ilena's eyes. Gordon was saying, "The story was that he died of a concussion, but actually he died of liver failure. Once he got in the hospital he just disintegrated . . . he had hepatitis . . . he'd been taking heroin. . . . It was a hell of a thing, Ilena. . . ."

She pressed her fingers hard against her eyes.

"Don't cry, please," Gordon said, stricken.

A pause of several seconds: the two of them in a kind of equilibrium, two lovers.

"Would you like me to drive you back to your hotel?" Gordon said.

She went at once to get her coat. Backing away, always backing away . . . she stammered a few words to Father Hoffman, to the dean and his wife, words of gratitude, confusion. Good-by to Detroit! *Good-by, good-by.* She shook hands. She finished her drink. Gordon helped her on with her coat—a stylish black coat with a black mink collar, nothing like the clothes she had worn in the old days. Out on the walk, in the soft falling snow, Gordon said nervously: "I know you're going to be married. Lyle Myer. I know all about it. I'm very happy. I'm happy for you. You're looking very well."

Ilena closed her eyes, waiting for her mind to straighten itself out. Yes, she was normal; she had gone to an internist in Buffalo and had been declared normal. *You are too young to be experiencing menopause,* the doctor had said thoughtfully; *the cessation of menstrual periods must be related to the Pill or to an emotional condition.* She thought it better not to tell Gordon all that. "Thank you," she said simply.

"I'm sorry they told you about Emmett," Gordon said. "There was no reason to tell you. He liked you so much, Ilena; he hung around my office after you left and all but confessed he was in love with you . . . he kept asking if you wrote to me and I said no, but he didn't believe me . . . he was always asking about you. . . ."

"When did he die?"

"Last spring. His liver gave out. Evidently it was just shot. Someone said his skin was bright yellow."

"He was taking heroin? . . ."

"God, yes. He was a wreck. The poor kid just disintegrated, it was a hell of a shame. . . ."

He drove her back downtown. They were suddenly very comfortable together, sadly comfortable. Ilena had been in this car only two or three times in the past. "Where is your wife?" she asked shyly. She watched him as he answered—his wife was visiting her mother in Ohio, she'd taken the children—no, things were no better between them—always the same, always the same—Ilena thought in dismay that he was trivialized by these words: men were trivialized by love and by their need for women.

"I've missed you so much . . ." Gordon said suddenly.

They walked through the tufts of falling snow, to the hotel. A gigantic hotel, all lights and people. Ilena felt brazen and anonymous here. Gordon kept glancing at her, as if unable to believe in her. He was nervous, eager, a little drunk; an uncertain adolescent smile hovered about his face. "I love you, I still love you," he whispered. In the elevator he embraced her. Ilena did not resist.

She felt her body warming to him as toward an old friend, a brother. She did love him. Tears of love stung her eyes. If only she could get her head straight, if only she could think of what she was supposed to think of . . . someone she was supposed to remember. . . . In the overheated room they embraced gently. Gently. Ilena did not want to start this love again, it was a mistake, but she caught sight of Gordon's stricken face and could not resist. She began to cry. Gordon clutched her around the hips, kneeling before her. He pressed his hot face against her.

"Ilena, I'm so sorry . . ." he said.

She thought of planets: sun-warmed planets revolving around a molten star. Revolving around a glob of light. And the planets rotated on their own, private axes. But now the planets were accelerating their speed, they wobbled on their axes and the strain of their movement threatened to tear them apart. She began to sob. Ugly, gasping, painful sobs. . . . "Don't cry, please, I'm so sorry," Gordon said. They lay down together. The room was hot, too hot. They had not bothered to put on a light. Only the light from the window, a dull glazed wintry light; Ilena allowed him to kiss her, to undress her, to move his hands wildly about her body as she wept. What should she be thinking of? Whom should she remember? When she was with Lyle she thought back to Gordon . . . now, with Gordon, she thought back to someone else, someone else, half-remembered, indistinct, perhaps dead. . . . He began to make love to her. He was eager, breathing as sharply and as painfully as Ilena herself. She clasped her arms around him. That firm hard back she remembered. Or did she remember? . . . Her mind wandered and she thought suddenly of Bryan, her husband. He was her ex-husband now. She thought of their meeting at that civil-rights rally, introduced by mutual friends, she thought of the little tavern they had gone to, on State Street in Madison, she thought of the first meal she'd made for Byran and that other couple . . . proud of herself as a cook, baking them an Italian dish with shrimp and crabmeat and mushrooms . . . yes, she had been proud of her cooking, she had loved to cook for years. For years. She had loved Bryan. But suddenly she was not thinking

of him; her mind gave way to a sharper thought and she saw
Emmett's face; his scorn, his disapproval.

She stifled a scream.

Gordon slid from her, frightened. "Did I hurt you? Ilena?"

She began to weep uncontrollably. Their bodies, so warm, now
shivered and seemed to sting each other. Their hairs seemed to
catch at each other painfully.

"Did I hurt you? . . ." he whispered.

She remembered the afternoon she had fainted. Passed out
cold. And then she had come to her senses and she had cried,
like this, hiding her face from her lover because crying made it
ugly, so swollen. . . . Gordon tried to comfort her. But the bed
was crowded with people. A din of people. A mob. Lovers were
kissing her on every inch of her body and trying to suck up her
tepid blood, prodding, poking, inspecting her like that doctor in
Buffalo—up on the table, naked beneath an oversized white
robe, her feet in the stirrups, being examined with a cold sharp
metal device and then with the doctor's fingers in his slick rubber
gloves—checking her ovaries, so casually—*You are too young
for menopause,* he had said. Was it the pills, then? The birth-con-
trol pills? *This kind of sterility is not necessarily related to the Pill,*
the doctor had conceded, and his subtlety of language had enchanted Ilena. . . .

"Don't cry," Gordon begged.

She had frightened him off and he would not make love to her.
He only clutched at her, embraced her. She felt that he was
heavier, yes, than she remembered. Heavier. Older. But she could
not concentrate on him: she kept seeing Emmett's face. His frizzy
hair, his big glasses, his continual whine. Far inside her, too deep
for any man to reach and stir into sensation, a dull, dim lust began for Emmett, hardly more than a faint throbbing. Emmett, who
was dead. She wanted to hold him, now, instead of this man—
Emmett in her arms, his irritation calmed, his glasses off and
set on the night table beside the bed, everything silent, silent.
Gordon was whispering to her. *Love. Love.* She did not remember that short scratchy beard. But she was lying in bed with an
anxious, perspiring, bearded man, evidently someone she knew.

They were so close that their blood might flow easily back and forth between their bodies, sluggish and warm and loving.

She recalled her husband's face: a look of surprise, shock. She had betrayed him. His face blended with the face of her student, who was dead, and Gordon's face, pressed so close to her in the dark that she could not see it. The bed was crammed with people. Their identities flowed sluggishly, haltingly, from vein to vein. One by one they were all becoming each other. Becoming protoplasm. They were protoplasm that had the sticky pale formlessness of semen. They were all turning into each other, into protoplasm. . . . Ilena was conscious of something fading in her, in the pit of her belly. Fading. Dying. *The central sexual organ is the brain,* she had read, and now her brain was drawing away, fading, dissolving.

"Do you want me to leave?" Gordon asked.

She did not answer. Against the hotel window: soft, shapeless clumps of snow. She must remember something, she must remember someone . . . there was an important truth she must understand. . . . But she could not get it into focus. Her brain seemed to swoon backward, in an elation of fatigue, and she heard beyond this man's hoarse, strained breathing the gentle breathing of the snow, falling shapelessly upon them all.

"Do you want me to leave?" Gordon asked.

She could not speak.

Bernard Malamud was born in Brooklyn and attended City College and Columbia University. He has taught at Oregon State University and Harvard and is now teaching at Bennington College. He has published five novels and two collections of short stories. For *The Magic Barrel* he received a National Book Award, and for *The Fixer,* a National Book Award and the Pulitzer Prize. His latest novel, *Tenants,* was published in 1971.

TALKING HORSE

Q. Am I a man in a horse or a horse that talks like a man? If the first, then Jonah had it better in the whale; more room all around; also he knew who he was and how he had got there. About myself I make guesses. Anyway, after three days and nights the big fish stopped at Nineveh and Jonah took his valise and got off. Not Abramowitz, still at hand, or on board, after years; he's no prophet. On the contrary, he works in a circus sideshow full of freaks—though recently advanced, on Goldberg's insistence, to the center ring inside the big tent in an act with his deaf-mute master—Goldberg himself—may the Almighty forgive him. All I know is I've been here for years and still don't understand the nature of my fate; in short, if I'm Abramowitz, a horse; or a horse including Abramowitz. Why is anybody's guess. Understanding goes so far and no further, especially if Goldberg blocks the way. Maybe it's because of something I said or thought or did, or didn't do, in my life. It's easy to make mistakes. As I say, I have my theories, glimmers, guesses, but can't prove a thing.

When Abramowitz stands in his stall, his hoofs booming nervously on the battered wooden planks as he chews in his bag of hard yellow oats, sometimes he has thoughts, far-off recollections, they seem to be, of young horses racing, playing, nipping at each other's flanks in green fields; and other disquieting images that resemble memories; so who's to say what's really the truth?

I've tried asking Goldberg, but save yourself the trouble. He gets green in the face at questions, very uptight. I can understand —he's a deaf-mute from way back; he doesn't like interference with his plans, or thoughts, or the way he lives, and no surprises except those he invents. He talks to me when he feels like it, which isn't so often—his little patience has worn thin. Lately he relies too much on his bamboo cane—whoosh across the rump. There's plenty of oats, and straw, and water, and once in a while a joke to make me relax; but usually it's one threat or another followed by a flash of pain if I don't do something or other right, or something I say gets on his nerves. It's not necessarily this cane that slashes like a sword; his threats have the same effect, like a zong of lightning through the flesh; in fact the blow hurts less than the threat—the blow is momentary, the threat you worry about. But the true pain, at least to me, is when you don't know what you wish to.

Which doesn't mean we don't communicate. Goldberg taps out Morse code messages on my head with his big knuckle— crack crack crack; I feel the vibrations go through the bones to the tip of my tail—when he tells me what to do next or he threatens how many lashes for the last offense. His first message, I remember, was NO QUESTIONS. UNDERSTOOD? I shook my head and a little bell jingled on a strap under the forelock. That was the first I knew it was there.

TALK, he knocked on my head, "You're a talking horse."

"Yes, master." What else could I say?

My voice surprised me when it came out high through the tunnel of a horse's neck. I don't exactly remember the occasion— go remember beginnings. My memory I have to fight to get an early remembrance out of. Maybe I fell and hurt my head on a rock or was otherwise stunted? Goldberg is my deaf-mute owner; he reads my lips. Once when he was drunk and looking for company he tapped me that I used to carry goods on my back to fairs and markets before we joined the circus; before that I thought I was born there.

"On a rainy, snowy, crappy night," Goldberg Morse-coded me on my skull.

"What happened then?"

He stopped talking. I should know better but don't.

I try to remember that night, and certain hazy thoughts cross my mind, which might be some sort of story I dream up when I have nothing to do but chew my oats. It's easier than remembering. The one that comes to me most is about two men, or horses, or men on horses, though which might be me I can't say except that Goldberg rides on my back every night in the act. Anyway two strangers meet, somebody asks the other a question, and the next thing you know they're locked in a fight, either hacking at each other's head with their swords or braying wildly as they tear their flesh; or both at the same time. If riders, or horses, one is thin and poetic, the other a fat stranger wearing a black crown. They meet in a stone pit on a rainy, snowy, crappy night, one wearing his cracked metal crown that weighs heavy on his head and makes his movements slow, and the other has his ragged colored cap; all night they wrestle by weird light in the slippery stone pit.

Q. "What's to be done?"

A. "None of those accursed questions."

In the morning one of us wakes with a terrible pain. It feels like a wound in the neck but maybe like a headache. He remembers a blow he can't attest to. Abramowitz, in his dream story, suspects Goldberg stuffed him into a horse because he needed a talking one for his act and there was no such thing. I wish I knew for sure.

NO QUESTIONS. WHEN ARE YOU GOING TO LEARN?

That's his nature; he's a lout, though not without a little consideration when he's depressed and drinking from his bottle. That's when he taps me out a teasing anecdote or two. He has no friends. Family neither of us talks about. When he laughs he cries.

It must frustrate the owner that all he can say aloud is four-letter words like geee, gooo, gaaa, gaaw, and the circus manager who doubles as ringmaster, in for a snifter, looks embarrassed at the floor. At those who don't know the Morse code Goldberg grimaces, glares, and grinds his teeth. He has his mysteries. He keeps a mildewed three-prong spear hanging on the wall over a stuffed pony's head. Sometimes he goes down in the cellar with an old candle and comes up with a new one, yet we have electric lights. Though he doesn't complain about his life, he worries and cracks his knuckles. Maybe he's a widower, who knows? He doesn't seem interested in women but he sees to it that Abramowitz gets his chance at a mare in heat, if available. Abramowitz engages to satisfy his physical nature, a fact is a fact, otherwise it's no big deal; the mare has no interest in a talking courtship. Furthermore, Goldberg applauds when Abramowitz mounts her, which is humiliating.

And when they're in their winter quarters the owner once a week or so dresses up and goes out on the town. When he puts on his broadcloth suit, diamond stickpin, and yellow gloves, he preens before the full-length mirror. He pretends to fence, jabs the bamboo cane at the figure in the glass, twirls it around one finger. Where he goes when he goes, he doesn't inform Abramowitz. But when he returns he's usually melancholic, sometimes anguished, didn't have much of a good time; and in this mood may hand out a few loving lashes with that nasty cane. Or worse, make threats. Nothing serious but who needs it? Usually he prefers to stay home and watch television. He is fascinated by astronomy, and when they have such programs on the educational channel he's there night after night, staring at pictures of stars, galaxies, infinite space. He also likes to read the *Daily News* but tears it up once he's done. Sometimes he reads this book he hides on a shelf in the closet under some old hats. If the book doesn't make him laugh outright it makes him cry. When he gets excited over something he's reading in his fat book, his eyes roll, his mouth gets wet, and he tries to talk through his thick tongue; but all Abramowitz hears is geee gooo gaaa gaaw. Always these words, whatever they mean, and sometimes gool goon geek gonk, in various combinations, usually gool with gonk, which Abramowitz thinks means Goldberg. And in such states he has been known to kick Abramowitz in the belly with his heavy boot. Ooof.

When he laughs he sounds like a horse, or maybe it's the way
I hear him with these ears. And though he laughs once in a while,
it doesn't make my life easier, because of my condition. I mean I
think here I am in this horse. This is my theory though I have my
doubts. Otherwise, Goldberg is a small stocky figure with a thick
neck, heavy black brows, each like a small moustache, and big
feet that swell up in his shapeless boots. He washes his feet in the
kitchen sink and hangs up his yellowed white socks to dry on the
whitewashed walls of my stall.

In winter they live in the South in a small, messy, one-floor
house with a horse's stall attached that Goldberg can approach,
down a few steps, from the kitchen of the house. To get Abramowitz in he is led up a plank from the outside, and the door shuts
on his rear end. To keep him from wandering all over the house
there's a slatted gate to just under his head. Furthermore the stall
is next to the toilet and the broken water closet runs all night. It's
a boring life with a deaf-mute except when Goldberg changes the
act a little. Abramowitz enjoys it when they rehearse a new
routine, although Goldberg hardly ever alters the lines, only the
order of answer and question. That's better than nothing. Sometimes when Abramowitz gets tired of talking to himself, asking
unanswered questions, he complains, shouts, calls the owner dirty
names. He snorts, brays, whinnies shrilly. In his frustration he
rears, rocks, gallops in his stall; but what good is a gallop if there's
no place to go, and Goldberg can't, or won't, hear complaints,
pleas, protest?

Q. "Answer me this, if it's a sentence I'm serving, how
long?"

A.

Once in a while Goldberg seems to sense somebody else's
needs and is momentarily considerate of Abramowitz—combs
and curries him, even rubs his bushy head against the horse's. He
also shows interest in his diet and whether his bowel movements
are regular and sufficient; but if Abramowitz gets sentimentally
careless when the owner is close by and forms a question he can
see on his lips, Goldberg punches him on the nose. Or threatens
to. It doesn't hurt any the less.

All I know is he's a former vaudeville comic and acrobat. He did a solo act telling jokes, with the help of a blind assistant, before he went sad. That's all he's ever tapped to me about himself. When I forgot myself and asked what happened after that, he punched me in the nose.

Only once, when he was half drunk and giving me my pail of water, I sneaked in a fast one which he answered before he knew it.

"Where did you get me, master? Did you buy me from somebody else?"

I FOUND YOU IN A CABBAGE PATCH.

Once he tapped my skull: "In the beginning was the word."

"Which word was that?"

Bong on the nose.

NO QUESTIONS.

"Watch out for the wound on my head or wherever it is."

"Shut your mouth or your teeth will fall out."

Goldberg should read that story I once heard on his transistor radio, I thought to myself. It's about a poor cabdriver driving his sled in the Russian snow. His son, a fine boy, caught pneumonia and died, and the poor cabby is unable to find anybody to talk to so as to relieve his grief a little. Nobody wants to listen to his troubles. The customers insult him if he opens his mouth to talk. So finally he tells the story to his bony nag in the stable. And the horse, munching oats, listens patiently as the weeping old man tells him about his boy he has just buried.

Something like this could happen to you, Goldberg. Or something similar since you have no son. Maybe a nephew?

"Will you ever free me out of here, master?"

I'LL FLAY YOU ALIVE, YOU BASTARD HORSE.

We have this act we do together. Goldberg calls it, "Ask Me Another," an ironic title where I am concerned.

In the sideshow days people used to stand among the bearded ladies, fat men, Joey the snake boy, and other freaks, laughing in astonishment and disbelief at Abramowitz talking. He remembers one man staring into his mouth to see who was hiding there. Ho-

munculus? Others suggested it was a ventriloquist's act even
though the horse told them Goldberg was a deaf-mute. But in the
main tent the act got thunderous storms of applause. Reporters
pleaded for permission to interview Abramowitz, and he had
plans to tell all; but Goldberg wouldn't have it. "His head will
swell up too big," he had the talking horse say to them. "He will
never wear the same size straw hat he wore last summer."

For the performance the owner dresses up in a balloony red-
and-white polka-dot clown's suit with a pointed clown's hat and
has borrowed the ringmaster's snaky whip, an item Abramowitz
is skittish about though Goldberg says it's nothing to worry over,
little more than decoration in a circus act. No animal act is
without one. People like to hear the snap. He also ties something
like an upside-down feather duster on Abramowitz's head that
makes him look like a wilted unicorn. The little circus band ends
its brassy "Overture to William Tell"; there's a flourish of trum-
pets, and Goldberg cracks the whip as Abramowitz, with his
loose-feathered, upside-down duster, trots once around the spot-
lit ring and then stops at attention, facing clown-Goldberg, his
left foreleg pawing the sawdust-covered earth. Then they begin
the act; Goldberg's ruddy face, as he opens his painted mouth to
express himself, flushes dark red, and his melancholy eyes under
black brows protrude as he painfully squeezes out the abominable
sounds, his only eloquence.

"Geee gooo gaaa gaaw?"

Abramowitz's beautifully timed response is:

A. "To get to the other side."

There's a gasp from the spectators, a murmur, perhaps of
puzzlement, and a moment of intense expectant silence. Then at
a roll of the drums Goldberg snaps the long whip and Abramowitz translates the owner's idiocy into something that makes sense
and somehow fulfills expectations; though in truth it's no more than
a question following a response already given.

Q. "Why does a chicken cross the road?"

Then they laugh. And do they laugh! They pound each other
on the head in helpless laughter. You'd think this trite riddle, this
sad excuse for a joke were the first they've heard in their lives.

And they're laughing at the translated question, of course, not the answer, which is the way Goldberg has set it up. That's his nature for you. It's the only way he works.

Abramowitz used to sink into the dumps after that, knowing what really amuses everybody is not the old-fashioned tired little riddle, but the fact it's put to them by a talking horse. That's what splits the gut.

"It's a stupid little question."

"There are no better," Goldberg said.

"You could try letting me ask one or two of my own."

YOU KNOW WHAT A GELDING IS?

I gave him no reply. Two can play at the game.

After the first applause both performers take a bow. Abramowitz trots around the ring, his head with panache held high, and when Goldberg again cracks the snaky whip, he moves nervously to the center of the ring and they go through the routine of the other infantile answers and questions in the same silly ass-backwards order. After each question Abramowitz runs around the ring as the spectators cheer.

A. "To hold up his pants."

Q. "Why does a fireman wear red suspenders?"

A. "Columbus."

Q. "What was the first bus to cross the Atlantic?"

A. "A newspaper."

Q. "What's black and white and red all over?"

We did a dozen like that, and when we finished up, Goldberg cracked the foolish whip, I galloped twice more around the ring, then we took our last bows.

Goldberg pats my steaming flank and in the ocean-roar of everyone in the circus tent applauding and shouting bravo, we leave the ring, running down the ramp to our quarters, Goldberg's personal wagon van and my attached stall; after that we're private parties till tomorrow's show. Lots of customers used to come night after night, even following us to the next town to watch the performance, and they still laughed at the riddles though they had memorized them by now. That's how the season goes, and nothing much has changed one way or the other except that recently

Goldberg, because the manager was complaining, added a couple of silly elephant riddles to modernize the act.

A. "From playing marbles."

Q. "Why do elephants have wrinkled knees?"

A. "To pack their dirty laundry in."

Q. "Why do elephants have long trunks?"

Neither Goldberg nor I like the new jokes, but they're the latest style. I keep in my mind that we could do the act without jokes. All you need is a talking horse.

One day Abramowitz thought he would make up a riddle of his own—it's not that hard to do. So that night after they had finished the routine, he slipped in his new joke.

A. "To say hello to his friend the chicken."

Q. "Why does a yellow duck cross the road?"

After a minute of confused silence everybody cracked up; they beat themselves silly with their fists—broken straw hats flew all over the place; but Goldberg, in unbelieving astonishment, glowered at the horse. His ruddy face turned almost black. When he cracked the whip it sounded like a river of ice breaking up. Realizing in fright that he had gone too far, Abramowitz, baring his big teeth, reared up on his hind legs and took several steps forward against the will. But the spectators, thinking this was an extra flourish at the end of the act, applauded wildly. Goldberg's anger eased, and lowering his whip he pretended to laugh. He beamed at Abramowitz as if he were his only child and could do no wrong, though Abramowitz knew the owner was furious.

"Don't forget WHO'S WHO, you crazy horse," Goldberg, with his back to the audience, quickly tapped out on Abramowitz's nose.

He had him gallop once more around the ring, mounted him in an acrobatic leap from the ground onto his bare back, and drove him madly to the exit.

Afterwards he Morse-coded with his hard knuckle on the horse's bony head that if he pulled anything like that again he would personally deliver him to the glue factory.

"Where they will melt you down to size. What's left over goes into dog food cans."

"It was only a joke, master," Abramowitz explained.

"To say the answer was OK, but not to ask the question all by yourself."

Out of stored-up bitterness the talking horse replied, "I did it on account of it made me feel free."

At that Goldberg whacked him hard across the neck with his murderous cane. Abramowitz, choking, staggered, but did not bleed.

"Don't, master," he gasped, "not on my old wound."

Goldberg went into slow motion, still waving the cane.

"Try it again, you tub of guts, and I'll be wearing a horsehide coat with a fur collar, gool, goon, geek, gonk." Spit collected in the corners of his mouth.

Understood.

Sometimes I think of myself as an idea, yet here I am in this filthy stall, standing with my hoofs sunk in my yellow balls of dreck. I feel old, disgusted with myself, smelling the odor of my bad breath as my teeth in the feed bag grind the hard oats into a foaming lump, while Goldberg smokes a cigar as he watches television. He feeds me well enough, if oats is your dish, but hasn't had my stall cleaned for a week. It's easy to take revenge on a horse if that's the type you are.

So the act goes on every matinee and night, keeping Goldberg in good spirits and thousands in stitches, but Abramowitz had dreams of being out in the open. They were strange dreams, if dreams; he isn't sure what they are, or come from—thoughts of freedom, or maybe self-mockery? Whoever heard of a talking horse's dreams? This occurs to him now and then. Goldberg hasn't said he knows what's going on, but Abramowitz suspects he knows more than he seems to, because when the horse, lying in his dung and soiled straw, awakens from a dangerous reverie, he hears the owner muttering in his sleep in deaf-mute talk.

Abramowitz dreams, or does something of the sort, of other lives he might live, let's say of a horse that can't talk, couldn't conceive the idea, is perfectly content to be just a horse without problems of speech. He sees himself, for instance, pulling a light wagonload of ripe apples along a rural road. There are leafy beech trees on both sides and beyond them broad green fields full of wild flowers. If he were that kind of horse, maybe he might retire to graze in such fields. More adventurously, he sees himself a racehorse in goggles, thundering along the last stretch of muddy track, slicing through a wedge of other galloping horses to win by a nose at the finish; and the jockey is definitely not Goldberg. There is no jockey; he fell off.

Or if not a racehorse, if he has to be practical about it, Abramowitz continues on as a talking horse but not in circus work anymore; and every night on the stage he recites poetry. The theater is packed and people cry out oooh and aaah, what beautiful things that horse is saying.

Sometimes he thinks of himself as altogether a free man, someone of indeterminate appearance and characteristics, who, if he has the right education, is maybe a doctor or lawyer helping poor people who need help. Not a bad idea for a useful life.

But even as I am dreaming, or whatever it is I'm doing, I hear Goldberg talking in my sleep:

As for number one, you are first and last a talking horse, not an ordinary one who can't talk; and I have got nothing against you that you can talk, Abramowitz, but on account of what you say when you break the rules.

As for a racehorse, if you could take a good look at the broken-down type you are—overweight, with heavy sagging belly and a thick uneven dark brown coat that won't shine up no matter how much I comb or brush you, and four hairy thick bent legs, plus a pair of slight cross-eyes, you would give up this foolish idea you can be a racehorse before you do something ridiculous.

As for reciting poetry, who wants to hear a horse recite poetry? That's for the birds.

As for the third and last dream, or whatever it is that's bothering you, that you can be a doctor or lawyer, you better forget it, it's not that kind of world. A horse is a horse even if he's a talking horse; don't mix yourself up with human beings, if you know what I mean. If you're a talking horse, that's your fate. I warn you, don't be a wise guy, Abramowitz. Don't try to know everything, you might go mad. Nobody can know everything; it's not that kind of a world. Follow the rules of the game. Don't rock the boat. Don't try to make a monkey out of me; I know more than you. We got to be who we are, although this is hard for you as well as me. But that's the logic of the world. It goes by certain laws even though that's a hard proposition for some to understand. The law is the law, you can't change the order. This is the way things are put together. We are mutually related, Abramowitz, and that's all there is to it. If it makes you feel any better, I will admit to you I can't live without you and I won't let you live without me. I have my living to make and you are my talking horse I use in my act to make my living, plus so I can take care of your needs. The true freedom, like I have always told you, though you never believe me, is to understand that and live with it so you don't waste your energy resisting the rules. All you are is a horse who talks, and believe me, there are very few horses that can do that; so if you are smart, Abramowitz, it should make you happy instead of always and continually dissatisfied. Don't break up the act if you know what's good for you.

As for those yellow balls of your dreck, if you will behave yourself like a gentleman and watch out what you say, tomorrow the shovelers will come, and after, I will hose you over personally with warm water. Believe me, there's nothing like cleanliness.

Thus he mocks me in my sleep, if that's what it is. I have my doubts that I sleep much nowadays.

In short hops between towns and small cities the circus moves in wagon vans. The other horses pull them, but Goldberg won't let me, which wakes up disturbing ideas in my head. For longer hauls, from one big city to another, we ride in red-and-white circus trains. I have a stall in a freight car with some nontalking horses with braided manes and sculptured tails, from the bareback riders' act. None of us are much interested in each other. If they think at all they think a talking horse is a show-off. All they do is eat, drink, piss, and crap all day. Not a single word goes back or forth among them.

The long train rides generally give us a day off without a show, and Goldberg gets depressed and surly when we're not working the matinee or evening performance. Early in the morning of a long train-ride day he starts loving his bottle and Morse-coding me nasty remarks and threats.

"Abramowitz, you think too much, why do you bother? In the first place, your thoughts come out of you and you don't know that much, so your thoughts don't either. In other words, don't get ambitious. For instance, what are you thinking about now, tell me?"

"Answers and questions, master—some new ones to modernize the act."

"Feh, we don't need any new ones, the act is already too long."

He should know the questions I am really asking myself, though better not.

Once you start asking questions one leads to the next and in the end it's endless. And what if it turns out I'm always asking myself the same question in different words? I keep on asking myself why I can't ask this coarse lout a simple question about anything. By now I have it figured out that Goldberg is afraid of questions because a question could show he's afraid people will find out who he is. Somebody who all he does is repeat his fate, if you know what I mean. It's thinking about his that made me better understand my own. Anyway, Goldberg has some kind of past he is afraid to tell me about, though sometimes he hints. And when I mention my own past he says forget it, think of the future. What future? On the other hand, what does he think he can hide from Abramowitz, a student by nature, who spends most of his time asking himself questions Goldberg won't permit him to ask, putting one and one together, and finally making up his mind—miraculous thought—that he knows more than a horse should, even a talking horse, so therefore, given all the built-up evidence, he is positively not a horse. Not in origin, anyway.

So I came once more to the conclusion that I am a man in a

horse and not just a horse that happens to be able to talk. I had
figured this out in my mind before; then I said, no it can't be. I feel
more like a horse bodywise; on the other hand, I talk, I think, I
wish to ask questions. A. Not a horse but a man. Q. Who else does
the same? So I am what I am, which is a *man* in a horse, not a
talking horse. Something tells me there is no such thing, even
though Goldberg, pointing his finger at me, says the opposite.
He lives on his lies, it's his nature.

Abramowitz's four legs wobbled with emotion at the thought.

After a long day of traveling, when they were in their new quarters that night, finding the rear door to his stall unlocked—Goldberg grew careless when depressed—acting on belief as well as
impulse, Abramowitz cautiously backed out. Avoiding the front of
Goldberg's wagon van he trotted across the fairgrounds on which
the circus was situated. Two of the circus hands who saw him trot
by, perhaps because Abramowitz greeted them, "Hello, boys, mar-
velous evening," did not attempt to stop him. Outside the grounds,
though exhilarated to be in the open, Abramowitz began to wonder
if he were doing a foolish thing. He had hoped to find a wooded
spot to hide in for the time being, surrounded by fields in which he
could peacefully graze; but this was the industrial edge of the city,
and though he clop-clopped from street to street, there were no
woods nearby, not even a small park.

Where can somebody who looks like a horse go by himself?

Abramowitz tried to hide in an old riding-school stable and was
driven out by an irate woman. In the end they caught up with him
on a station platform where he had been waiting for a train. Quite
foolishly, he knew. The conductor wouldn't let him get on though
Abramowitz had explained his predicament. The stationmaster
then ran out and pointed a pistol at his head. He held the horse
there, deaf to his blandishments, until Goldberg arrived with his
bamboo cane. The owner threatened to whip Abramowitz black
and blue, and his description of the effects was so painfully vivid
that Abramowitz felt as though he had been slashed into a bloody
pulp. A half hour later he found himself back in his locked stall,
his throbbing head encrusted with dried horse blood. Goldberg
ranted in deaf-mute talk, but Abramowitz, who with lowered

head pretended contrition, felt none. To escape from Goldberg he knew he must first get out of the horse he was in.

But to exit a horse as a man takes some doing. Abramowitz planned to proceed slowly and appeal to public opinion. It might take months to do what he must. Protest. Sabotage if necessary. Revolt! One night after they had taken their bows and the applause was subsiding, Abramowitz, raising his head as though to whinny his appreciation of the plaudits, suddenly cried out to all assembled in the circus tent, "Help! Get me out of here, somebody! I am a prisoner in this horse! Free a fellow man!"

After a silence that rose up like a dense forest, Goldberg, who was standing to the side, unaware of Abramowitz's passionate cry—he picked up the news later from the ringmaster—saw at once from everybody's surprised and startled expression, not to mention Abramowitz's undisguised look of triumph, that something had gone seriously wrong. The owner at once began to laugh heartily, as though whatever it was that was going on was more of the same, part of the act, a bit of personal encore by the horse. The spectators laughed too, and again warmly applauded.

"It won't do you any good," the owner Morse-coded Abramowitz afterwards. "Because nobody is going to believe you."

"Then please let me out of here on your own account, master. Have some mercy."

"On that matter," Goldberg rapped out sternly, "I am already on record. Our lives and livings are mutually dependent, one on the other. You got nothing substantial to complain about, Abramowitz. I'm taking care on you better than you can take care on yourself."

"Maybe that's so, Mr. Goldberg, but what good is it if in my heart I am a man and not a horse, not even a talking one?"

Goldberg's ruddy face blanched as he Morse-coded the usual NO QUESTIONS.

"I'm not asking, I'm telling you something very serious."

"Watch out for hubris, Abramowitz."

That night the owner went out on the town, came back dreadfully drunk, as though he had been standing with his mouth open where it had rained brandy; and he threatened Abramowitz with the trident spear he kept in his trunk when they traveled. This is a new torment.

Anyway, the act goes on but definitely altered, not as before. Abramowitz, despite numerous warnings and various other painful threats, daily disturbs the routine. After Goldberg makes his idiot noises, his geee, gooo, gaaa, gaaw, Abramowitz purposely mixes up the responses to the usual ridiculous riddles.

A. "To get to the other side."

Q. "Why does a fireman wear red suspenders?"

A. "From playing marbles."

Q. "Why do elephants have long trunks?"

And he adds dangerous A.'s and Q.'s without permission despite the inevitability of punishment.

A. "A talking horse."

Q. "What has four legs and wishes to be free?"

At that nobody laughed.

He also mocked Goldberg when the owner wasn't carefully reading his lips; called him "deaf-mute," "stupid ears," "lock mouth"; and whenever possible addressed the public, requesting, urging, begging their assistance.

"Gevalt! Get me out of here! I am one of you! This is slavery! I wish to be free!"

Now and then when Goldberg's back was turned, or he was too lethargic with melancholy to be much attentive, Abramowitz clowned around and in other ways ridiculed the owner. He heehawed at his appearance, brayed at his "talk," stupidity, tyranny. Sometimes he made up little songs of freedom as he danced on his hind legs, exposing his private parts. And sometimes Goldberg, to mock the mocker, danced with him—a clown with a glum painted smile waltzing with a horse. Those who had seen the act last season were astonished, stunned by the change. They seemed concerned, uneasy.

"Help! Help, somebody help me!" Abramowitz pleaded, but nobody moved.

Sensing the tension in and around the ring the audience sometimes booed the performers, causing Goldberg, in his red-and-white polka-dot suit and white clown's cap, great embarrassment, though on the whole he kept his cool during the act and never used the ringmaster's whip. In fact he smiled as he was being insulted, whether he "listened" or not. There was a sly fixed smile on his face, and his lips twitched. And though his fleshy ears flamed like torches at the gibes and mockeries he endured, Goldberg laughed to the point of tears at Abramowitz's sallies and shenanigans; many in the big tent laughed along with him. Abramowitz was furious.

Afterwards Goldberg, once he had stepped out of his clown suit, threatened him to the point of collapse, or flayed him viciously with his cane; and the next day fed him pep pills, and painted his hide black before the performance so that people wouldn't see the wounds.

"You bastard horse, you'll lose us our living."

"I wish to be free."

"To be free you got to know when you are free. Considering your type, Abramowitz, you'll be free in the glue factory."

One night when Goldberg, after a day of profound depression, was listless and logy in the ring, could not get so much as a limp snap out of his whip, Abramowitz, thinking that where the future was concerned glue factory or his present condition of life made little difference, determined to escape either fate; he gave a solo performance for freedom, the best of his career. Though desperate, he entertained, made up hilarious riddles, recited poems he had heard on Goldberg's transistor radio which sometimes stayed on all night after he had fallen asleep; he also told stories and ended the evening with a moving speech.

He told sad stories of the lot of horses, one, for instance, beaten to death by his cruel owner, his brains battered with a log because he was too weakened by hunger to pull a heavy wagonload of wood. Another concerned a racehorse of fantastic speed, a sure winner in the Kentucky Derby, had he not, in his very first race, been doped by his owner who had placed a fortune in bets on the next best horse. One was about a flying horse shot down by a hunter who could not believe his eyes. And then Abramowitz told a story of a youth of great promise, who, out for a stroll one sunny spring day, came upon a goddess bathing in a stream. He gazed at her bare beauty in amazement and longing; seeing him staring at her she let out a piercing scream. The youth took off at a fast gallop, realizing, before he had got very far, from the noise of his snorting and the sound of pounding hoofs as he ran, that he was no longer a youth of great promise but a horse running.

Abramowitz then cried out to the faces that surrounded him, "I am also a man in a horse. Is there a doctor in the house who can help me out?"

Dead silence.

"If not a doctor, maybe a magician?"

No response except nervous laughter.

He then delivered an impassioned short speech on freedom for all. Abramowitz talked his brains blue, ending once more with a personal appeal. "Help me to recover my original form. It's not what I am but what I wish to be. I wish to be what I really am, which is a man."

At the end of the act many people in the tent were wet-eyed and the band played "The Star-Spangled Banner."

Goldberg, who had been asleep in a sawdust pile for a good part of Abramowitz's solo act, roused himself in time to join the horse in a bow. Afterwards, on the enthusiastic advice of the circus manager, he changed the name of the act from "Ask Me Another" to "Goldberg's Varieties." And wept, himself, for unknown reasons.

Back in his stall after the failure of his most passionate, most inspired pleas for assistance, Abramowitz butted his head in frustration against the stall gate until his nostrils bled in his feed bag. He thought he might drown in his blood and didn't much care. Goldberg found him lying on the floor of the stall, half in a faint, and revived him with aromatic spirits of ammonia. He bandaged his nose and spoke to him in a fatherly fashion.

"That's how the mop flops," he Morse-coded with his fingertip, "but things could be worse. Take my advice and settle for a talking horse, it's got distinction."

"Make me either into a man or make me either into a horse," Abramowitz moaned. "It's your power, Goldberg."

"You got the wrong party, my friend."

"Why do you always say lies?"

"Why do you always ask questions you can't ask?"

"I ask because I am. I wish to be free."

"So who's free, tell me?" Goldberg asked.

"If so," said Abramowitz, "then what's to be done?"

DON'T ASK. I WARNED YOU.

He threatened to punch his nose; it bled again.

Abramowitz later that day began a hunger strike which he carried on for the better part of a week; but Goldberg threatened force-feeding with thick tubes in both nostrils, and that ended that. Abramowitz almost choked to death at the thought of it. The act went on as before, and the owner changed its name back to "Ask Me Another." When the season was over the circus headed south. Abramowitz trotted along in a cloud of dust with the other horses.

Anyway, I have my thoughts.

One fine autumn day, Goldberg washed his feet in the kitchen sink and hung his smelly white socks to dry on the gate of Abramowitz's stall before sitting down to watch astronomy on educational television. To see better he had placed a lit candle on top of the TV set. But he had carelessly left the stall gate open and Abramowitz, surprised to discover he had not given up, hopped up three steps and trotted through the messy kitchen into the living room, his eyes flaring. Confronting Goldberg staring in awe at the universe on the screen, he reared with a bray of rage to bring his hoofs down on the owner's head. Goldberg rose to protect himself. Hopping up on the chair he managed with a grunt to grab Abramowitz by both his big ears as though to lift him by them, and the horse's head and neck, up to an old wound, came off in his hands. Amid the stench of blood and bowel a man's pale head popped out of the hole in the horse. He was in his early forties, with fogged pince-nez, intense dark eyes, and a black moustache. Pulling his arms free, he grabbed Goldberg around his thick neck with both bare arms, holding on for dear life. As they tugged and struggled, Abramowitz, straining to the point of madness, slowly pulled himself out of the horse up to his navel. At that moment Goldberg broke his grip and, though the astronomy lesson was still going on, disappeared. Abramowitz made a few discreet inquiries, later, but no one could say where.

Departing the circus grounds, he cantered across a grassy soft field into a dark wood, a free centaur.

Rosellen Brown's poems have appeared in many magazines, including *Atlantic, Poetry,* and *Nation.* Her book of poems *Some Deaths in the Delta* was a National Council on the Arts Selection for 1970. She has had stories in the *New American Review, Tri-Quarterly, Hudson Review, Quarterly Review of Literature,* and other magazines. Miss Brown is gathering together a series of stories about the people in "Mainlanders," among others, into a book to be called *The Ice Cream Block.* She lives with her husband and two young daughters in Orford, New Hampshire, and teaches part-time in a rural Vermont school.

MAINLANDERS

My friends Ines, Gloria and Isabel, between them, have thirteen children, boys named after fathers present and absent, girls bearing fresh hopes into a generation of *Americanos,* shining in the names of movie stars, at home in South Brooklyn. Every one of them has a crumbless kitchen, against great odds; a kitchen of flowers and the obedience of dogs and children. Their rooms are dense with glass fish and gilt frames, busy with a great many hearts beating, hands flying. They spend hours combing their daughters' dark hair ungrudgingly; stirring with a tinny spoon two kinds of rice and salty *baccalao.* They do not burn candles from the *Botanica* or visit a spiritist but they will tell you, if you ask, that everyone was happier when their mothers did, even if it meant crazy fears and wearing a black hand on your wrist from the day you were born. *We sang, we danced, the parties never ended. Now I don't want my children out of the house or I might not see them again. Or want to see them. Today your house is never so full of comadres and when they come—we sit in the dark of a cave and watch a little dead blue light dancing.* They are womanly and independent of their men, making demands only beyond the point when the future dims and dips under the horizon. Then they ask for assurance loud and open and straight. Most of them are not with their first husbands.

One morning Cherry announces, holding back on the threshold between two rooms, that her husband threatened to kill her last night. And he means it, she says; he showed her the pistol, just out of hock.

Two weeks later, when we hear that Cherry has taken the children and gone to her mother in New Jersey, they are stunned. No one can think why she'd have left him. *He put too damn much money in that car of his,* Isabel tells us. *And too much time, she was always complaining he liked the car better than her.* I remind them of the morning she told us about the gun.

Isabel says *I wasn't here that day.* Ines says *That must have been when I was on the phone.* Elsa says she was in and out a lot that morning. Gloria just sits and looks at me, shaking her head.

The long school block is an unrelenting tangle—no one ever sees who it is who's been generous enough to give the homebound children their dead cars for souvenirs. They are the children's castles; creative playthings. Across moats of broken windshield glass, the second graders spin the steering wheels, they hoot and bounce on the burned-out back seats. It is the adults who eat the flesh of the cars—take home the mirrors, hubcaps, everything that twists or lifts off; the children can still get footholds on the skeleton and they aren't chrome-hungry. For a while you drive your car around the block the long way so you won't have to see the boneyard. But now there is half a Ford hulked at the corner and soon even the curb of the long way around will be lined with flung bones and tin flesh dangling.

It all happened twelve or fifteen years ago and in smiling beery recollection it sounds casual and benign. Hector is safe on the other side; he has made it and can vouch for the others too: none of them is dead, only one is in jail, and that for taking somebody else's rap, which must be a special form of success. A point of pride: none of their girls ever got hooked—they had their junkies, on and off, but the girls were clean. The Padres were real, though, he insists, and meant business, chains and knives to prove it. Peculiar, Hector muses: they were the only integrated gang in Brooklyn! Isn't that anyone's idea of brotherhood? They included in the blood fellowship the blue-eyed brownstone son of a Jewish judge whose chambers must have been up at the other end of Court Street, where the state and the borough of Brooklyn dreamed they had things under control.

The seams began to loosen and then to rip for the best of reasons, when Spanish dancing came into a power of its own; he and the other Puerto Ricans in the Padres went downtown to the ballrooms. In fact, they couldn't stay away: gang fights, running into the dark on sneakered feet with blood on the knuckles, was no longer the only pure joy. When Leonard Bernstein and Jerome Robbins came to see them dance and write down bits of their conversation in little leather notebooks, their teeth must already have been filed halfway. When *West Side Story* opened and they saw what they had become onstage (saw in suits and after-shave from the eighth row orchestra) and were proud, not cheated of themselves, that file touched the nerve of the street boy in them and severed it for good.

Hector and Gloria (who's been his all these years, since he was a Padre) spend themselves, time and money, keeping their boy and girl from seeing out the window past the clotheslines. In green chalk the wall at their corner warns THE BOYS FROM BERGEN STREET LAMF (to be read no other way than it was intended: *Likamuhfuckuh!*). Their son is almost old enough to begin to see his possibilities. He indulges his father with pieties about the unappealing habits of The Boys, who are noisy, dirty, disrespectful, and goes out of his way to make friends with the biggest Boy's little brother.

All the ways there are to live seventeen years in one spot. Carmen's bubble. She moves, pretty, dark, pointy at the elbows, up and down the long flights to her grandmother's fourth-floor-front, where she has a bed in a corner of the living room. She is an adventurer among her friends—her boyfriend occasionally takes her to 42nd Street. The others, though. They are not merely rooted to the cement up and down the block: they *are* the ground they poke up out of, one can't imagine them being plucked out of it and transplanted, unless to an identical block. This is a secret they keep well: no one who lives in Brooklyn—near downtown, where the stores are!—can look stranded down a rutted country lane in the year 1971. They curse like men at the ugly street, with its pavement uneven as the ocean, and garbage over the pail rims. What's more, they look as though they are prepared to travel— eye make-up thick with impossible invitations; pants flared in proper response to the necessities of the year; and nothing about them which admits poverty except (leaving aside their hopes, their expectations, and the unfilled spaces in their minds) mouths full of blighted teeth, which can't be hidden behind pleats or new-new vinyl. Other than that, their only isolation from the other avid shoppers they pass on Fulton Street, or so it seems, is their Spanish accent. But they were born in Brooklyn, all of them, and they do not know Spanish. Only the names of foods they cannot cook. The farthest they dare to go (they say, want to go) is school, and they go there and back like programmed machines. A few times last year, Carmen tells me, she went out to Staten Island with a friend whose brother had the good fortune to live in a big green park. It was an institution for the retarded and it seemed to me the grass was poor compensation for all he would never have. But she was far from depressed at the sight of the children in their caged lives. She wanted to go back.

She brought me a problem once from her school. She dared not trust herself to read it correctly so she showed it to me, copied out dutifully in her loose-leaf book (for which subject she couldn't remember):

LIST 5 REASONS BEHIND MAN'S DESIRE TO ESCAPE THIS WORLD.

I leaned hard against the doorpost and told her I couldn't really help her much with that.

She has another year of school. Then she wants to become a
nurse, either in the army (it is hard to imagine her very girlish
suppleness in brown—or is it gray or navy—with shoulder pads)
or she will take a mail order course on her own. She has been
eyeing an ad for a nursing "diploma" in the back of her catechism
book. She will learn something from those fruitless dealings—I
wish, I wish I could tell her so she would hear me—but it will not
be nursing.

Carmen is getting married. She has known the boy since the
sixth grade and she says he is very kind—that is, she adds, un-
embarrassed, he is not Spanish. Because she does not want to be
beaten and deserted, as her father and every other man she knows
up and down the block have proved themselves solely capable of
doing. (Her father has already given her his wedding present,
she tells me. She has just seen him for the first time since she was
two years old—he lives perhaps a half-mile away—and, no, he
hasn't given her his blessing but something more important: his
admission that he has no rights in the matter, neither to bless her
nor to curse her. She admits she has been terrified of the meeting.) She is, she says, very very lucky. "Going to get married" in
this case means, for what it is worth, declaring herself the girl
who is officially waiting for a boy named Happy to get free of the
army in a couple of years, and to get past Vietnam. The half-chil-
dren in her womb have a couple of years, then, to get ready.

The one tangible thing the intention is worth at this point is a
solemn exchange of rings—his only a $50 affair which she hopes
they will let him wear even in his uniform, hers a classic diamond (pear shaped) for upwards of five hundred as-yet-un-
earned dollars. She spends all her waking and probably her
dreaming hours imagining it. Whether she dreams of Happy himself she does not tell me. Therefore: swallowing what I tell myself
is merely a culture-bound nausea at the idea of beginning married life in mutual indebtedness to a salesman of stones, I suggest
to Carmen that she shop around a bit before she commits herself to a dusty, unprepossessing (but expensive) chip of rock
glimpsed only in the window of the Kredit jewelers around the
corner, where it sits winking in mirrors. Now I am as innocent as

Carmen, it turns out, though that is my guilt; it is only her misfortune—how can she be otherwise? I suggest to her that she shop for her diamond in the jewelry district, that great stone quarry in the 40s off Fifth Avenue. Carmen has no idea where those streets are, or even *that* they are. She has never even heard of Macy's. She has never been out of Brooklyn on the "F" train, not across the river into the city, that quick commute that takes seven minutes when the trains are running right. (Yes, it runs to Coney in the other direction, and she's been out that way. And the "A" train took her to *El Barrio,* Spanish Harlem, once with her mother but she didn't like that—she was happy to know it was there but wasn't planning to return.)

She misses two dates to make the trip but finally, afraid to evade it any longer, she shows up at my house, late but willing. We go into the city. (I am writing down everything we do, at her insistence: which train, which direction, which stairway, which exit, in case she ever has to go back on her own.) We conclude our business, $450 worth and a bargain at that, though to me an invisible one weighing less than a carat, and I delighted to be as uninformed about faceting and appraisals as she is—and look for a place to have lunch. Carmen is walking proudly next to me with the receipt for her down payment in her pocket. (She has a little dowry of savings from her baby-sitting, and keeps it in a dresser drawer. *Banks charge to keep your money,* she insists, though credit buying is—isn't it?—free.) She has been lavished with more attention and respect than any of the Brooklyn cut-throats would ever squander on a poor P.R.; her eyes, under their weight of ballerina's stripes and shadings, are glimmering with light of fifty-eight genuine facets. She says *Hey, I heard of a place once we could go if it's around here somewhere. This restaurant, I think it's called The Astronaut. You put money in these places in the wall. . . ."* While we're looking for the one on 47th Street, I tell her, tears in my eyes, that if she likes it, she'll find another three long blocks from her house.

Gloria, Ines and Isabel are sitting, elbows on the table, silt-black coffee in the cup, toothy with anger. *Marie, Marie, Marie, is hav-*

ing a baby. So. She has betrayed them. They have clawed their way to a sanity about this thing (except for Ines, whose life has been complicated by many men, two children each, no more ever, unless of course by another husband)—boosted each other over a wall of private secrets, public regulations—and she has flown in its gleaming, aseptic face. Her littlest one still crawls on a splintery floor, the older ones out at the elbows and pockets to everyone's shame but Marie's. They shake the dregs of coffee like miners looking for gold; a gilt light sways and dances across the stamped tin ceiling. If they could go back with Marie to the very moment—the instant when life flew out of her like a dangerous spark—they would haul her away by the ears and feet and sit with her under a wall somewhere, cool against the brick, until she remembered how she was a virgin once. But here they are, too late, like mourners, and she has broken the ranks and run off by herself. *Friends don't do you no good,* says Isabel. *Damn the dark* is what she is thinking, *and men when you can't see their faces*. She clicks her tongue wetly like someone about to spit, and swallows cold dirt from the bottom of the cup.

Ines says she can get coats, suits, a whole line of men's clothes— 36, 38, 40—very cheap. She sells it for extra kitchen money. *Where do you get it, Ines?* She smiles, looks across the coffee cups at no one, looks back to see if I am smiling too.

He opened the store with banners and signs welcoming himself, promising SPANISH FAVORITES!!! as though every corner hadn't had a dusty store or two for years: Varela's, Rodriguez Family Grocery, Maximo's Bodega, and all those that never bothered to name themselves. In the window lies the salt cod, beached on a five-pound sack of rice, going gritty on the motes in the air. A thin-haired tiger cat prowls as close to it as she dares and compromises, folding herself up day after day at the foot of the bread-rack that stands near enough to be redolent of aging fish. Near the back, under the detergents, there is one discreet shelf of candles for the assuaging of saints and the destruction of enemies. Out of the dark the kindergarten colors glow in their tall glasses, the reds, greens, pinks, blues (PEACEFUL HOME, [alleged] MONEY DRAWING CANDLE, SAFE CROSSING, 7 AFRICAN POWERS, WORK CANDLE, a dozen wordless black candles, a hissing cat, back arched, frosted over the wax) and the multicolor stripes, almost edible in their candied vividness.

Day after week after month he comes to work at seven, sometimes earlier; he pulls the gate across the front door at ten or eleven, seven days a week. In less than a day's work hunching behind the counter, his face avid for activity, he could go three-quarters of the way around the world.

From my window across the street—across a river of people never diverted from their business and the habits that take them to supermarkets or old stores full of old friends—I watch his banners wilt. When I go to him for something I've forgotten elsewhere, I can feel the air alter at the threshold: cheeses souring on months, even the cans and boxes stale at the edges, a film of dead time on their labels. His little savings wash into the sewer grating out front, and his small face begins to go pointy with fear. His mustache sharpens. His round and sunny wife, who cannot speak to any but the Spanish customers, is trying to learn how to ring up numbers. She puckers her brow like a child pleasing her parents, but she gets too little practice; and when an *Americano* stands at the counter with his beer or cigarettes or one can of tomato sauce, her husband sprints up to the adding machine to keep her from offending with her slowness. He works so hard at polishing and straightening that I expect hungry genies to spring out of the buffed counters with long grocery lists in their rich smoky hands.

It will be only a matter of a few weeks now: surely the miscalculations have begun to add themselves up in his meticulous ledger. I turn away, I can't go near his door, it is plague-ridden with his misfortunes. I restrain myself from calling down to him from my window as he douses the sidewalk from a pail of suds, once, and a second time: *Señor Rojas! You have been notified in case of emergency! Escape while you can! The A & P is coming with a black glove on its closed hand. There will be no clues. (Mira, believe me, Señor, how far away must one be to see it?) You will be found shaken to death, your fingers—your careful dreaming fingers—still on the register keys, the drawer wide open, none of your money gone.*

Isabel (and Paco and Nilda and Faye), Gloria (and Hector and Doris and Junior) and Ines (and Ismael and Tracy and Tanya, Chico and Nando, and a visiting niece, Yvonne), two dogs, a room full of fish tanks, a stray cat who eats in Ines' kitchen, and Hector's mother, live on a jut called Red Hook that points to the sea. They could trace, with a little patience, the gray street through beer cans to the river, wind with the river under the bridge, and go free from there. It isn't good for much, the ocean— a damp breeze in July, and maybe a couple of outings to the beach if somebody's car is working. Europe's across it and the air is never dull because of it: coffee burnt in Jersey; oily fish dead on the surface; burning rubber from the shipyard—*what in the hell do they do over there?*—and once in a while, better than flowers, a hint of endless, black, deep mountains of salt.

One day Junior came home late for supper. He had pieced together a story in a book at school, very vague, but he went over to the fenced-in riverbank to think about it and see if it made any sense. Somewhere, he had read, the streets are water and salt, the houses are water and salt, the people water and salt, and an old green island, real as Manhattan across the soot-gray inlet, is lost with all its gold and silver still heavy on it.

Patricia Zelver grew up in Medford, Oregon, and took her A.B. and M.A. at Stanford University. She is married to a City Planner and has two sons. Mrs. Zelver has published short stories in various magazines and is the author of two novels, *The Honey Bunch* and *The Happy Family*. She lives with her husband on the San Francisco Peninsula, and is at present working on a third novel.

THE FLOOD

It had been raining for a week. The rain melted the snow packs in the mountains, turning the streams into torrents; logging roads were flooded, upland farms inundated; Highway 99 across the Siskiyous was closed by slides. In town, the creek had overflowed, and the merchants on Creek Street put up sandbags. The wind blew in great gusts; the Norton News Sentinel said the river, ten miles out of town, was rising a foot an hour.

John Brigham decided he ought to call Hilda Butterwick before the lines went out.

"Look here, Hilda," he would say, firmly, "you better get into town. I'll reserve a room for you at the Hotel and I'll come out and get you."

That was it. Just a brisk statement, no more. Nothing about The Manse; though a new letter from one of Hilda's daughters, who lived in California, lay upon his desk: "Surely you can persuade her. . . . She would be so much more comfortable and, if anything happened, we could feel assured she'd get the proper care."

John had to chuckle when he read the letter. He felt the same way Hilda did about The Manse—going there would destroy your integrity as a citizen and human being. He belonged to this town;

he had grown up here and practiced law for forty-three years. The Manse was a recent modern monstrosity built upon the hill, just outside of town; it was a colony unto itself; it was even run by a bunch of outsiders—professional Presbyterian social workers. Not that he criticized the project; they provided a useful service and he even often advised his elderly clients to go there.

"But what about you, John?" Mildred Stone, a recently widowed lady asked him. "You're my age."

"Oh, I've got nothing against The Manse," John said. "It's a fine place, for most folks, but I'm not sure I'd fit in. I might want to pinch one of those pretty nurses they have, and get in trouble."

Milly had pretended to look shocked; then she giggled at his wickedness. They had known each other ever since Emerson Grade School days; he felt certain Milly would feel at home up there.

But Hilda Butterwick! If The Manse were his client, he'd have to advise them not to take her; all she would do would be to stir up trouble; that was her hobby, nowadays.

Besides, he was the last person to advise her about anything. He had considered writing back to her daughter and saying, "Appeal to Newman Hunter, not me. I am no longer in her favor." But, of course, you couldn't say a thing like that to children.

Hazel left at five-thirty. At six, John kicked out Olly Ferguson, who made John's office a home away from home. He didn't want anyone to hear, not even Olly, who didn't have all his marbles anymore, for he had publicly vowed never to speak to Hilda Butterwick again.

He put the call through. The Shady Cove operator answered.

"This is John Brigham," he said. "How are all of you doing out there?"

"Well, the lines are still up," she said. "But Benny's Cocktail Lounge had to close last night. It was too wet in there even for the soaks."

"Give me Hilda Butterwick."

"I thought you were never going to speak to her again."

"It's strictly a business matter," said John.

"Half the time she won't talk unless I tell her it's Newman Hunter, and sometimes she won't even talk to him!"

"We'll give it a try," John said.

The rural line buzzed; after a moment Hilda answered. John could hear the operator tell her Mr. Brigham was on the phone.

There was a long pause, then Hilda spoke. Her ordinarily throaty voice had a peculiar high sing-song rhythm. "This is a recorded announcement," she said. "Mrs. Butterwick is entertaining guests. At the sound of the gong you may leave a message." There was another silence. Then the Chinese gong, which Hilda had brought back from Hong Kong on one of her crazy trips around the world, echoed stridently in John's ear.

"Oh, for Christ's sake, Hilda, come off your high horse. I'm just calling to see if you need any assistance."

"Mrs. Butterwick asks for no charity, she is able to take care of herself," she replied in the same Recorded Announcement voice. Then she hung up.

"I told you so," said the Shady Cove operator, gleefully.

When John's rage had subsided a little, he decided he was glad he had called, despite the humiliation. Now, if Hilda drowned, he could say, I tried to rescue the old bag. Yes, I swallowed my pride and called her up and offered my assistance . . . But then Hilda wouldn't be around to know he had been right all along; as he'd been right about a lot of other things, too. Sadly, he realized that she was the only person he'd really want to tell. Goddamn Hilda Butterwick, he thought. She has destroyed the serenity of my old age.

The next evening there was a heavier storm with sixty miles an hour winds. The electricity and the phone service went out, and everyone sat around in Raymond's Bar, huddled up in coats and mittens and stocking caps; they played gin rummy by candlelight, and listened to the reports on a transistor radio about the river. Casper's Bridge, below Shady Cove was out. Schools all over the area were closed. Army helicopters were attempting to rescue people stranded in isolated mountain communities. The sheriff's men were evacuating people from Sam's Valley on the Left Fork. People with cabins on the river were beginning to come into town.

The Red Cross was setting up emergency shelters in the high school gym in town.

"How is Hilda?" Raymond asked John.

"How the hell should I know," he said. He thought he was catching a chill, and he felt morose. "She's not my client anymore, anyway," he added, so it would be on record. "She's going to Newman Hunter."

Newman Hunter was nine years younger than John. He had an office in the old brick Wells Fargo Building, all gussied up with gold scales and bar chairs and an antique safe and a black tufted leather sofa. He dressed in costume, like a movie gambler from the 90's, a red vest and a watch chain, a Stetson hat and boots. Whenever The News Sentinel did a feature on the town, they included a photograph of Newman, entitled "colorful local attorney." Since these activities were not properly lawyerish, the local Bar snubbed him. It was just like Hilda to be attracted to a charlatan like that.

Hilda, in her dotage, had discovered the law courts. She had pestered John, continually, to sue the United States government, the county, the Power and Light Company, even personal friends. She had done this, despite the fact that she knew John detested going to court, which meant putting on his hearing aid. Moreover, his experience in the law had taught him that most court cases were unnecessary. If you waited long enough, people either settled out of court or forgot their grievances. Time, itself, was on your side. But Newman was an actor, and enjoyed making court appearances, no matter how outlandish the cases were.

Now Hilda was giving Newman trouble; he wondered if she had used her Recorded Announcement voice on him. Yes, let Newman persuade Hilda to leave the Chalet, he decided. He could go out there in his movie outfit clothes and no doubt get a story in the News Sentinel about how he had endangered his life for his client.

At ten o'clock, John went home. He couldn't drive down Jackson on account of the creek; he had to take a circuitous route down Elm. It was raining buckets and the street lamps were out;

still, he could have driven the whole town blindfolded after all these years.

His small ordinarily comfortable bachelor home was freezing, and there was a leak in the kitchen roof. He scrambled around in the dark, and found a pot to put under it; then he groped his way into his bedroom, undressed quickly, down to his long underwear, threw some extra blankets on the bed and crawled in.

But it was still cold, his arthritis hurt, he couldn't use his heating pad, and there was no hot water for a hot water bottle. Moreover, he couldn't get Hilda off his mind. Recorded Announcement, indeed. Where had she picked that one up? Probably Newman had some new-fangled device like that in his office along with those phony antiques. He could hear the drip, drip, drip in the pot from the kitchen—a loud, lonely, ominous sound. The Manse, he had been told, had an emergency generator.

Well, if he were cold, Hilda would be colder, despite her Spartan ways. The Chalet was really just a big drafty barn. He had not set foot in it, now, for two years—not since she had thrown that moth-eaten marmot at him, after he had refused to sue Clayton Poole for the bridgework that troubled her. She had missed, and he had kept his poise. In cruel retaliation, he had told her she was growing senile; she should go to The Manse.

Perhaps he shouldn't have said that; perhaps the rupture had been partly his fault. He had let things get off on an unprofessional footing the year before that, when he had asked her to marry him. It certainly had not been her feminine charms; it had been her cooking, which he had to admit was good, and the attractions, though not the comforts, of the Chalet. Right away he had regretted his hasty words; marriage to Hilda Butterwick would have been like punishing himself for all those years of peaceful bachelor life. But his impulsive proposal, made after too many bourbons, had given her the upper hand. He had noted the gleeful look in her blue eyes when she turned him down. The look had implied that he would ask her again; instead he had felt the relief of a reprieved felon.

She had revenged herself, shamelessly.

"John thinks he'd like to move into the Chalet," she said, in his presence, at one of her parties, to Doc Storey. "But can you imagine him living without central heating?"

At other gatherings, she hinted by her manner at attempted intimacies. And one day in his office, right in front of Hazel, she had asked him how his bladder was working after his prostate trouble.

At the same time he was certain she had not wanted to marry him; since her husband's death she had openly cherished her new independence. She was merely disappointed that John had not given her a second chance to demonstrate this.

The next day, after a sleepless night, John put on his old fishing boots and his plaid mackinaw, which he had not worn for years, and drove into town. He could barely see and the water was almost up to his hubcaps. Main Street was blocked off, now.

At the Police Station, the Chief was out helping with the refugees, but Carl Swanson was at his desk. "Well, I see there's no fool like an old fool," he said cheerfully, when he saw John.

"I want you to make a check on Hilda Butterwick," said John.

"They're all being evacuated up at Shady Cove," Carl said. "It's a real mess. We've got two pregnant women and four new babies over at the gym."

"I want you to get in touch with the Sheriff and ask about Hilda. She's lived alone so long, she's kind of squirrelly. She probably doesn't even know how serious it is."

"I'll do that if you promise to go to Raymond's," Carl said. "He has a fire going, and enough people there to keep warm. I'll drop by and tell you what we've learned."

"Don't just shout it out loud in front of everyone," John said. "You come in and get me aside. It's a kind of, well, a touchy proposition."

"It shall be handled with the utmost delicacy," Carl promised, with a wink. "I'm just as scared of Hilda Butterwick as you are."

When the river began to rise, Hilda put on her tarp and waders, took a small stepladder and wrench, and, defying wind and rain, marched down to the boathouse. The ground beneath her feet was slippery, treacherous; the fir trees along the path were bent

half over; the willows near the water, more supple, swayed back
and forth. The river had widened grossly; it was brown and
swollen and racked by waves. The small deck of the boathouse
already had a half-foot of water washing over it. She could hear
the flat-bottomed river boat inside the shed, knocking and
straining against the walls like an imprisoned beast. There would
be sanding and varnishing to do when spring came.

She waded through the water on the deck and set up the
ladder, and took down the buffalo horns which were fastened to
the eaves. After this, she returned to the Chalet, hauled the veranda furniture indoors and stacked it in the Great Hall.

At seventy-five, she was tall, angular and still strong. Her
maiden name had been Christianson; she was of Viking-pioneer
blood. Her blonde hair had turned white; she cut it herself in an
old-fashioned, practical Dutch bob. She refused to wear glasses
except for reading; her faded blue eyes were like those pale fish
that swam in the dark recesses of underground caverns, keeping
their dark prehistoric secrets to themselves. The sun had thickened
her skin and coated it with liver spots; of this she was proud. How
much better it was than the transparent, fragile flesh of her contemporaries.

In her old age her clothes, like Newman's, had become costumes. In the daytime, around the Chalet, or for trips into Shady
Cove, she dressed in an old paint-spattered monkey suit which
her husband, Eddie, had used for chores; outdoors she wore a
pair of Big Mac men's boots, nicely broken in; indoors, a pair
of old Indian moccasins. When she entertained company, she
blossomed out in a dirndl skirt from Greece, a Peruvian llama
sweater, a red Spanish shawl, over her shoulders, long earrings,
and silver bangles on her spotted arms. She dotted her leathery
cheeks with rouge and mascaraed her eyes, but she did not believe in lipstick. In both costumes she walked with a forthright
stride; one foot after the other, a kind of mad purpose blazing
in her eyes.

In her youth, before she married Eddie Butterwick, she had
taught school up in Bridgeport; she had walked three miles to
and from her parents' home to the small country schoolhouse

every day. The first lesson in the morning, following this walk, was always calisthenics; deep breathing and proper elocution she considered important. Her ambition had been to become an actress—for years, after her marriage, and while she brought up her two daughters, she had organized and participated in the Norton Little Theatre group. Her brightest rôle had been Portia; she still knew most of the lines. But marriage had dragged her down, younger people gradually took over the Little Theatre and she was relegated to minor rôles. After having been assigned the part of a shepherdess in "As You Like It," she wrote a haughty note and resigned.

Eddie had never made much money; he was in insurance, but he had an uncle who had made a fortune in lumber. Just in time to fill the void left by the Little Theatre, this uncle died, leaving his money to Eddie and the Chalet to Hilda. He had never liked Hilda but, as he approached death, he realized that she, alone, would do honor to his house in the woods. His will read, "She will appreciate its character."

Hilda did. The Chalet was modeled on a German hunting lodge; it was adorned with mounted animal heads—moose, elk, buffalo, deer—and the brittle, varnished corpses of steelhead and salmon. Stuffed small animals and birds perched on bookshelves and end tables. An oil painting of a Modoc Indian chieftain in full war regalia hung over the great stone fireplace. The Chalet's drafty, raftered rooms, furnished with Navajo rugs and Indian trinkets, seemed made for an ancient warrior-king. Its site, over the wildest riffle on the Rogue, was splendidly savage.

Hilda made Eddie move into the Chalet, though his insurance business was in Norton, twenty-five miles away. Moreover, she refused to permit him to wire it for electricity; at night, she lit the kerosene lamps, herself; stalking from room to room, her shadow against the wall was like a giant priestess performing a magical rite.

For the first time in her life she felt her environment suited her; she was mistress of an establishment, not just a house. Unfortunately, Eddie was not around long enough to enjoy their altered circumstances; he died, leaving Hilda wealthy.

When Hilda was first widowed, her daughters in California suggested she move back into town. By way of an answer, she instituted her famous Chalet Sunday brunches—feasts of kippered salmon, creamed finnan haddie, broiled kidneys, blueberry muffins, and three kinds of homemade jam. John came early and made the gin fizzes. Until this time, she had not believed in strong drink; John weaned her on the gin fizzes, and she went on to become a connoisseur of bourbon, buying Jack Daniels in cases, which she stored in the attic.

One never knew who might turn up at her brunches. She asked whoever caught her fancy, without regard to their social position or how they would mix with the other guests. The David Hinks (Hinks Department Store), and the Carter Smiths (Rogue Orchards) and Dr. and Mrs. Storey mingled with Bill Blair, who ran the Shady Cove Gas Station, and did odd chores for her on the side, and Muriel Burke, the waitress from Benny's Cocktail Lounge and Riverside Café.

The guests were allowed to fish or merely sunbathe on her deck. But they had to respect the spirit of her gatherings. They had to love the river and appreciate the Chalet. Moreover, the conversations had to be on a high plane, involving either local natural history, of which she was an authority, or reminiscences of her past successes as an actress.

The conversation, however, did not preclude gossip, which she drank in greedily, as if she had been deprived of it at some important stage in her development. This was true; she had always scorned the personal and the trivial. Now, suddenly discovering it, as she had booze, she began to manipulate people in order to create situations. Capriciously, she would drop an acquaintance, and add another; her sense of drama gave the brunches a further dimension; people came as they would come to the theater, to be surprised.

But she was not made to enjoy her triumphs; a kind of reaction set up inside of her; she began to sense slights, suspect treacheries. When her guests left, she would stalk the veranda complaining to a contented, well-fed John of their stupidity, their shallow natures. Why did she bother? Why did she slave? They came only to feed their faces; there was nothing inside their brains. Since John came, too, partly for this reason, he remained tactfully silent. But perhaps she suspected treachery here too, for, at this time, she began her jaunts around the world. She traveled alone.

One spring, she visited Europe; another the Far East. She went to Mexico for Christmas and to Lapland in summer. When she returned, she organized slide lectures to which her guests were subjected; the curios she had collected were displayed, for the occasion, on the rustic plank table in the dining room, like wedding gifts. There were amber worry beads from Greece, a pre-Columbian vase from Mexico, an armless, beady-eyed putto from Venice, the gong from Hong Kong.

"There I am on the second camel," she would say. "That is my guide, Domingo, sitting in the boat. I am standing beside the bell tower. If you look closely you will see me next to the Corinthian column. That is our tent—the lioness came within three feet."

She had not traveled, now, for two years. "It is difficult to get away when you are engaged in litigation," she told people. Litigation was her new hobby. John had dampened her spirit in this pursuit, and she had flung the marmot at him, but with Newman Hunter she blossomed like a young girl. Termite inspectors, repair men, a distant neighbor with a barking dog, trespassers, who ignored her "No Hunting, No Trespassing" sign, were all brought to court. It was said, jokingly, that one should take out special Hilda Butterwick insurance before approaching her.

But this, too, was waning. Judges were growing impatient; even Newman had refused to take her last case against two teenagers who had dumped some rubbish on her land. She had suddenly felt very much alone.

Now, after bringing in the buffalo horns from the boathouse, she sat down in the peel peacock chair; it was her special chair, like a throne. In the glistening wet tarp and waders she looked like an ancient queen. She was thinking. Perhaps she had been hasty throwing the marmot at John. She had not hit him; her aim was not as good as it once had been. Still, at her age, one perhaps ought to cherish old friends, despite their weaknesses.

This thought gave rise to a new idea. Why not organize a group of people to go on hikes? Everyone was too sedentary these days; they only sat around and drank and ate. I know the trails for thirty miles around, she said to herself. I will lead. I will wear a whistle in case anyone gets lost. Also the sun helmet I bought in Calcutta. I'll call John first. When I present my idea he'll recognize my physical and mental fitness and eat his words about The Manse.

"If you can't hike because of your prostate, you can sit on the veranda and watch us off," she would tell him.

She would do setting-up exercises, first, to get into top condition. She got up with new determination. The rain was beating in gale sheets against the veranda window. The river made a loud mooing noise, not entirely unpleasant.

"No weaklings allowed," she would say to John. "You will be the one exception."

While she was thinking all this, her phone rang. It was the Shady Cove operator.

"John Brigham is on the line. He's calling to see if you need any help, Mrs. Butterwick."

Hilda froze. They had not spoken to one another for a year, and now he was spoiling all her plans by pretending that it was she, not he, who could not manage alone.

Once, a few weeks ago, she had called the Rialto Theatre in town to ask the management if they would be interested in a matinée lecture of her travels abroad. "Around the World with Hilda Butterwick," it would be called. She had been answered by a recorded announcement. This impersonal form of communication, which had infuriated her then, seemed just the way, now, to respond to John. She said, "Just a moment, please," and took the gong off the wall and dragged it over to the phone.

"Mrs. Butterwick asks for no charity," she said, and hung up. At that same moment there was a mighty crash. The Ponderosa pine, next to the house, had fallen across the veranda, crushing the railing in its descent. It lay, a fallen giant, its branches crumpled, its cones scattered around on the decking like ceremonial offerings. Its bulk barred the door and covered the lower half of the large window. The Ponderosa had been a favorite; an eagle had nested in its top branches for three summers; Hilda had watched the fledglings with her binoculars, feeling a possessive pride.

Bill Blair, who had offered to help her around the place, had insisted that the pine was dead. "It's no more dead than you or I," Hilda had said. And when he had kept after her about it, she ordered him off her premises forever.

She picked up a lamp and went into the kitchen and poured herself two shots of Jack Daniels, then returned to the peacock chair and stared gloomily at the great corpse. The water rose higher around it; the little cones drifted off, deserting their matrix. Soon the warm liquor began to cheer her; she commenced to plan the work to be done after the storm. The veranda decking was no doubt badly injured, too. She rose and threw another log upon the smoking fire, then poured herself another slug. Perhaps she would have a woodsawing party; it would be good for townspeople to use their muscles; afterwards, she would serve a hearty wholesome lunch—lentil soup with sour cream, sardines, stuffed eggs, dark rye bread, and several kinds of cheese.

At five o'clock, John listened to the news on Raymond's radio. Sixty miles of highway, twenty miles of railroad track, and three airports were under water. Five persons were lost, presumed dead in the mountain areas. Three men had been killed on helicopter rescue missions. At least a hundred houses and cabins and forty business establishments in Southern Oregon and Northern California had been swept away by the mighty torrents. Orchards and farms had been turned into lakes. Free surplus grain was being flown in for catttle; the Army Engineers were coming in to put up emergency bridges as soon as the storm abated. Six Air Force C119 cargo planes, carrying 21,000 pounds of telephone repair equipment would take off as soon as the weather permitted. Flood damage, so far, was estimated in the millions. It would take a year to dry out the redwood from the flooded drying yards. The Red Cross was appealing for blankets and bedding for the evacuees.

And, then, the local news—John listened eagerly. The water impounded behind Paradise Dam, at the headwaters of the Rogue, was due to spill over the top sometime this evening. Residents of Prospect and Shady Cove had all been advised to leave at once.

At five-thirty, Carl came in and took John aside. "They're sending a deputy over to Hilda's," he said. "If she's still there, they'll get her out." At six-thirty, he ordered a sandwich at the bar; at seven o'clock, a wet and cross Hazel strode into Raymond's and humiliated him in front of Olly by ordering him to go to the Hotel.

"They're taking everyone over sixty-five," she said, snappishly.

Then she waited, while he put on his mackinaw and boots and followed her out.

Hilda, warmed by drink, had slept well. When she awoke, the fire was out, but she was able to rekindle it. Then she dragged a stool to the window, and peering over the Ponderosa pine, surveyed the scene. The river had risen to the porch; the boat-house was gone. It was as if she were on an island in the midst of a brown, raging sea.

Actually, of course, she was on a peninsula; she knew it was possible to wade out the back door where the ground was higher, and where she kept her car. But the sense of being on an island pleased her more. She was like Robinson Crusoe, snug, domestic, caring for her needs with no help from anyone.

In her head, she checked her provisions. She had enough fire-wood for two weeks; her food supply was ample; she bought toilet paper and kerosene and Jack Daniels and canned good in wholesale lots, which she stored in the attic. Except for her yo-gurt, she was not dependent on the accouterments of civilization, as they were in town. With delight, she thought of John's kitchen, whose cupboards were apt to contain no more than a few cans at a time, whose refrigerator was always half empty. He had not been brought up right; his ancestors were not Viking kings.

Then, to occupy herself, she began to rearrange a drawer of slides in the dining room. She was neatly cataloguing them, pasting titles on the boxes. "Hilda Butterwick, Africa, 1964. Hilda Butterwick, Orient, 1960." As she lifted out the box from Scandinavia, she found an unopened letter from her elder daughter; it had been written a month ago.

"Dear Mother," it began, "if you absolutely refuse to go to that nice retirement home, then couldn't you take a little apartment in town and keep the Chalet for weekend visits?"

There was more, but she didn't bother to read it; she tore the letter up in a rage. An apartment! She would die in an apartment. A tiny box, surrounded by other boxes with people in them, like dolls in doll houses. She wouldn't be able to breathe. As for that nice retirement home—what did her daughter know about it? She could imagine the meals. Overdone roasts, soggy vegetables, store-bought rolls. Grace at meals. Organized recreation. A bus to take them into town. A youthful, middle-aged director. Hobby shops. Crafts. Water colors. Sunday night movies. Folk dancing. Sweaty palms!

The Chalet was her home, not for "weekend visits." It was her home, and she would never leave it to either of her daughters. Already she could see the "For Sale" sign up; the rush of realtors, curious neighbors, tourists, who didn't belong to the community. No, she would change her will. She knew John wouldn't do it, and now she doubted Newman. She would find another attorney, maybe leave it to the county as an historical monument, filled with her artifacts. Was the county to be trusted, she wondered? Would they preserve it, according to her wishes? This would have to be looked into as soon as the storm was over.

As soon as the storm was over, she would begin other projects, too. Perhaps organize a play-reading society. She would invite only people with fine voices. Well, she might invite John, who didn't have a fine voice, which was probably the reason he refused to appear in court for her; she would invite him out of charity.

They would read the classics. Shakespeare. Molière. Racine. She would be Portia, once again. The rôle had suited her.

The quality of mercy is not strain'd
It droppeth as the gen-tul rain from heaven.
Upon the place beneath; it is twice blest;
It blesseth him that gives, and him that takes.

Too bad, she thought, that more people did not take those immortal words to heart.

There was a knock on her back door; then a male voice shouted, "Anyone at home?"

Hilda quickly ducked into a nearby closet. It contained Eddie's uncle's guns. The intruder's heavy boots stalked through her house; in fury she pictured the mud upon her plank floors.

"Mrs. Butterwick!" the voice called.

Hilda popped out of the closet, holding a carbine; she had kept it loaded, one never knew what might happen these days. She held it firmly, its muzzle pointing at Bill Blair, sheriff's deputy. "I'll give you exactly two minutes to get out," she said.

"Hilda, listen, we're evacuating all the cabins on the River. The dam's going. Everyone's left but you. You've got to get out fast."

"No one's telling me what to do," she said, and marched toward him, the gun aimed at his middle. "I know the river, I've lived here for twenty years, I'll get out in my own good time if necessary."

"Your car won't start, Hilda, and you couldn't drive it if it did. If you won't come with me now, we'll have to get you out by force."

She laughed, haughtily; then she cocked the gun. Bill shrugged his shoulders and stamped out, slamming the back door behind him.

That afternoon, she sat on the high stool at the window, sipping Jack Daniels, and watched things come down the river. A door; a shed, with a rooster on top; pilings, lumber, a cow, a house trailer. Some she recognized. A piece of Casper Bridge, a roof from the Riverside Café, a small boat called *Honey Bun,* which belonged to the Sparks children, a mile upstream. It was like the end of the world, and she, the sole survivor. She found this thought exhilarating. When she finished the glass, she poured herself another.

The sheriff's men came for her at six o'clock. They tramped through the Chalet, calling her name. But she hid cleverly in the attic closet, holding her breath, not stirring a limb.

When they left, she went back downstairs. The water was seeping into the ground floor. She put on her tarp and waders and took the bottle of Jack Daniels and went back up to the attic. After awhile she could hear the water roaring through the house. Still holding the bottle, she climbed the ladder to the roof. It was dark and the wind and rain howled around her. She crouched behind the chimney, using the fire ladder on the roof as an anchor, and took another big drag of bourbon. Then the house gave a great shudder and slipped off its foundation into the waters. Hilda rode the roof, like a great bird, as far as Peanut Creek, a mile downstream, when she and the Chalet disappeared into the waves.

John executed Hilda's will; she had never written a new one as Newman's client. But long after the private memorial service, after the daughters had left, furnishings from the Chalet were brought into John's office. The Chinese gong, which had been found in a farmer's field; a bloated elk's head, which had floated into Shady Cove; the warped oil painting of the Indian brave, which some children came upon under a temporary army bridge.

John wrote the daughters; there was no reply. The objects remained in his office, gathering dust. They worried him. One afternoon he gathered them up and took them home and burned the elk's head and the oil painting in his incinerator. He left the gong, which wouldn't burn, for the junk man. Then he went into his empty house and fixed himself a good strong bourbon. He knew he could not live alone much longer, that he would end up at The Manse. He would play cards and go on field trips and tell dirty jokes to the nurses, while, all the time, he would feel the scornful eye of his old friend upon him. She had triumphed over him irrevocably; there would be no redress.

James Alan McPherson was born in Savannah, Georgia, in 1943. He received his B.A. from Morris Brown College, his LL.B. from Harvard Law School, and M.F.A. from the University of Iowa Writers Workshop. He is a writer of short stories and a journalist, and is now at work on a novel. Mr. McPherson has taught at the University of Iowa, the University of California at Santa Cruz, and Harvard summer school, and is presently a contributing editor for *The Atlantic Monthly*. He lives in Cranston, Rhode Island.

THE SILVER BULLET

When Willis Davis tried to join up with the Henry Street guys, they told him that first he had to knock over Slick's Bar & Grill to show them what kind of stuff he had. Actually, they needed the money for the stocking of new equipment to be used in a pending reprisal against the Conchos over on the West Side. News of a Concho spring offensive was in the wind. But they did not tell Willis this. They told him they had heard he had no stuff. Willis protested, saying that he was ready to prove himself in any way but this one. He said that everyone knew Slick was in the rackets and that was why his bar had never been hit. As a matter of fact, he did not know this for certain, but did not really want to do the job. Also, no one could remember having seen Slick around the neighborhood for the past three years.

"Slick ain't in no rackets!" Dewey Bivins had screamed at Willis. "You just tryin' to get outta it on a *humble!* Slick died of t.b. over in Jersey two years ago. And don't come tellin' me you don't know that." Dewey was recognized as the war lord of the group, and there were many stories circulating, some dating several years back, about the number of dedicated Concho

assassins who were out to get him. Some said that at least two
of the Concho membership had taken a blood oath and waited
at night in the darker areas of Henry Street for Dewey to pass.
Others maintained that the Concho leadership, fearing disproportionate retaliations, had given orders that Dewey, of all
the Henry Street guys, should go unmolested. Dewey himself argued that at least four guys were looking for him, day and
night, and liked it known that he walked the streets unarmed, all
the time. In fact, each time he was seen walking, his reputation
grew. People feared him, respected his dash, his temper, the way
he cocked his purple beret to the side. The little fellows in
the neighborhood imitated his swagger. He was a dangerous enemy, but a powerful associate. So Willis decided to give it a
try.

But first he went around to see Curtis Carter, hoping to get
him to go along. Carter wanted no part of it. "I know for a fact
that Slick ain't dead," he pointed out. "You'd be a fool to mess
with his establishment."

"Aah, *bull*shit!" Willis replied. "When was the last time you
seen Slick? There's another guy runnin' the joint now." But
his voice was not as convincing as he wanted it to be. And Carter
was not moved, not even when Willis suggested that this job
could lead to a closer association for both of them with the
Henry Street guys.

Carter was not impressed. "If Slick takes after you," he said,
"how can them guys help you run any faster than you'll have to
run by yourself?" Willis did not like to think about that possibility,
so he called Carter a ball-less son of a bitch and announced that
he would do it alone.

But now that he was forced to do it alone, Willis began to really
wonder about Slick's connections with the rackets. He remembered hearing stories about Slick in the old days. These stories
frightened him. And even with Slick gone for good, the bar might
still be covered. He wanted to ask around about it, but was afraid
of calling attention to himself. Instead, he made several brief

trips into the place to check out the lay of the land. The bar opened sometime between 11 and 12 o'clock, when Alphaeus Jones, the bartender, came in; but it did no real business, aside from the winos, until well after three. He figured that two o'clock would be the best time. By then the more excitable winos would have come and gone and the small trickle of people who went in for the advertised home-cooked lunch would have died away. Alphaeus Jones took his own lunch around one-thirty or two, sitting on the stool at the end of the counter, just in case any customer entered. And the cook, Bertha Roy, whom Willis recognized as a neighbor of his aunt's in the projects over on Gilman, left the place around that same time to carry bag lunches to the ladies at Martha's Beauty Salon down the block. This kept her out of the place for at least half an hour. He did not want Bertha to see him, so he decided the best time would be the minute she left with the lunches.

Again he went to Curtis Carter, begging for help. Curtis worked in an autoparts warehouse about four blocks away from Slick's. Willis told him that the job would be much softer if they could pull it off together and then make a run back to the warehouse to hide out until after dark. But Curtis still did not want any part of the operation. He made a long speech in which he stressed the importance of independent actions, offering several of his own observations on the dependability of the Henry Street guys; and then disclosed, by way of example, that he already had a nice steady income produced by ripping off, from the stock room, new accessories and mended parts, which he sold to a garage over on the West Side. "There ain't no fair percentage in group actions," he concluded, the righteousness of a self-made man oiling his words. Willis called him a milk-fed jive and said that he was after bigger stuff. Curtis checked his temper and wished him luck.

The following afternoon, Willis waited across the street, leaning against the window of a barbershop and smoking a cigarette, until he saw Bertha Roy come out the door with the lunch bags. When he was sure that she was not going to turn around and go back, he threw the cigarette into the gutter and crossed over, trying to work up a casual amble. But his knees were much too close together. He pushed through the door, sweeping with his eyes the few tables against the wall on his left. The place was empty. Alphaeus Jones, a balding, honey-colored man with a shiny forehead, looked up from his lunch. A blob of mustard from the fish sandwich he was eating clung to the corner of his mouth. "What you want?" he asked, chewing.

Willis moved closer to the end of the bar and licked his lips. "What you got?" he asked.

Jones raised his left arm and motioned to where the sunlight glittered through the green and brown and white bottles on the shelves behind him. With his other hand, he raised the fish sandwich and took another bite. Willis licked his lips again. Then he shook his head, trying hard to work the amble up into his voice. "Naw, man," he said, his voice even but still a bit too high, "I mean what you got in the register?" And he made a fist with his right hand inside the pocket of his jacket.

Jones eyed him, sucking his teeth. Then he said, "A silver bullet." And, looking up into the space above Willis' head, his right hand lifted the sandwich again. But just before it reached his mouth, he looked Willis directly in the face and asked, impatience hurrying his voice on, "You want it, Roscoe?"

"It ain't for *me*," Willis said very fast.

"Ain't for nobody else. You the first fool to come in here for years. You want it now, or later?"

Willis thought it over. Then, ever so slowly, he took his right hand out of his jacket pocket and laid both hands, fingers spread, on the bar.

Jones sucked his teeth again. "You done decided?" he asked.

"A beer," Willis said.

When he reported to the Henry Street boys what had happened, Dewey said: "You a silver-bullet lie!" The other guys crowded round him. They were in the storage basement at 1322 Henry. There was no door. "Chimney" Sutton, high on stuff, stood by the stairs leading up to the first floor, smashing his fist into his open palm. Besides needing the money for the coming offensive, they did not like to have an initiate seem so humble in his failures. "First you come with that mess about Slick," Dewey said. "Now you say old Jones bluffed you outta there on a bullshit tip." He paced the floor, making swift turns on his heels and jabbing an accusing brown finger at Willis, who slumped in a green-metal chair with his head bowed. Sutton kept slamming his fist. The others—Harvey Gomez and Clyde Kelley—watched Willis with stone faces. "I know what your problems is," Dewey continued. "You just wanna get in the club without payin' no dues. You didn't never go in there in the first place."

"That ain't true," Willis protested, his hands spread out over his face. "I'll pay. You guys know how bad I wanna get in. But there wasn't no sense in takin' a chance like that. A guy would have to be crazy to call a bluff like that," he said, peering through his fingers at Dewey. "I tell you, his hands was under the counter."

"Aah, get off my case!" Dewey shouted. He jerked his head toward the stairs where Chimney Sutton was standing, still pounding his fist. Willis slid off the chair and eased across the room. Sutton was about to grab him when he saw Dewey wave his hand down in a gesture of disgust. Sutton moved a few inches away from the bottom step. Willis got out of the basement.

He hurried away from Henry Street, thinking it through. He still wanted to get into the organization. He felt that a man should belong to something representative. He was not against people going to work or joining churches or unions if these things represented them. But he wanted something more. And the Henry Street guys were not really bad, he thought. The papers just made them out to be that way. Several of them were family men. Dewey himself had been a family man at one time. That showed that they respected the family as an organization. But this by itself was not enough. There was not enough respect in it. And after a while you realized that something more was needed. Willis was not sure of what that thing was, but he knew that he had to try for it.

In the late afternoon, he went back around to the warehouse to see Curtis Carter. It was near closing time, but Curtis was still sorting greasy valves and mufflers into separate piles on the floor. His blue overalls were dirty and rust-stained. When Curtis saw him come in, he motioned him over to the john in the rear of the shop, where McElrath, the manager, could not hear them. "You do it?" Curtis asked, his voice hollow with suppressed excitement.

"No."

Curtis grinned. He seemed relieved. His mouth was smeared with black grease from his hands. "Couldn't get up the balls by yourself, huh?"

Willis told him about the silver bullet.

Curtis laughed aloud and said, "That's some more jive. Jones wouldn't never shoot nobody in there. In the afternoon they wouldn't have no more than fifty dollars in the register, anyhow. You think he wanna get in the news for somethin' like that?"

Now Willis felt bad. He knew that, from all angles, Curtis was right. He could see that Curtis knew it, too. He began to feel cheated, tricked, a laughingstock. "What can I do now?" he asked. "The guys are gonna be hard on me 'cause I didn't deliver."

"I told you so in the first place," Curtis said. "Now you go'n get it, no matter whichaway you turn. Don't think that old Jones go'n keep his mouth shut about what happen today."

"What can I do?" Willis asked, his lowered voice begging support.

"Get yourself some protection," Curtis said. "Maybe try a new approach."

"Like what?"

Curtis, still with the air of an objective advisor, told him about some guys with a new approach. They were over on the West Side. He offered no names but gave Willis the address of an office that, he suggested, might be friendly to Willis' situation.

On Wednesday morning, Willis took the bus over to the office. Once he had located it, he began to suspect that he might have been given the wrong address. This office had the suggestion of real business about it, with large red lettering on the window that read: W. SMITH ENTERPRISES. When Willis entered, he saw two new hardwood desks and tall gray file cabinets on either side of the small room. On the floor was a thin, bright-red wall-to-wall carpet; and behind one of the desks sat a man who wore a full beard, with a matching red shirt and wide tie. The man was watching him and looking very mad at something. Willis approached the desk, holding out his hand as he introduced himself. The man ignored the hand and continued to look very mad. The new hand-carved name plate on the desk said that his name was R. V. Felton. He was the only person in the office, so Willis had to wait until Felton was through surveying him. Finally, still not seeming to focus on the physical presence before him, the man named Felton asked: "What you want?"

Willis said what he had been told to say: "I got a problem in community relations."

R. V. Felton looked even madder. His cheeks puffed out. His nose widened as he sat erect in the brown-leather chair. Then, as if some switch had been clicked on, he began to speak. "Well, brother," he said, "that's our concern here. This office is committed to problems vis-à-vis the community. That's our only concern: an interest in the mobility of the community." His voice, as he talked, seemed tightly controlled and soft, but his hands suddenly came alive, almost on their own, it seemed to Willis, and began to make grandiose patterns in the air. The index finger of his right hand pumped up and down, now striking the flat palm of his left hand, now jabbing out at Willis. The hands made spirals, sharp, quick cutting motions, limber pirouettes, even while the fingers maintained independent movements. "There are profound problems that relate to community structure that have to be challenged through the appropriate agency," he continued. "We have friends downtown and friends in the community who see the dynamics of our organization, vis-à-vis the community, as the only legitimate and viable group to operate in this sphere. They support us," he said, his eyes wandering, his hands working furiously now, "we support the community dynamic, and together we all know what's going down. That's our dynamic. Dig it?" And he fixed a superior eye on Willis' face.

"Yeah," Willis said.

Now R. V. Felton relaxed in the chair and lifted a pencil

from the new brown holder at the edge of his desk. "Now, brother," he said, "suppose you articulate the specifics of your problem."

At one-thirty that same afternoon. Willis, with R. V. Felton behind him, walked into Slick's Bar & Grill. Bertha Roy was back in the kitchen, preparing the bag lunches; at the end table in the far left corner of the room, a single customer was getting drunk. Jones was pulling his own lunch out of the kitchen window with his back to the door. When he turned and saw that it was Willis standing by the bar, he smiled and asked, "A born fool, hey?"

R. V., looking especially mean, came up to the bar and stood beside Willis. Jones sighed, laid the plate on the bar and dropped both hands out of sight. "How much this place earn in a week?" R. V. demanded. He had puffed out his cheeks and chest, so that he now looked like a bearded Buddha.

"We eat steady," Jones told him, still smiling.

Bertha Roy looked out at them from the kitchen, her sweating face screwed up in puzzlement.

R. V. sighed, intimating ruffled patience. "A fat mouth make a soft ass, brother," he said to Jones.

"What you boys want?" Bertha called from the kitchen. Her voice sounded like a bark.

"Tend your pots, Momma," R. V. called to her. Then he said to Jones: "How much?"

"You better get on out," Jones told him.

Willis, standing beside R. V., tried to look as mad. But his cheeks could not hold as much air, and without a beard, he did not look as imposing.

"Now, listen here, brother," R. V. said to Jones. "As of this minute, I declare this joint nationalized. Every dollar come in here, the community get back twenty-five cents, less three cents for tax. Every plate of food pass over that counter, the community get ten percent of the profit, less two cents tax. Paying-up time is Friday mornings, before noon. You can play ball or close down now."

"Can I ask who go'n do the collecting for the community?" Jones asked, his voice humble.

R. V. snapped his fingers twice. Willis moved in closer to the bar. "This here's our certified community collector vis-à-vis this bar," R. V. announced. "Treat him nice. And when he come in here on Friday mornings, you *smile*."

"Why wait for Friday?" Jones asked. "I'll smile right now." And he raised his hands from under the bar. He was holding a 12-gauge shotgun. "See how wide my jaws are?" he asked. "I'm smiling so much my ass is tight. Now, what about yours?" And he lifted the gun and backed off for range.

"Let's go, man," Willis said to R. V. He was already moving toward the door.

But R. V. did not move. He held up one long finger and began to wave it at Jones. "A bad move, brother," he said.

"Why don't you boys go on home!" Bertha Roy called from behind Jones. "You oughtta be *shame* of yourselfs!"

"Bertha, you don't have to tell them nothin'," Jones said over his shoulder. "They'll be goin' home soon enough."

Willis was already at the door. He did not mind being the first one out, but then, he did not want to leave without R. V. "Let's go, man," he called from the door.

"Tomorrow's Thursday," R. V. said to Jones, ignoring Willis. "We'll be in to inspect the books. And remember, if you get any ideas about disrupting the progress of our dynamic here, there'll be some action, vis-à-vis *you*." Then he turned sharply and walked toward Willis at the door.

The drunk over in the corner lifted his head from the table and peered after them.

"You boys need a good whippin'," Bertha Roy called.

Jones just watched them go, smiling to himself.

That night, Willis went into Stanley's pool hall and told Dewey Bivins what had happened. He explained that since R. V. Felton and his organization had taken over, there would be a guaranteed cut of 12 percent for him, Willis, every Friday. And since he had decided to join up with the Henry Street guys, rather than with

R. V., this would mean a weekly income of from $20 to $30 for the gang. He said that he envisioned new uniforms for the guys, better equipment and a growing slush fund for more speedy bail bonding. But Dewey did not seem to share his enthusiasm. He laid his cue on the table, frowned and asked, "Who is these guys, anyhow? They don't live round here. This here's *our* territory."

Willis tried to explain, as concretely as possible, the purposes of the organization. And though he made a brave effort to repeat, word for word, the speech that R. V. had given him, he could tell that without the hand movements, it sounded uninspiring. In fact, Dewey said as much even before Willis had finished. "That's bullshit!" he said, his face going tight. "They ain't go'n pull that kind of shit round here. Any naturalizin' that's done, *we'll* be doin' it!"

"Nationalization," said Willis.

"And we'll be doin' it, not them phonies."

"But then I'll be in trouble," Willis explained. "These guys have already taken over the job. If I let you take it from them, they'll be after *me*."

"That's your problem," Dewey said, his eyes showing a single-mindedness. "You wanna be with them or us? Remember, we live round here. If you join up with them, the West Side ain't go'n be far enough away for you to move." He allowed a potent pause to intervene, then asked, "Know what I mean?"

Willis knew.

The following morning, he waited outside the barbershop across the street from Slick's. He smoked, walked up and down the block several times, then got into a throw-to-the-wall game with the boy who worked in the shop. He lost 17 cents, and then quit. The boy went back into the shop, shaking the coins in his pocket. Willis waited some more. He had planned to go in with the group that arrived first; but as the wait became longer and longer, he began to consider going in alone and apologizing to Jones for the whole thing. He decided against this, however, when he saw Bertha Roy leaving to deliver the lunch bags. The place seemed unsafe with her gone.

Finally, a little after two, R. V. Felton and another fellow drove up in a dark-blue Ford. R. V., behind the wheel, was wearing green sunshades. He double-parked and kept the motor running while his man got out and went into Slick's. Willis crossed over and leaned against the car. R. V. was looking especially mean. He looked at his reflection in the rearview mirror, and then looked at it in the side mirror. Willis waited patiently. Finally, R. V. said, "We talked it over. Six percent for you."

"You said twelve!" Willis protested.

"Six," R. V. said. "This here's a small dynamic. Besides, I had to cut Aubrey in on your share. You'll get twelve, maybe more, when you line up some more of these blights on the community."

"I don't wanna get involve no more," Willis said.

"I figured that. That's why it's six."

Willis was about to make further protests when Aubrey came back to the car. He opened the door on the curb side, leaned in and said, "R. V., you better come on in, man. That dude done pull that heat agin."

"Aah, fuck!" R. V. said. But he got out of the car, pushing Willis aside, and followed Aubrey into the bar. Willis entered behind them.

Jones was standing behind the bar, holding the shotgun.

"You want some trouble, brother?" R. V. asked.

"There ain't go'n be no trouble," Jones said.

"Then let's have them books."

"We don't keep no books," Jones said.

"A strange dynamic," R. V. said, pulling on his beard. "Most strange."

Jones cradled the gun butt against the bend of his right arm. "And here's somethin' stranger," he said. "If I was to blast your ass to kingdom come, there wouldn't be no cops come through that door for at least six hours. And when they come, they might take me down, but in the end, I'd get me a medal."

Now R. V.'s lips curled into a confident grin. He shook his head several times. "Let me run something down for you, brother," he said. "First of all, we are a nonprofit community-based grassroots organization, totally responsive to the needs of the community. Second"—and here he again brought his fingers into play

—"we think the community would be very interested in the artic-
ulation of the *total* proceeds of this joint vis-à-vis the *average*
income level for this area. Third, you don't want to mess with us.
We got the support of college students."

"Do tell," Jones said. "Well, I ain't never been to college myself, but I can count to ten. And if you punks ain't down the
block when I finish, that street out there is gonna be full of
hamburger-meat." He braced his shoulder and lifted the gun.
"And one last thing."

"You better say it quick, then," R. V. told him.

"I'm already way past five."

Willis, backing off during the exchange, had the door almost
open when it suddenly rammed into his back. Before he could
turn around, Dewey Bivins and Chimney Sutton pushed him
aside and stepped into the room. As Sutton pushed the door
shut again and leaned his back against it, Willis glimpsed Bertha
Roy, her face a frightened blur, moving quickly past the window
and away down the block. He turned around. Dewey, a tight fist
pressed into either hip, stood surveying the room. Both he and
Sutton were in full uniform, with purple berets and coffee-colored
imitation-leather jackets. Dewey swung his gaze round to Willis,
his eyes flashing back fire. Alphaeus Jones, still in the same spot
behind the bar, held the gun a bit higher.

"Who are these dudes?" R. V. asked Willis.

Willis, trying to avoid Dewey's eyes, said nothing.

"Who the hell are *you?*" Dewey asked.

"Nine," Jones said.

Willis was still trying for the door. But Sutton moved up behind
him, forcing Willis to edge almost to the center of the room.

Dewey walked closer to R. V. "Where's the money?" he demanded.

R. V. began to stroke his beard again. He looked more puzzled
than mad. "Brother," he said, "there's some weird vibrations
in here. What we need now is some unity. Think of the ramifications that would evolve from our working together. This
here's a large community. The funds from this one joint is pure
chicken shit compared to the total proceeds we could plow back

into community organizations by combining our individual efforts into one dynamic and profound creative approach."

"Yeah?" asked Dewey, his head cocked to the side.

R. V. nodded, looking less puzzled. "Our organization, for example, is a legitimate relevant grass-roots community group," he said, making hyphens with his downturned fingers. "We have been able to study the ramifications of these here bloodsucking community facilities. We have the dynamic. You have the manpower. Together we can begin a nationalization process—"

"You a naturalizin' lie!" Dewey screamed. *"We* the only group operate round here. You better take that bullshit over to the *Conchos."*

"Let's git 'em," Chimney hissed, moving forward and pounding on his fist.

Jones grinned and raised the gun.

The room tensed. Chimney and Dewey stood close together, almost back to back. Similarly, Aubrey inched closer to R. V. and both stood facing Chimney and Dewey, their backs to Jones. Eyes narrowed in assessment, hands began to move toward pockets, fingers twitched. Dewey turned to Willis, standing near the door. "Which side *you* on?" he asked through his teeth. Without answering, Willis began to move toward the center of the room.

"Hey, Alphee!" someone said.

They all looked. A man was coming through the door. "Hey, Alphee," he said again, seemingly unaware of the fury he had temporarily aborted, "a cop out there writin' a ticket on that car that's double-parked. The owner in here?" He walked past the group and over to the bar, his face betraying no curiosity.

"Could be," Jones told him, now lowering the gun. "But you know how these big-time businessmen can fix tickets."

The man smiled, then, in the same loud voice, asked "What you doin' with that gun, Alphee?"

"Fixing to swat some flies," Jones answered.

Now the man turned and looked at the five in the middle of the room. "Them?" he asked, nodding his head as he surveyed the faces.

Jones smiled. "That's right."

The man smiled, too. He was dressed in a deep-green suit and starched white shirt open at the collar. "Which one's the big businessman, Alphee?" he asked, the suggestion of amusement tugging at the corners of his mouth.

"You got me," Jones said.

"Is it you?" the man asked R. V. "You the only one in here don't look like a bum."

"Lemme take 'em, R. V.," Aubrey said.

But R. V. didn't answer. He was obviously in deep thought.

Dewey and Chimney began to look troubled. Willis' mind was racing. He looked out the window. The cop was standing with his left foot on the bumper of the car, writing. He began to wish that Bertha Roy would come back or that the cop would finish quickly and then go away.

"Now, a *real* businessman," the man was saying to no one in particular, "he would own him at least six cops, a city councilman, one and a half judges and a personal letter from the mayor. He wouldn't have to worry about one little old cop writin' a ticket." He paused and the smile left his face. "You own anything like that?" he asked R. V.

"Let's go, man," R. V. said to Aubrey in a low voice.

The man walked over and slapped R. V. across the face. "You own anything like that?" he asked again, his voice suddenly dropping the hint of amusement.

R. V. stiffened and drew back his fists. The man slapped him again. "What you wanna do that for?" R. V. whimpered.

"Floor the mother!" Dewey said. "He come in here tryin' to take over."

The man turned to Jones. "Who's that?" he asked.

"Some of them punks that hang out on Henry Street."

"Get out," the man said to Dewey.

"For what?" Dewey asked. "We on *your* side."

"No you ain't," the man said. "Now, get out before I change my mind."

Dewey and Chimney headed for the door. Willis followed them.

"Not you," the man called after Willis. "You with these other businessmen, ain't you?"

Dewey turned at the door. "Yeah," he said, malice in his voice, "he ain't wearin' our uniform."

"I told you to get out," the man called.

"You go'n let him talk that way?" Chimney asked Dewey.

"Shut up!" Dewey hissed at him, an unfamiliar fear in his eyes.

Willis watched them go out the door. He felt trapped. Now there was only Bertha to hope for. Through the window, he could see that the cop had already left the car. Turning to the room, he saw R. V. and Aubrey standing unnaturally straight, like mechanical toys. R. V.'s lips were pushed out, but now the mean look had been replaced and R. V. was sulking like a little boy. The man stood at the bar, seemingly engaged in some private conversation with Jones. But after a few seconds, he turned to R. V. again. "Alphee, here, says I should just let you fellows go. He got a good heart and don't want to see you boys in any more trouble." Then he hit R. V. again, this time a quick, hard blow with his fist. R. V. screamed as the knuckles thudded into his face. "Waste him, Aubrey!" he moaned, his face turning deep brown.

But Aubrey did not move. He was looking past the man. Willis looked, too, and saw Jones holding the shotgun again and smiling. "Ten," Jones said.

R. V.'s head fell. He backed off, roughly pushing Aubrey aside. "You go'n be sorry you done that," he muttered, fighting to contain his rage. "We got—"

"Give the boys a beer before they go, Alphee," the man said.

"Let 'em pay," Jones said, following R. V. with the gun.

The man smiled. "Just a regular businessman, huh?"

"We don't want nothin' from here," Aubrey said. R. V. was standing behind him, nursing his face. He didn't say anything.

"Then take that dummy out of here," Jones ordered.

R. V. and Aubrey slowly moved toward the door. Again, Willis followed.

"Not him," Jones said. "He been in here three times already. I want to make sure he don't come back."

Willis stopped. The two others went on out, R. V. pausing only long enough at the door to say, "You ain't seen the last of our dynamic," and to shake his fist vengefully.

"Punks," Jones said.

Now Willis stood alone, frightened and frozen, eager to be going, too. He faced the man. "I didn't know," he said, his voice little more than a tremble.

"Know what?" the man asked in a softer tone.

"That this place was covered by the rackets."

The man laughed. He closed his eyes and kept the laugh suppressed in his throat. He laughed this way for almost a minute. "You hustlers kill me," he said at last. "All that big talk and you still think a black man can't have no balls without being in the rackets."

"I didn't know," Willis said again.

"Aah, *go on* and get out!" Jones said.

"Let him have a beer, Alphee," the man said, still containing his laughter.

"No," Jones said. "Go and get out. You give me a pain."

"They just young," the man told Jones.

"The hell with that," Jones said.

Willis moved toward the door. Any moment he expected them to call him back. But all he could hear as he moved was the jerking laughter coming up from deep inside the man as he made low comments to Jones. When he was going out the door, he heard Jones say, "Sure, I was young. But I ain't never been no *fool*."

Willis ran down the block. As he passed Martha's Beauty Salon, Bertha Roy saw him and raced to the door. "You!" she called after him. Willis turned. Bertha's face was stern and her eyes flashed. "Your momma oughtta give you a good whippin'," she said.

Willis pretended he had not heard and ran faster down the block.

After attending Andover and Harvard, **John Malone** spent several years in Europe, returning in 1965 to New York, where he now lives. Other short stories have appeared in *New American Review, Evergreen Review* and *Transatlantic Review.* His first novel, *The Corruption of Harold Hoskins,* is being published in the spring of 1973.

THE FUGITIVES

Man and Woman, Circa 1971

When the doorbell rings, my wife and I are screaming at one another. I have, she claims, boiled a brisket of beef in her brown rice pot, contaminating it irretrievably. She has, there is no doubt about it, invaded my studio while I am painting. My studio is as sacrosanct as her rice pot, any day. So we are both screaming, my face getting purple (she informs me), hers very white.

The doorbell becomes more insistent. Whoever is pushing it can probably hear us screaming, around the corner of the house. The windows to the studio are open.

"Answer the door," I say.

"Answer your own goddamn door," says my wife.

I get up to do so, but usher her out of the studio ahead of me. She is in a mood to slash canvas.

The Revolutionary

His jeans, if he were to remove them, would surely stand up by themselves.

The rest of his costume follows suit:

Cowboy boots encrusted with mud, the leather cracked and peeling.

A faded peacoat.

Denim shirt.

Beard.

And shoulder length hair.

Even so, by his scraggly teeth and the messianic glint in his eye, I recognize a friend from the past.

"I've come from Philadelphia," says Henry, casting a glance over his shoulder.

Investigators Must Investigate

"Certainly he was here," I say to them. "But it was weeks ago."

"Did you realize that you were harboring a known criminal?"

When was it, I wonder, that 'alleged' came to mean 'known'?

But I say merely, "One of the pleasures of living out here in the country is that you never have to see a newspaper."

"You have a television set," they point out.

"I only use it to watch baseball," I tell them. "I'm a Red Sox fan."

The investigators exchange a look. Painters cannot be baseball fans in their cosmology, it seems.

"Why didn't you report that he'd been here, when you later found out that he was on the run?" One investigator asks most of the questions. The other stares, attempting to intimidate.

"It seemed beside the point. It was days later, and I had no idea where they had gone. I thought it would be a waste of my time and yours."

"You were wrong," says the intimidator. "In this business, there's always some useful piece of information you can pick up. Even if it's not about the accused."

Happy Men Take Pride In Their Accomplishments

"What in hell were you doing in Philadelphia?" I ask, holding the door wide for my friend to enter.

Henry glances once again over his shoulder. There is nothing to see but fields and trees and sky. My nearest neighbor lives a mile and a half away.

"Don't you read the papers, man?"

He sounds almost piqued. Gently, I explain that I avoid the news.

"Oh, yeah, well, I was blowing up a draft office," says Henry, entering my house, his voice as raucous as of old.

"Really?" I say, flinching at the volume and subduing my dismay. "Do they know you were in on it?"

"Sure, man. The Feds are after me. Isn't that something?"

I am glad for him in a way. A celebrity at last. Once, he had wanted to be an artist, with a capital 'A'. Now that he is a revolutionary (with, I am sure, a capital 'R') I suppose that it could only be a cause for shame to remain anonymous. It is, after all, the age of publicity.

My wife, drawn no doubt by Henry's stentorian glee (he has always abhorred anonymity, it occurs to me, and his voice is a sign of it) has drifted into the hall.

"You mean the F.B.I.?" she says.

A City Girl

My wife is not happy here in the country.

She consented to move only because it meant that she could grow organic vegetables in the backyard and raise organic chickens in the tool shed.

In all but her ecology, she is a city girl.

She desires noise pollution even as she rejects the other kinds.

The country makes her nervous, it is far too quiet.

At night it is so still you can hear the crickets cheep.

I believe, besides, that she misses women's lib.

A Meeting of Minds

"Jane, this is Henry Grant." I do not trouble to identify Jane as my wife. It is a word she despises. Besides, the matter should be clear to Henry. No mistress would treat a man with the contempt Jane reserves for me.

"Hello, Henry."

"Alias Sonny Berman," says Henry, showing his scraggly teeth in a grin. I recall that Henry never was happy with his own name; too mundane.

"What are they after you for?" asks Jane, eyeing him speculatively.

"He blew up a draft office," I explain.

"Well," she says, "it's nice to meet a man with some guts."

My choices are limited. "You want to stay with us?"

Henry nods, suddenly serious, conspiratorial. "Overnight. I don't think they're even on my trail. I'll get out before dawn."

Investigators Must Speculate

"How did you meet Henry Grant, alias Sonny Berman?" they ask me.

"The first time I saw him he was wearing brand new loafers."

The investigators sit stony-faced. "Where was that?"

"At school."

"Which school?"

"Andover. It's a prep school."

The investigators exchange glances, as though a suspicion had been confirmed.

"Why did you mention his loafers?"

"It was by way of observing that people change."

"He was different then?"

"Yes. He wanted to be a writer."

"A writer?" The eyes of the investigators glisten. "What did he write?"

"Stories, poems, plays. Everything. He wrote all the time."

"You read these—stories?"

"Quite a lot of them. I was the art editor of the school literary magazine. He was two years behind me in school but he turned in so many pieces they made him an assistant editor. I got to know him. We became friends."

"Close friends?"

"I suppose. But I graduated, and went on to college. So I only saw him occasionally over the next two years."

"Did he go to the same college?"

"Yes."

"Was he still doing this—this writing—then?"

"Some. But he'd lost the spark. They'd made him editor-in-chief of the magazine at Andover. The exercise of editorial power, and worrying about things like printers' costs and selling advertising space to the local coffee shop took all the romance out of it for him. It stifled him. But then, that's what prep schools are for, to exorcise any strain of creativity from the future leaders of our land. It's their function in society. Andover was always one of the best at the job."

The silent investigator speaks. "Did you ever have sexual relations with the accused?"

I do not wish to annoy my visitors. But I cannot help myself. I laugh in their self-important faces.

They look deeply offended.

"I'm sorry," I say. "I shouldn't laugh. Most prep schools also look upon writing and painting as forms of sexual deviation. Anything that isn't directly related to money sounds queer to them."

"You deny that you ever had sexual relations with him?"

"I would never compete with my wife," I say, smiling benignly at them.

The Loving Cup Is Shared

Henry has arrived in the late afternoon. That means that we can immediately sit down and start drinking.

The liquor cabinet is well stocked.

I offer Scotch, vodka, bourbon, etc.

Henry asks if there is any red wine.

Otherwise he will take beer.

It wouldn't do, of course, for a revolutionary to sit around drinking Scotch. The President, for Christ's sake, probably drinks Scotch.

Unfortunately, though, the only red wine I have in the house is a couple of cases of an excellent 1959 Bordeaux. It is not that I begrudge a good bottle of wine to Henry. But I don't want to insult his revolutionary fervor with a chateau label. I decide to disguise its quality, and decant a bottle into a pitcher. I am sure Henry judges such questions by appearances and not by his palate.

Jane too will take wine.

Usually she drinks vodka martinis.

If I am lucky, she may join the movement and end up behind bars. Probably, knowing my wife, it is just Henry's grotty sex appeal that is working on her. In spite of spindly legs and a cock the size of a toothpick, Henry has an aura of virility. He lolls back in an easy chair with one leg up over the arm, dribbling red wine into his beard.

Jane is entranced.

Investigators Ask Too Many Questions

"Did Grant have any drugs with him when he was here?" I am asked.

"Not that I know of."

"You're sure about that?"

"Positive."

The pause is brief. "Have you ever taken drugs yourself?"

"I thought you were investigating Henry Grant. If you're investigating me, I'll call my lawyer."

"Why should you need a lawyer?" They ask it very quickly.

"Because I'm dealing with an agency that refers to men as criminals before they've been brought to trial."

The pause is much longer. The investigators stare at me, as though deciding whether or not to get tough. It is the kind of silence affected by actors playing underworld captains in the movies, at those moments when they are contemplating having someone rubbed out.

"When did you last see Grant, before this visit?" The tone of

voice makes it clear that they are, by their lights, being exceedingly patient with me.

"In Paris, five or six years ago."

"Was Grant taking drugs then?"

"I don't believe that's any of your business."

For the first time, the investigators smile. "A grand jury will be called in this case eventually. You realize that we could have you subpoenaed."

I would just as soon the investigators did not smile.

"If I'm called before a grand jury I'll decide at that time whether or not I have a duty to speak. I don't believe I could tell you anything that would be at all important in connection with his alleged activities in Philadelphia."

"Well then, let's put it another way. If in fact Grant is proved to have been involved with blowing up the draft office, would you say that you approved or disapproved of his action?"

"Of course I wouldn't approve. I'm absolutely against violence of any kind. It's stupid, as well as illegal."

The investigators look surprised, as though I had disappointed them. "Then why," I am asked, "are you being so difficult? Why are you protecting your friend?"

"Let's just say that one good turn deserves another."

"So that's it. What did he do for you?"

"He persuaded my wife to run away with him."

There is a silence.

Then, hesitantly, the intimidator speaks. "Are you putting us on, mister?"

Exits

Jane comes into my room and turns on the overhead light, which I never use. I awake immediately. It is 4:00 A.M.

"I'm leaving," she says.

I blink at the sudden brightness. They have had several hours together. After dinner I returned to my studio, giving them an opportunity to explore further their instant interest in one another. Clearly, they have made the most of their time.

"Where are you going?" I ask.

"With him."

"Yes, Jane. But where? Or aren't I sufficiently trusted?"

"North Africa, eventually."

"You'll like the couscous, I imagine. It's usually made with meat, however."

Jane shrugs, as though food did not matter. I wonder if she will take her rice pot with her.

"It's nice at least to have unchauvinistic sex again," she says.

"Does that mean you fuck him? Besides, I thought you'd decided to become a lesbian."

"I may still. But this seems a more interesting possibility for the moment."

"Just so long as you're happy. But you would have made a splendid lesbian. You have just the right combination of arrogance and querulousness."

"I'm only going to take a few clothes," Jane says. "Maybe I'll send for some things later."

"All right. Why don't you give Henry a pair of my trousers."

"Why?"

"I'd like to have those jeans of his."

"As a fetish? I always thought you were basically queer."

"I'm interested in them aesthetically, not sexually."

"Okay, I'll ask him."

"Tell him I'd regard it as a fair exchange."

"I'll just bet you would," says Jane.

The Investigators Do Not Comprehend

"Did Grant discuss his political activities with you?"

"Not his activities. Just his ideas."

"His ideas? Did he give you any idea where he might strike next?"

"It wasn't that kind of conversation. It was an intellectual argument, over drinks and dinner."

"But he did indicate he was for violent action?"

I hesitate.

I phrase my answers carefully. It would distress me to be accused of taking revenge on a man who ran away with my wife.

"He didn't say what he, personally, was planning, or even indicate that he was planning anything. All he did was try to explain to me the reasoning behind the tactics of some of the radical groups. I don't think they all agree with one another."

"What was the, uh, reasoning, he described?"

"Simply that if there was enough violent protest, the repressive actions of the government would become so severe that even the 'silent majority', as some people call it, would become radicalized."

The investigators turn once again to consult one another in silence. "Typical leftist dogma," mutters the intimidator finally.

"Do you agree with this line of reasoning?" I am asked.

"No." I shake my head emphatically. "I told Henry that I thought his belief in the silent majority, while touching, was rather naive. Being by definition gutless—people are only silent because they're afraid to rock the boat—it seemed to me that in a truly repressive society, people would just scrabble around like crazy to get their sons into West Point, or at least the police academy, in the hope that they might end up with a dictator in the family. That's better than my son the dentist any day."

The investigators look down at the pads in their laps, on which they have been scribbling my replies from time to time. They turn to look at one another, and the intimidator holds up an envelope and shrugs.

"There seems to be some discrepancy," I am informed. "You say you don't agree with the radical ideas of your friend. Yet we have information that you are not fully in support of existing forms of government in this country."

"What information?"

"We don't know who supplied it. But it's in the dossier. The full facts will be on file at the Bureau."

"There are people who would lie about me."

"All right. We'll ask you the question. Do you or don't you

believe that radical changes in our governmental forms are needed?"

"I believe that some radical changes are needed, certainly. But violence is not the way to get them."

"How would you go about it, then?"

"I believe in the subversion of art."

"The what?"

"Some kind of subversion," says the intimidator.

"Of art. The subversion of art. Art influences people on a subconscious level, so they aren't as much on the defense against it."

"Art?"

The investigators do not believe in the subversion of art. That is just as well for me, I am certain.

"Art?"

They take their leave.

They even apologize for taking up so much of my time.

In a more conventional era, they might have regarded me as dangerous, I suppose. But there are, in this time, too goddamn many other radicals in the woodpile to pay any attention to subversion through art, for Christ's sake.

Revolutionary Artifacts

When I saw Henry in Paris, during the height of his drug period, he showed me a notebook he had written under the influence of mescaline. Although he had, sometime before, given up all ambition of pursuing bourgeois success as a writer, he had apparently retained some drive to express himself. It was a bound notebook, of the kind that French schoolchildren write their lessons in. Henry had filled its pages with a procession of squiggly lines, drawn in ballpoint. They looked like this:

On every third or fourth page there was a stray word or two: a color, as in red, an obscenity, as in fuck, or a god, as in Allah.

In recreating the notebook I cannot claim to have produced an exact representation, of course, but the impact, I hope, will be much the same. This notebook that I have prepared lies open on a small black podium inside a clear plexiglass box some six feet in height. In this box I have also placed a brand new pair of Weejun loafers, size 7½C, and Henry's jeans. I have sprayed the jeans with a clear plastic solution that does indeed enable them to stand up by themselves. I call this construction REVOLU-TIONARY ARTIFACTS, and it will go on exhibit, together with a number of recent paintings, at the beginning of next month.

The investigators finally having left, I am taking advantage of the hour or so of remaining daylight to work on the final painting I intend to complete before the coming exhibition. The work is going well.

I may even be able to finish this canvas before evening.

If so, I will break out a bottle of wine from my case of Bordeaux. Just after the investigators left, I took a steak out of the freezer to thaw. With it I believe I shall have some brown rice. Jane did indeed leave her pot behind, and I am fond of brown rice when it is not forced upon me.

I feel very much at peace, very sure of my course as I work steadily away in the afternoon light.

It is very quiet here in the country.

Alice Adams grew up in Chapel Hill, North Carolina, and graduated from Radcliffe. Since then she has lived mostly in San Francisco. Miss Adams, the author of a novel *The Fall of Daisy Duke,* is working on a collection of short stories and on a new novel.

THE SWASTIKA ON OUR DOOR

Normally, Karen Washington took a nostalgic interest in stories about, and especially pictures of, her husband's former girls. They had all been pretty, some beautiful. And they reminded her that her successful and preoccupied lawyer husband had once been a lively bachelor, vigorously engaged in the pursuit of women. But the large glossy picture of Roger and his brother, Richard, who was now dead, and a girl, that she found on the top shelf of her husband's shirt closet disturbed her considerably. Why had Roger put it there? She was not jealous—she did not suspect him of having perpetuated an old liaison—but she felt left out. Why had he chosen not to tell her about this particular beautiful girl, in her high-collared dress?

To the left was fat Roger, grinning and blinking into the flashbulb, having raised his glass of wine to the night-club camera— a man out on the town, celebrating, having a good time. "The jolly Roger." With his peculiar private irony Richard had sometimes called his brother that. On the right was skinny, tortured Richard, staring at his brother with a gaze at the time stern and full of an immoderate love. Between them, somewhat recessed, was the long-necked, beautiful, dark girl, who was looking at Richard as though she thought he was either marvellous or crazy. Or perhaps she herself looked crazy. In the bright, flat light her collar made an odd shadow on her cheek, and her eyes were a strange shape—very narrow and long, like fish.

Karen sneezed from the dust. It was the maid's day off, and she was doing the closets. She was a poor housekeeper, and did not like to be reminded of that fact, of which both the dust and the presence of the picture on an untouched shelf did remind her. Retreating from the closet, she put the picture on her husband's dressing table, meaning to ask him about it that night. Karen was a big, dark, handsome girl, descended from successful generations of Berlin bankers; her father, the last of the line, had come to San Francisco in the twenties, well before Hitler, and had been prominent in the founding of a local bank. She had already, in ten years of marriage to Roger, produced five sons—five stalwart big Washingtons who had never known their difficult doomed Southern uncle, Uncle Richard, cartons of whose books were stored, still unpacked, in the basement.

Karen remembered Richard well, although she had only seen him twice in the month between her engagement party and his death. But over the years Roger had talked often of his brother, with anger and guilt, affection and a vast regret. She thought of Richard for a great deal of that day as she moved about the narrow, unwieldy, and expensive Victorian house on Pacific Avenue, bought when Richard died and they inherited his money. The house from its northern windows had oblong views of the bay and the bridge, of Sausalito and the hills of Marin County. That day, that March, there were threatening rain clouds, a shifting kaleidoscope of them, gray streaked and smudged with darker gray.

Karen had felt and still did feel an uncomfortable mixture of emotions in regard to Richard, one of which was certainly the guilty impatience of the healthy with the sick. Richard had been born with a defective heart, ten months after Roger's healthy and normal birth, and had suffered greatly during his lifetime. But beyond his irremediable physical pain he had seemed, somehow, to choose to be lonely and miserable. He lived in a second-rate downtown hotel even after he got his money; he was given to brief, sad love affairs, generally with crazy girls ("Affairs with

psychopaths are a marvellous substitute for intimacy," he had
been heard to say). He only bought books and records; his
clothes were impossible.

Like many secure and contented people, Karen could be somewhat unimaginative about the needs of those who were not content—of those who were, in fact, miserable. To her credit, she
knew this, and so she sighed as she moved incompetently about
her house; she sighed for Richard and for her own failure to
have understood or in any way to have helped him.

Karen's deficiencies as a housekeeper were more than made
up for by her abilities as a cook, or so her husband and most of
their friends thought. That afternoon, as heavy dark rains en-
shrouded the city and the bay, Karen made a superior moussaka,
which was one of Roger's favorites. Richard had also liked it,
the one time he came to dinner before her marriage, and Karen
was pleased to remember that she had at least done that for him.

Then, just as she had finished, from upstairs she heard the
youngest child begin to whimper, waking up from his nap, and
she went up to get him, to bathe and dress him before the older
boys all tumbled home from school.

The kitchen maid would come at three and stay until after
dinner, since Roger liked a formal evening meal.

Karen was dressing, and lost in a long skirt that she tried to
pull down over her increasing thighs, when Roger came in and
asked her about the picture.

"What's that doing out here?" "Here" was "heah;" Roger had
kept his Southern voice, though less strongly than Richard had.

Her head came out of the dress, and she bridled at the annoy-
ance in his tone. "Why not? It was up on your top shirt shelf."
At worst, in some atavistic Germanic way, Karen became coy.
"Some old girl friend you haven't told me about?" she said.

Roger was holding the picture, blinking at it in the harsh
light from Karen's makeup lamp, holding it closer and closer to
the bulb as though he would burn it if the picture did not reveal
all that he wanted to know.

"She's beautiful," said Karen. She came to look over his shoulder, and pressed her cheek against his arm.

"She was Richard's girl. Ellen. You remember, the one who came to Mount Zion Hospital when he was dying. After that was taken." He pointed unnecessarily at the picture. "We were celebrating his money, after he finally sold his land. That was the night he met her."

Karen was quiet, looking at the peculiar girl, whom she now vaguely remembered having heard about, and at Richard, whom no large sums of money had ever cheered, and at jolly Roger.

"What a creepy girl," Roger said. "Richard's worst. She finally had to be locked up. For all I know she still is."

"Oh." Karen shuddered.

Roger put the picture down with a heavy sigh. He was fatter now than when it was taken; his neck was deeply creased with fat, and his big cheeks drooped.

Then abruptly he turned around and embraced Karen with enthusiasm. "What's for dinner?" he asked. "Did I smell what I think I did?"

Because Richard had been sick so much and had been tutored, he and Roger ended by finishing high school in the same June of 1943, and that July they entered Harvard together, two Southern 4-Fs in giddy wartime Cambridge—fat Roger, who had a punctured eardrum, and thin, sick Richard. They both reacted to the scene with an immediate and violent loneliness. Together, they felt isolated from all those uniforms, from the desperately gay urgency of that war, and from the bright New England climate.

Roger's fat and Richard's illnesses had also isolated them in childhood; they were unpopular boys, who spent most of the afternoons at home reading or devising private games. But to be isolated and unpopular in a small town where everyone knows you is also to be surrounded—if not with warmth at least with a knowledge of your history. There is always the old lady approaching on the sidewalk who says, "Aren't you Sophie Washington's boys? I declare, the fat one is the living spit of your grandfather." Or the mean little girl in the corner grocery store who chants softly, "Skinny and fat, skinny and fat, I never saw two brothers like that."

They had, too, an enormous retreat from the world—the huge Washington house, full of books everywhere. And the pale mother and father, who had been and continued to be surprised at finding themselves parents, who retreated from parenthood to long conversations about the histories of other Southern families. "It was a perfect background for eccentrics of the future," Richard later told Ellen.

Both Roger and Richard had chosen history as their field of concentration at Harvard. During those summer afternoons and into the gaudy fall, while R.O.T.C. units drilled in the Yard and pretty Radcliffe girls in sloppy sweaters and skirts, white athletic socks, and loafers lounged on the steps of Widener Library, Richard and Roger studied furiously in their ground-floor rooms in Adams House, and at night they went to movies. Every night a movie, in suburbs as far-lying as the subway system would carry them, until one night when the only movie they had not seen twice was "I Wanted Wings," in Arlington. So they stayed home and for a joke read chapters of "Lee's Lieutenants" aloud to each other, which was not one of the texts for History I but which was the only book in the room they had not already read. It had been an off-to-college present from their not very imaginative mother. In stage Southern accents they read to each other about Fredericksburg and Chickamauga, Appomattox and Antietam.

Roger had a photographic memory, of which Richard was fiercely proud. His own memory was erratic; he easily memorized poetry but he had a lot of trouble with names and dates, with facts. As they walked across the Yard in the brilliant September air, Roger recited several pages from that book, still in that crazy, exaggerated accent—". . . and before the Northern armies could marshall their forces . . ."—while Richard gambolled beside him, laughing like a monkey.

The next January, which was the beginning of their sophomore year, they were taking a course called Philosophic Problems of the Postwar World. With everyone else they stood around outside Emerson Hall, waiting for the hour to sound. Richard was overheard to say to Roger, in that crazy Southern voice, "As I see it, the chief postwar problem is what to do with the black people."

At the end of that year Roger had four A's and Richard had two A's, a C, and a D, the D being in Biology. They had no friends. Richard regarded their friendlessness as a sign of their superiority; no one else was as brilliant or as amusing as his brother, and thus they were unappreciated. Roger didn't think much about that sort of thing then. He was solely concentrated on getting top grades.

Those Harvard years were, or perhaps became in memory, the happiest of Richard's life. He had Roger's almost undivided attention, and it was a time when Roger laughed at all his jokes.

Aside from the Southern joke that was their mainstay, they developed a kind of mad irony of their own—an irony that later would have been called sick, or black. Roger's obesity came into this. "You must have another hot dog. You won't last the afternoon," Richard would say as Roger wolfed down his seventh hot dog, at lunch at a corner stand. And when Roger did order and eat another hot dog they both thought that wildly funny. Richard's heart was funny, too. At the foot of the steps of Widener he would say, "Come on, I'll race you up to the top," and they would stand there, helplessly laughing.

That was how Richard remembered those years—big, fat Roger tilted to one side, chuckling hugely, and himself, dark and wiry and bent double, laughing, in the Cambridge sun. And he remembered that he could even be careless about his health in those years; he almost never hurt. They went for long walks in all the variously beautiful weathers of Cambridge. Years later, in California, Richard would sigh for some past Cambridge spring, or summer or fall. Roger remembered much less; for one thing, he was in later life so extremely busy.

They were reacted to at Harvard for the most part with indifference; other people were also preoccupied, and that is how, in general, Harvard is. However, Roger and Richard did manage to be irritating. To the then current remark "Don't you know there's a war on?" they both had been heard to respond, "Sir, the War has been over for almost a hundred years." And those were "liberal" years: racism, or what sounded like it, was very unpopular. No one made jokes about black people—no one but Roger and Richard.

One night Roger and Richard came back from the movies (a revival of a "Broadway Melody" in Dorchester; Roger loved musicals) to find that someone had put a swastika in black chalk on the door of their room. Richard was enchanted; in a way it was the highest moment of his life. All his sense of the monstrosity of the outside world was justified, as well as his fondness for drama—he was persecuted and isolated with his brother. "Roger," he said very loudly and very Southernly, "do you reckon that's some kind of Indian sign they've gone and put on our door?"

Roger laughed, too, or later Richard remembered Roger as laughing, but he recalled mainly his own delight in that climactic moment. They went into their room and shut the door, and after them someone yelled from down the stairwell, "Southern Fascists!" Richard went on chortling with pleasure, lying across the studio couch, while Roger walked thoughtfully about the room— that big, bare room made personal only by their books and some dark curtains now drawn against the heady Cambridge spring night. Then Roger put a Dietrich record on the player.

That was more or less that. The next day the janitor washed the chalk off, and Roger and Richard did not speculate as to who had put it there. Anyone could have.

But a week or so later Roger told Richard that he was tired of history; he was switching his field of concentration to economics. And then he would go to law school. "Fat makes you already eccentric," he said. "And eccentrics have to be rich."

"In that case I'll switch to Greek," Richard countered furiously, "and remain land-poor."

And that shorthand conversation made perfect sense to both of them.

They both did what they said they would, except that soon after their graduation (Roger *summa cum laude* and Phi Bete) Richard had a heart attack that kept him in the hospital at home in Virginia, off and on for a couple of years, fending off his anxious mother and writing long, funny letters to Roger, who seemed to be enjoying law school.

So it worked out that by the time Richard went back to Harvard for his master's in Greek literature Roger had got out of law school and gone to San Francisco, where he began to succeed as a management consultant to increasingly important firms. He was too busy even to come home for the funerals of his parents, who died within a month of each other during his first winter in San Francisco. They had, they thought, divided their land equally between their two sons. Roger sold his immediately for thirty thousand, and believed he had done very well. He urged Richard to do the same, but Richard, lazily or perversely, held on to his until five years later, when an encroaching freeway forced the sale and he got a hundred thousand.

Richard did not enjoy his second time at Harvard, except in the sense that one enjoys a season of mourning. He was terribly lonely, he missed Roger vividly, everywhere in Cambridge, and his heart hurt most of the time.

It was not until the early fifties that Richard got his teaching job in a small college near San Francisco and saw his brother again. And then he came into his money, and met Ellen.

In his downtown hotel, Richard had a large room that the maid was not allowed to enter. ("Then why live in a hotel?" practical Roger had asked.) The room was stacked everywhere with books, with records and papers. Richard took most of his meals in the hotel dining room; after he came home from a day of teaching; he rarely went out. He was not well; much of the time he felt dizzy, and he ached, but it was hard to gauge the degree to which his isolation was forced upon him. If Roger, for example, had had a bad heart, he would undoubtedly have had it continually in the midst of a crowd.

Indeed, in the years since Harvard Roger had become gregarious. Professionally, he was hyperactive; his entire intelligence and energy were occupied. People whose lawyer or adviser he was also asked him to dinner, and he became known as a very courtly if somewhat ponderous bachelor as well as an astute businessman. Roger was greedy for company; he revelled in his invitations, his cocktails and dinners, and his girls.

Girls who fell in love with Richard were girls with whom Roger had not been successful; that was how Richard met girls. In one of their rare conversations about women, Roger remarked on Richard's perfect score. Richard had never been turned down.

"But with how many ladies have I—uh—attempted to prove my valor?" Richard asked in the parody Southern manner that he sometimes tried to continue with Roger. "Four—or is it three? I sometimes lose track of these—uh—astronomicals."

Ellen made five.

One May afternoon, a few months after they had met, Richard lay down across some tufts of new grass on the bank of a duck pond in Golden Gate Park watching Ellen, who was out wading among the ducks. Like a child, she held her skirt bunched up in front of her at the top of her long, thin, childish legs. Water had spattered the shabby gray flannel; Ellen visibly didn't care. She splashed out toward some brown ducks who were peacefully squatted on the surface of the pond. They fled, scuttering across the water, submarining under, as Ellen screamed out, "See! They know I'm here!"

Her long fish-shaped eyes that day were almost blue with excitement. When she was unhappy or simply remote, they were gray.

At the farther edge of the pond were willows, now thickly green with spring; they grew out into the water in heavy clusters. And all around the pond were tall eucalyptus trees, shedding their bark in long strips, that scented the air with lemon as the breeze fluttered their sad green scimitar leaves above Richard's head.

Out of the water, Ellen became a detached and languorous girl, who sat on the grass not far from Richard, clutching her arms about her knees and watching him curiously, listening to that tormented and violent Southern talk.

"Interest! *Interest!*" was what Richard was saying. "My own brother, my *heir,* and he offers me interest on a loan. 'My God,' I told him, 'you're my brother, take all the money, but for God's sake don't offer me interest.'"

Above the trees pale-gray clouds drifted ceremoniously across the sky. Half closing her eyes, Ellen turned them into doves— flocks and flocks of soft, gray doves.

"God, if I'd only sold the bloody land when Roger sold his," said Richard for the tenth or perhaps the hundredth time that day. "And got only thirty thousand like him instead of this bloody hundred."

Richard's frenzy and the intensity of his pain had oddly a calming effect on Ellen. Unlike most people, who were frightened or impatient or even—as Roger now was—bored, Ellen experienced with Richard a reduction of the panic in which she normally lived. Rather reasonably she asked him what she had often been told but had forgotten. "Why didn't you sell it then?"

"I preferred to be land-poor." This was in the old stage Southern voice. *Ah pruhfuhd.* Then, "Christ, I didn't want the money. I still don't. If I could only just give it to him. Without dying, that is." And he laughed maniacally.

By this time, in the mid-fifties, pain had deeply lined Richard's face. There were heavy lines across his forehead, lines down the sides of his nose and beside his wide, intensely compressed mouth. Many people, especially Roger's more recent friends, considered Richard crazy. He was difficult to be with, and this became increasingly true. "He has grown quite impossible," Roger would say.

"What does he think it means to be brothers?" Richard demanded ferociously.

"How much money did he want?" Ellen asked mildly.

"Twenty thousand!" Richard shrieked. "At six per cent! My brother!"

His voice scared the ducks more than all of Ellen's splashings had; they scattered in a wild and hasty disorder, flapping their wings and crying out.

Ellen crawled over to where Richard lay. With one finger she stroked his eyelids closed, then kissed them—one, then the other. Richard sat up and grasped for her; he clutched her violently against his chest. "God," he said. "If you knew how lovely you are. Everything you do." Then he said, "You really should marry me. I could guarantee you instant widowhood." He was given to these embarrassing references to his death.

Ellen pulled away from him and huddled herself about her knees again, staring out glumly across the pond at the still retreating ducks. She said, "If you only knew how ugly I am."

He cackled with pleasure in her. And in his joke—"In that case, you're going to have a very hard time getting to New York. United doesn't fly any ugly girls."

Ellen giggled for a minute, then stopped abruptly. All of her gestures were like that—jerky and discordant. "I may not even go to New York," she said. "It takes so much nerve."

Ellen was a mathematician—"of all things," as most people said. Her Oakland Baptist John Birch Society father, especially, said that, and often. Ellen was gifted and had been offered a fellowship at Columbia.

"Stay here," Richard said. "Let me keep you. God, won't anybody take my money?"

The melodramatic note in that last told Ellen that Richard was going to talk about Roger again, and she sighed. She liked it better when he was reading poetry to her, or when he didn't talk at all and played records—Telemann and Boccherini, Haydn and Schubert—in his cluttered room.

But Richard said, "Roger wants to invest in some resort land near Lake Tahoe, with some of his rich new German friends. Do you know the altitude at Tahoe? Six thousand feet. I wouldn't last a minute there. How to explain why his brother is never invited for weekends or summer vacations? I am socially unacceptable to my brother—isn't that marvellous?"

Richard's eyes were beautiful; they were large and clear and light brown in that agonized face. They exposed all his pain and anger and despair—his eyes and his passionate, deep Southern voice. He was really too much for anyone, and certainly for himself. And there were times, especially when he ranted endlessly and obsessively about Roger, when even Ellen wanted to be away from him, to be with any dull and ordinary person.

Ellen had met Roger at a Berkeley cocktail party, and she had had dinner with him a couple of times before the night they celebrated Richard's money at the silly, expensive restaurant where the picture was taken. Ellen had not liked Roger very much. He was exceptionally bright—she recognized and responded to that—but she was used to very bright people, and all the money-power-society talk that Roger tried to impress her with alarmed her. "You could marry extremely well if you wanted to," Roger told her. "With your skin and those eyes and those long legs. But no one should marry on less than thirty thousand a year. It can't be done." Then he had laughed. "You'd probably rather marry a starving poet, wouldn't you? Come and meet my crazy brother, though, even if he has just come into money."

And so Richard and Ellen met and in their fashions fell in love.

Now, feeling dizzy, Richard lay back on the bright-green grass and stared up through the maze of silvered leaves to the gray procession of clouds. His sickness sometimes made him maudlin; now he closed his eyes and imagined that instead of the pond there was a river near his feet, the James River of his Virginia childhood, or the Charles, at Harvard, with Roger.

Not opening his eyes but grinning insanely to himself, he asked Ellen, "Did I ever tell you about the night they put the swastika on our door?"

Of course Richard lent Roger the money, with no interest, and their diminishing relationship continued.

Occasionally, even in the midst of his burgeoning social life, Roger was lonely; he hated to be alone. Sometimes, late at night, he would telephone Richard, who always stayed up late reading and playing records. These conversations, though never long, were how they kept in touch.

At some point, a couple of years after Richard had met Ellen, Roger began to talk about a girl named Karen Erdman, and Richard knew that she was the one he would marry. But Roger took a long time deciding. Karen was a patient girl. Richard did not meet Karen until the engagement party, but he was so intuitively attuned to Roger that he could see her and feel the quality of her presence—that big, generous, and intelligent girl who adored his brother.

"The question seems to be," Richard said to Roger over the phone, "whether you want to marry at all. If you do, obviously Karen is the girl you should marry."

"I have a very good time as a bachelor," Roger said. "But it takes too much of my time. You break off with one girl and then you have to go looking for another, and at first you have to spend all that time talking to them."

"God, what a romantic view! In that case perhaps you should marry."

"But she wants children. I find it almost impossible to imagine children."

"Sir, what kind of a man would deplore the possibility of progeny?" Richard asked in their old voice.

"I can't decide what to do," said Roger. Then, as an after-thought: "How is Ellen?"

"Marvellous. She has managed to turn down four fellow-ships in one year."

"She's crazy."

"You're quite right there."

"Well. Good night."

"Good night."

A heavy, engraved invitation invited Richard to the Erdmans' engagement party for their daughter. "Oddly enough," Richard said to Ellen. "Since they're being married at Tahoe, I'm sur-prised they didn't do the whole thing up there. Or simply not mention it until later. God knows I don't read the society pages."

Richard was not asked to bring Ellen.

The Erdman house, in Sea Cliff, was manorial. Broad halls led into broader, longer rooms; immense windows showed an enor-mous view of the bay. And the décor was appropriately sump-tuous—satins and velvets and silks, walnut and mahogany and gilt. Aubusson and Louis XV. For that family, those were the proper surroundings. They were big, dark, rich people who dressed and ate and entertained extremely well.

In those crowded, scented, overheated rooms, Richard's pale, lined face was wet. He went out so infrequently. The profusion and brilliance of expensive clothes and jewels, the tables of elaborate food made him stare. He stood about in corners, trying to cope with his dizziness and wildly wondering what he could find to say to anyone in that company. Lunatic phrases of gallantry came to him. Could he say to the beautiful blond across the room, "I just love the way you do your hair, it goes so well with your shoes"? Or to the tall, distinguished European who was actually wearing his decorations, "I understand you're in money, sir. I'm in Greek, myself. Up to my eyes in Greek." No, he could not say anything. He had nothing to say.

Roger's new circle included quite a few Europeans: refugees like his father-in-law-to-be, Mr. Erdman's friends, and transients— visiting representatives of banks, commercial attachés and consuls. The rest were mainly from San Francisco's solid merchant upper class—German-Jewish families who had had a great deal of money for a long time. They didn't read much but they were knowledgeable about music and they bought good paintings on frequent trips to Europe. Among those people Roger looked completely at home; even his heavy Southern courtliness took on a European flavor.

Mrs. Erdman was a very pretty woman, with smooth, dark hair combed back in waves, and round, loving eyes as she regarded both her husband and her daughter. Richard found this especially remarkable; he had never known a girl with a nice mother and he imagined that such girls were a breed apart. Ellen's mother had jumped under a train when Ellen was thirteen.

Mrs. Erdman wanted to be nice to Richard, once it was clear to her who he was. The two boys were so unlike that it was hard to believe they were brothers. "I'm so sorry that you won't be able to come up to the lake for the wedding," she said sympathetically.

"But who'd want a corpse at a wedding?" Richard cackled. "Where on earth would you hide it?" Then, seeing her stricken face and knowing how rude he had been, and how well she had meant, he tried again. "I just love the way you do your hair—" But that was no good either, and he stopped in midsentence.

Mrs. Erdman smiled in a vague and puzzled way. It was sadly

obvious that poor Richard was insane. And how difficult for Roger that must be.

Roger was beaming. His creased fat face shone with pleasure, which, for the sake of dignity, he struggled to contain. Having decided to marry, he found the idea of marriage moving, and he was impressed by the rightness of his choice. He was now in love with Karen, and he would love her more in years to come. He was even excited by the idea of children—big, handsome Californian children who were not eccentric. He stood near the middle of the enormous entrance hall, with Karen near his side, and beamed. He was prepared for nothing but good.

Then suddenly, from the midst of all that rich good will, from that air that was heavy with favorable omens, he heard the fierce, loud voice of his brother, close at hand. "Say, Roger, remember the night they put the swastika on our door?"

There was a lull in the conversations as that terrible word reverberated in the room. Then a hum began to fill the vacuum. Feeling himself everywhere stared at, and hearing one nervous giggle, Roger attempted a jolly laugh. "You've been reading too many books," he said. "Karen, darling, isn't it time we went into the other room?"

It is perhaps to the credit of everyone's tact that Richard was then able to leave unobtrusively, as the front door opened to admit new guests.

A month later, two months before the June wedding at Lake Tahoe, Richard had a severe heart attack, and he died the next day at Mount Zion Hospital, with Ellen and Roger at his bedside.

They had been watching there at close intervals for the entire day, and they were both exhausted. Even their customary wariness in regard to each other had died, along with Richard.

"Come on, let me buy you some coffee," said Roger, fat and paternal. "You look bad."

"So do you," she said. "Thanks. I'd like some coffee."

He took her to a quiet bar in North Beach, near where she was then living, and they sat in a big, recessed booth, in the dim late-afternoon light, and ordered espresso. "Or would you like a cappuccino?" Roger asked. "Something sweet?"

"No. Thanks. Espresso is fine."

The waiter went away.

"Well," said Roger.

"Well," echoed Ellen. "Of course, it's not as though we hadn't known all along. What was going to happen."

The flat reasonableness of Ellen's tone surprised Roger, and he looked at her with a little suspicion. Ellen was never reasonable. But there was nothing visible on her white face but fatigue and sadness.

Roger said, "Yes. But I wonder if we really believed it. I mean, Richard talked so much about dying that it was hard to believe he would."

The coffee came.

Stirring in sugar, regarding her cup, Ellen said, "People who talk about jumping under trains still sometimes do it. But I know what you mean. We somehow didn't behave as though he would die. Isn't that it?" She lifted her gray eyes to his blinking pale-blue ones.

He took the sugar, poured, and stirred. "Yes, but I wonder what different we would have done."

In the same flat, sensible tone Ellen said, "I sometimes wouldn't see him when he wanted to. I would be tired or just not up to it, or sometimes seeing someone else. Even if the other person was a boring nothing." She looked curiously at Roger.

He responded with a little flicker of excitement. "Exactly!" he said. "He was hurt and complained when I went to boring dinners or saw business friends instead of him, but I had to do that. Sometimes for my own protection."

"Yes," said Ellen, still very calm, with an oblique, upward look at Roger.

"People grow up and they change," Roger said. "I could hardly remember all that time at Harvard, and he always wanted to talk about it."

"Of course not," she said, staring at him and holding her hands tightly together in her lap, as though they contained her mind.

Roger was aware that he was acting out of character; normally, he loathed these intimate, self-revelatory conversations. But he was extremely tired and, as he afterward told himself, he was understandably upset; it is not every day that one's only brother dies. Also, as he was vaguely aware, some quality in Ellen, some quality of her listening, drove him on. Her flat silence made a vacuum that he was compelled to fill.

"And remember that time a couple of years ago when I wanted to borrow the money?" Roger said. "He was so upset because I offered him interest. Of course I'd offer him interest. Otherwise it wouldn't have been fair."

"Of course not," said Ellen, looking deeply into his eyes. "Everyone has to pay interest," she said reasonably.

"It was the least I could do," Roger said. "To be fair to him. And I couldn't spend the rest of my life thinking and talking about how things were twenty years ago."

"Of course not," Ellen said again, and soon after that he took her home and they parted.

But in the middle of that night Roger's phone rang, beside his wide bachelor bed, and it was Ellen.

"Swine! Filthy, fat swine!" she screamed. "Horrible fat ugly murdering swine. You killed him with your never time to see him and your fat German business friends always around you and your all-American swine success. How lovely he was and suffering and you found him not socially acceptable to your new swine friends and you couldn't believe his heart and now you can get filthy blubber fatter on his money. . . ."

She seemed to have run down, and into the pause Roger asked, "Ellen, do you need money? I'd be more than happy—"

She screamed, but it was less a scream than a sound of total despair. Then she hung up, and a few weeks later Roger heard that she had had a complete breakdown and was hospitalized —perhaps for good.

After the excellent dinner of moussaka, salad, and strawberries in cream, Karen and Roger settled in the living room with strong coffee and snifters of brandy. It was an attractive, comfortable, if somewhat dishevelled, room—very much a family room. Karen's tastes were simpler than those of her parents. Her furnishings were contemporary; the fabrics were sturdy wools or linen, the broad sofa was done in dark-brown leather.

Roger leaned back; he blinked and then sighed, looking up to the ceiling. Roger had been talking, as he rarely did, about his Virginia boyhood—that house full of books near the quiet James River, his parents, his fragile younger brother.

"I sometimes wish," said Roger, "that I'd taken the time somewhere along the line to have learned a little Greek. It seemed to give Richard so much pleasure."

"But, darling, when would you ever have had the time?"

"That's just it, I never had the time."

"I wonder what has happened to Ellen," Karen said. "Do you think she's still put away?"

"I'm not sure I'd even want to know," said Roger. "I forgot to tell you that she called me the night he died."

"Really? No."

"Yes, she was quite hysterical. I think she was angry because she knew I was Richard's heir." By now Roger had come to believe that this was indeed the case. "Yes," he said. "She probably thought I should give her some of his money."

In the large, safe room, beneath other large rooms where her sons were all sleeping, Karen shuddered, and together she and Roger sighed, for Richard's pain and death and for poor lost Ellen's madness.

"Here," said Karen, "have more coffee. Poor darling, you look as though you need it."

"You're right. I do." And Roger reached out to stroke his big wife's smooth, dark cheek.

Judith Rascoe was born in San Francisco and grew up in California and Idaho. She got her B.A. from Stanford, and her M.A. from Harvard. In the spring of 1973 a collection of her short stories and a novella will appear under the title *Yours, and Mine*. Miss Rascoe is now living in Los Angeles.

A LINE OF ORDER

And over all this chaos of history and legend, of fact and supposition, he strove to draw out a line of order, to reduce the abysses of the past to order by a diagram. STEPHEN HERO

There is a compulsion worse than nostalgia: to return to a scene of past unhappiness, as if one expected it to turn out right—this time! When I went back to Sand River my cousins were there, and their own lives trailed around them like unfinished quilts. But to my surprise Saint Agnes School was gone, torn down, all its possibilities lost. Once I read several books about nuns and convent schools; they were nothing like Saint Agnes. Now Saint Agnes School has disappeared. Its grounds are rubble, weeds, rubble. I walked back and forth across the leveled block, but the rubble was beaten so small that not even one whole brick was left.

"The Sisters don't look like Sisters anymore," my cousin Joan said.

They dress, I am told, in dowdy blue and black, utility sheers, stout shoes, hats of an old-fashioned military cut. There's a car pool to Gleeson High School, where there are young, Tiparillosmoking, joking priests to teach the boys and girls (strictly a day school). The mothers, I gather, are worried that their children will marry Negroes. "I've talked to the Negro people," says Father Larry Shuler, "and they want to marry their own."

Not a board, not a brick. I can convince nobody, scarcely myself, that Saint Agnes School was once an establishment of substance in a wealthy district. (On the houses across the street there are signs now: ROOMS.) I never saw it in that heyday, of course, but my mother did.

I walked back and forth across the rubble, looking for Saint Agnes lamb, a stone lamb, painted white; it used to stand in a niche over the front door of the school, over the arc of stone letters—*Saint Agnes School.*

My father came back from the Pacific when the war was finished and asked for a divorce. My mother gave it to him. We had been living with her parents on a little farm in Wilson, almost fifty miles from Sand River, and I'd been happy there. I was ready to start school with Bobby Lyons and Norma Mary Metz; already, that summer, we had begun to study the yard of the local public school—the Warshaw School. My grandmother would walk us there in the evenings and sit on a bench near the teeter-totter while we tried the swings. The Warshaw School had an enormous black-metal fire slide—we called it a fire escape, but it was in fact an enormous iron tube that went at an angle from the second floor down to the ground. In case of fire, my grandmother said, children could be thrown into the tube, by which they'd slide to safety. Bobby Lyons climbed into the lower mouth of the fire slide and shouted and pounded. "I can't wait to go down that old thing," he said.

"I hope there's a fire," Norma Mary said boldly.

"There won't be any fire," my grandmother said. We had to agree with her, for the Warshaw School was built all of brick, the only brick building in town besides the Methodist church, and it stood upon a wide field of asphalt. My grandmother led us home in the near dark; heat lightning licked across the sky at the end of Fourth Street. "The lightning'll catch the school on fire some day I bet," Bobby Lyons said.

"It will not," my grandmother said. "But they'll have a fire drill one day and you'll get to go down the fire slide." And then changing her mind: "Oh, I hope they don't. It must be nasty filthy dirty in that old pipe."

"Fire drill!" Bobby Lyons yelled, running ahead, sliding on the pebbles on the summer-beaten road. "Fire drill!"

But my mother realized that she would have to go to Sand River to find a new husband, and I would go to Sand River and board at Saint Agnes School, which had been one of the finest Catholic schools in the Rocky Mountains (my mother said). The sisters taught good manners (my grandmother said). "I was a damn fool to marry outside the Church!" my mother said to my grandmother; they agreed it had been an unlucky thing to do. My grandmother had gone to Saint Agnes School, and she remembered with pleasure the school parties and processions. Once she had walked from Saint Agnes School to Saint Michael's Cathedral, a mile along Bannock Street, wearing a white gown and roses wreathed upon her head, a handmaiden of the Blessed Virgin. The daughters of silver millionaires had gone to the school in those days, and French and Irish priests came from San Francisco to give lectures on moral theology and literature—

These things I know now, but then I listened to my mother and my grandmother and thought of: velvet, silver, roses. My grandmother in her petticoat. French—which for some reason meant "clean" to me; perhaps there was a French laundry in Sand River. I thought of Christmas; when I went to Saint Agnes School, I decided, it would be like Christmas morning. There would be candles and carols, and everything would be new. My mother drove to Sand River one weekend and came back with new clothes: white cotton undershirts, brown stockings and garter belts, white blouses, two navy-blue smocks, and a navy-blue sailor coat with four brass buttons and a navy insignia, embroidered with scarlet thread, on the left sleeve.

In September, twenty-five years ago, it was a hundred degrees at noon, and by ten o'clock in the morning the hot light was already beginning to penetrate the vault of poplar leaves that hung over my grandparents' yard. In one corner of the yard there was a concrete well of sorts, a little box that poured water into a ditch no wider than my body, and I followed my grandfather to this well, where he opened the gate, and then followed him along the ditch as he made cuts with a shovel to let the water flood the lawn. The water was cold at first, and I was afraid of the earthworms his shovel revealed, but soon the lawn was covered with an inch of water; I ran back and forth across the shallow lake, kicking up plumes of water and watching the drops form in the air before they fell again. A shift of the wind brought the smell of alfalfa from the field behind us; from my enormous grotto I could see the sun-dazzled field and a man on a tractor cutting the alfalfa.

At noon my grandfather banked the ditch again and the water soaked down under the grass and my footsteps were erased as the blades sprang back. Norma Mary Metz came walking down the glaring dirt street and I met her at the corner. She had sweat on her face.

"Are you through with school?" I asked.

"I have to go back after lunch. I can't talk to you. I just have an hour to eat lunch, and I want to go back and play with Carol. I'm going to get my mama to fix me a lunch in a lunch box. The school food is icky. Why aren't you in school? You're supposed to be in school."

"You cried the first day," I said.

"I didn't."

I said, "I saw you when your mother brought you back."

"Wayne Harrison pulled my braids," she said.

"I'm going to school tomorrow."

"Then I can wait for you and we'll walk together."

"No, you can't. I'm going to a boarding school in Sand River."

"I just thought bad kids went to boarding schools," she said. "What did you do?"

"I didn't do anything; it's not for bad kids."

Later, when it was time for Norma Mary and Bobby Lyons to come back from school, I hid in the woodshed.

Then it began to storm. My mother and grandmother came

hurrying down the street with packages in their hands, shouting for my grandfather and me to get the chairs in off the lawn, while behind them thunderheads reared over the trees, showing their black bellies, and the wind started lifting the branches of the poplars. When we got inside the back porch I could hear the trees very loudly. All summer they roared in the sunshine, but in a storm it was as if waves were breaking over us, and I could hear soughs and creaks and cracks. Then my grandmother told me to keep off the back porch, for she was afraid that a limb would break and fall through that flimsy roof. Then the rain came, tearing the leaves from their twigs, and my grandfather ran to the woodshed and brought back a bucket of coal and a bucket of kindling, while my grandmother stood at the back door, holding her flying hair away from her face.

After dinner my grandfather went to sleep in his chair next to the radio, and all I could hear were the railroad clock and the rain and women's voices from the bedroom. I went out to the sleeping porch, where the canvas over the screens was bulging in the wind. My grandmother kept the victrola in there; I cranked it up and put on a record:

> He's got
> Curly hair
> I never cared for
> Curly hair
> But he's got
> Curly hair
> And that's my weakness now.

I watched myself tap-dancing, barefoot, in the wardrobe mirror.

My Uncle Dwight drove us to Sand River the next afternoon, and by the time we arrived, it was almost dark. "Just go out on Bannock," my mother said. She rolled down her window; the green, aromatic smell of elm spray filled the car. The streets were lined with enormous elms, with big houses sunk in ample gardens. "Here we are," my mother said. Uncle Dwight stopped in front of a four-story Victorian building, constructed of brick and orna-

mented with ironwork, standing by itself as proprietor of a whole
block. The building, in its turn, was dominated by its bell tower,
which began as a porch for the door, continuing up the front of
the building, and then rose alone into the sky, lifting a gold cross
above the shadowing elms to the last ray of sunlight.

My mother led me up the walk while Uncle Dwight followed
with my suitcase and my blue tin trunk, but after setting the
trunk down in the hall he shot back to the car. The floors and Ed-
wardian woodwork beamed with polish; a hemp runner, very
narrow, showed where one might walk, either straight ahead to
the end of the hall where a niche held a large statue of Our
Lady of the Immaculate Conception, or to the right and up a
broad staircase. Midway down the corridor a door opened and a
tall, heavy nun came forward to greet us, her face as immobile
as the moon in a halo of starched linen. "Hello," she said, "I'm
Sister Mary Stephen." Abruptly my mother caught me and kissed
me again and pointed out my trunk to Sister Stephen, and Sister
Stephen assured my mother in a hearty voice that I would have a
wonderful time. "There's a little girl waiting for you," Sister Stephen said. "Her name is Patsy and she wants to know when you
arrive." Impatient now, I gave my mother a last kiss and watched
her go out the front door. The front door closed. I followed Sister
Stephen up the stairs.

She led me into a dormitory on the second floor: white walls,
white ceiling, white iron beds, white dressers, white curtains, and
ten little girls in white nightgowns that hung to their ankles.
When she put my suitcase on the bed and opened it, I found that
it smelled of freshly washed nightgowns too, and soap. Sister
Stephen told me to undress under my nightgown; all the other
girls, briefly informed of my name, were doing the same thing,
and they looked like moths struggling in cocoons while Sister
Stephen moved among them, undoing braids and unbuttoning
dresses.

Patsy had coppery hair in a single long braid down her back;
she was not allowed to speak to me, but as a gesture of welcome
she reached down, grabbed the hem of her nightgown, and pulled
it up, revealing a round little bare body. There was a rush of

giggles, like raindrops blown against a window, and then silence.
Sister Stephen explained that we were about to go to the bathroom, that we would do what we had to do, then wash our hands
and faces and brush our teeth; we must not talk or make noise,
and we must not drink any water, because this would mean we'd
have to get up in the night. Standing in my robe and slippers,
holding my towel and washcloth and toothpaste and toothbrush
and cup, I was afraid of the whiteness and silence. I saw Sister
Stephen pinch the arm of a girl who was dawdling.

I was given a place in the procession to the bathroom, and once
there I was careful not to swallow a drop of water. When we returned, Sister Stephen told us to kneel, and with our noses in
the sides of our long-legged beds, we prayed in unison to Mary
and then to our guardian angel:

> Angel of God, my guardian dear
> To whom God's love entrusts me here,
> Ever this day be at my side
> To light and guard, to rule and guide.
> Amen.

A scene from the dormitory: I am lying on my bed, repeating the
alphabet to myself (I have just learned it), trying out different
rhythmic groupings of the letters, settling finally on the synco-
pated ABCD EFG HIJK LMNOP—QRS TUV Double-youuuuuu X YZ

A scene from the classroom: Sister Stephen, in the yellow light of
a dark afternoon, is printing the words *hat, bat, cat* on the board,
and I am reading them and savoring the shape of the vowel in my
mouth, trying to remember other words for the list. I liked the
classroom. I was neither quick enough to be bored nor slow
enough to fall behind. The rules of grammar, punctuation, and
penmanship protected me; I could understand them. Two years
before, I had made a game of writing the letters of the alphabet,
which I could write but not read, in any order at all on sheets of
paper. When I covered a sheet I took it to my mother and asked
her if I had written any words. Now, at six, I had real words to

write as I wished, and with a big yellow pencil I made the shapes
of printed small letters, each of which had assumed a character:
dwarfish *a*'s, submarine *p*'s, talkative *e*'s, and *d,* who I thought
was like the joker in a pack of cards.

A scene from Sunday: I am standing in the parlor, listening to my
mother, but I cannot look at her. She asks me, "Are you having a
good time here?"—or something like that, perhaps, "I'll bet you're
having a good time here, aren't you?" I say yes because that is the
right thing to say. In a few weeks I have learned that I must always do the right thing. At breakfast time that Sunday Sister Stephen had led us, as usual, to the long breakfast table in the basement. The table was rather frightening in the early morning: long
and crowded with cheap, heavy china, nickelplated knives, forks
and spoons, pots, jugs—all with a hard shine from the bare bulb
overhead. And overhead too the steampipes like the gnarled roots
of a tree, as if we were eating deep underground, under the tree.
The steam hissed and gurgled above us. I no longer wanted to eat
breakfast, because every morning the moment came when I had
to pick up my cup, break the film with my lips, and drink down
the chocolate that was tepid, thick, and very sweet. At first I had
said, "Please, I don't want to drink it." Sister Stephen insisted. I
refused. She commanded. I drank it and at once threw up. "That's
nasty! That's disgusting!" she cried, and my punishment was to
stay in the basement for an hour after the others had left.

"Do you like Sister Mary Stephen?" my mother asks.

"Yes, I like her a lot," I say.

After a while one of the Sisters comes into the parlor, and this
is the signal that visiting hours are over; it is suppertime. When
my mother leaves I remember that I was going to ask her if I was
an orphan. One of the day pupils told me that boarding pupils
were orphans, but I didn't think this was true.

It was not a large school. Perhaps fifty girls, from six-year-olds to
thirteen-year-olds, boarded there, and the single building held
them all and classrooms and chapels and nuns besides. The school

occupied a block; behind the building there was a yard with spaces marked off for games and an adjoining garden with a grotto to the Virgin Mary built of big, clumsy stones. The girls in the first three grades could go only in the yard or in the building; but during the day we were joined by day pupils, both boys and girls, for classes and games. These others presumably lived near the school—some of them may have lived no more than a block away—but for me the world outside the school's walks ceased to exist. I was completely incurious about the homes of the day pupils. Yet every doorway and statue and stone ornament and pebble of the school was of the greatest interest, and I was always touching, smelling, even—when no one was looking—tasting a patch of brass or a knob of wood. I remember the tin that covered a big table in the basement—a sheet of tin folded under the edges of the table and tacked into place. On that table were laid slices of bread spread with margarine and apricot jam for the morning collation. I remember the word "collation": a new word, long and full of sound and having a pleasant meaning. I passed my hand along the smooth blood-red brick until it reached the basement window; then I bent down and watched the kitchen girls laying out slices of bread, the top of each slice like the top of a valentine heart.

I remember the Virgin Mary's bare foot pressing the head of a serpent.

I remember how we walked two by two in front of Sister Stephen to the cathedral on Sunday to hear Mass. Patsy told me that if I rubbed my hands together and then blew on them, they would get warm; I still do this, even though it does not warm my hands—perhaps I do it because I liked Patsy.

Now and then the older girls—the thirteen-year-olds, I suppose —said they would brush and braid our hair, and this was a particular treat because their dormitory was redolent of privilege: each girl had a dresser twice as large as mine and a screen of white cloth to form a cubicle about her bed. The privacy of those cubicles seemed to me the most desirable thing in the world from the first moment I saw them.

A fat girl with a pageboy lifted me onto a stool. "What've you got to say for yourself?" and she began to brush my hair, grabbing a handful in her fist and brushing it until the brush crackled and stray hairs, alive with electricity, crawled over my cheek and down my neck. I hated it, and in order not to think about it I imagined having a cubicle of my own, a curtained and inviolable space. I could read there, or cry. At night, in our dormitory, there was a dim light, and when somebody was crying anybody could see her. If the crying went on, eventually a light would go on behind the screen at the end of the room, a shadow would rise in silhouette behind the screen, and then Sister Stephen appeared in shawl and nightdress and stamped through the dormitory to the weeper's bedside: "Wake up. You're having a nightmare. Hush now. Go back to sleep." A few times somebody admitted that she wanted her mother. "Your mother isn't here," Sister Stephen said, her voice like a stick; she was teaching us something about the world. How quickly we learned what she taught us!

"Do you want me to tell you a story?" said the girl who was brushing my hair.

"Yes," I said, pleased. I knew what kind of story she would tell.

"This is a true story, now," the girl said. The brush went down my hair very, very slowly. "There was this fraternity and they wanted to test the new members, you know? So they found this big old, awful old haunted house, really spooky, and they said to the boys, 'You have to spend the night in this old haunted house.' And meanwhile they got a medical student to give them the arm of this black man and they hung up the black man's arm in the house and made voices going, 'I want my arm back!' And the next day they went in and found one of the boys was dead and the other was crazy and his hair had turned white just overnight!"

"Tell me another story."

The older girls also knew a story about people who strapped panthers' claws to their hands and murdered travelers, and a story about a man who fell into a hay-baling machine. The little girls screamed when they listened to these stories; then, with our hair brushed and braided and the braids tied with elastic and plaid ribbons, we walked back to our own dormitory and waited for Sister Stephen to lead us downstairs to breakfast.

That year the snow began early, in the middle of October, and it was decided that I was too sickly—or too likely to be sickly—to be allowed to play in the snow. I had not been sick and I resented this confinement, but now it seems more reasonable to me, for I must have become, in those few weeks at Saint Agnes, an unprepossessing and listless child. I was infected with a sort of nervous apathy; I cried a good deal and played with my food and daydreamed and did not listen the first time. "I want you to hear me the first time!" Sister Stephen insisted. For some reason I still find inexplicable she wanted us to have spirit. She liked disobedience, and I remember the cold look with which she took her leave of me when the day's lessons were over and I stayed behind in the classroom while the other children went to play in the snow. "Goodbye, Sister," I said.

"Goodbye," she said. "Turn out the light." She waited a moment, frowning at me, as if to provoke me to something—to demand I be allowed outside? I went to the window and leaned on the sill. From the second-story classroom window I could see the snow gather under the lights in the schoolyard. Children in snowsuits made snowmen and threw snowballs and lay down in the untrodden patches and waved their arms to make angels. Standing in the window, I waved my arms too, imagining the soft resistance of the snow. A long time later a buzzer sounded loudly: the voice of the building. The little figures in snowsuits left the yard and disappeared through the lighted doorway.

But eventually I disobeyed. I don't remember how. Probably I whispered when we were supposed to be silent or didn't pay attention or wriggled in my seat in class—a lot of time was spent ordering children not to wriggle. Not to sway back and forth behind their desks, or curl their feet up under them or shift from spot to spot on the curved oak seat. In any event, a day came when we were told that our class would get to see a cartoon film, and after lessons we were led down the hall not to the dormitory but toward the stairs; "up there" the film would be shown. And then something happened and then Sister Stephen suddenly pulled me out of the line and held me immobile while the others passed.

"I warned you," she said.

"I won't do it again," I said, already having forgotten what I'd done.

"But you did do it again! You disobeyed me deliberately!" She jerked my arms, and I flung up my hands and cried, "Please." And then the combination of her own anger and my cowardice carried her past the edge of reason and she slapped my face with the back of her hand and cried, "There! And if your nose bleeds, don't blame me!" My nose began to bleed at once, and she shoved me into an empty classroom and went out, locking the door behind her. I was used to my nose bleeding and it did not frighten me, but the blow had filled me with a drowning sense of terror, and I wept and coughed, covering my face and hands with blood. Some time later an elderly nun came in to me and led me to the bathroom and told me to wash my face. I looked in the mirror and saw blood all over my mouth and hands.

"Now wash your face," she said. Her voice was kind, and she touched my face very gently with a rag dipped in warm water. "If you cry your nose will bleed again."

"Sister Stephen hit me," I said. She frowned at my tattling; then she told me that I was all right, that I should be good, and that things were all better now. She was puzzled, I think, and she did not bring me back to Sister Stephen at once but walked me to the dormitory, which was empty and dark. "You won't be afraid if I leave you here?" she asked. "No," I said, truthfully, and without another word, without thanks, I left her and went to my bed and lay down and listened to her footsteps walk away.

When the other little girls came back, I said nothing and they asked me no questions—nor did I expect any, and it is only now that I realize how odd it was that there were no friendships among the little girls. We had lost interest in other human beings. Three or four girls began to wet their beds again. One tall, big-eared girl would go into fits of hysterical anger and bite whoever was nearest her. The worst day was laundry day; our stockings and garters, pants and undershirts, petticoats and nightgowns were all thrown into a large cloth laundry bag. We had to stand silently while Sister Stephen inspected these clothes for signs of wear or worse. One day she reached into the bag, pulled out a pair of pants, read the name tag, and then waved the pants for all to see: "This little girl does not know how to wipe herself properly. She is *filthy.*" And then she pointed at a chunky, red-headed little girl with a boyish face: "These are *yours.* I don't want to see this nasty sort of thing again." All the color went out of the girl's face making her freckles seem like the marks of a disease. Sister Stephen flung the pants back in the bag, picked it up, and left the room, while the rest of us started to chant, "Nasty! Nasty! Nasty!" The red-headed girl walked over to her bed and hung onto the covers with both hands and cried, while the rest of us, silent now, stared at her—at the small shoulder-blades, like the back of a young frog.

It took a while, but one by one we learned that Sister Stephen was pleased when somebody received a gift from home. The red-headed girl, for instance, got a tin weaving frame, a square of tin like a fence for a doll's house, the tin cut into teeth so that yarn could be woven back and forth and up and down. When you finished a hundred squares you could make a blanket, she said. Sister Stephen was delighted with this; she helped the red-headed girl to thread the loom and showed her how to weave the piece of looped wire that served as a bobbin through the warp of green wool. The red-headed girl was allowed to work with her little loom for a few minutes every night after we all got undressed and into our nightgowns, but when she had made two or three squares and lost interest, Sister Stephen lost interest in her and again scolded her as readily as she scolded the rest of us.

My turn came when one of my aunts sent me a pair of small plaster angels—baby angels, one in pink and one in blue, kneeling in prayer. "Aren't these wonderful," Sister Stephen said. "You must show them to everybody." And I passed them around and now the other little girls were indifferent, while Sister Stephen was full of enthusiasm. "They're lovely!" she said, and her big farm-girl's face got quite pink. "Put them on your dresser where we can see them!"

As a consequence, when our parents came on Sundays we begged for gifts. "I want a paint set!" "Can I have a little teeny doll?"

One or two girls had already been taken away from the school. The other mothers were uneasy.

"Are you having a good time?" my mother asked me again.

"Oh, yes," I said. I had begun to dread this question.

"I brought you a paint set," she said.

"Thank you!" I said. The first thing I did when she left was to show the paint set to Sister Stephen, who smiled and admired the wide choice of colors.

I wish I could explain Sister Stephen. I can see her: a big woman in a heavy serge habit, with big freckled hands, a big face, seemingly without eyebrows or lashes because these were so pale, and huge blue eyes, so large, so blue and enormous the pupils, that I was sickened by them—by their enormous stare. Sometimes when the light from a window touched her face her eyes were so opaquely blue, so huge, that she seemed blind, like a marble statue. She had a heavy voice and stood habitually with her arms folded and her chin tucked down against the hard white edge of the wimple.

But of her nature, I can only guess. She seemed ruder, more excitable than the other nuns, and I would hazard now that she was a farm girl from somewhere in the Midwest, and ill-at-ease and resentful among the half-hearted Catholics of the West, who even got along with Protestants and Mormons. It is so easy to imagine wearying, uncomfortable visits from the old bishop, Bishop Gleeson, to the shabby drawing room the sisters kept for themselves. Bishop Gleeson was of my grandmother's time, and he would remember when Saint Agnes School was full of the daughters of silver kings and copper kings. All up and down Bannock their houses stood: silver mines, copper mines, gold mines paid for the porte-cochères and the turrets and piazzas. Gold from Idaho City plated the cross on the Saint Agnes tower. But now the mines were closed. Up in the mountains snow falls on the fenced, abandoned workings; watchmen sit in their houses looking at the snow fall on the road—tonight they'll call the city to say they're closing it up for the winter. The daughters of the silver kings are old women and spend the winter in Palm Springs.

Sister Stephen stares at the bishop, amazed he cannot tell the difference between his time and hers. She could walk him to the window some Sunday and show him the sort of people who have their kids in Saint Agnes School: divorced women, farmers from away upcountry, people who've had a girl go wild on them. Even the Basques, when they get a little money ahead, send their children to the Sacred Heart sisters in Portland.

And so, when a mother or a relative sends a child a gift, Sister Stephen is reassured that the child has not been forgotten, that *she* has not been forgotten, left thankless with a few little girls whose parents have forgotten them. If a child has no visitors, if no cards or gifts come, Sister Stephen is repelled: what has happened to the child? what perversion of life does the child represent? Every night she tells the little girls to kneel and to pray, and her strong voice urges their voices louder. But nothing happens, no extraordinary grace is shed upon the school or the children or her own bewildered spirit.

At Christmas my mother and her new beau took me to my grandparents' house, and there I found all the grownups full of nervous optimism because this was the first Christmas after the war: "We can be thankful at least the war's over," they said to each other. The snow fell and fell past the windows and covered the lawns. "Of course you can play in the snow!" they said to me, and wrapped in a rabbit-fur coat I was handed to my cousins, who put me on their sleds and pulled me over hillocky gardens and brought me home again. "There you are!" my grandmother exclaimed. The rabbit-fur coat lay on the blue Chinese rug. I was led to the kitchen, right up to the woodstove my height, fat, hot; my grandfather lifted the stove lid and dropped in a handful of pine needles "for the smell" and then on top of the lid went a kettle "for a toddy." My Uncle Dwight came in from the back porch, smoking a cigar, and I could hear his hunting dogs pawing and slipping on the linoleum of the porch. "We'll fix you a toddy,"

Uncle Dwight said; he put a spoon and a half of bourbon in a glass tumbler and picked up the teakettle. "But first," he said, putting the kettle back on the stove, "first let's have something extra special in this." He opened a cupboard, brought out a little cardboard box, and shook two pieces of rock candy into my hand. "What do you say we put this in?"

"Not all of it."

"Then one piece," and he dropped one piece, big sugar crystals clustered on a string, into the tumbler, covered it with boiling water, and gave it to me: "Here's your toddy now." And delighted by the sweet smell of bourbon, I dropped the other piece in and fished it out again. "That'll make you sleep now," he said.

I slept, under a down satin comforter, and woke up in the night sometimes to find myself alone; then I would get out of bed and go first to the window where I could see the light from the front parlor falling across the snow, and then to the door, where I could hear the grownups' voices chattering on and on—not their words, but the rising and falling tones, the musical shape of questions and silences.

Sometimes when I was eating breakfast my grandmother asked me if I wanted to play with Bobby Lyons or Norma Mary Metz, but I said I didn't want to.

"Just before you came Norma Mary asked if you'd be here for Christmas," my grandmother said.

"She has so many friends at school," my mother said.

"Yes," I said.

"You'll see them again soon," my grandmother said.

"Yes, I will."

"She misses them," my mother said.

Finally they convinced themselves that I missed my school friends very much, and so late New Year's Day my mother and her new beau drove me back to Sand River and Saint Agnes School. When we started to get out of the car my mother's eyes filled with tears. "I wish you didn't have to go back so soon," she said, and looked at me imploringly.

"I don't have to go back now," I said.

"Yes, but I know you want to," she said, and with a little snuffle she brushed away the two tears and licked her lips and led me briskly up the walk. A nun I'd seen very seldom answered the bell: "Why, what an early bird!" she said. "Have you had your supper?" she asked when my mother had left.

"Yes, Sister."

"Well, what will we do with you?"

I was, it seemed, the only girl who had come back yet.

"Wait here," she said, and after a long time Sister Stephen came down the stairs.

"The other girls aren't back yet," Sister Stephen said. "I don't know what we're supposed to do with you." She picked up my suitcase. "You'll have to go to bed." Then she sped me up to the dormitory and stood silently in the doorway as I unpacked my case and undressed. She led me to the bathroom. She led me back to the dormitory. She listened to my prayers. "Good night," she said, and walked off down the hall. I lay awake for a long time, listening for voices, but I heard nothing but the whispers of the radiators.

The next morning, after a solitary breakfast in the kitchen, I was told I could play in the basement recreation room—a large, low-ceilinged room with a bare floor and three sagging couches, crooked lamps, tables, jigsaw puzzles in half-broken boxes, and squinting windows covered with heavy screens.

The day wore and wore. There was soup for lunch.

"Is anybody back?" I asked the cook.

"Nobody yet," she said. "Look at the snow, will you?" As soon as she said it, the snow stopped too. I went back to the recreation room to play with a jigsaw puzzle, but it was too difficult for me. I climbed up on the back of one of the couches so that I could look out a window. The floor creaked and Sister Stephen came into the room. "Get off that sofa," she said. "Who said you could do that?"

"Nobody," I said.

"Do you think you can climb on furniture?"

"No," I said. "I'm sorry."

" 'No, Sister,' " she said.

"Why are they all gone, Sister?" I asked her.

"They're home with their families because the term hasn't

started," she said. "Do you think you can climb on sofas at home?"

"Then why am I here?" I asked.

"You're here because your mother doesn't want you," she said. "You're a bad girl and she doesn't want you."

Then she walked away.

I was nailed to the spot with humiliation; the other girls would come back and discover this awful secret. They would make fun of me—they might even make fun of my mother because she had made such a mistake, letting Sister Stephen know. All the presents in the world: embroidery frames, paint boxes, holy cards, figurines, miraculous medals—all were worthless; nothing could ransom my humiliation. Looking at the seam of snow across the window I felt a chill, a hot, dreamy chill, rush under my skin as if it were transparent. The next day when the others came back, I caught a cold.

For several days I would not admit it. Everybody seemed sickly. As we bumped into each other on the processions from dormitory to bathroom, from dining room to classroom, I felt hot breath on my face, the hectic warmth of other bodies. My heart caught cold first; it bumped faster and faster; it lurched awkwardly when Sister Stephen moved close to me, when her habit shadowed the corner of my eye and her cold hand pressed my shoulder: "Pay attention," she said. "Watch where you're going." It was very cold now and the old furnaces were not adequate, and sometimes at night one little girl or another, her face hot and her feet cold, would droop exhausted over the white washbasin and squirt hysterical tears while the toothbrush went around and around in her mouth. "You're acting like a big baby!" Sister Stephen cried in outrage. We all understood this and agreed with her. I, for one, lay in bed silently haranguing my guardian angel; he could and must help me not to be a baby. After a while I could feel his wings close around me—thick, soft, and heavy like the wings of wild geese my Uncle Dwight shot—and I swooned into their powdery darkness.

My breath got squeaky, my voice faded.

"What's the matter with you?" Sister Stephen demanded.

"Nothing, Sister," I said, and shut my mouth tight.

And then one day after dinner she took one girl by the back of her collar and stretched her to her toes, inviting us to look at her unfastened garter, unraveled braid, dirty hands, and spotted knees. "You are here," said Sister Stephen, "because your mother doesn't want to take care of you, and you can't take care of yourself."

I peeked sideways and other girls were peeking too, partly relieved because our shame was now shared, partly the more hopeless because obviously this was why we were all here; our sentences were not arbitrary or mistaken . . .

"Your mother doesn't want you," said Sister Stephen, early and often; she was no longer informing us of this fact but reminding us. I began to have a dream about my Aunt Bernice: we were driving in her car and the door on my side fell open and I started to fall out. I begged and begged Aunt Bernice to stop the car, to slow down at least so I could close the door, but she refused and began to wrestle with me, and at last I realized that she wanted me to fall out of the car; then I began to scream at her that she must not do that because my mother would be angry with her— but by that time Aunt Bernice had turned into an enormous dead dog and lay inert and cold in the meadow grass. In another dream I walked up to a mirror and looked at my face and it had become a hollow shell, like a Halloween mask, the skin all tight, yellow, and stiff like an empty bug's carcass left in a spider web. I sat up in bed shrieking. But I made no sound. The dormitory was silent. I wanted and waited for the light to go on behind the screen but it did not go on.

"What's the matter with you?" Sister Stephen asked.

I tried to say "Nothing," but this time I coughed instead. She put her big cold hand on my forehead and then told me to go to bed. That afternoon the bare trees wobbled behind the windows whenever I woke up. After I had been awake for a few minutes, I began to cough again. Finally Sister Stephen brought me a glass of water. "Don't cough," she said.

I didn't blame her for hating my coughs. They began as a little trickling in my throat, like the small pebbles and dust particles that precede an avalanche; then suddenly my whole chest seemed to cave in with explosions of noise. The coughs were like shouts, and after each paroxysm I was scared and worn out. I sipped at the tepid, musty water. My eyes felt as if I had been staring at the sun.

That night I woke up and began to cough. The noise was unbearably loud. I crammed sheets into my mouth and sucked at the wet, spitty linen. At the end of the dormitory the light went on. She came to me wearing a long, coarse white nightgown, with her hair hanging down the back of her neck and a flashlight in her hand. After telling me to drink some water she shone the light in my face; when I coughed again she whispered furiously, "You're just doing this to annoy me."

"I can't help it," I whined.

"Stop it!"

I tried. A cough expanded in my chest now like a broken steel spring. I pressed my lips together but it was too strong, it broke loose, and I began to cry.

"You can't sleep here, disturbing everybody," she said. "Put on your robe and your slippers."

I did as I was told and followed her out of the dormitory and into a smaller room where there was only one bed.

"This is the infirmary," she said.

It was a fine place. My meals came on trays, and nuns and a doctor and two jigsaw puzzles came to my room. When the door was shut for the night I could lie back on the pillows and cough as long and as loudly as I had to. Then my mother came and said I could come home for a few days.

"I like it here," I said, one jigsaw puzzle to go.

"I know, but it will only be for a few days," she said.

The next morning one of the older girls helped me put on my clothes and braided my hair and led me up the stairs that wound toward the bell tower, past windows that were like lightning flashes, showing bare trees and chimneys crowned with snow. We found my blue tin trunk amidst the others, but we took only my suitcase; yet I pretended I was leaving forever and longed to make the older girl believe this. As we went downstairs the stairway seemed to grow larger with my imagined sense of freedom. In the dormitory I emptied the drawers of my dresser and wrapped the plaster angels in a clean petticoat. "Goodbye," I said to everybody. My mother and Aunt Bernice were in the hall, waiting to take me away. When we went out the door the air carried an electric smell from the fallen snow.

It was the middle of a winter afternoon. I was sitting on the rug in the middle of the living room in Aunt Bernice's house looking at *The Book of Knowledge*. The pages were heavy and shiny; they reflected the long-slanting sunlight. My mother came into the room and knelt down on the rug.

"Do you miss your friends at school?" she asked.

"No," I said.

"Don't you want to see Sister Stephen?" she asked.

"No," I said.

I began to turn the pages of the book with deliberate slowness so that everything would seem all right and normal, because then I could say—and said—"Sister Stephen slapped me. She made my nose bleed and said it wasn't her fault, but it was her fault. She said you didn't want me. She says that to everybody when you do something wrong, she says your mother doesn't want you, right in front of everybody."

My mother jumped up and said in a cold voice, "You aren't going back to that school. That's settled. That's all finished."

Then I wanted to tell her the story again, but she told me that it was finished, that she promised I would never have to go back there again, and so I kept quiet. When several days passed I asked again if I had to go back to the school and she said no again. Finally one evening she came back from downtown and said she had been to the school to tell Sister Superior about Sister Stephen and that it turned out Sister Stephen was tired and didn't like to take care of children. "Poor thing," my mother said to Aunt Bernice. "The poor woman is—" and then tapped her finger on her temple. "They won't let her take care of any children anymore, believe you me."

"But they didn't do anything," I said—or burst out with, rather, thinking I *knew,* I *knew* what had happened, only I *knew.*

"They didn't know," Aunt Bernice said.

Two years later Saint Agnes School stopped taking boarding students.

I went to another school and had a good time, but I could not forget Sister Stephen. One night I took out the plaster angels and smashed them with a hammer, but this made me feel worse than ever. Then I began to have a dream I would have for years: I found myself back in school, but up in the bell tower, high above the moonlit snow and the black tree boughs, and I ran down the dark stairways and through the yellow-electric halls, putting the nuns to flight and waking up all the little girls in their white nightgowns and chasing them into a fire slide like the one on the Warshaw School.

And then I must tell one more dream. A few years ago I was explaining the idea of purgatory to somebody, and I remembered how Sister Stephen explained it: each sin, she said, was like a nail driven into a clean white plank. One could remove the nail but the scar was still there. That night I dreamt there was something in my breast—an arrow, a burning point of light. Then my mother died and the arrow fell out of my breast and grew dimmer, dimmer, and winked out. Sister Stephen was there and I begged and begged but she would not speak to me.

Raymond Carver was born in Clatskanie, Oregon, and grew up in Yakima, Washington. His stories have appeared in *Esquire, Harper's Bazaar, The Iowa Review, Perspective, North American Review, December, Best American Short Stories 1967, Best Little Magazine Fiction 1971 and 1972,* and elsewhere. He has published two books of poetry: *Near Klamath* and *Winter Insomnia.* In 1970 Mr. Carver received a National Endowment for the Arts Grant and in 1971 the Joseph Henry Jackson Award. He is presently Lecturer in Creative Writing at the University of California, Santa Cruz. During 1972–73 Mr. Carver will be a Wallace Stegner Creative Writing Fellow at Stanford.

WHAT IS IT?

Fact is the car needs to be sold in a hurry, and Leo sends Toni out to do it. Toni is smart and has personality. She used to sell children's encyclopedias door-to-door. She signed him up, even though he didn't have kids. Afterward, Leo asked her for a date, and the date led to this. This deal has to be cash, and it has to be done tonight. Tomorrow somebody they owe might slap a lien on the car. Monday they'll be in court, home free—but word on them went out yesterday, when their lawyer mailed the letters of intention. The hearing on Monday is nothing to worry over, the lawyer has said. They'll be asked some questions, and they'll sign some papers, and that's it. But sell the convertible, he said, today, tonight in fact. They can hold onto the little car, Leo's car, no problem. But they go into court with that big convertible, the court will take it, and no argument.

Toni dresses up. It's four o'clock in the afternoon. Leo worries the lots will close. But Toni takes her time dressing. She puts on a new white blouse, wide lacy cuffs, the new two-piece suit, new heels. She tranfers the stuff from her straw purse into the new patent-leather handbag. She studies the lizard makeup pouch and puts that in too. Toni has been two hours on her hair and face. Leo stands in the bedroom doorway and taps his lips with his knuckles, watching.

"You're making me nervous," she says. "I wish you wouldn't just stand," she says. "So tell me how I look."

"You look fine," he says. "You look great. I'd buy a car from you anytime."

"But you don't have money," she says, peering into the mirror. She pats her hair, frowns. "And your credit's lousy. You're nothing," she says. "Teasing," she says, and looks at him in the mirror. "Don't be serious," she says. "It has to be done, so I'll do it. You take it out, you'd be lucky to get three, four hundred, and we both know it. Honey, you'd be lucky you didn't have to pay *them*." She gives her hair a final pat, gums her lips, blots the lipstick with a tissue. She turns away from the mirror and picks up her purse. "I'll have to have dinner or something. I told you that already, that's the way they work, I know them. But don't worry, I'll get out of it," she says. "I can handle it."

"Jesus," Leo says, "did you have to say that?"

She looks at him steadily. "Wish me luck," she says.

"Luck," he says. "You have the pink slip?" he says.

She nods. He follows her through the house, a tall woman with a small, high bust, broad hips and thighs. He scratches a pimple on his neck. "You're sure?" he says. "Make sure. You have to have the pink slip."

"I have the pink slip," she says.

"Make sure."

She starts to say something, instead looks at herself in the front window. She studies their reflection in the window, and then shakes her head.

"At least call," he says. "Let me know what's going on."

"I'll call," she says. "Kiss, kiss. Here," she says, and points to the corner of her mouth. "Careful," she says.

He holds the door for her. "Where are you going to try first?" he says. She moves past him and onto the porch.

Ernest Williams looks from across the street. In his Bermuda shorts, stomach hanging, he looks at Leo and Toni as he directs a spray onto his begonias. Once, last winter, during the holidays, when Toni and the kids were visiting his mother's, Leo brought a woman home. Nine o'clock the next morning, a cold foggy Saturday, Leo walked the woman to the car, surprised Ernest Williams on the sidewalk with a newspaper in his hand. Fog drifted, Ernest Williams stared, then slapped the paper against his leg, hard.

Leo recalls that slap, hunches his shoulders, says, "You have someplace in mind first?"

"I'll just go down the line," she says. "The first lot, then I'll just go down the line."

"Start at nine hundred," he says. "Then come down. Nine hundred is low bluebook, even on a cash deal."

"I know where to start," she says.

Ernest Williams turns the hose in their direction. He stares at them through the spray of water. Leo has an urge to cry out a confession.

"Just making sure," he says.

"Okay, okay," she says. "I'm off."

It's her car, they call it her car, and that makes it all the worse. They bought it new that summer three years ago. She wanted something to do after the kids started school, so she went back selling. He was working six days a week in the fiber-glass plant. For a while they didn't know what to do with the money. Then they put a thousand on the convertible, and doubled and tripled the payments until in a year they had it paid. Earlier, while she was dressing, he took the jack and spare from the trunk and emptied the glove compartment of pencils, matchbooks. Blue Chip stamps. Then he washed it and vacuumed inside. The red hood and fenders shine.

"Good luck," he says, and touches her elbow.

She nods. He sees she is already gone, already negotiating.

"Things are going to be different," he calls to her as she

reaches the drive. "We start over Monday. I mean it." Ernest Williams looks at them and turns his head and spits. She gets into the car and lights a cigarette. "This time next week," he calls again. "Ancient history." He waves as she backs into the street. She changes gear and starts ahead. She accelerates and the tires give a little scream.

In the kitchen Leo pours Scotch and carries the drink to the backyard. The kids are at his mother's. There was a letter three days ago, his name penciled on the outside of the dirty envelope, the only letter all summer not demanding payment in full. We are having fun, the letter said. We like Grandma. We have a new dog called Mr. Six. He is nice. We love him. Good-bye.

He goes for another drink. He adds ice and sees that his hand trembles. He holds the hand over the sink. He looks at the hand for a while, sets down the glass and holds out the other hand. Then he picks up the glass and goes back outside to sit on the steps. He recalls when he was a kid his dad pointing at a fine house high on the hill above the road, a tall white house surrounded by apple trees and a high, white rail fence. "That's Finch," his dad says admiringly. "He's been in bankruptcy at least twice. "Look at that house." But bankruptcy is a company collapsing utterly, executives cutting their wrists and throwing themselves from windows, thousands of men on the street. They still had furniture. They had furniture and Toni and the kids had clothes. Those things were exempt. What else? Bicycles for the kids, but these he sent to his mother's for safekeeping. The portable air-conditioner and the appliances, new washer and dryer, trucks came for those things weeks ago. What else did they have? This and that, nothing mainly, stuff that wore out or fell to pieces long ago. But there were some big parties back there, some fine travel. To Reno and Tahoe, at eighty with the top down and the radio playing. Food, that was one of the big items. They gorged on food. He figures thousands on luxury items alone. Toni would go to the grocery and put in everything she saw. "I had to do without when I was a kid," she says. "These kids are not going to do without," as if he'd been insisting they should. She joins all the book clubs. "We never had books around when I was a kid," she says as she tears open the heavy packages. They enroll in the record clubs for something to play on the new stereo. They sign up for it all. Even a pedigreed terrier named Ginger. He paid two hundred and found her run over in the street a week later. They buy what they want. If they can't pay, they charge. They sign up.

His undershirt is wet, he can feel the sweat rolling from his underarms. He sits on the step with the empty glass in his hand and watches the shadows fill in the yard. He stretches, wipes his face. He listens to the traffic on the highway and considers whether he should go to the basement, stand on the utility sink, and hang himself with his belt. He understands he is willing to be dead.

Inside he makes a large drink and he turns the TV on and he fixes something to eat. He sits at the table with chili and crackers and watches something about a blind detective. He clears the table. He washes the pan and the bowl, dries these things and puts them away, then allows himself a look at the clock.

It's after nine. She's been gone nearly five hours.

He pours Scotch, adds water, carries the drink to the living room. He sits on the couch but finds his shoulders so stiff they won't let him lean back. He stares at the screen and sips, and soon he goes for another drink. He sits again. A news program begins, it's ten o'clock, and he says, "God, what in God's name has gone wrong?" and goes to the kitchen to return with more Scotch. He sits, he closes his eyes, and opens them when he hears the telephone ringing.

"I wanted to call," she says.

"Where are you?" he says. He hears piano music, and his heart turns.

"I don't know," she says. "Someplace. We're having a drink, then we're going someplace else for dinner. I'm with the sales manager. He's crude, but he's all right. He bought the car. I have to go now. I was on my way to the ladies and saw the phone."

"Did somebody buy the car?" he says. He looks out the kitchen window to the place in the drive where she usually parks.

"I told you," she says. "I have to go now, Leo."

"Wait, wait a minute, for Christ's sake," he says. "Did some-body buy the car or not?"

"He had his checkbook out when I left," she says. "I have to go now. I have to go to the bathroom."

"Wait," he yells. The line goes dead. He listens to the dial tone. "Jesus Christ," he says as he stands with the receiver in his hand.

He circles the kitchen and goes back to the living room. He sits. He gets up. In the bathroom he brushes his teeth very carefully. Then he uses dental floss. He washes his face and goes back to the kitchen. He looks at the clock and takes a clean glass from a set that has hands of playing cards painted on each glass. He fills the glass with ice. He stares for a while at the glass he left in the sink.

He sits against one end of the couch and puts his legs up at the other end. He looks at the screen, realizes he can't make out what the people are saying. He turns the empty glass in his hand, and considers biting off the rim. He shivers for a time and thinks of going to bed, though he knows he will dream of a large woman with grey hair. In the dream he is always leaning over tying his shoelaces. When he straightens up, she looks at him, and he bends to tie again. He looks at his hand. It makes a fist as he watches. The telephone is ringing.

"Where are you, honey?" he says slowly, gently. He can hear music again.

"We're at this restaurant," she says, her voice strong, bright. "We're having dinner."

"Honey, which restaurant?" he says. He puts the heel of his hand against his eye and pushes.

"Downtown someplace," she says. "It's nice. I think it's New Jimmy's. Excuse me," she says to someone off the line, "is this place New Jimmy's? This is New Jimmy's, Leo," she says to him. "Everything is all right, we're almost finished, then he's going to bring me home."

"Honey?" he says. He holds the receiver against his ear and rocks back and forth, eyes closed. "Honey?"

"I have to go," she says. "I wanted to call. Anyway, guess how much?"

"Honey," he says.

"Six and a quarter," she says. "I have it in my purse. He said there's no market for convertibles. I guess we're born lucky," she says and laughs. "I told him everything. I think I had to."

"Honey," Leo says.

"What?" she says.

"Please, honey," Leo says.

"He said he sympathized," she says. "But he would have said anything." She laughs again. "He said personally he'd rather be classified a robber or a rapist than a bankrupt. He's nice enough, though," she says.

"Come home," he says. "Take a cab and come home."

"I can't," she says. "I told you, we're halfway through dinner."

"I'll come for you," he says.

"No," she says. "I said we're just finishing. I told you, it's part of the deal. They're out for all they can get. But don't worry, we're about to leave. I'll be home in a little while." She hangs up.

In a few minutes he calls New Jimmy's. A man answers. "New Jimmy's has closed for the evening."

"I'd like to talk to my wife," Leo says.

"Does she work here?" the man asks. "Who is she?"

"She's a customer," Leo says. "She's with someone. A business person."

"Would I know her?" the man says. "What is her name?"

"I don't think you know her," Leo says.

"May I ask who is calling?" the man says.

"That's all right," Leo says. "That's all right. I see her now."

"Thank you for calling New Jimmy's," the man says.

Leo hurries to the window. A car he doesn't recognize slows in front of the house, then picks up speed. He waits. Two, three hours later, the telephone rings again. There is no one at the other end when he picks up the receiver. There is only a dial tone.

"I'm right here," Leo screams into the receiver.

Near dawn he hears footsteps on the porch. He gets up from the couch. The set hums, the screen glows. He opens the door. She bumps the wall coming in. She grins. Her face is puffy, as if she's been sleeping under sedation. She works her lips, ducks heavily and sways as he cocks his fist.

"Go ahead," she says thickly. She stands there swaying. Then she makes a noise and lunges, catches his shirt, tears it down the front. "Bankrupt," she screams. She twists loose, grabs and tears his undershirt at the neck. "You son of a bitch," she says, clawing.

He squeezes her wrists, then lets go, steps back, looking for something heavy. She stumbles as she heads for the bedroom. "Bankrupt," she mutters. He hears her fall on the bed and groan.

He waits awhile, then splashes water on his face and goes to the bedroom. He turns the light on, looks at her, and begins to take her clothes off. He pulls her from side to side undressing her. She says something in her sleep and moves her hand. He takes off her underpants, looks at them closely under the light, and throws them into a corner. He turns back the covers and rolls her in, naked. Then he opens her purse. He is reading the check when he hears the car come into the drive.

He looks through the front curtain and sees the convertible in the drive, its motor running smoothly, the head lamps burning, and he closes and opens his eyes. He sees a tall man come around in front of the car and up to the front porch. The man lays something on the porch and starts back to the car. He wears a white linen suit.

Leo turns on the porch light and opens the door cautiously. Her makeup pouch lies on the top step. The man looks at Leo across the front of the car, and then gets back inside and releases the hand brake.

"Wait," Leo calls and starts down the steps. The man brakes the car as Leo walks in front of the lights. The car creaks and groans against the brake. Leo tries to pull the two pieces of his shirt together, tries to bunch it into his pants.

"What is it you want?" the man says. "Look," the man says, "I have to go. No offense. I buy and sell cars, right? The lady left her makeup. She's a fine lady, very refined. What is it?"

Leo leans against the door and looks at the man. The man takes his hands off the wheel and puts them back. He drops the gear into reverse and the car moves backward a little.

"I want to tell you," Leo says, and wets his lips.

The light in Ernest Williams' bedroom goes on. The shade rolls up.

Leo shakes his head, tucks his shirt again. He steps back from the car. "Monday," he says.

"Monday," the man says, and watches for sudden movement.

Leo nods slowly.

"Well, good-night," the man says, and coughs. "Take it easy, hear? Monday, that's right. Okay, then." He takes his foot off the brake, puts it on again after he has rolled back two or three feet. "Hey, one question. Between friends, are these actual miles?"

The man waits, then clears his throat. "Okay, look, it doesn't matter either way," the man says. "I have to go. Take it easy." He backs into the street, pulls away quickly, and turns the corner without stopping.

Leo tucks at his shirt and goes back in the house. He locks the front door, and checks it. Then he goes to the bedroom and locks that door and turns back the covers. He looks at her before he flicks the light. He takes off his clothes, folds them carefully on the floor, and gets in beside her. He lies on his back for a time and pulls the hair on his stomach, considering. He looks at the bedroom door, outlined now in the faint outside light. Presently he reaches out his hand and touches her hip. She does not move. He turns on his side and puts his hand on her hip. He runs his fingers over her hip and feels the stretch marks there. They are like roads, and he traces them in her flesh. He runs his fingers back and forth, first one, then another. They run everywhere in her flesh, dozens, perhaps hundreds of them. He remembers waking up the morning after they bought the car, seeing it, there in the drive, in the sun, gleaming.

Jane Mayhall was born in Louisville, Kentucky. She went to Black Mountain College in North Carolina, the Middlebury Music School in Vermont, and the New School for Social Research, New York City. She has taught at the New School for Social Research; Morehead State College, Morehead, Kentucky, and Alice Lloyd College, Pippa Passes, Kentucky. Miss Mayhall has published three books, *Cousin to Human* (a novel), *Ready for the Ha Ha* (a book of satires), and *Givers & Takers* (poems). Her poems, plays, and essays have appeared in literary and feminist magazines, and she is completing a book on American Women Writers, and a second novel. Miss Mayhall is married to the writer, Leslie Katz, and lives in Brooklyn.

THE ENEMY

When I first met him, he looked like a handsome, red-haired snake. But no, I will go back. . . .

When I read his first published story, which had already created a sensation, I was struck by nothing but its cruelty. But at the time, I felt obliged to keep my trap shut. "Just think of it, how daring!" somebody said. Or words to that effect. We were at a New York party. "A Jew, writing antisemitic literature." A girl across the room gave an unexplained giggle. My stomach turned. It was 1947. Just the right year, just the right timing. And by god, I thought, I'll bet he knows this. I'd never met the young man who had been in the war, I'd no doubt we shared the same dislike for sanctioned killing, and he was making himself famous by hitting the right perversity, which everyone with any ambitions or pretentions to literary fame would catch on to in a moment. It was the next thing to wearing a swastika, with the millions of Jews scarcely buried. How smart, how chic. My stomach turned. But silently, I kept silent. Or, rather, to whom could I speak? Intuitions are the sponge-boats of the unlucky. I was also a writer and—of no importance, unless you think it—a female, and about the same age as my enemy, the Young Famous. He was already famous, and I could sense his being buoyed up by the tides of political disenchantment, and the backwaters of meanness, and (this is harder to say) the natural reaction to the sufferings of the many martyrs.

Because, oh clever enemy, he had pounced on the little fact that not all martyrs are especially saints. He had tracked down the nastiest nifty. So, a man is eligible for dying in a gas chamber? Well, look, he's not so great. He cheats his partner, he scratches his tail, he urinates in the bathroom. Methodically the young Author brought out the hilarious facts. And shamelessly, he "uncovered mounds of maggots." Brave? No, shameless. But the world wanted to be shameless. Who was their best example? Well, that man of simple tastes. Adolph Hitler, himself. What better literary flavor than to extol the one you opposed? But you do it on the sly, by ironic indirection. Almost flirtatiously. And with a touch of the renegade.

An appetite for meat that was mostly gamy.

The devil smiling into cocktails. I became somewhat obsessed. Everything seemed to connect with bad public influences. I remember at a downtown bar, in 1949, overhearing two people (I can't remember what they were like) describing details of a gruesome car accident they'd seen. I can still hear the gloat in their voices, the expressive, complacent enjoyment.

Meanwhile I, this uncredited writer, thought of myself (though I didn't discuss it) as a kind of sour-grapes, pettish and irritated fool. The price of being published only seldom. Either my time was past, or it hadn't come. There was no easy way to assess it. At parties, at least one person would bring up our scandalous Author. Everyone said: "He writes that way because (1) he had an unhappy childhood, (2) he is telling the truth, (3) he's a smooth operator." But even the last was uttered in tones of respect. And oh—believe me, said the fools (then, I perceived I was *not* a fool) "sadism can never be dull."

The years went crashingly by. Can I say anything, without relating it to the whole of society? Here are some random quotes from my 1956 notebook: "The attempt to combat old horror seems to exist in the creation of new horrors. There is some ghastly, mental form of justification going on. The idealization of monstrous behavior. In some ways I understand it. In other ways, I feel it is all superficial and crazy." And later, "They are talking of antiart and novelty. And likewise, the use of criminal ideas for intellectual rejuvenation. Why does this concept seem so bourgeois to me? The tabloids are cashing in, and the scream-titled movies. Some smart cookie knows the cash value of something."

I felt warped and consumed, spinning out more impossible sentences. There was scarcely a movement of thought that didn't fall into a vast, unhappy web. But I couldn't quite fix the source of my resentment.

"The sneer, the mock and the fart, as good as gold in the bank."

And, "It isn't barbarism that is being preached us, but another kind of slick, canny use of decay."

I looked at these words, almost blindly. Because even as I had written them, for the least read story, in the least read book, I could see how hollow-sounding, even precious they seemed. Behind my frontal lobes, there was always that shadowy companion. My adversary was turning out "good dramatic situations" like cream. And he had a formula, I noticed. It was in pretending, at the beginning of a novel, to like people, his girl, his little brother, his mother—then showing (without comment) how rotten they really were. Except, his beliefs about being rotten weren't exactly mine. In one of his stories, the fiancée of the hero accidentally drops an unused Kotex on the floor. It's a high point of exposé, showing how comic and unlovely women actually are. The hero is rightfully repelled, and in time escapes the girl. But not before giving her a sermon on how much more he loves her than she does him. Literarily, the scene was a "breakthrough." "With all the laughs and zingy guts" (said a critic) "of life itself."

Should some arch female writer have written: "Love the girl, love her Kotex"?

But, inverse Victorianism. And what the hell did the closet equipment matter. If she'd dropped an aluminum pan, would it have made any difference? The guy didn't want her anyway. But good god, and god, again. The idea of a "breakthrough," and so shabby, infantile. And the audience on its knees, picking up the salacious tidbits. Stupid children.

I was once more in the intolerable web. It was like a private *cause célèbre*. I comforted myself by reading Lermontov, who said: "In decent company as in a decent book open abuse cannot occur." But, the remonstrance, oddly enough, I felt was directed at myself. Never mind that all the successful and published villains were doing dirt on life, exaggerating and de-emphasizing, using the mores of the crowd, prejudices and ugly appetites, never mind the spurious images, and the evil they committed, they did it with an art. In them, there was some myth-making ability, and the use of hidden weapons. While I, for whatever I was, wanted to straightly cry out my stern, subjective abuse.

Finally, I met him at a Writers' Colony. It was just outside Philadelphia, one of those short-lived enterprises on somebody's converted farm. I remember the day and fine weather; between the silver birch leaves was a dancing play of wind. Down the hill, he came sauntering. He walked, I thought, like a man who wore silken underwear. Some of my bias seemed confirmed.

He was courteous and oily, a snake of remarkable attraction. I mustn't be rude, I said to myself. And not a coward, either. I was not a coward, but I was amazed at the pressure of bona fide world opinion; all of those volumes selling. Books translated into Italian, French, Danish, Japanese. For some reason, all that notoriety and power seemed housed in his gleaming white teeth. Correlations melded; his eyes, like the eyes of some red-haired people, were entrancingly pale, deep set. But, it was the insidious *savoir faire*—that made me feel abashed. How can you attack a villain, whose every nuance is embedded in a kind of intellectual foam rubber, the wisecrack, sarcasm, evasion?

A smiling snake, with a murderous tooth.

I was, I knew, taking the whole thing too seriously. We spoke a few words and separated, continuing our opposite paths. He hadn't been a snob, nor had I expected him to be. I went back to my room and got ready for dinner. On the second floor of main quarters, I had a little niche. Through the dark, shaded windows the light was summery, soft. This was a particular Writers' Colony, and I mourn that it's now defunct. Only a few months since, the chief donor (an heir to a cough medicine fortune) ran out of funds. But while it lasted, the going was good; and for me, more than an economic convenience. It was like a sort of European farm monastery, and I thrived on it. Time, and conditions for work. I presumed that, in the same way, it served as a like retreat for my free-to-choose Author. Else, why was he there? We were buddies in the stew together. But, that wasn't my real thought.

I was slightly amused at the process. How your mind gets stuck on a symbol and won't let go. But that's what life is about, isn't it? Whether you admit it or not, you're opposed to some things and in favor of others; interpretings follow. And hence. All of my fantastic moral resentment seemed geared to a central figure. It was nonsense, but it was natural. I poured myself a half-tumbler of bourbon, and sat down in a chair to think, thoughts galloping like waves across the sea.

I couldn't help but believe that writers, and everyday people too, *can't* be unconscious of the effects of what they do. Nabokov says art is not prophetic. A beautiful idea, but maybe not so true? The damage of consequences. If, writing a book, or even in your personal life, you set up a mouth-smacking scene of violence, or some imbecilic cruel character evaluation, some weak-minded persons, or young ones, will want to imitate the orgy. With my Famous Author—a joke, the word "my," but so linked was he to the stresses in my brain—under all the clear documentary sentences (though I'd always fancied strains of a pornographic Somerset Maugham), behind all the furniture of the ordinary, kids eating popcorn, couples having sexual intercourse, old men spitting in the gutter, there was always that little germ of *demeaning,* and the secret in his wheat. The germ, and the worm; and the inviolate snake. Call it anything you want, the message was hate. His hero hated Jews. He also hated sex, but of course in the guise of the funny-ugly, all those side-splittingly awkward positions. The coitus of contempt, my dear, my dear!

I got up, thoughts running acid. In the four corners of the room there was nothing to counter my dreams. But damn it, they were true. No less substantial than guns and chairs, people's lousy attitudes.

But why important to me?

"Cultivate your own damned garden."

In the silence of the room, I heard my voice. Me, myself and the bourbon. How Jesus Christ embarrassing. The room, off to itself; I was sure nobody'd heard. No matter, but incriminating. A blind for doing nothing, spouting mottos at the ceiling! All such inanities I condemn. Starved hopes, and muddy illusions. I went to the bureau and combed my hair.

But, the only thing in his books (a final recap, so often had I been through this mad excursion), the only things he'd ever made slightly pleasant, in the art of subliminal discourse, pleasant *and* comely, I thought, were: good-looking clothes, rich homes and automobiles. . . .

I arrived at the downstairs dining room, with a spent conscience. Literally, my animus was burned up. How to waste your own private time. The big plank table where we ate was all filled, with one seat at the very end; which I took. My Enemy sat across, looking humble. He had a trick a lot of writers have, I think I have it myself, of disappearing into the woodwork. The rest of the company was acting agreeable; the rough-coated animal world. How inflections do deceive. How much of what I say could be termed avoiding issues, when it's capillary rage sieved off from a wound.

But momentarily I had distance. And the assemblage that night seemed cheerful. Conversation flowed in little groups. A buff-colored hurricane lamp had been brought in to light the table; and down with writers' gloom. And more, to that whiff of rustic elegance, of pewter bowls and Liberty Bell glass, to the unspoken and hibernate calm—had been added the tranquilizing and invisible presence of some offstage person or personages, the lurid angels of success boiling up their magic potions. I don't mean on Broadway, or in Hollywood, but in those far-fetched and philosophical caves of secret cause and reason, where excitement and the ingredients of public taste are savagely stirred and brewed, to whet the majority of emotions, and in what kitchens of the ordinary, that delicious *pot au feu;* and I think that was underneath it, the old conglomerates, and the sense of evil power and the beauties of the system, along with a genuine commonality of the artist's profession, and whatever it was, there were continuous cordial outbursts, dredged-up prolific talk; and the bubble and glow of corresponding interests.

Meanwhile, our prime Celebrity sat, eating his food in that abject, gentleman's silence.

I don't know how the conversation started. A middle-aged Yale poet I will call O'Leary, seated at the elbow of the Author, was attempting a compliment. I half-listened and I didn't, such things travel by osmosis. I knew the poet, who looked like a rosy-cheeked country parson. His work was dour and trim. But that's neither here nor there. In himself, he was unworldly, good-natured. Mixed with others, he might become something else. But flattery, in this case, was not self-seeking. O'Leary was presuming to fill a gap, bringing up an anecdote to show how famous, practical and witty was the man at his side. The details had been picked up from somewhere, I didn't learn the source.

But it seemed that last month the Author, in deep freeze incognito, had visited a midwest college town. When stepping out of his car, he had been instantly recognized by a young college girl. Upon seeing him, she had flipped. "Oh," she said, "aren't you—?" and she gave his name, "and didn't you write—?" To which he acquiesced, she had mentioned his latest novel. "Oh," she said. "I just thought that book was wonderful. I read it seven times. What do you think of that?" The guileless, wide-eyed question. The book's topic had been incest, "an incitement to incest" (to quote a corny blurb). Oh, my rummage brain, in context, *I'd thought* disappointing. A force-feed, heartless vaudeville stunt. But, at least he'd dared to write it, servicing the uninformed. . . . But, what did he think of that? "Seven times!" the Author had answered.

"I think you must be crazy. I think you ought to have your head examined."

I conceded as I listened; it was a likeable, cogent story. Only a sour-head could miss that vitality of reply. A frank, honest rebuff. And there were comic overtones. It was like a Freudian Chinese box. The framework "outside the culture" and WHAT the book was about. You could see how he kept it simple, like a kind of obscene Kathleen Norris. I'm not being uncharitable, the counterparts are true. But mostly the virtue worked in how he'd handled the girl. Easing out of the awkward moment, with some friendly character. The hero kind, but firm.

Most of the table reacted with sounds of approbation. It was a sort of harmless in-the-know, and didn't affect anything else. The faces, I noted, were smiling. Only the Author looked uncomfortable. He hadn't peered up. Though the attention was centered on him.

"And so, what was she like?" A woman at the end indulged the question.

I shy at the gratuitous, and thought he would also. Merely— I don't know why. He seemed modest, uncompromising. And hadn't looked up from his plate.

But the eyelashes fluttered slightly. He sent a clear, gray glance. I hadn't noticed before the extent of penetration.

"What was she like—?" He appeared to ruminate. "Well, I'd say," he brought the words out slowly, "she had hair."

"Hair?" The woman laughed uncertainly. She didn't know how to take it. "But all girls today have hair—."

He gave a stunning, beautiful smile. His face, incredibly, seemed thinner. At once, my premonitions of the serpent world returned.

"That," he said, "isn't what I mean. She had hair—" he implied a little shudder, "she had hair where it usually wouldn't be."

"Oh, come off it. Where?" I heard an unlikely chuckle. It came from a man two plates down. He was a somber "distinguished novelist," a difficult, struggling person whose reputation rested on one "penultimate" work. The lamplight glittered on his thick eyeglasses.

The Author made a gesture. He had put down knife and fork, and was running his hands up and down his own coat sleeves. It was terribly grotesque and funny. His voice was rich with teasing.

"Arms,—" he said, and the underground torrents held back by the greatest effort. He pulled himself together with a sort of wicked humor, strangely mingled like a sound of joking vomit. "Uh-uh-ar-rms!"

"Arms?" The woman at the end of the table gave way. Her control was lost in giggles. "B-but, there's nothing wrong with—" she couldn't keep from laughing, "—nothing wrong with th-that."

"Oh," his voice was rapier steady. "You don't *know*. Have you ever seen an unwashed beagle? Each spike of spikey hair—" he bit the sibilance. "Then—you *know*. Like, kind of bunched-up, r-ruffled—"

Laughter swept the table.

"But with her," he said, "that's just the way it grew!"

O'Leary began to chortle. His face had turned beet red.

"You're—" he sought the compliant word, "you're kidding!"

The Author shook his head, mysterious, negative. He delivered another smile. I don't know how to describe it, that species of erudition. He had a quality of lasciviousness and disgust that went straight to the nerve roots. I am not exaggerating. But meanwhile, oddly, too, there was something honorable. That pale, tender glance, unused to vulgar nonsense. Though he was doing the finger-act again, running hands up and down his arms.

Which produced bolts of tinny laughter. Hysterical, not pleasant? Maybe I'm mistaken. The more unfolding the others became, the more I closed my shell.

"I remember—" he sat back with a look of confidence. No, he really seemed boyish and trusting. Or, rather like a blond cowboy; at the age of forty-seven, he had a lanky, young man's build, and must keep himself (I thought) well-exercised. "I remember," he said, "the girls when I went to school. You know? Like in the fifth grade. Wow, and some of them—my god! The hairy wonders."

Sophomoric, weird and strange. Could it have happened anywhere else? I suppose so, the group impulse; just enough and not

too much. A few others had started to talk, gaiety presiding. He'd
set a terrific precedent, and examples stood out and always followed the given theme. Nobody really meant it, and all just acting
silly. From the wells of memory, some hair-encrusted female.
O'Leary came up with a sudden Gaelic backlog, including a
"loathsome Irish lass" with hair from knees to thighs. The table
screamed and snickered, and nearly applauded. Meantime, the
Author was laughing behind his half-cupped palm. I didn't know
how he did it. But I perceived the chameleon flashes. It was very
close to successful writing. The strangling of reality for the fine,
twisted phrase. . . .

*Saying a thing, not because it's true, but for the attention it
brings.*

Sometimes it isn't possible to record adult behavior. People just
get carried away. And the preposterous as it happens, to them,
seems ordinary. Afterwards, nobody thinks anything irrational
occurred. Though what was being said was really nuts. I couldn't
share their fun. It all seemed false and wrong. Still, mundane
comparisons took over. I had no stake in the game. I was, in fact,
reasonably non-hirsute (as "hairless as an Allegheny cockroach,"
my mind went flailing out on purging clauses) and what the hell
difference did it make?

I, too, like the Author, remembered girls at school. They were
Irish, German, Italian. I grew up in an industrial city. As far as
malicious commentary goes, what does it ever matter? Some of
the girls I used to know had hair on arms, *and they weren't ob-
noxious.* They were young, nice human persons. But, I couldn't
say this out loud. Nor, of the mind traversed to other connecting
planes. I remembered a boy I was in love with once (we must
have all been about fourteen)—I accidentally saw him caress
another girl's skin. She was Irish, and had long black lashes; her
eyes were a green-type blue. And the dark down of her arms—
was to him alluring. Could such facts be exposed at this table? Of
course, they couldn't. We live in an age of prosecuting sickness. I
was jealous, and I saw how he liked her. It killed me, but I did.
She was a darling, bright, sexy little kid.

This is not the digression it seems. It's people who count, and not epidermal wrappings. Momentarily, I had to refer to my own little jungle childhood, to get my brains back on how things *actually had been.*

I wasn't all that calm. My heart was ferociously pounding. "Listen," I said. "Listen—"

But what was I going to say? I hadn't the remotest idea. My mouth was dry as if I'd been running against a strong wind.

"Listen—" I managed to get his attention.

I craved to be devious, it seemed the only way.

"Listen," I said (with a repose I didn't feel), "the trouble is: none of you have explained enough."

"About what?"

"About—the money."

"What?"

"I mean—" I could hear in my voice an insane levity. "I mean, the money you were all talking about when we first sat down."

My Adversary glanced at me, perplexed.

"Money?" His tone was gentle. "But—nobody mentioned money." He glanced around the table. "At least, I don't think anybody did."

I insisted that they had, and wished they'd go on about it.

"Because, what everybody said was all so fascinating!"

As irony, the speech was a flop. But I was under my own compulsion. I didn't know why I was doing it. I didn't, either, feel excessively feline. Just angry, confused and numb. My heart was heavily pounding.

Awhile longer, I continued with the nonsense. A few—I noticed the woman at the very end—O'Leary and some others were eyeing me quizzically. But none seemed prompted to investigate the error. Only my Enemy was accommodating.

"I assure you," he said, "nobody uttered a word. In fact, well —that simply wasn't the subject. Isn't it funny, though, how you got that? When we were talking. . . . I really can't imagine. . . ."

His head tilted down. Puzzlement, good will. I wasn't scored for the childish masquerade. He appeared to believe me. I was struck by the matter-of-factness. There was something about the expression. It was the same enthusiastic candor I'd assumed, a short

while ago, was a hate-filled bunch of lies. He hadn't meant any
harm. You just take what you find. For all I'd blamed, he hadn't
caused the world. He was no more responsible—than a child in
the market place. Who was my Enemy? There are no enemies.
Only sloughs of puny wisdom, bad luck. It is the sentimentality of
women, to credit deeds with a motive? I was my own enemy. Shift
the integers. "People aren't people, only symptoms." Any trite excuse will do the trick. The fun house of conceit. "I have the conceit of the maladjusted. He was the humility of preferred ideas."
But, who was I to think there was a choice? The Author sat across
in a pose of innocence. The light, smooth brows lifted in a faint
arc.

Later, I walked out through the hall to the back porch. The sky
was nearly night. There was a nice moist smell from the grass. I
stopped to enjoy it, and to look across the fields. A figure came up
behind me. I hadn't expected another encounter; I saw the famous
profile clearly. It was, in the half-dark, a rather elongated face,
that fashion admires today. In a cigarette ad I've seen, there's a
very strong likeness; the fault isn't his. Shadows for eyes, and a
longish, oversized head, hair combed to the nape of the neck. The
balances make it seem handsome.

"By the way, a word." I heard the familiar voice. The Author
addressed me from the far side of the porch. The tone was tactful,
friendly. Just keeping the record straight. "It was you," he said,
"who mentioned it. Nobody else brought it up." He didn't repeat
the word, money.

"Yes," I said. "I was the one who did."

Diane Johnson was born in Moline, Illinois. She attended Stephens College in Missouri, the University of Utah, and the University of California, where she now teaches. Miss Johnson lives in Berkeley, California, with her husband and four children. Her most recent books are *Burning,* a novel, and *Lesser Lives,* a work of Victorian biography.

AN APPLE, AN ORANGE

Twice a week Rosie Vedder got down on her knees, like a great blue and gold hassock, to scrub her kitchen floor, but she would not scrub another woman's floor in this position. That was a point she always carried at the outset.

"Too much work," she would say, looking at the lady with imperious, pale eyes as if challenging her to deny it. "You get me the the kind of mop with the sponge on the end and the kind of thing you have not to wring out with your hands." And if the lady protested, which American ladies were mostly too timid to do, she would add, "If you can put your hands in it, the water is not hot enough. I am a very clean woman and I know. You got to use very hot water."

Her person inspired confident visions of cleanliness. She was big, heavily pink, with a knotted coronet of faded gold braids and the perennial odor of bleach, in which she seemed to slake herself, protecting against dirt the way one might use citronella against mosquitos. The indignant expression of her slightly protruding eyes had perhaps been caused by dirt; she pursued it like a vengeful goddess, and wore things down with cleaning. Rosie kept her house, and the houses of her ladies, the way she would have liked the whole world to be—shining, level, soap-tasting, safe.

In Los Angeles she had a better house than she had in Holland, and she had gotten it for herself, without a man. A little house with a kitchen and a bedroom, and a slatted porch in the back where the refrigerator was. All the floors, even in the living room, were green linoleum, and this was ugly but very easy to keep clean. Sometimes when the sun was hot on the windows the house had an old smell, so that Rosie would remember that many things had happened here before the house was hers, things with men, too, and a bitter feeling of helplessness would seal her ears and eyes, and she would trancelike scrub the place, trying not to think about the unassailable accretions of former lives within her rooms. But at other times when her kettle steamed too long and fogged the windows all around inside, and the steam trailed down in little mineral streaks which she would have to wash, some other day, she felt especially cozy. Her steam was permeating every crack and board and the whole house was somehow sealed and hers. Then she would be seized by a panic of precarious love.

In the evenings though she was very tired she would watch television and crochet and think of her special plan, to divorce her husband back in Holland. This was why she was taking in a boarder, though she hated the idea of a boarder, damp towels and alien tracks; it was to be a temporary arrangement only, just until she paid for her divorce. She had crossed an ocean to live alone, and would not abridge this priceless freedom except to win it absolutely. Freedom, unrestraint, were passions seeded in her heart when she was young, had grown as she did in bulk, years and power, and now this flowering. At the age of fifty-three, her children scattered and breeding, she had said goodbye to the tyrannical old Dutch husband with his messy habits, thin legs, disgusting demands, and sailed to America. She was a woman of spirit, as they had found to their amazement. But she was a practical woman too. Sharing her little house with a refined, clean, non-smoking, paying woman on a temporary basis would in the long run hasten her complete independence. She knew a divorce was probably unnecessary; poor spineless little Dutch men who think themselves too old to cross oceans are small threat to vigorous free women in America. She was being divorced because she would like the feeling. And someday, when perhaps a letter would come saying Papa is sick, it would have no claim on her. She would shrug.

What would she do when she was free? The idea hung unformed but luminous in her mind; she could imagine gazing unimpeded at broad landscapes, with, indistinctly, a person, some love or companion, perhaps the chic and witty woman she had seen once in a dove-grey suit alight from a train. Or someone, speaking to her at her elbow. She never could see this person, but she could hear her speaking. They leaned over a ship's rail, they peered from the little square golden windows of a westward flying plane. Rosie smiled with a measure of self-tolerance at her own notions, so incompatible with her age and bulk, and yet she would not give them up. Boss of herself, traveller.

One of her daughters had followed her to America and had double-jumped the rules of cultural assimilation by marrying well and not minding that her mother was a scrub-lady. It had been this daughter who thought of the boarder, and found one. She represented the idea to her proud mother as "helpfulness"; Rosie would be helping a homeless woman who had been put out of her live-in housekeeping job. She had come all the way from China for this job and now had no place to go.

"A China woman? Here to *my* house?" Rosie had said at first, as if it were impossible, and then, "Is she a very clean woman?"

"She is a very clean woman, Mother, and the Foleys think very highly of her as a person, it's just that it hasn't worked out for them, she isn't too good with children or something."

"Hum," Rosie said, and secretly thought better of the China lady. And it would be somebody to talk to, as long as this was a clean woman. Ja, all right. "Thirty-five dollars a month she would have to pay, and half the light and water," and it was arranged.

She almost changed her mind on the day of Anna Lim's arrival, when it rained and she began to think about tracks on the bright floor, dripping puddles from the feet of strangers, damp luggage. She had not bargained for people bringing rain. Her hand was on the telephone when she saw the car pull up in front of the house, and then it was too late. She put some newspapers on the floor. Her daughter's neighbor, Mrs. Foley, a brisk anxious woman in a raincoat appeared at the door bearing apologies, thanks, spattered paper sacks full of clothing. Beyond, a face peered motionless out of the wet car window, watching Mrs. Foley carry satchels, and Rosie Vedder stood sourly at the door staring into the rain, making a barricade of her disapproving face.

The Chinese woman at length climbed out of the car and moved slowly up the walk, through the wet, without lifting her feet. She had the gait of the discouraged or the sick. Sickness occurred to Rosie in a rush of displeasure; she could not take care of someone complaining and helpless. The idea of sickness filled her with the same physical revulsion that dirt did, and she stared at the little woman as if she expected some affliction to show up luminous under her strong glare. The Chinese woman looked down at her own feet and at the puddles through which she indifferently sloshed, and did not meet Rosie's eyes.

Mrs. Foley led her in and sat her on the sofa, patted her, patted Rosie, hovered and finally dashed out into the rain again, wearing an expression of great relief. Rosie watched the disconsolate person huddled on the sofa, but said nothing until the neighbor drove away. Then she came closer, trying to decide about her. She at first seemed to be young, she was so little, but then Rosie saw that she was closer to her own age, tiny and pale, with a face of glass. She was not sick, Rosie saw, only timid. She had flat brown eyes, intent with fright, and the faintest of lines on her tight skin. She sat stiffly. Rosie was seized by an instinctive hospitable urge, something in her that did not want another person, however foreign and strange, to look so miserable in her house.

"Well, Anna Lim," she said, sitting down in her comfortable chair, as if for a good chat, "that woman did not like you at her house, eh? She was a bossy lady, I could tell." She expected that Anna would have a side to tell.

"No, I am no good," said Anna, and stirred inside her green coat.

"Ah? Well. A person in America does not have to live-in, like a slave. Work hard, you can have a house, like me, be free, be independent. But she wanted too much work, that one, I can always tell them. Yes?"

"Oh yes, she wanted everything. Cook, clean, iron. She even wanted me to polish the silver." A note of passion trembled in the flat voice, but she still stared at the floor. Rosie was mystified; to polish silver did not seem excessive. She tried to meet Anna on another ground.

"Well, you are China," she said, "but you speak English very good."

"Yes," said Anna. She spoke it with a perfect cultivated British accent.

"Better than me," laughed Rosie. "I learn it too old. But you aren't so young, are you?"

"I'm fifty," said Anna. She looked up, at this, for the first time, and seemed pleased to answer a personal question. Her face opened, and she seemed ready to answer more, but Rosie was on her feet.

"I will make you a cup of coffee," she said, and went to the kitchen.

Having decided to share her home, Rosie tried to do it handsomely. She kept to herself the bedroom and the bedroom closet, but she moved her umbrella and coat out of the entry closet so that Anna might put her few things there, and she allowed Anna to tape some pictures on the living room wall above the sofa, her bed, even though they did not conform to Rosie's ideas of decoration. Two were photographs of a slim youth, Anna's nephew on Formosa, and one was a colored picture of Christ.

The nephew, as it appeared during the evenings that followed, was Anna's only relative, and in Rosie's opinion he was a poor excuse for one; there was nothing interesting about him and he never wrote. Still he was something for them to talk about. They did not have much. They could not seem to speak of their own lives. Rosie thought China the strangest and most contrary country she had heard of, and could not bear to listen to such odd reminiscences. And Anna, infuriatingly, was too incurious and passive

ever to ask about Holland. They tried once to talk about the
war, but it was not interesting. Anna had not suffered much, she
said, and that was all she would say. For Rosie the war always
dissolved into one hard memory, something done to her by two
German soldiers, which she could not think of yet without her
breath quickening with impotent hatred.

"Germans are animals," was all she would say of it. "And
there was no butter for five years."

Although they did not talk much, they were comfortable and
companionable. A room with someone in it, female and clean, had
a lighter, flowery feel. And Anna was as tidy as Rosie could wish.
There were no signs of her unless you were looking right at her.
When she had finished her bath, the tub would be dry, even; apparently she dried off the tub with her towel. Rosie would go to
work in the morning and return at night to find Anna sitting in the
spot where she had left her, nothing ever moved, nothing used or
disarranged. It seemed as if Anna did nothing at all, all day. She
was like a vase of faded blossoms, and like blossoms this was
faintly easeful to the heart.

Her indolence was almost the only thing about Anna that
bothered Rosie. She was incapable of indolence herself, and mis-
trustful of it in others; she nagged Anna to look for a job. She read
to her aloud from the want-ads and even composed a little adver-
tisement for Anna to post at the supermarket. But Anna only
shook her head and said in her British governess voice she would
prefer to wait a little while. Rosie concluded from this that poor
Anna's spirit was still bruised from her experience with Marie's
neighbor, and did not press the matter much at first. She too had
worked for difficult ladies.

She was concerned, though, about Anna's finances. She knew
how they stood because Anna had entrusted her with the keeping
of her savings, four hundred dollars—an impressive, fat fold of
bills which Rosie counted admiringly and put away beneath her
handkerchiefs in the top bureau drawer.

"Anna, you are a very sensible woman after all, I believe,"
she had said. "If I had four hundred dollars—well, what? Two
hundred dollars for the divorce, then I am a free woman, no one

can touch me. And then I would put the rest away, or maybe I would go someplace on a trip. Rosalinda Vedder, traveller." She had gone off to the kitchen for the coffeepot thinking about this. She was not a foolish woman, man-hunting on cruise ships. Not a foolish buyer of souvenirs. She had not yet thought of quite the right place to go, but she had the vision of it, heard the soft voice.

"Of course your money will be gone before you know it, if you get no job soon," she said, coming back. "Thirty-five dollars to me each month, half the food, half the lights. In four or five months it will be gone."

"That's a long time," said Anna. Her confidence in Providence seemed to Rosie unjustified, so because Anna did not seem to worry about her future, Rosie had to. Each time she lifted her handkerchiefs she felt the thickness of Anna's roll of money, and would warn and remind and scold Anna's complacency.

One day she put her hand in the drawer and was immediately aware that a lot of Anna's money was gone. She thought first of theft, and of being blamed herself, and let out a shriek that brought Anna running to her.

"Your money is gone! See, it is almost all gone." Her hand holding the flat packet was shaking. Anna, who had never touched her, reached out and took Rosie's hand. Her face was calm, in command, confident. The touch of her little hand was warm. Rosie found herself surprised at this.

"Don't worry. I know, I took the money myself, to give to my school. It's a surprise, you'll be so pleased."

"What school?" Rosie asked, withdrawing her hand, not liking the sound of this.

"It's a school for office work. I'll learn to type and use the telephone switchboard. Then I can get an office job," said Anna, smiling. "I have been planning to do this, you see, and now I will start on Monday."

"What's the matter with houskeeping jobs," said Rosie. "I can get you plenty of jobs."

"I just don't like—I'm no good. I suppose I don't have the strength," Anna said.

"No, you are too little," Rosie said, but then she tried to

imagine Anna's thin little shoulders hunched above a typewriter—Anna, who never seemed to understand the simplest things, taking orders from a loud man in an office. She was filled with disgust for the pitiful notion and for a man who would take Anna's money and promise to teach the typewriter to a poor old woman.

"How much of your money gave you them?" she asked.

"Two hundred dollars. But of course when you have learned office work you can earn much more in one month."

"Oh, no," Rosie cried out, horrified. "You could get a divorce for two hundred dollars. You are just a stupid woman. You will never get an office job. You are fifty years old. You just throw the money away."

"No, it will be better," smiled Anna. "You'll see."

"*You* will see," said Rosie, much agitated, and stalked to the kitchen. She was unable to think of anything better to do for poor foolish Anna than to make her a cup of coffee.

Anna began school on Monday. They walked to the bus stop together every morning after that, and it was pleasant. Rosie held her golden head high, regarding with a cheerful fresh morning smile the early faces that they met, and Anna beside her took two of her tiny steps to keep pace. She wore her green coat, a foot too long for her, and her head was bent so that the knot of her hair at the nape of her neck was the tallest thing about her. She faithfully carried her little notebook under her arm, and Rosie felt as if she were walking a child to the school bus. She waved after Anna good-humoredly enough, but her resentment at the thieving school never vanished.

For one thing, besides being impractical and thieving, the school was making Anna very tired. When Rosie came home each evening at five-thirty, her steps scarcely slower than when she had gone out and her cheeks and hands bright red, she would find Anna waiting in the living room, bent over her notebook, frowning and pressing her forehead, exhausted. Rosie could not help but pity the poor little creature. She scowled and scolded about the school, but she fixed supper for them both without comment. Anna ate tremendously and was grateful. Her face was radiant through its weariness, it was as if no one had ever been good to her before.

"Thank you," she would always say. "That was a wonderful supper. You are very good to me. I can never repay you."

And she never did. Rosie began to notice this after a terrible day when she slipped and fell on the wet kitchen floor at work for Mrs. Baker. She didn't mention this to Mrs. Baker, nor to Anna, nor even to herself did she for a time admit it, but she had hurt her back. She noticed over the next few days that working was hard. There was one special pain that shot up her spine when she bent over, and another that tore into her shoulder blades when she straightened. It hurt to reach things on high shelves and it hurt to push a mop. At the end of a day she was exhausted by trying to modify her movements, and by the pain. Anna never seemed to notice this. She just sat at the table, working in her notebook, looking up at Rosie with a welcoming smile of dependence and joy.

By Wednesday Rosie allowed herself, as soon as she got home, the luxury of an ostentatious limp, but Anna did not notice this limp, nor hear aggrieved mutterings in the kitchen as she got supper. On Friday evening, in her resentment, Rosie was clumsy, dropped some potatoes too hard into boiling water and was scalded on the forearm by the splatter. She hissed in pain, and Anna came padding in.

"I have burned myself, do you see?" Rosie shrieked at her. "It is a wonder I have not burned myself before. Why can you not do this, cooking, when you know I am not feeling good?"

"No. I did not know," whispered Anna. "I am so sorry." She looked as if it were she who had been burned. "Please go in the living room. I will fix dinner. I am sorry, but I am so slow and stupid. I have been so unkind to my dear friend," she said.

Rosie limped off, nursing her arm and her resentment. She sat on the sofa and closed her eyes. Her bones seemed to settle and her legs were heavy. The burn smarted, the back pained.

"I am getting old," she said aloud; it was a frequent remark with her, but for almost the first time, a sense of her treacherous, ailing flesh made her believe it and distorted her image of herself as a woman free and unencumbered, before whom adventures lay. She suddenly wanted to see Kati and Peter, the two children left in Holland, of whom she seldom thought. The arm puffed and stung. Her eyes stung angrily.

Anna took her hand. Rosie had not heard her come. "Let me put some butter on your arm," she said, and gently rubbed soft butter over the burn stroking and stroking the poor arm. Rosie closed her eyes again.

"Thank you, Anna. I am just a poor old woman."

"Poor, poor Rosie," said Anna, in a soft, solicitous, crooning voice, like a Chinese song.

Anna was busy for a long time in the kitchen but she finally brought Rosie a plate of food. She gave her a napkin to spread over her lap.

"What is this?" Rosie asked, pleased at the attention.

"Meat and vegetables, prepared in the Chinese fashion," Anna said. Rosie ate slowly, watching the television, until she could not bear to keep still anymore.

"I have never eat such food!" she burst out. "The meat is all in little pieces mixed up in with the vegetables. The vegetables are hardly cooked. You don't even know how to cook! Oh, Anna, I tell you." She put her plate on the floor by her chair and adjusted herself to glare at Anna better. "You give all your money to the school, you are not strong enough to do housework and you cannot cook right—you are a completely foolish woman."

Anna sighed and shook her head. "When I get my office job, perhaps I can give you more money if you will do the cooking."

"Ach, no, I do not want your money. I am a very fair woman. I will tell you. You cook supper for you, I will cook supper for me. That is fair. Then we have no argument. And you help me clean on Saturdays. You have been here a month and never have you helped me clean on Saturday." And Anna agreed.

That night when they had gone to bed, Rosie heard a soft step in the bedroom, heard her own tiny gasp of fear, and then realized it was Anna. She whispered to her in the dark, to make sure. "Anna?"

"Yes," Anna whispered, "I could not go to sleep. I am so unhappy. Please tell me you are not unhappy with your Anna." The poor little old woman. She had a sweet smell, like an old doll out of an attic. Impulsively, Rosie clasped her, like a doll.

"No, you are all right," Rosie muttered, and turned away, ready for sleep again, and Anna crept off. But then Rosie lay awake, and felt a new anger press inside her, so that she could not sleep.

After that when Rosie came home from work she would fix a little plate of food for herself, a potato and a piece of meat and cabbage. Then Anna would go in and cook and eat whatever she ate, and wash her plate and put it away again, so that Rosie never knew what she ate. On Saturdays they would clean and then go to the market, each buy her groceries separately, take them home. Anna put hers in one side of the refrigerator, one end of the cupboard, Rosie the other. At the market Rosie would grumble to Anna of her extravagance. She ate odd things from little cans, very costly, and slices of expensive meat. "What will you do when the money is gone?" and Anna would smile archly and say, "An office job, remember, where I will not have to scrub and clean."

One afternoon Rosie came home late, nearly seven, because she had stayed late to fix supper for the family, and she was feeling tired, and her back still bothered her. She had been thinking of the nice cold baked apple waiting for her in the refrigerator, but when she looked for it it was gone. Her heart pounded, as if it were gold that was gone, or something precious, or as if she had found someone dead.

"Anna," she said, "an apple I was going to have for my supper . . ." Anna came into the kitchen with a strange, bright look on her face. Rosie's pale blue eyes were terrible. "Have you taken it?" Anna did not hesitate.

"Oh, my friend, I am sorry," she said. "Yes, I did. I ate it, and I did not think you would mind. I . . ."

"Well, I do mind," Rosie, very hungry, snapped at her. "By God, I do mind. Is stealing apples what they do in China?" She had supper of boiled potatoes in the kitchen and would not talk to Anna. Later in the night she thought she heard the little

Chinese woman crying in her bed. She lay awake, half expecting Anna to come in to be forgiven, but this did not happen.

The next day as they walked to the bus, Anna put her hand on Rosie's arm.

"Stealing is what they do in China when they are hungry," she said in a low voice. "I suppose they do that anywhere. But I was wrong to take something from my only friend. It is just that I am so wicked."

Rosie had the awful idea that Anna would start to cry again right there on the bus stop, so she shook the little hand off and said, "Well, never mind, one apple is not so much. But you should not take things from me, in my house. But you should not be hungry either. We will talk of it tonight."

Then Anna's bus pulled up, and Rosie turned away, pretending not to notice that Anna had dropped her precious notebook into the wet gutter and had to carry it dripping and ruined onto the bus.

When Rosie got home she found Anna copying into a new notebook the little marks and squiggles she learned at school, like Chinese writing. Rosie had thought those lines would come easier to Anna than to an American woman. Anna's thin greying hair strayed from its knot and the tight skin across her flat little cheeks was damp with weariness and concentration.

"Have you not much money left now?" Rosie said, picking up the conversation as if it were her sharp sewing scissors to poke little Anna.

"No," Anna sighed, putting down her pen. "Soon I hope I will get my office job. I have three more weeks left at school."

"You have forty dollars left, ha?" Rosie said. She had kept careful track.

"No, only thirty. I gave ten dollars to my church."

"To your church! So you go hungry? So you steal from me? Is that what your church likes?!"

"Oh, no, I am sure it would not. I have said I am very sorry. You have forgiven me, and so will God." She smiled.

"Ah, don't bring it all up now. Thirty dollars! You have to

give me that on Monday, also the light bill. What will you use for food?"

"I don't know," Anna said, still smiling.

"That's it! You don't plan! So it is, you give your money away, you have no job." Rosie's voice began to rise and shake in her wrath at the impracticality. "I never will understand you. You are so stupid." Anna shrugged and smiled, but when she spoke her soft voice also shook. She stood up and tightly held to the chair.

"Yes! I am 'so stupid.' No, I am not! You are always telling me that I am stupid and wasteful and wasted and weak. I am not. You despise me because I am not good at scrubbing floors, well scrubbing is good enough for you, you are a peasant anyway. I know about peasants, there are enough of them in China. But I am not one of them. I have had to do a lot of things, but I know what I am. I am not a young woman but I am not too old to make my life better. I am very good at my school, better than the young girls. The young girls laugh, but you should not laugh. You are a cruel uneducated woman. Well, I will work in an office and you will be a scrub lady. Poor old Anna, she has no one, she has never had a man, she is 'China,' you said. But you will see!"

Rosie only gave one outraged cry and stamped off to her bedroom. "You tell me I am so old," Anna shouted outside the door. "I am the same, I am the same inside as I ever was, and I am trying. I am still trying. I have very much of my life yet to live."

"Go to bed," Rosie called in a terrible voice, and then when Anna said nothing more, she undressed herself in a trembling hurry, pulled her nightgown over her big body, over her big soft breasts, all in the blindest hurry, and covered herself up tightly in bed. In the morning she got up, made her bed and sat on the edge of it, waiting for Anna. She knew what to expect. Anna knocked and then crept in, very tiny and yellow in her long white nightgown. She knelt down at Rosie's knees and stared. She put her hands on Rosie's big knees, a gentle touch, like a healer's on the sore old knees.

"I am sorry," she began. "I am very wrong and very stupid.

I have said cruel things to my only friend. Please forgive me. I am very old, and no one has ever loved me, and I have said stupid things to you. Look." She got up and went to the drawer in Rosie's chest and got her money. "Here is thirty dollars. I have some food and some bus tokens. Please let me stay a short time when this is gone. I will soon get a job, I will pay you more." Her lips were like a little line of Chinese writing.

Rosie took the money. She was frowning. She smoothed her dress over her knees. "I will tell Mrs. Baker I am sick today," she said. "You go work for her instead. Twelve dollars. See, I give you my work." Not a bad idea, it would be nice to stay home. But Anna shook her head. Her voice rose higher.

"No, I could not. But you are very kind. I do not deserve you. You are the best woman I know. Let me stay. Wouldn't you miss your Anna? I would miss you. We are old, and we should not be alone. It is a bad thing to be alone in life."

Something in this thin wail pierced Rosie further. It is a bad thing to be alone in life. She thought of Anna's light, warm fingers and old childlike face. "We are alone in life anyway," she said. "I am going to work now." She felt herself sigh, like a bellows, involuntarily.

Then she cleaned Mrs. Baker's house until no dirt could be spied in it anywhere and the windows shone like air, and rolls were in the oven, which made Mrs. Baker say she could never do without her. Rosie sniffed.

"You can never depend on other people," Rosie said. Then, before she left Mrs. Baker's, she called her daughter and told her to find another place for Anna.

Marie called two evenings later. Anna was studying as usual. "I think I should have glasses," she said, rubbing her eyes. "My eyes hurt, and sometimes my head aches so; do you think I should have glasses?"

"Glasses cost money," Rosie began, and then the phone rang.

"A woman up the street will take Anna. Martha Roberts. Her own girl had to leave, maybe for two months, sickness in the family. And Martha has five kids, so she needs somebody right away."

"That's good. This is a nice lady?"

"Oh, sure, she's all right. Anna will have a nice room and all. Martha could come after her tonight."

"Ja, thank you, I will tell her." Rosie hung up and turned to Anna.

"Well, I have a nice job for you," she said. Anna looked up, not understanding.

"That was my daughter. I told her you can stay here no longer and she finds you a nice lady to work for."

"What do you mean? You said I could stay here!"

"No, I did not say that. You did not understand. You have no money, you have to have work. Now comes a nice lady to take you. Nice house. She lives up by my daughter. My daughter lives on a nice street, and you will have a room to yourself. Plenty to eat."

"When? What are you saying?" Anna cried, pressing her little hands against her little flat chest.

"This lady will come for you tonight. It will be a good thing, Anna. You need to work."

"But I will get a job! I have told you. The school helps me to get a job when I graduate."

"Office work," Rosie snapped. "I told you not to throw your money away on that thing."

"Oh, I will not go," Anna said, her eyes darting with fear. "I have told you. I cannot go. I cannot miss my school, I . . ." She put out one hand and fumbled behind for her school notebook. Her voice became soft and quiet again.

"Please, Rosie dear, I know I have been such a trouble to you, but I love you, I am your friend. You are the only person who has ever been kind to me. I mean that. You mean more to me than my own nephew, my nephew, he has never done anything for me. You have done so much."

"Well, I do yet one more thing. I get you a good job. You better pack your things, Anna." But Anna sat still on the couch. Rosie went to Anna's closet and began to bring the clothes out, and put them in her suitcase. "You do this," Anna said presently, "so that I will not graduate. Because you said I would never graduate." Her voice was flat and her tears were gone. "You are a wicked woman. You take away my life."

When Mrs. Roberts arrived Anna was nearly ready. Rosie was carefully unsticking the photographs from the wall over the couch. Anna watched, quiet, smiling at Mrs. Roberts, her eyes very blank. "Shall I have my own room?" she asked Mrs. Roberts presently. The woman liked the sound of Anna's cultivated British accent.

"Oh, yes!" she assured her, and was assiduous about carrying out the suitcase, some sacks and boxes. Rosie watched them from the door. Anna followed Mrs. Roberts to the car, holding herself straight. Mrs. Roberts opened the door for her and carefully helped her in. Anna was smiling her shy and fragile smile. She did not look at Rosie anymore. Rosie with a heart like bitter stone scrubbed the marks of tape from the wall where the pictures had hung, and then she ate the orange Anna had left in the refrigerator.

John Cheever lives in Ossining, New York, and teaches at Sing Sing. Among his books are *The Wapshot Chronicle, The Wapshot Scandal,* and *Bullet Park.*

THE JEWELS OF THE CABOTS

Funeral services for the murdered man were held in the Unitarian church in the little village of St. Botolphs. The architecture of the church was Bulfinch with columns and one of those ethereal spires that must have dominated the landscape a century ago. The service was a random collection of Biblical quotations closing with a verse. "Amos Cabot, rest in peace/Now your mortal trials have ceased. . . ." The church was full. Mr. Cabot had been an outstanding member of the community. He had once run for governor. For a month or so, during his campaign, one saw his picture on barns, walls, buildings and telephone poles. I don't suppose the sense of walking through a shifting mirror—he found himself at every turn—unsettled him as it would have unsettled me. Once, for example, when I was in an elevator in Paris, I noticed a woman carrying a book of mine. There was a photograph on the jacket and one image of me looked over her arm at another. I wanted the picture, wanted, I suppose, to destroy it. That she should walk away with my face under her arm seemed to threaten my self-esteem. She left the elevator at the fourth floor and the parting of these two images was confusing. I wanted to follow her, but how could I explain in French—or in any other language—what I felt? Amos Cabot was not at all like this. He seemed to enjoy seeing himself and when he lost the election and his face vanished (except for a few barns in the back country, where it peeled for a month or so), he seemed not perturbed.

There are, of course, the wrong Lowells, the wrong Hallo-
wells, the wrong Eliots, Cheevers, Codmans and Englishes, but
today we will deal with the wrong Cabots. Amos came from the
South Shore and may never have heard of the North Shore
branch of the family. His father had been an auctioneer, which
meant in those days an entertainer, horse trader and sometime
crook. Amos owned real estate, the hardware store, the public
utilities and was a director of the bank. He had an office in the
Cartwright Block, opposite the green. His wife came from Connecticut, which was, for us at that time, a distant wilderness on
whose eastern borders stood the city of New York. New York was
populated by harried, nervous, avaricious foreigners who lacked
the character to bathe in cold water at six in the morning and to
live, with composure, lives of grueling boredom. Mrs. Cabot,
when I knew her, was probably in her early 40s. She was a short
woman with the bright-red face of an alcoholic, although she was
a vigorous temperance worker. Her hair was as white as snow.
Her back and her front were prominent and there was a memora-
ble curve to her spine that could have been caused by a cruel cor-
set or the beginning of lordosis. No one quite knew why Mr.
Cabot had married this eccentric from faraway Connecticut—it
was, after all, no one's business—but she did own most of the
frame tenements on the East Bank of the river, where the workers
in the table-silver factory lived. Her tenements were profitable,
but it would have been an unwarranted simplification to conclude
that he had married for real estate. She collected the rents herself.
I expect that she did her own housework and she dressed simply,
but she wore on her right hand seven large diamond rings. She
had evidently read somewhere that diamonds were a sound in-
vestment and the blazing stones were about as glamorous as a
passbook. There were round diamonds, square diamonds, rectangu-
lar diamonds and some of those diamonds that are set in prongs.
On Thursday afternoon, she would wash her diamonds in some
jeweler's solution and hang them out to dry in the clothesyard.
She never explained this, but the incidence of eccentricity in the
village ran so high that her conduct was not thought unusual.

Mrs. Cabot spoke once or twice a year at the St. Botolphs

Academy, where many of us went to school. She had three subjects: "My Trip to Alaska" (slides), "The Evils of Drink" and
"The Evils of Tobacco." Drink was for her so unthinkable a vice
that she could not attack it with much vehemence, but the
thought of tobacco made her choleric. Could one imagine Christ
on the cross, smoking a cigarette? she would ask us. Could one
imagine the Virgin Mary *smoking?* A drop of nicotine fed to a pig
by trained laboratory technicians had killed the beast. Etc. She
made smoking irresistible and if I die of lung cancer, I shall
blame Mrs. Cabot. These performances took place in what we
called the Great Study Hall. This was a large room on the second
floor that could hold us all. The academy had been built in the
1850s and had the lofty, spacious and beautiful windows of that
period in American architecture. In the spring and in the autumn,
the building seemed gracefully suspended in its grounds, but in
the winter, a glacial cold fell off the large window lights. In the
Great Study Hall, we were allowed to wear coats, hats and gloves.
This situation was heightened by the fact that my great-aunt Anna
had bought in Athens a large collection of plaster casts, so that we
shivered and memorized the donative verbs in the company of at
least a dozen buck-naked gods and goddesses. So it was to Her-
mes and Venus as well as to us that Mrs. Cabot railed against the
poisons of tobacco. She was a woman of vehement and ugly prejudice and I suppose she would have been happy to include the
blacks and the Jews, but there was only one black and one Jewish
family in the village and they were exemplary. The possibility of
intolerance in the village did not occur to me until much later,
when my mother came to our house in Westchester for Thanks-
giving.

This was some years ago, when the New England highways had
not been completed and the trip from New York or Westchester
took over four hours. I left quite early in the morning and drove
first to Haverhill, where I stopped at Miss Peacock's School and
picked up my niece. I then went on to St. Botolphs, where I
found Mother sitting in the hallway in an acolyte's chair. The
chair had a steepled back, topped with a wooden fleur-de-lis.

From what rain-damp church had this object been stolen? She wore a coat and her bag was at her feet.

"I'm ready," she said. She must have been ready for a week. She seemed terribly lonely. "Would you like a drink?" she asked. I knew enough not to take this bait. Had I said yes, she would have gone into the pantry and returned, smiling sadly, to say: "Your brother has drunk all the whiskey." So we started back for Westchester. It was a cold, overcast day and I found the drive tiring, although I think fatigue had nothing to do with what followed. I left my niece at my brother's house in Connecticut and drove on to my place. It was after dark when the trip ended. My wife had made all the preparations that were customary for my mother's arrival. There was an open fire, a vase of roses on the piano and tea with anchovy-paste sandwiches. "How lovely to have flowers," said Mother. "I so love flowers. I can't live without them. Should I suffer some financial reverses and have to choose between flowers and groceries, I believe I would choose flowers. . . ."

I do not want to give the impression of an elegant old lady, because there were lapses in her performance. I bring up, with powerful unwillingness, a fact that was told to me by her sister after Mother's death. It seems that at one time, she applied for a position with the Boston police force. She had plenty of money at the time and I have no idea why she did this. I suppose that she wanted to be a policewoman. I don't know what branch of the force she planned to join, but I've always imagined her in a dark-blue uniform with a ring of keys at her waist and a billy club in her right hand. My grandmother dissuaded her from this course, but the image of a policewoman was some part of the figure she cut, sipping tea by our fire. She meant this evening to be what she called aristocratic. In this connection, she often said: "There must be at least a drop of plebeian blood in the family. How else can one account for your taste in torn and shabby clothing? You've always had plenty of clothes, but you've always chosen rags."

I mixed a drink and said how much I had enjoyed seeing my niece.

"Miss Peacock's has changed," Mother said sadly.

"I didn't know," I said. "What do you mean?"

"They've let down the bars."

"I don't understand."

"They're letting in Jews," she said. She fired out the last word.

"Can we change the subject?" I asked.

"I don't see why," she said. "You brought it up."

"My wife is Jewish, Mother," I said. My wife was in the kitchen.

"That is not possible," my mother said. "Her father is Italian."

"Her father," I said, "is a Polish Jew."

"Well," Mother said, "I come from old Massachusetts stock and I'm not ashamed of it, although I don't like being called a Yankee."

"There's a difference."

"Your father said that the only good Jew was a dead Jew, although I did think Justice Brandeis charming."

"I think it's going to rain," I said. It was one of our staple conversational switch-offs used to express anger, hunger, love and the fear of death.

My wife joined us and Mother picked up the routine. "It's nearly cold enough for snow," she said. "When you were a boy, you used to pray for snow or ice. It depended upon whether you wanted to skate or ski. You were very particular. You would kneel by your bed and loudly ask God to manipulate the elements. You never prayed for anything else. I never once heard you ask for a blessing on your parents. In the summer you didn't pray at all."

The Cabots had two daughters—Geneva and Molly. Geneva was the older and thought to be the more beautiful. Molly was my girl for a year or so. She was a lovely young woman with a sleepy look that was quickly dispelled by a brilliant smile. Her hair was pale-brown and held the light. When she was tired or excited, sweat formed on her upper lip. In the evenings, I would walk to their house and sit with her in the parlor under the most intense surveillance. Mrs. Cabot, of course, regarded sex with utter panic. She watched us from the dining room. From upstairs there were loud and regular thumping sounds. This was Amos Cabot's rowing machine. We were sometimes allowed to take walks together if we kept to the main streets and when I was old enough to drive, I took her to the dances at the club. I was intensely—morbidly—jealous and when she seemed to be enjoying herself with someone else, I would stand in the corner, thinking of suicide. I remember driving her back one night to the house on Shore Road.

At the turn of the century, someone decided that St. Botolphs might have a future as a resort and five mansions complete with follies were built at the end of Shore Road. The Cabots lived in one of these. All the mansions had towers. These were round with conical roofs, rising a story or so above the rest of the frame buildings. The towers were strikingly unmilitary and so I suppose they were meant to express romance. What did they contain? Dens, I guess, maids' rooms, broken furniture, trunks, and they must have been the favorite of hornets. I parked my car in front of the Cabots' and turned off the lights. The house above us was dark.

It was long ago, so long ago that the foliage of elm trees was part of the summer night. (It was so long ago that when you wanted to make a left turn, you cranked down the car window and *pointed* in that direction. Otherwise, you were not allowed to point. Don't point, you were told. I can't imagine why, unless the gesture was thought to be erotic.) The dances—the assemblies—were formal and I would be wearing a tuxedo handed down from my father to my brother and from my brother to me, like some escutcheon or sumptuary torch. I took Molly in my arms. She was completely responsive. I am not a tall man (I am sometimes inclined to stoop), but the conviction that I am loved and loving affects me like a military bracing. Up goes my head. My back is straight. I am six foot, seven, and sustained by some clamorous emotional uproar. Sometimes my ears ring. It can happen anywhere—in a Keisang house in Seoul, for example—but it happened that night in front of the Cabots' house on Shore Road. Molly said then that she had to go. Her mother would be watching from a window. She asked me not to come up to the house. I musn't have heard. I went with her up the walk and the stairs to the porch, where she tried the door and found it locked. She asked me again to go, but I couldn't abandon her there, could I? Then a light went on and the door was opened by a dwarf. He was exhaustively misshapen. The head was hydrocephalic, the features were swollen, the legs were thick and cruelly bowed. I thought of the circus. The lovely young woman began to cry. She stepped into the house and closed the door and I was left with the summer night, the elms, the taste of an east wind. After this, she avoided me for a week or so and I was told the facts by Maggie, our old cook.

But other facts first. It was in the summer and in the summer, most of us went to a camp on the Cape run by the headmaster of the St. Botolphs Academy. The months were so feckless, so blue, that I can't remember them at all. I slept next to a boy named DeVarennes, whom I had known all my life. We were together most of the time. We played marbles together, slept together, played together on the same backfield and once together took a ten-day canoe trip during which we nearly drowned together. My brother claimed that we had begun to look alike. It was the most gratifying and unself-conscious relationship I had known. (He still calls me once or twice a year from San Francisco, where he lives unhappily with his wife and three unmarried daughters. He sounds drunk. "We were happy, weren't we?" he asks.) One day another boy, a stranger named Wallace, asked if I wanted to swim across the lake. I might claim that I knew nothing about Wallace, and I knew very little, but I did know or sense that he was lonely. It was as conspicuous, more conspicuous than any of his features. He did what was expected of him. He played ball, made his bed, took sailing lessons and got his lifesaving certificate, but this seemed more like a careful imposture than any sort of participation. He was miserable, he was lonely and sooner or later, rain or shine, he would say so and, in the act of confession, make an impossible claim on one's loyalty. One knew all this, but one pretended not to. We got permission from the swimming instructor and swam across the lake. We used a clumsy side stroke that still seems to me more serviceable than the overhand that is obligatory these days in those swimming pools where I spend most of my time. The side stroke is lower class. I've seen it once in a swimming pool and when I asked who the swimmer was, I was told he was the butler. When the ship sinks, when the plane ditches, I will try to reach the life raft with an overhand and drown stylishly, whereas if I had used a lowerclass side stroke, I would live forever.

We swam the lake, resting in the sun—no confidences—and swam home. When I went up to our cabin, DeVarennes took me aside. "Don't ever let me see you with Wallace again," he said. I asked why. He told me. "Wallace is Amos Cabot's bastard. His mother is a whore. They live in one of the tenements across the river."

The next day was hot and brilliant and Wallace asked if I wanted to swim the lake again. I said sure, sure, and we did. When we went back to camp, DeVarennes wouldn't speak to me. That night a northeaster blew up and it rained for three days. DeVarennes seems to have forgiven me and I don't recall having crossed the lake with Wallace again. As for the dwarf, Maggie told me he was a son of Mrs. Cabot's from an earlier marriage. He worked at the table-silver factory, but he went to work early in the morning and didn't return until after dark. His existence was meant to be kept a secret. This was unusual but not—at the time of which I'm writing—unprecedented. The Trumbulls kept Mrs. Trumbull's crazy sister hidden in the attic and Uncle Peepee Marshmallow—an exhibitionist—was often hidden for months.

It was a winter afternoon, an early winter afternoon. Mrs. Cabot washed her diamonds and hung them out to dry. She then went upstairs to take a nap. She claimed that she had never taken a nap in her life and the sounder she slept, the more vehement were her claims that she didn't sleep. This was not so much an eccentricity on her part as it was a crabwise way of presenting the facts that was prevalent in that part of the world. She woke at four and went down to gather her stones. They were gone. She called Geneva, but there was no answer. She got a rake and scored the stubble under the clothesline. There was nothing. She called the police.

As I say, it was a winter afternoon and the winters there were very cold. We counted for heat—sometimes for survival—on

wood fires and large coal-burning furnaces that sometimes got out
of hand. A winter night was a threatening fact and this may have
partly accounted for the sentiment with which we watched—in
late November and December—the light burn out in the west.
(My father's journals, for example, were full of descriptions of
winter twilights, not because he was at all crepuscular but because
the coming of the night might mean danger and pain.) Geneva
had packed a bag, gathered the diamonds and taken the last train
out of town—the 4:37. How thrilling it must have been. The diamonds were meant to be stolen. They were a flagrant snare and
she did what she was meant to do. She took the train to New York
that night and sailed three days later for Alexandria on a Cu-
narder—the S.S Serapis. She took a boat from Alexandria to
Luxor, where, in the space of two months, she joined the Moslem
faith and married the khedive.

I read about the theft the next day in the evening paper. I delivered papers. I had begun my route on foot, moved on to a
bicycle and was assigned, when I was 16, to an old Ford truck. I
was a truck driver! I hung around the linotype room until the papers were printed and then drove around to the four neighboring
villages, tossing out bundles at the doors of the candy and stationery stores. During the world series, a second edition with box
scores was brought out and after dark, I would make the trip
again to Travertine and the other places along the shore.

The roads were dark, there was very little traffic and leaf
burning had not been forbidden, so that the air was tannic, melancholy and exciting. One can attach a mysterious and inordinate
amount of importance to some simple journey and this second
trip with the box scores made me very happy. I dreaded the end of
the world series as one dreads the end of any pleasure and had I
been younger, I would have prayed. "CABOT JEWELS STOLEN"
was the headline and the incident was never again mentioned in
the paper. It was not mentioned at all in our house, but this was
not unusual. When Mr. Abbott hanged himself from the pear tree
next door, this was never mentioned.

Molly and I took a walk on the beach at Travertine that Sunday afternoon. I was troubled, but Molly's troubles were much

graver. It did not disturb her that Geneva had stolen the diamonds. She only wanted to know what had become of her sister
and she was not to find out for another six weeks. However,
something had happened at the house two nights before. There
had been a scene between her parents and her father had left.
She described this to me. We were walking barefoot. She was
crying. I would like to have forgotten the scene as soon as she
finished her description.

Children drown, beautiful women are mangled in automobile
accidents, cruise ships founder and men die lingering deaths in
mines and submarines, but you will find none of this in my ac-
counts. In the last chapter, the ship comes home to port, the children are saved, the miners will be rescued. Is this an infirmity
of the genteel or a conviction that there are discernible moral
truths? Mr. X defecated in his wife's top drawer. This is a fact,
but I claim that it is not a truth. In describing St. Botolphs, I
would sooner stay on the West Bank of the river, where the
houses were white and where the church bells rang, but over the
bridge there was the table-silver factory, the tenements (owned by
Mrs. Cabot) and the Commercial Hotel. At low tide, one could
smell the sea gas from the inlets at Travertine. The headlines in
the afternoon paper dealt with a trunk murder. The women on the
streets were ugly. Even the dummies in the one store window
seemed stooped, depressed and dressed in clothing that neither
fitted nor became them. Even the bride in her splendor seemed to
have gotten some bad news. The politics were neofascist, the factory was non-union, the food was unpalatable and the night wind
was bitter. This was a provincial and a traditional world enjoying
few of the rewards of smallness and traditionalism, and when I
speak of the blessedness of all small places, I speak of the West
Bank. On the East Bank was the Commercial Hotel, the demesne
of Doris, a male prostitute who worked as a supervisor in the factory during the day and hustled the bar at night, exploiting the
extraordinary moral lassitude of the place. Everybody knew Doris
and many of the customers had used him at one time or another.
There was no scandal and no delight involved. Doris would charge

a traveling salesman whatever he could get, but he did it with the regulars for nothing. This seemed less like tolerance than like hapless indifference, the absence of vision, moral stamina, the splendid ambitiousness of romantic love. On fight night, Doris drifts down the bar. Buy him a drink and he'll put his hand on your arm, your shoulder, your waist, and move a fraction of an inch in his direction and he'll reach for the cake. The steam fitter buys him a drink, the high school dropout, the watch repairman. (Once a stranger shouted to the bartender: "Tell that son of a bitch to take his tongue out of my ear"—but he was a stranger.) This is not a transient world, these are not drifters; more than half of these men will never live in any other place, and yet this seems to be the essence of spiritual nomadism. The telephone rings and the bartender beckons to Doris. There's a customer in room eight. Why would I sooner be on the West Bank, where my parents are playing bridge with Mr. and Mrs. Eliot Pinkham in the golden light of a great gas chandelier?

I'll blame it on the roast, the roast, the Sunday roast bought from a butcher who wore a straw boater with a pheasant wing in the hatband. I suppose the roast entered our house, wrapped in bloody paper, on Thursday or Friday, traveling on the back of a bicycle. It would be a gross exaggeration to say that the meat had the detonative force of a land mine that could savage your eyes and your genitals, but its powers were disproportionate. We sat down to dinner after church. (My brother was living in Omaha at that time, so we were only three.) My father would hone the carving knife and make a cut in the meat. My father was very adroit with an ax and a crosscut saw and could bring down a large tree with dispatch, but the Sunday roast was something else. After he had made the first cut, my mother would sigh. This was an extraordinary performance, so loud, so profound that it seemed as if her life were in danger. It seemed as if her very soul might come unhinged and drift out of her open mouth. "Will you never learn, Leander, that lamb must be carved against the grain?" she would ask. Once the battle of the roast had begun, the exchanges were so swift, predictable and tedious that there would be no point in reporting them.

After five or six wounding remarks, my father would wave the carving knife in the air and shout: "Will you kindly mind your own business, will you kindly shut up?"

She would sigh once more and put her hand to her heart. Surely this was her last breath. Then, studying the air above the table, she would say: "Feel that refreshing breeze."

There was, of course, seldom a breeze. It could be airless, midwinter, rainy, anything. The remark was one for all seasons. Was it a commendable metaphor for hope, for the serenity of love (which I think she had never experienced)? Was it nostalgia for some summer evening when, loving and understanding, we sat contentedly on the lawn above the river? Was it no better or no worse than the sort of smile thrown at the evening star by a man who is in utter despair? Was it a prophecy of that generation to come who would be so drilled in evasiveness that they would be denied forever the splendors of a passionate confrontation?

The scene changes to Rome. It is spring, when the canny swallows flock into the city to avoid the wing shots in Ostia. The noise the birds make seems like light as the light of day loses its brilliance. Then one hears, across the courtyard, the voice of an American woman. She is screaming. "You're a goddamned, fucked-up no-good insane piece of shit. You can't make a nickel, you don't have a friend in the world and in bed you stink. . . ." There is no reply and one wonders if she is railing at the dark. Then you hear a man cough. That's all you will hear from him. "Oh, I know I've lived with you for eight years, but if you ever thought I liked it, any of it, it's only because you're such a chump you wouldn't know the real thing if you had it. When I really come, the pictures *fall* off the walls. With you it's always an act. . . ." The high-low bells that ring in Rome at that time of day have begun to chime. I smile at this sound, although it has no bearing on my life, my faith, no true harmony, nothing like the revelations in the voice across the court. Why would I sooner describe church bells and flocks of swallows? Is this puerile, a sort of greeting-card mentality, a whimsical and effeminate refusal to look at facts? On and on she goes, but I will follow her no longer. She attacks his hair, his brain and his spirit, while I observe that a light rain has begun to fall and that the effect of this is to louden the noise of traffic on the *corso.* Now she is hysterical—her voice is breaking—and I think that at the height of her malediction, perhaps, she will begin to cry and ask his forgiveness. She will not, of course. She will go after him with a carving knife and he will end up in the emergency ward of the *polyclinico,* claiming to have wounded himself; but as I go out for dinner, smiling at beggars, fountains, children and the first stars of evening, I assure myself that everything will work out for the best. Feel that refreshing breeze!

My recollections of the Cabots are only a footnote to my principal work and I go to work early these winter mornings. It is still dark. Here and there, standing on street corners, waiting for buses, are women dressed in white. They wear white shoes and white stockings and white uniforms can be seen below their winter coats. Are they nurses, beauty-parlor operators, dentists' helpers? I'll never know. They usually carry a brown paper bag, holding, I guess, a ham on rye and a Thermos of buttermilk. Traffic is light at this time of day. A laundry truck delivers uniforms to the Fried Chicken Shack and in Asburn Place there is a milk truck—the last of that generation. It will be half an hour before the yellow school buses start their rounds.

I work in an apartment house called the Prestwick. It is seven stories high and dates, I guess, from the late Twenties. It is of a Tudor persuasion. The bricks are irregular, there is a parapet on the roof and the sign, advertising vacancies, is literally a shingle that hangs from iron chains and creaks romantically in the wind. On the right of the door, there is a list of perhaps 25 doctors' names, but these are not gentle healers with stethoscopes and rubber hammers, these are psychiatrists and this is the country of the plastic chair and the full ashtray. I don't know why they should have chosen this place, but they outnumber the other tenants. Now and then you see, waiting for the elevator, a woman with a grocery wagon and a child, but you mostly see the sometimes harried faces of men and women with trouble. They sometimes smile; they sometimes talk to themselves. Business seems slow these days and the doctor whose office is next to mine often stands in the hallway, staring out the window. What does a psychiatrist think? Does he wonder what has become of those patients who gave up, who refused group therapy, who disregarded his warnings and admonitions? He will know their secrets. I tried to murder my husband. I tried to murder my wife. Three years ago, I took an overdose of sleeping pills. The year before that, I cut my wrists. My mother wanted me to be a girl. My mother wanted me to be a boy. My mother wanted me to be a homosexual. Where had they gone, what were they doing? Were they still married, quarreling at the dinner table, decorating the Christmas tree? Had they divorced, remarried, jumped off bridges, taken Seconal, struck some kind of truce, turned homosexual or moved to a farm in Vermont where they planned to raise strawberries and lead a simple life? The doctor sometimes stands by the window for an hour.

My real work these days is to write an edition of *The New York Times* that will bring gladness to the hearts of men. How better could I occupy myself? The *Times* is a critical if rusty link in my ties to reality, but in these last years, its tidings have been monotonous. The prophets of doom are out of work. All one can do is to pick up the pieces. The lead story is this: "PRESIDENT'S HEART TRANSPLANT DEEMED SUCCESSFUL." There is this box on the lower left: "COST OF J. EDGAR HOOVER MEMORIAL CHALLENGED. The subcommittee on memorials threatened today to halve the $7,000,000 appropriated to commemorate the late J. Edgar Hoover with a Temple of Justice. . . ." Column three: "CONTROVERSIAL LEGISLATION REPEALED BY SENATE. The recently enacted bill, making it a felony to have wicked thoughts about the Administration, was repealed this afternoon by a stand-up vote of 43 to 7." On and on it goes. There are robust and heartening editorials, thrilling sports news and the weather, of course, is always sunny and warm, unless we need rain. Then we have rain. The air-pollutant gradient is zero and even in Tokyo, fewer and fewer people are wearing surgical masks. All highways, throughways, freeways and expressways will be closed for the holiday weekend. Joy to the world!

But to get back to the Cabots. The scene that I would like to overlook or forget took place the night after Geneva had stolen the diamonds. It involves plumbing. Most of the houses in the village had relatively little plumbing. There was usually a water closet in the basement for the cook and the ashman and a single bathroom on the second floor for the rest of the household. Some of these rooms were quite large and the Endicotts had a fireplace in their bathroom. Somewhere along the line, Mrs. Cabot decided that the bathroom was her demesne. She had a locksmith come and secure the door. Mr. Cabot was allowed to take his sponge bath every morning, but after this, the bathroom door was locked and Mrs. Cabot kept the key in her pocket. Mr. Cabot was obliged to use a chamber pot, but since he came from the South Shore, I don't suppose this was much of a hardship. It may even have been nostalgic. He was using the chamber pot late that night when Mrs. Cabot went to the door of his room. (They slept in separate rooms.) "Will you close the door?" she screamed. "Will you close the door? Do I have to listen to that horrible noise for the rest of my life?" They would both be in nightgowns, her snow-white hair in braids. She picked up the chamber pot and threw its contents at him. He kicked down the door of the locked bathroom, washed, dressed, packed a bag and walked over the bridge to Mrs. Wallace's place on the East Bank.

He stayed there for three days and then returned. He was worried about Molly and in such a small place, there were appearances to be considered—Mrs. Wallace's as well as his own. He divided his time between the East and the West banks of the river until a week or so later, when he was taken ill. He felt languid. He stayed in bed until noon. When he dressed and went to his office, he returned after an hour or so. The doctor examined him and found nothing wrong.

One evening Mrs. Wallace saw Mrs. Cabot coming out of the drugstore on the East Bank. She watched her rival cross the bridge and then went into the drugstore and asked the clerk if Mrs. Cabot was a regular customer. "I've been wondering about that myself," the clerk said. "Of course, she comes over here to collect her rents, but I always thought she used the other drugstore. She comes in here to buy ant poison—arsenic, that is. She says they have these terrible ants in the house on Shore Road and arsenic is the only way of getting rid of them. From the way she buys arsenic, the ants must be terrible." Mrs. Wallace might have warned Mr. Cabot, but she never saw him again.

She went after the funeral to Judge Simmons and said that she wanted to charge Mrs. Cabot with murder. The drug clerk would have a record of her purchase of arsenic that would be incriminating. "He may have it," the judge said, "but he won't give it to you. What you are asking for is an exhumation of the body and a long trial in Barnstable and you have neither the money nor the reputation to support this. You were his friend, I know, for sixteen years. He was a splendid man and why don't you console yourself with the thought of how many years it was that you knew them? And another thing. He's left you and Wallace a substantial legacy. If Mrs. Cabot were provoked to contest the will, you could lose this."

I went out to Luxor to see Geneva. I flew to London in a 747. There were only three passengers; but, as I say, the prophets of doom are out of work. I went from Cairo up the Nile in a low-flying two-motor prop. The sameness of wind erosion and water erosion makes the Sahara there seem to have been gutted by floods, rivers, courses, streams and brooks, the thrust of a natural search. The scorings are watery and arboreal and as a false stream bed spreads out, it takes the shape of a tree, striving for light. It was freezing in Cairo when we left before dawn. Luxor, where Geneva met me at the airport, was hot.

I was very happy to see her, so happy I was unobservant, but I did notice that she had gotten fat. I don't mean that she was heavy; I mean that she weighed about 300 pounds. She was a fat woman. Her hair, once a coarse yellow, was now golden, but her Massachusetts accent was as strong as ever. It sounded like music to me on the upper Nile. Her husband—now a colonel—was a slender, middle-aged man, a relative of the last king. He owned a restaurant at the edge of the city and they lived in a pleasant apartment over the dining room. The colonel was humorous, intelligent—a rake, I guess—and a heavy drinker. When we went to the temple at Karnak, our dragoman carried ice, tonic and gin. I spent a week with them, mostly in temples and graves. We spent the evenings in his bar. War was threatening—the air was full of Russian planes—and the only other tourist was an Englishman who sat at the bar, reading his passport. On the last day, I swam in the Nile—overhand—and they drove me to the airport, where I kissed Geneva—and the Cabots—goodbye.

Josephine Jacobsen was born in Coburg, Canada, of American parents. She lives in Whitefield, New Hampshire, and Baltimore, Maryland, with her husband, Eric Jacobsen; they have one son, Erlend, a poet and teacher. She is currently serving her second term as Poetry Consultant to the Library of Congress.

A WALK WITH RASCHID

When the muezzin began to call, James got out of bed and went to the window. Tracy shifted as he did so, murmuring and giving a light shiver, and he pulled the sheet over her body which looked bright in the moonlight; the iron grillwork barred it.

The call, a rough, unhuman, melancholy, hornlike sound, fell and rose, with a breathstopping pause between phrases. It appeared to take up, in a strange tongue, an unsettled theme. That it referred to a god could never be doubted. It insisted, accused, identified, summoned. No matter that he couldn't get so much as his toe into Moule Idris, shoeless or shod.

They had turned off the fountain just below, and the tiled courtyard, where he and Tracy and Mr. and Mrs. Neeson had sipped mint tea at noon in a daze of color, was absolutely still. The bone-blue of the medina slept; anyway, was silent. Not a bawl, not a bark. That extraordinary voice, not like a reed or a ram's horn, but more like both than a voice, proceeded powerfully up and down its ways. Were the tanners asleep, bright yellow and red, peacefully stinking? Did the single-toothed coppersmith rise and kneel to the east? Did it wake Raschid? At the thought of Raschid asleep or awake in that visible bone-blue city, James thought immediately of Oliver, asleep or awake in a home once as familiar to James as his fingers, now distant in a variety of ways. This had happened three or four times. Beyond the fact that Raschid and Oliver both belonged to the human species, and were ten-year-old males, it was hard to see a connection.

Shivering a little in the three o'clock air, he heard the phrase end, on a wild deep braying gasp; a pause, and then a high climb. He stared through the grill at the blaze of moonlight; all the dark seemed to have contracted into the cypresses. A small dizzy sense of ridiculousness wafted over him: James Gantry, naked, immaculately shaved, hearing the news of Allah and his Prophet, while his wife, bright as a minted penny, slept behind him, and his honeymoon rose in the blanched Moroccan night. Here every known thing seemed to have its alien echo: his feet, the brilliant geometry of the tiles; Tracy, the carved and gilded and painted bed; his son's pale-faced, square-set image; Raschid.

Raschid wore a striped djellabah; it was too small, but looked dignified. He never (when James had seen him) raised the hood. He had small bones, extended eyelashes, and a left thumb flattened in some mishap. His eyes (differing in this from his face, which was somber), were light-hearted in their darkness; unlike those of Oliver, which were of a pale and steadfast blue.

Hastily choosing the lighter confusion, James pressed down on the thought of Raschid. He didn't understand Raschid. Political prejudice aside, he did consider Arabs decorative; and then, Oliver's lack of childish charm had only lucklessly sharpened James' love of it. So he was prepared for that aspect of Raschid. But although he was gloomily convinced that the man who wasn't a scoundrel was apt to be a boob, he didn't want to be a boob, and he was alert for Raschid's angle. It could hardly be other than money, and when James found it apparently wasn't, he was thrown into unease. The whole of Fez contributed to this.

Fez was all there, close, breathing, smelling and moving, and yet he felt unsure what was real, where, exactly, the fraud began. The dyers and tanners were real; standing high above the stench, on narrow pitted steps with Tracy gamely clutching his elbow, the guide waiting, and Raschid gesticulating one step below, he saw them, inside their own lives; but, too, in some circle of Dante's. And in the cavern of trays, the coppersmith with his one tooth and serene eyes, looked at once like a tourist's artisan, and a disguised and saintly magician.

Raschid had cut himself out from the horde of children by an incident common between the sexes, and not unknown between adults and children strange to each other—a sudden wordless intimacy, based on a mutual attraction solid as an electric shock.

Raschid's reaction, James perfectly well knew, was inevitably rooted in a lack in the past, and a hunger for the future. His own, he faced with a familiar stale qualm, was at least the former. The future, now, was Tracy. He had never been truly equipped to love Oliver, if love entailed satisfaction. But, unrejected, he would have offered as fine substitutes as his nature would provide and guilt could prompt. But he *had* been rejected; first somewhere in secret, and then verbally. It was odd how clearly he knew that it was he who had been rejected, rather than Louise who had been chosen. If Louise had never found their son a very interest-compelling subject, she had maintained with him, during the periods when he attracted her attention, a mild-mannered friendliness. There were children who *did* interest her; but any comparisons which she may have made in silence, or in dreams, never resulted in maternal animosity.

It had always been hard for Oliver to speak; and it was Tracy who had got him through the ordeal of his decision, by her ability to listen, an ability as native and as finely-honed as her tennis game. How a child of his and Louise's could be that inarticulate, passed James' understanding. Though he secretly thought of Louise's articulateness as facile (perhaps because it worked so well on her newly-privileged kindergarten listeners), there it was. Oliver gave, always, the impression of weighing. He was a sort of small, human, heavily-constructed pair of scales, the results of whose balances were never disclosed. After the permissible baby age, he had been caught now and then telling stories, all involving possessions, material or animal; but until James had looked at them in the light of Tracy's sunny honesty, he had not called them lies. Like Tracy, he spontaneously believed lying to be the meanest of the vices. "Know the truth, and the truth shall make you free." It was Tracy's only biblical quotation.

One hot September afternoon she had said it to him, running her cool fingers over the pink shells of her toenails. James, waiting in his brown hateful bed-sitting room; Oliver, redelivered to the house which for twelve years had been James' home. Tracy had been standing at the window: he thought she appeared like Mercury, the gods' lissome and terrible messenger. She came over to the daybed, kicked off her pumps, curled up and seized her toes. Over them, half humorously, half tearful, she quoted her maxim.

"Well?" said James.

"He wants to stay with Louise."

The curious shaft, like dry ice, that burned through him, he could not have diagnosed for his life.

"I don't believe it."

"He told me so. In so many words."

There was a silence. Tracy kept it; she never blundered.

"Well," he said at last. "How hard was it—for him, I mean?"

"Very, I think," said Tracy softly. She looked, for her, tired, and James rushed toward her in his mind's eye. How much she gave, how little, without denigrating herself, she asked. She had not demanded commitment. Now that she had it, she would have shaped herself to another woman's heavy and taciturn child, if that was what James and Oliver wanted. Oliver had liked her at once. He was always looking for a new thing to belong to him, James glumly thought, and it was Tracy who had lifted from all three of them that most savage incident of a split marriage—self-declaration by offspring. Louise, conditioned to consult, in her warm-soup voice, finger-painters versus block-builders, had kindly said, "Oliver should choose, himself. He's ten. It's only a limited choice, it's not as though he'd never see the other."

"A child that age, even a *frank* child," Tracy had said as she and James turned it gently over and over, "can't get words around huge things, the things its life is made of. If you ask him about motorbike parts, or batting averages, it's a piece of cake. But fool, awful questions, like 'do you love your mother?' 'are you mad at your father?' . . . What we've *got* to have is the truth, that's the only thing that'll hold up. He can say to me 'my father' or 'my mother.' To you, or Louise, he'd have to say 'you.' That's where, perhaps, I helped. Getting 'loyalty' out of it. Poor Oliver. Christ, the things people do in the name of loyalty. Pulling live tissue apart. I said it was a temporary pattern; just that. No great, permanent decision. That you and Louise wanted to stand enough aside to give him room to breathe and think. This way, he needn't say to either, 'I don't want to live with you.' "

"It's just," said James lamely, "that he seems so remote from Louise."

Tracy laid her weary head back against the brown cushions of the daybed.

"Louise really only likes them at the pre-judgment age," she said astutely. "It makes her nervous to be sized up. Children are death on that."

"Did he say anything about me?" he after a while asked.

"Bang!" went knuckles on the door. James rose; it was their ice. Conveniently later she said gently, "He was embarrassed. He's only ten. And he sometimes finds it hard to be honest. This was one of the hard times."

James raised his amber glass and drank. Tracy, too, raised her glass. "To Oliver," she said slowly. They drank. Suddenly a wild relief—the die cast, that inn of decision in which the mind sleeps well—flooded James. "To Morocco," he said. But the second toast was too soon for Tracy. She set her glass softly by the ice-bucket, and closed her green eyes.

The chanting had stopped. The muezzin had gone back to wherever he had come from. The moonlight had withdrawn; Tracy was only a dark corner. James, who had sat down on a sighing hassock, got up. A light burst out in a kitty-cornered window in the lower garden, and Mrs. Neeson, in flamingo chiffon panels, went across it. How very gorgeous, James thought meanly. Mrs. Neeson was too much for him. The effect was flawless, but though effortless in appearance, seemed to spring from a vast hidden machinery. Surely Nubian slaves must have toiled for centuries, computers made hairline decisions, sleep, reading and eating have been forsworn for plans. Was Mr. Neeson the machinery?

Mrs. Neeson's references were too oblique and intimate to be name-dropping; nothing so cut-rate fell from her lips. The Palais Jamai, reprieved by quaintness and the lovely tokens of old Moorish lusts, amused her in an endearing way. "How we do envy you dear old number seven," she had said at once. "We cabled just too late." Tracy, with her candid gaze, had subsequently re-examined their small lustrous room. "Well, now we have the Good Housekeeping Seal," James said nastily. It had amused him that Mrs. Neeson should cause Tracy to reassess anything.

Did that flamingo vision arise, from the first sweet sleep of night, to perform esoteric rites of beautification? Or was she merely en route to the bathroom? The light still burned. The medina still slept. In an orgy of pre-dawn slackness, James wondered, abashed, if Raschid dreamed of the American who spoke French, who, infinitely powerful, infinitely just, was an enormous, sudden friend. James was as beautiful as Raschid; though, at thirty-three, it would never have occurred to him that this was true.

In the morning, the courtyard tiles shone from the hose. The fountain, released, sprang up and fell, and distant noises came from the medina.

Raschid came to the outer entrance about ten o'clock. James, who had gone out to treat with a taxi-driver, saw his striped djel-labah swerve out of the medina-alley. The taxi driver said at once, "The guides will get police if he keeps does so. He can't guide. Beggars, beggars."

"He is not a beggar," said James shortly. He decided to ignore the taxi-driver's opinions. "At eleven-thirty, then," he said haugh-tily, and turned toward Raschid.

Day before yesterday, when he had first joined them—dou-bling their steps quietly along the stony way, regarded sideways by a James enchanted, apprehensive, waiting for the story, the brown small palm—he had worried about James' French. "Vous com-prenez?" he asked, drawing up his short nose as though smelling language deficiencies. "Vous comprenez ce que j'ai dit?" Then he began to worry about Tracy, but not much. "Expliquez à votre femme," he said once or twice rather perfunctorily, as if she might be dangerous if too much excluded.

He made the stale standard joke, pushing a donkey aside, "Ce sont les petits taxis de la medina!" and his eyes laughing at James, at himself, at the donkeys, at the prostrate jest, took James into a dazzling intimacy.

At the end of their stroll through the bleak biblical landscape of stones, bare earth and bleached sun, James extracted a handful of change. Instantly a cloud passed over Raschid's brown eyes, muddying their color. He put both hands behind his back and looked sullenly down at his feet under the djellabah's dirty edge.

"J'ai voulu faire votre connaisance," he said. "C'était tout simplement ça."

Amazed, pleased, uneasy, James had returned his dirhams to his pocket.

"What did he say?" asked Tracy, smiling at Raschid.

"He said he wished to make my acquaintance, that was his only purpose."

They shook hands with him, first James, then Tracy, and he asked James when he would care to go through the medina. They were going the next morning, said James, but with a guide, it was already arranged. Raschid murmured something in Arabic. Then he lifted his head and said clearly in French, looking James straight in the eye, that he would like, once, to take them himself into the medina. They would go to certain places the guide would not have time for; then, when that was finished, they would go to une restaurante typique, très typique, très petite, très bonne, and there they would faire déjeuner ensemble. "Demain, peut-être?"

That they could not do, Tracy, easily snared, having committed them to lunch with the Neesons. "Alors, le jour après . . ." said Raschid.

"Hélas, nous allons à Meknes."

"Alors, le jour après ça . . ."

"But that's our last day," said Tracy, guessing.

James said to her in rapid English, "We could go in the afternoon, late, and have supper instead of lunch. I'd really like to. That would leave practically the whole day free."

"Good," she said instantly. She grinned affirmatively at Ras-

chid; but his face, direly balanced between their glances, stayed
dark until James committed them: "Eh bien, d'accord. A quatre
heures et demi. Après, nous pouvons diner ensemble. Le jour
après le lendemain."

The next day he came with them and their outraged guide. He
pointed now and then, but did not speak except to say, with
taciturn authority, "Moule Idris, c'est le plus beau de tous."

As they peered over the shoulders of a picture-snapping com-
patriot, into that vast, ordered, brilliant coolness, Tracy said a
little crossly, "I don't see why they let people take *pictures* and
not go in—if they take their shoes off, I mean. My husband went
into one in Alexandria," she told the guide.

He gave them a bland frown. "Fez is a more holy city," he said.
"Very holy." Raschid stared at James to see how he received
this statement.

Disoriented, they trudged behind their towering and animated
guide: coppersmiths, tinsmiths; souks; weavers, tanners, dyers.
They debouched, helpless, into lavish rooms at the end of sinister
entrances; undesired rugs, glowing like radiant signals, unfurled
by rapid boys; mint tea; unstuffed hassocks, cast upon the floor to
sink in gorgeous slow motion; mint tea. They flattened themselves
against stone to let donkeys pass. The donkeys' aristocratic legs
supported immense piles of planks, towering baskets, piles of
colored cloth. "Ce sont les petits taxis de la medina," said the
guide.

Tracy, all gold and green, in white linen, stayed cool and happy.
James was battling a sense of disequilibrium. It seemed to have
darted like a shadowy fish in deep water ever since the hour
when he had heard the muezzin's raucous wandering call, when
he had been alone at the window. He was summoned, yet he was
not. He could touch people at any minute—indeed, it was impossible not to; but he should have been closer, or more distant. This
way, it needed to be a travelogue, a chapter: the medina, Fez. The
place hummed, milled, teemed; all the travelogue words. But the
eyes that met his, over yaskmak and under turban, slid over
human material borne past them by a guide.

His elbow was jerked; on his arm the soiled brown hand with the

smashed thumbnail rested, pressing. "Voilà! C'est notre restaurante future. Quand nous faisons ensemble notre promenade."

He could see nothing but a blind darkness beyond an open
doorway; and they were past it, anyway. But it was an engagement; and it was as though at last he were identified.

They had not gone to Meknes, after all. Something had upset
Tracy, and she lay all day, qualmish and languid, not even much
reading. She urged James to go anyway, but he suddenly realized
how much he did not want to. He wanted to stay still. The Neesons
had gone to Meknes, causing Tracy to remark, childishly, that if
she *were* going to be sick, it seemed like a good day.

James sat in the shadow by the fountain and read *The Tale of
Genji.* Ravished by a paragraph, he stared from his shade into a
daze of sun. He jumped up, and went in to read to Tracy about
the little maids going into the dim early garden, carrying their
cricket-cages; but she had fallen asleep, her pale hair lightly
snarled on the punched-up pillow. He stared at his future, awed.
The simple, unambiguous, exquisite, and here-present future. He
went back, through the cool splendors of the hall, into the courtyard, sat down and read the passage again. But this time it had
thinned out. He shut the book, and then as two couples paused,
staring lovingly around them, raised it.

He had not heard his muezzin again, except the night before,
when, a semi-circular foursome, they were having coffee in the
small bar. Then, though faint, the hard distant wail had caused
them slightly to raise their voices.

It annoyed James that he did not enjoy the Neesons. He
credited them with being out of the run; *more* of something, if
not of something different. Mr. Neeson, who looked as though
he had had his blood painlessly extracted and then been sealed
again, had a small, pungent speech. It admitted of no qualifica-
tions, but it was lively. Mrs. Neeson, whose anecdotes, never
blasting, were pleasantly penultimate, glowed and breathed. Perhaps Mrs. Neeson had all that blood?

A friend of hers, a more-than-promising young French film
director (formerly a Godard protégé, but now intransigently in-
dividualistic), was, or might be, at Marrakesh; the Neesons were

waiting for a call. Against the embroidered cushions, Mrs. Neeson appeared to have been incarnated from an absolutely first-class original. Lustrously, she leaned toward James, with a luminous-lipped air of barely pre-coital chic.

"He's very ready," she said. "Very open-ended. But there's a terrific thrust. He used color-change for mood long before Antonioni."

"Film is exciting," said Tracy. James saw with love that she felt uncertain, but not totally docile, in her habitual self-underestimation.

"It's the camera. It's knowing how not to interfere with what the camera sees." A turbaned head appeared at her shoulder; it was the Mamounia, calling from Marrakesh.

The Gantrys were halfway up the stairs when she returned. "Jean-Paul!" she cried softly after them. "It was! His art man is going to do some sketches of a palace in Meknes, and we're going back to Meknes, and meet him at a friend's place outside, where we can go for cocktails, and then drive on late to Rabat, all of us."

Back at the foot of the stairs again, the Gantrys glanced at each other, reapproaching the bar. Could she mean "all"?

"I've told him about you both." So she did. "And you were going to Rabat anyway, the next day."

James said at once, "How nice of him, and of you. But tomorrow, we can't." He saw Tracy's eyes cloud. "We're tied up," he nevertheless said. It sounded lame. Somehow he could not get a grip on Raschid which could produce him for the Neesons in the guise of an engagement.

But Mrs. Neeson was incurious and easy. "Oh dear, if we'd only known a bit sooner."

Behind the big carved door of Number 7, James said guiltily, "Why on earth don't you go? You can take a car back here."

Tracy had crossed to the window-grille. The fountain was still playing. "Darling, don't be ridiculous. 'Jean-Paul' doesn't want to see me. It might have been fun—but not just me, with them."

He joined her at the window. The cypresses pointed straight at great many stars.

"I mean," said James, "he's been counting on it for three days. A kid that age . . ."

"Heavens, yes," she instantly agreed. "We couldn't change him to lunch, you don't suppose?"

He was somehow relieved that evidently it wasn't that she hankered for the Neesons in exchange for Raschid, as that she had a generous appetite for both. "We can't get *hold* of him. I've no idea where he lives, in the medina. Do you know," he said, surprised, "I can't even remember his last name. He told me twice, but Arabic names . . ." But it still seemed to him strange.

"Oh well," said Tracy mildly, and taking her kimono she disappeared into the bathroom, through whose open overhead arch he could hear her running the shower and cheerfully whistling.

He dreamed of Mercury. The god's heels, conventionally wing-tipped, barely rested on the kindergarten floor. The small black faces stared, not truly frightened. "And *this*," said Louise's breathy voice, "is *Mercury*. He is a messenger. He is the gods' *messenger*. He is a god, too. He is the god of lovers, and of thieves. We will draw that thing on his head. With our crayons. It is a helmet. A *golden helmet*. Oliver, will you turn him sideways for us, please." As Oliver moved to do so, James woke, coldly clear. Mercury had been beautiful. The small black faces had been beautiful; open, dark, turned like royal pansies toward Louise's sun. Louise's son. James' son. Not that pale, really, not in real life; not that squat, not that shut.

He had had one tantrum, Louise wrote. Only one. He bought a snake, sent from an unscrupulous snake-farm in Florida. It had to be fed live mice. Regularly. The whole thing was psychologically wrong at the moment. Cruel, stupid and inefficient. She had returned the snake, collect. Oliver had exploded. He had called her a white mouse. A white rat. For the snake to eat. He wanted to live with his father. His father was, actually, coming to take him away.

Louise, rancorless, and encouraged by this purging, had reminded him of his choice. It was a lie. He began to weep. He had never never said that, never, never. She had not said, "Then why hasn't your father come to get you?" And a little later, when she came back to the room, he hugged her violently and explained that he had said it because his snake had been returned. He had chosen her because he loved her. Since then he was friendly, and was saving for a Siamese kitten.

For an awful day James had wondered if, in his rage and frustration, Oliver had lived through minutes of believing his own invention; that he had summoned a father who, silently, never arrived; received a disprized home, nursed a secret he could never admit. Tracy had gone quite white over this story. But she did not think that, even in his rage, Oliver believed it. "That's his weak spot. It's because he's inarticulate, I'm sure. He lies sometimes, like about the raccoon—because he can't fully express things."

Faces such as Raschid's did not, basically, need words; but he had them, correct, lucid, formal. It was a curious rendezvous; beyond the afternoon, the walk, the dinner, the farewell, what did Raschid want? A different memory? A promise? A bond outside his arc? Yes, he had brothers, he had answered. Six. Two sisters. No father. (Gone? Dead?) An aunt. A mother.

What sort of present could Raschid be given? He was extraordinarily intelligent. He spoke well. He had fire, grace. He was dirty; but small boys got dirty. But this was settled dirt. And the djellabah was mildly ragged. Would he like James to meet his mother? To what purpose? Was this really a friendship? Wild as that seemed. What would they eat? What on earth would the restaurant through that dark doorway be like? But then the inner shops. . . . He felt a tremendous hot gaiety, a sense of some light-hearted reprieve, that spilled into his sleep. He was amused to find he was thinking in terms of "not letting Raschid down."

Their last day came over the gardens like a single jewel. After lunch they went down to the lower level to say goodbye to the Neesons, later departing for Meknes and Jean-Paul. The Gantrys had an hour before Raschid's arrival. The lower garden was cool and dusty; the Gantrys, faced with a long, sunny trek, slumped peacefully in wicker chairs. Tracy thought of the postcards she had meant to get. "I could do it now," she said. "Oh sit still," said Mrs. Neeson affably, but Tracy went on mournfully remembering that she would *not* want to write them tonight, and God knew, not be-

fore leaving early in the morning. Finally, she went to get them.
When she came back, some time later, she was dissatisfied. Having
searched, she had ended up with pictures taken from curious
angles, denigrating the courtyard and its views. Nevertheless, she
scribbled laxly, stopping to sigh, in the fragrant heat.

At quarter past four, James rose. "Well," he said, "have a fine
trip. I hope . . ." But the Neesons were coming up, too. At five,
the car for Meknes would be there; they would wait by the fountain. "Those streets must be death, in this sun," said Mrs. Neeson.
It was hotter in the upper courtyard, an intimation of outside.

"You go and see," said Tracy to James. "He mightn't be there
yet."

James secretly had a feeling that he would have been there for
some time. He went out through the flower-beds, past the lily-pool,
along the tiled way, to the outside glare. Raschid had not yet arrived. There were two taxis (neither the one driven by Raschid's
foe), a motorcycle, loiterers in the narrow shade thrown by the
wall. He went back to the courtyard. Tracy had finished her
cards. She stuffed them in her purse, slung it on her shoulder, and
looked ready.

Suddenly James was anxious. It was like one of those dreadful,
contrived stories in which at the last moment someone is run over,
his mother falls dead, he is arrested, or locked in a windowless
room.

"He *must* be there now," said Tracy. She had evidently explained things to the Neesons, since they looked only interested.
"If your small Arab doesn't show, you'll get to Rabat with us yet,"
said Mrs. Neeson amiably.

"It's twenty-five to five," said Tracy. "You know he'd be there
by now. Go see."

One of the taxis was gone. The shade along the wall had
widened. He could not see Raschid. Perhaps he had come during
James' return to the courtyard and dashed away for a minute.
James' breath felt odd. I am *not* meeting a general to negotiate
for peace, he reproved himself, a little amused and puzzled. The
taxi-driver stared at him. James looked fiercely at the ground; the
man knew perfectly well that his cab was not wanted. Then he

raised his eyes quickly to his watch. It was a quarter to five, and a weight like a concrete block fell on him. Something *had* happened. And he would never know. That was the only part that was really bad. The truth, he thought, joking, can't make me free if I don't know it. Couldn't Raschid have sent him word? But he knew that an alley tart would have had more chance of penetrating the late sultan's harem, than Raschid or a friend, of penetrating the courtyard.

A taxi drew up, and two black and enormous women got out, one magnificent in royal blue, the other towering in a bone-crushing pink. They were mammoth, handsome, ferociously powerful. They began pulling bundles from the taxi, roped huge mounds, baskets, bags with knotted necks. Their driver had disappeared into the medina. James looked gratefully at this diversion. Raschid had no watch. Time, to an Arab child . . . But he did not believe it.

The taxi-driver reappeared from the medina entrance, followed by a man in a soiled white djellabah, leading two donkeys. The man and the driver began to load the bundles onto the donkeys, higher and higher; last came a roped trunk. Finally, when only the hung heads and delicate legs were visible, the man struck each donkey a blow with a large stick and they lurched, and then swayed, sagging, forward down the sloping alley and out of sight. The taxi backed, ground gears, rushed off. The driver of the parked taxi addressed James.

"Berbers," he said. "Berbers. No damn good." He spat from the taxi window. "Bad people around," he said.

James looked at him. The man stared into his eyes. "Bad boys, too," he said. "That boy, he kicked your wife."

"What?" said James.

"He kicked her," repeated the driver. "Police fix him soon, I say it. She speak to him nice, and he yelling, Non, non, non. And then she try to give him something. Give him American money. Goddam fool, he kick and yell."

"I don't know what you are talking about," said James.

"Not one hour gone by," said the taxi-driver with care. "Not one hour. He yelling at her, *menteuse, menteuse!* That's 'liar' he

says. In French, crying and yelling. Then he pull up his hood, and
kick her leg and run away. She smile at me, this way," he lifted
his shoulders to his ears. "Very nice lady, not to get police."

James went over to the alley and looked down it. The Berbers
and their donkeys had disappeared; other figures, other donkeys,
strode and swayed. Hooded heads turned corners. Under a djella-
bah-hood, dark eyes, now turned a light, steadfast blue, raced
away, raced away. The wall had cut off the sun, and a faint fresh
coolness rose from the stones. As the taxi-driver watched him, he
turned back and went toward the courtyard.

David Shaber was born in Cleveland. He taught at Allegheny College and Smith College before coming to New York, where he has written articles for *Holiday, Cosmopolitan* and other magazines, as well as several screenplays for major studios. His work has also appeared in *The Best Short Plays* series, *Venture, Transatlantic Review, Prize Stories 1961* and *Prize Stories 1962*. He is currently at work on a novel.

SCOTCH SOUR

That was the summer he felt he had no options; whatever came his way he felt obliged to do. If there were a research project he had to take it, or a course he had to give it, even though his own dissertation lay on his desk like a stone that would not roll one way or the other, and the course meant two Siberian weeks at an adult camp in Vermont. If there were a girl he had to get a haircut and ask her for drinks regardless, if an offer to sub-let his apartment he had to be sensible about that, too, and be stuck up at the country place for seven solid weeks alone. None of it was what he wanted, but he did it all, anyway. Because he had gone so long without anything, and he did not know how else to change the way things had gotten to be with him.

The women, especially. In the sixteen months since he had come home that Monday and found her gone, in the fifteen-and-a-half months since he had learned where she slept that famous week-end, in the fifteen months and thirteen days since he had agreed with his analyst that was not the issue and told her he understood, and in the fifteen months and ten days since she had done it again; in the fifteen months and nine days since he began to realize the wedding might be off, in the fourteen-and-a-half

months since he had reluctantly abandoned the delays and excuses
which he called patience and insight and had asked her to move
her clothes out of the apartment, in the fourteen months and
one week since he had given her a chance to reconsider; in the
eleven months since he had stopped expecting to hear from her,
in the ten months since he had stopped expecting to run into her,
and in all the other dragging months after that which stretched
behind him like a desert dotted here and there with dry, blank
forms, he had gone from nothing to nothing to nothing again.
And the months of that summer had been the driest of all.

It was almost with anticipation that he had picked up the
telephone in the beginning, reaching for those promising names
he had squirreled away in the pouches of his mind against the day
when he might once again be back in the world. But somehow the
first two girls he managed to find simply stood him up, and when
he reached back into the pouches again they were unexpectedly
empty. Nor, he discovered, did he know where to find anything
else to put in them; now that he had come back to the world,
the world seemed no longer to be there. In the four years he had
been out of circulation his students had grown too young for him
(eleven years' difference was one thing but fifteen was another),
no one gave parties anymore, and there seemed to be no natural
way for him to meet anybody. He went vainly through three old
address-books two times each, then called what friends he still
had left who were single, but it turned out they were up against
the same thing he was and had no numbers to spare. And after
one shuffle *manqué* with a razor-back free lance public relations
girl in his building and two shuddering experiences with computer
dating, like a cornered animal that exposes its soft under-throat
to the harriers at its heels, he had finally that summer given himself up to the eager mercies of his married friends, though he
knew what that would be. Mostly the husbands were useless, giving him only the fringes of their own best fantasies. And the wives
were, if anything, too helpful.

"Listen," he would say finally over the phone from the country
after about ten minutes of empty conversation at toll rates, "Lis-

ten, the truth is, I'd like to meet somebody—you know what I mean?"

"Oh," the wife would say. "You mean you'd like to meet somebody."

"I just decided," he would say, "that you don't meet anybody unless you make an effort. And you can't make an effort unless you make an effort, right?"

"Oh, absolutely," the wife would say.

"So do you happen to know anybody I could call?"

"Well, what kind of girl would you say you're looking for?"

At the beginning of the summer he would answer. "You know, good company, bright, attractive—nothing special," and they both would laugh. A few weeks later he changed it to, "I don't care, as long as she's beautiful." And by the middle of July he would simply say, "Oh, I don't know. Somebody nice."

"Well," the wife would say, "that should be easy."

And so in the afternoons one, two, sometimes even three days a week, he would go upstairs at three to change (when it should have been at two-thirty if he were to be on time) and drive in to meet nice girls at the St. Moritz or the Algonquin or other places he could not afford. And after the dinner or the movie was over and he had asked them for another date because he didn't know how not to, he would drive back to Connecticut and watch part of the second late movie and get into bed at four and oversleep the next day and not sit down at the desk until twelve-thirty or one. Sometimes he would go to bed with them and sometimes he wouldn't. (For a while he tried to try not going too far on the first date to see if that would make any difference. The difference was that if he did, when he got back to the country he would be tired enough to sleep without the second movie.)

In this way he had already that summer been through the slim divorcee named Penny who had three children and was deaf in one ear—she took the hearing-aid off before they made love, belligerently daring him not to do right by her and of course he hadn't, on the third date they had a huge row while she stood in his driveway holding the mousse she had bought as a surprise for dessert and one dark night two weeks later he had left the empty pannikin in her mail-box in Katonah; plus a Long Island beauty with two children and one hammer thumb who denied him (she was waiting for love) and a short Zionist nurse who did not but never forgave him because he fell asleep afterwards when she wanted to talk about her conflicts, and she woke him and they lay with their hands folded on the covers and discussed her anger until the birds began to chirp and he could drive her all the way back to the city in atonement. Not to mention one dim evening with a girlish ex-wife in mini-skirts though when he put his tongue in her mouth he could feel the gutta percha ridge of the restoration at the rear of her upper teeth, and another with a psychiatric-social worker who kept looking at him all night and shaking her head and smiling and calling him by his whole name, "Henry Bleier, Henry Bleier," then stood in her doorway saying "Why do I feel you pulling away from me?" as he backed down the stairs promising to call. And others, and others. Sometimes he would even ask them to the country for the week-end in some attempt to assume the old shape the days once had, then to spend endless boring hours driving to Stratford or around upper Westchester and while he drove trying to reason his way through it all, beginning with the premise, of course, that somehow it was his fault.

Periodically he thought of giving up and periodically he did, and did nothing. But the end of each day alone in the country surprised him, closing in without remedy. He sat at the desk as though inside a giant sun dial while the sun marched around the house coming first through one window then another, until it got behind the barn and the twilight would begin. And he knew that if he drove to the movies in Norwalk it would only be worse coming home afterwards. So he would barbecue big steaks he could not finish and watch the light fade and go in the house and turn on the television set and lie on the sofa and think there must be someone he could call. Once he said out loud, "God, isn't there anybody?" but it only made him feel foolish. And sometimes he would try to cry because he thought it might make him feel better. But he could not cry. And in a day or two he would think of a fresh wife he hadn't tried and would call and ask her if she knew someone he could meet.

Somewhere around the middle of July he decided maybe it was that he had been asking the wrong people to fix him up. So he had cast around for different fixers and through his dentist (his gums had always been a problem) he had actually found a model named Laurel Something who was analyzed and really about to solve some of her major problems. Unfortunately she was involved herself at the moment with a widower and his two children in Quogue, but between mouthfuls (Luchow's, eighteen dollars plus tip and a parking ticket when they got back to the car) she gave him the names of two wonderful girls. The first turned out to be a fashion coordinator who was just about to move in with her boss. And at six o'clock on a miserably sticky August afternoon Henry stood looking for something to lean on in the Oak Bar of the Plaza while he waited for the Judy Something who was the second and would be his third of the month and the eleventh of the summer.

She was supposed to be the prettier of the two, and at first he was also anxious to meet her for certain other voodoo reasons— mainly that the middle four letters of her last name (it was something like Malven or Nalven) were the same as those of a girl he once had a crush on in high school. But it had taken so long to reach her, sitting over the phone in the country, staring at the oil company calendar on the kitchen wall and counting ten rings every day for three weeks (sometimes he would find himself holding the receiver and hearing it ring and could not remember whose number he had dialed); and by the time she finally answered he couldn't remember what he felt. But she said she had short brown hair and would be the one in the pink dress and the harried look, and he said he would be wearing a blue cord suit and suggested the Plaza because he was afraid the waiters at the St. Moritz were beginning to recognize him.

On the way in he had allowed himself to wonder if she really could be good-looking, and if she were would it be too much to ask her to the country for the week-end right away. And he had definitely decided it would be too much, definitely, but of course she wouldn't be good-looking anyway so there was nothing to worry about. And then, though he had been a good fifteen minutes late, an apprehensive circuit of the room had revealed no pink dresses with brown hair. So he had stood mutely at the bar until the bartender saw how politely he was waiting, and then asked for a Scotch sour. He would have liked to be known as a person with certain immutable, slightly out-of-the-way tastes and things about him, you could say O he never this or O he always that. At the age of thirty-four he was still looking for them, he was still searching for a style without knowing that the search itself was one, and lately he had taken to trying Scotch sours. And so, sipping his drink, he stood now both with hope and without it, watching the door open and close, open and close, and the people come in.

Each one who arrived seemed to join another. The bar seemed full of couples touching each other somewhere, hand to hand in the middle of tables, shoulders pressing here, elbows there, hips, forehead leaning to forehead, temple to temple, a roomful of social Siamese twins. As he peered over the rim of his glass, everything seemed to dwindle back from the little asterisks that were the points of contact. But still no pink dresses with brown hair.

Then the door opened again and there appeared just inside it O such a face. And glanced around. And, My God, hesitated. A sun-tanned olive madonna of a face haloed with dark hair, with brown hair, not ten paces from where he stood. Somewhere beneath the face he had a glimpse of creamy caramel arms and throat scooped from the shell of an aching pink dress. And above it there were eyes and eyebrows and a nose that all went together, plus lips that puckered on his heart and drew the blood right from it; a face that cut into his side like a wild pain, it hurt him when he drew breath. He knew it couldn't be her, there were a million reasons why it couldn't be, she was too young, too pretty, oh he knew, her hair was too long—but still the way it rose across her forehead graphed the joy he felt. And he knew, but she stood in the doorway so long that a fierce hope rose in him despite himself. Like a boy in dancing class gathering his pumps beneath him, he straightened slowly. And still she hesitated, a lovely pink-and-

brown petal floating just inside the door. And still. Then smiled—
oh!—and seemed, incredibly, to be moving toward him. Until he
caught where her eyes were and turned and saw the man who
was waiting behind him with the upraised hand, then turned back
and because he could not stop himself smiled and nodded a little
anyway at the face as it went past. He stood smiling a moment
afterwards as though for someone else because he did not want to
look foolish. And suddenly he thought, Listen, I won't decide
about asking her for the week-end now, I'll be spontaneous about
it.

"God, I'll bet you're gonna murder me," said a voice behind
him. He swung around startled, "Henry, right?"

There was this girl.

"I'm Judy," she said. "Hi."

Henry just looked at her.

"You came in the wrong way," he said finally.

"I guess what I did was I went to the dining room by mistake,"
said the girl. "So they just told me to come in the other door. Boy,
half an hour late. I'll bet you'd just like to murder me."

"You came in the wrong way," Henry said again. "I wasn't
watching that way."

He felt like a man who has fallen off a roof and broken his bones.
His skin was still intact but everything inside was cracked, in some
frozen way everything was broken but still pressed together with
the breath squeezed out, and he could not tell how his fingers,
he had no feeling at the ends of his fingers. But somehow he got
across the room with her, and the Captain pulled a table out from
the banquette and the girl slid in. And Henry remembered to ask
if she was okay, then lowered himself into the chair opposite her
one broken bone at a time. She ordered some kind of gin sling,
and he said he was all right with what he had and just sat
there inside himself, and as soon as it was safe looked out at her
through the periscopes of his eyes.

It wasn't even that she was awful, it was just that she wasn't
anything, except (maybe) the promise of being old. There was
some kind of mouth and face that were harmless enough. But she
was old in little ways, as though she were aging back from the

edges—something in the way her shoulders simply hung out of her sleeveless cotton dress, weight without shape, something in the blunt fingers, the square ankles, the latticework sandals with the stockinged toes sticking out and the hair-do that took him back to Miss Himmel in the Second Grade, all skinned up to a dibby-dabby cluster of tiny curls perched on the top of her head in that neat, glandless femininity of school-teachers. She reminded him of Miss Himmel; everywhere his eye fell on her there was something earnest and dull. And on the back of her right hand and the outer side of her left arm just above the elbow were a series of roundish reddish crusts with a smear of white stuff dried over them. Through the white stuff he could just see the faint lick of moisture shining around the edges of each crust. He looked away quickly.

"Pretty clever, huh?" she said, waggling the hand at him. "Poison oak." She shrugged. "I don't know what it is with me, but I get everything that comes along. Can you believe that all I did was sit on some grass, and bingo. And then of course I couldn't keep my hands off it, naturally, and scratched myself and it spread like crazy. At first it almost drove me wild—I had to wear a glove for over two weeks." Very carefully with the other hand she squeezed the arm as close as she could to the blotches without actually touching them. Her fist opened and clenched tightly. "But it's almost better now." With a visible effort she took her hand away. "Should I put the glove back on? I could put it back on, if this bothers you."

"No, no," he said quickly. "It doesn't bother me." And looked away.

"Boy, I must really be some prize package anyway," said the girl, and lifted the hand with the blotches to tuck a stray wisp back into the strangled bunch of curls. "I should be ashamed of myself, but I was so late I didn't even stop to look in a mirror."

"You look okay to me," said Henry.

"I can imagine."

"No, really, you do, you look fine."

She looked at him a moment. Then she shrugged and took a long swallow of her drink. "Gee, I dearly needed that," she said.

"I'm terribly sorry to be so late, but I'm just fit to be tied. I mean, did you ever have the urge to kill?" Without waiting for a reply, she sighed, "Oh, it's my boss. I could just kill him, I'm so fit to be tied." Henry shifted his weight in the chair. There was something about the word boss that sounded like the salesgirls' restroom in the five-and-ten. "I'm almost embarrassed to tell you," the girl went on without pause, "But see, after stewing about it for months I finally pulled myself together this morning and asked for a raise. And then I waited all day for him to say something. I even finished my work early and just sat around, waiting and waiting. And then finally at almost six o'clock, when I should have been gone at five-thirty anyhow, at almost six o'clock he just breezes out of his office as innocent as you please and says, 'So long, Judy, have a nice week-end.' Have a nice week-end. I just sat there and curdled."

"Maybe he forgot." He wondered vaguely what they were talking about.

"Oh, he didn't forget. He just wanted to make me stew a little more, and I'm such a dummy I let him do it. Don't worry, he didn't forget. Actually, see, it isn't just a raise raise, it's a big raise." She looked at him timidly from under her eyes. "Twenty-five more a week." And then rushed on as though he were about to say something, which he wasn't—"It nearly scared me to death to ask for it, but I've been there so long, nine years, I felt I had to do something." She paused a moment. "I guess it is a pretty big raise, isn't it?"

"Sounds reasonable to me," said Henry, thinking *nine years*. And he saw her further and further for what she was, just a secretary on the edge of being an old maid who wore sweaters and kept track of when everybody went to lunch and worried about who was entitled to the desk by the window.

"I don't know, I might leave or something. Maybe I should leave."

In the silence Henry realized it was his turn again. "Well, what kind of a job would you want?"

"Anything that pays twenty-five more a week," said the girl, and laughed. "Oh, I'm just making noise—I suppose it's a pretty

good job, really. I really run the office. He can't do a thing without
me, and he knows it, that stinker." She sat back. "Anyway, this
isn't very scintillating of me—to sit here and talk about my stupid
job. I'm sorry."

Henry gestured automatically. "Listen, if it's on your mind, it's
on your mind."

The girl looked at him again and smiled slightly.

"You're very nice, aren't you?" she said.

"Yes," said Henry, "I'm very nice. But I guess that's my problem." He said it with more emphasis on *my* than *problem,* and
smiled because he wasn't sure of what might be happening on his
face.

There was a silence while she swizzled her drink and he
swizzled his.

"So . . ." said the girl.

"So," said Henry. "So."

More than anything he wanted to leave, to get up and get out
and get into the car, to go, to flee, to flee flie flow flum.

"Would you like another drink?" said Henry.

He was sitting sideways at the table with one leg crossed over
the other, but there was not even anything else in the room he
could look at. The only thing he could really see in the corner
which he faced were the two grimly painted middle-aged women
posing for each other at the next table. Like two Lenten *gigantes*
their eyes were wrinkled caverns of blue shadow, their mouths
coated with a thick red that bled into the many little lines, above
their lips. They had been served something in frosted glasses, and
when they bent to drink every strand of their rigid silver-blue
hair bent absolutely with them. While the girl went on talking he
nodded occasionally and looked at the two women and snapped
his mixer in half, relishing the sharp little plastic pain against his
finger, anything to keep his eyes open.

He could not understand why he was so tired. He heard her
voice saying things but everything came at him through waves
of distance, trying to answer was like talking under water; now
and then he heard his voice out there somewhere, but that was all.
He did not smile as he usually did. He did not poise alertly on the

peaks of her sentences, ready to leap-frog them nimbly between
his legs and skip down into the next valley of sentences which
would be his, he did not even say any of the things he usually said.
(He did not think of them as things he usually said but he usually
said them nonetheless, things such as When I look at your face
now I can see how you used to look as a baby or It's interesting
the way you use your hands, you really enjoy touching things, don't
you.) Instead her words seemed to roll erratically at him like
large, slow, feathery balls, brushing his fur as they bumbled by.
And while she talked he sat there inside himself and nodded and
thought, If I could just close my eyes and go to sleep right here.
Why can't I just close my eyes and go to sleep right here?

There was one flicker perhaps, when on one of his visits to the
conversation he came back to find she seemed to be saying something about her job and her name.

"—Because let's face it, they go together. With a name like
that, what else can you expect?"

"Why, what's wrong with your name?"

"Just listen to it. Just once, carefully. Ju-dee. It's so ordinary,
so goody-girl. All Judy's have straight hair and thick legs. And
bad skin." She stared ruefully, as though she had looked through
a little window into herself and for a moment seen herself as she
really was.

And Henry, touched despite himself, was moved to say, "Oh, I
don't think Judy's so bad. There's something, something straightforward about it."

"Dull, you mean."

"No, straightforward. Honest. And such girls are rare, believe
me."

"Oh yeah, rare."

"Besides, names don't mean anything," said Henry.

"Yes, they do," said the girl doggedly. "And Judy is Judy."

"Well, what would you like it to be? Esmerelda. Daphne—
what?"

"Oh, I don't care. I used to think something like Bim maybe, or
Gigi. Something perky, gay—I don't know, something that
would inspire me."

"You think you need inspiring?"

"Listen, what I need—" she started. "Just never mind what I need." She poked her mixer at him. "You shouldn't be so nice, you know that?"

For a moment then he had looked at her, wondering what the waist was like beneath the plain cotton and was there some way you could do it without touching, measuring how the dress could lift over the white smears as it came off. And wondering if it did would the plainness come off with it, would the plainness fall away to reveal something beneath that was beyond plain, something bone-naked and ultimate and sweet. Maybe if you explained clearly ahead of time, you could do it without touching. Then he looked again at the flat, limp cotton and realized just as clearly that he didn't want to. He just didn't want to.

And so for the rest of the time he swung himself sideways again and nodded and sucked his ice to stay awake and studied the blue ladies at the next table and also certain independent marvels such as how their lipstick could leave a smear on the frost of their glasses at the time the frost of their glasses left a smear on their lips. Until at last he could look at his watch and say he hated to break this up but he did have a slight drive ahead of him.

And the girl said God she'd forgotten he lived in the country and apologized again for being late and hoped he wasn't fit to be tied. And he said it was all right, actually he had to come in anyway but he really ought to be getting back, and she asked was it just a house he had up there, or what. And he said it was just a house that actually he and this girl had taken for week-ends at the time because actually he'd been going with this girl. At the time. And then he paused guiltily and felt he had to say, "Maybe you'll see it for yourself sometime"—largely because he didn't want her to know he had already decided she never would.

"Is it very far?" asked the girl.

"Oh no, not really—about an hour, an hour and a half on the train, that's all. What you do is change at Stamford and I drive over to New Canaan and meet you. You'll see, if you come up, some week-end maybe." He was looking for the waiter.

"That's very nice of you to offer," said the girl cautiously. "It sounds like fun."

"My pleasure. Maybe sometime when you're free sometime."

The girl looked at him.

"Well," she said, "this week-end would be good for me. How would it be for you?"

"This week-end?" said Henry, caught with one hand still in the air for the waiter. "Oh, you mean *this* week-end?"

But before he could say whatever it was he was going to say because he didn't know what else to say, he was interrupted by a glossy middle-aged balloon of a man who busheled up alongside his elbow, fluttering his manicured hands and crying loudly to the two blue ladies, "Well, NORma, Norma-Norma—and my God don't TELL me Hazel; it's actually that crazy Hazel." He had a little moustache tweezed beneath his nose and was draped in slacks and a tropical sports-jacket, a prairie expanse of orange plaid that sloped out to button on the precise equator over his belly. Now, amid unguent Estee Lauder blushes and little clucks and cries from the women of Oh Freddy and Honestly Freddy and Freddy you're terrible, the man proceeded to bulge his way into the slot between the two tables with his back to Henry, then bent to kiss the one called Hazel—and as he did so the rear vent of his jacket parted and two vast gray dacron globes hung themselves out over Henry's glass. Still peering dimly at the girl across the table like a man trying to get the number of the truck that has just hit him, Henry glanced up, leaned exaggeratedly out of the way and frowned, more at the distraction to his numbed concentration than anything else. And remained leaning and frowning while the man squeezed the rest of the way through the tables, got himself turned around and finally sank down diagonally across from him on the banquette. Whereupon the man hung one plaid arm around crazy Hazel, leaned over the table with a conspiratorial finger to his lips and said loudly, "But exCUSE me, Kids, I forgot we have to whisper. Because we seem to be upsetting His Highness next door here."

At first Henry continued to smile dully at the girl. Then gradually through the dusty charcoal layers of his mind the words from the next table filtered drop by drop until they were all gathered in a little pool at the bottom and he looked at them. Then looked again. The girl was saying that if she took the ten o'clock train she could make a whole day of it, and Henry turned his head stiffly to the next table and said very distinctly, *"What* was that?"

The man looked at him.

"What was that you said?" repeated Henry. His voice seemed very loud.

"Why, something bothering you?"

"Freddy," said one of the blue ladies faintly.

"I just want to know what you said, that's all."

"You heard me, Sonny."

"Freddy, please," the lady said again, plucking at his sleeve.

"Oh, why don't you just—" Henry searched, "—just shut up, *Big Mouth.*" And was instantly dismayed it was all he could find.

"Maybe you'd like to step outside," said the man.

It was all so unreal, so flat and corny that suddenly Henry wanted to giggle. He hadn't any idea what button to aim for or which fist to put before the other or even made a fist to strike anything other than himself in over thirty years. It was unreal, it was recess-time at school, but something warm and prickly dredged through him and broke open in the pit of his stomach, and he didn't care. He absolutely didn't care about anything except the satisfactory rasping sound the chair made as he promptly pushed back from the table.

"Come on."

Henry looked at the man; the man looked at him. For an instant he had to stifle an impulse to stick out his tongue; and then somewhere from the side of his eye he happened to notice the girl across from him. To his surprise she was flattened against the banquette, her blotched hand pressed to her mouth, her eyes white and wide.

The man blinked. "Fine," he said. "Fine." Then he cleared his throat. "Just as soon as I finish my drink."

"Whenever you're ready," said Henry lightly. He turned back to the table, tingling as though he had just had his weight on something that had been asleep. The girl was waiting for him with her eyes still wide, offering to exchange them with his in relief; but he only smiled. Uncertainly, she arched her eyebrows toward the next table, but Henry kept his right where they were, dead level, and spoke only of schedules and stations and changing at Stamford. And when he was good and ready he asked for the check.

That turned out to be the end of it, of course. As they stood to leave, the man at the next table mumbled something about one drink too many, but Henry barely heard. He was not, to tell the truth, paying much attention. And he was still smiling as he walked out behind the uneasy back of the girl who had looked at his face a few moments earlier and hunkered back against the wall, as well she might. As well she might.

Curt Johnson is a free-lance writer/editor living in Western Springs, Illinois. In 1959 he published a novel *Hobbledehoy's Hero,* and since then he has had forty-five short stories published. He also edits and publishes the magazine *December* and has edited *Short Stories from the Literary Magazines* with Jarvis Thurston and *Best Little Magazine Fiction* with Al Greenberg.

TRESPASSER

West and a little South of De Valls Bluff is Little Rock, the capital of Arkansas, a city with many, many lawyers. East and a little north of the Bluff is Brinkley and Forrest City and more like them and finally Memphis, the cotton capital of the world. The cab-drivers in Memphis boast about the beauty of Memphis girls. "Be down about eleven or twelve tonight," they will tell you, "and see what a Southern Belle looks like."

Forrest City and Brinkley and the rest of them have their points of civic pride also. In Forrest City it's the duck-hunting on the Languille bottoms. The limit is four in season, but if you live in Forrest City you go out and come back with twenty and thirty and go out again for more.

In De Valls Bluff they brag about the White River fishing. The White River runs just east of town and there is supposed to be some of the best fishing in the world there: blue channel cat and bass and bream and—for those who want them—alligator gar. Fishing for alligator gar is done for the sport of it. You hook a gar and it comes boiling up out of the water and fighting all the way in. It sounds and then runs at you, gills open, and surfaces again and sounds and so on. But when it's landed all you have is a long, heavy ugly catch of scales. You don't ordinarily eat gar; you do eat bass and channel cat.

Occasionally the White River crowds over its banks and floods the low lands. It used to be that at times even the old highway into the Bluff got flooded over. When the river subsides it leaves ponds and small lakes behind and these hold captive fish which are easy feeding for those gars also left behind.

The Bluff itself is situated on high ground, so its citizens don't have to worry much about being flooded out. In fact, many of them look forward to a flood now and again because there is less food in the ponds left behind than in the river and, therefore, better fishing. But there are people on the east bank of the White, the low side, who are inconvenienced very much by the flooding.

One old man, elderly at least, had a shack in the timber a little over 200 yards from the east bank and every year he had a wet time of it. In the really bad years, ever since the new highway, you could get in to his cabin by land only two or three weeks out of the fifty-two. This man, Thomas, had been in France during World War One. When he came back he first worked as a handyman in the Bluff. Then the Depression forced him to move his wife and belongings out of town across the river to government land, where living was free.

He built a house from mill scraps and next to his house he placed an eight-foot-square tank made out of old metal road signs. He stocked the tank with worms and went into business. Every day he sat beneath a tarp stretched between his house and the tank, waiting for customers. He developed an extraordinary sense of patience; his wife, with him.

When the old highway was still in use and a fisherman wanted a nickel's worth of worms, he turned off the highway to "Buzz's Place"—spelled BUS'S PLASE on the old man's sign.

At the bottom of the Depression, the White River, during one of its floods, threatened to change its course entirely. When it finally went down again the Army Engineers were called in. The Engineers lined the banks with rip-rap and sank rock on mats in the river and drove pilings and after that the river held its course.

Then the Engineers paved a section of new highway paralleling the old on higher ground to the south and finished their project by constructing a new bridge into the Bluff.

During this construction Thomas worked fifteen hours a day. Other than his service in France during World War One, it was the only steady job he ever held. When the work was completed he went back to his post in the chair under the tarp, only now—from the new highway—there was no convenient turnoff to his stand so his business dropped to almost nothing.

The next year, the Army, as a reward for its efforts in checking the river, was permitted to use the abandoned section of the old highway in a demolition exercise. Its experts buried tons of high explosive under the old highway and moved Thomas and his wife into temporary quarters over the rear of a tavern in the Bluff and then they set off their charges. There was a loud explosion and many fish in the ponds next to the old highway were killed by the concussion, but not much real damage was done except that the reinforcing rods of the old highway were left jutting from its surface.

When the Army left, Thomas and his wife moved back to their home. They cleaned up the litter in their yard and shored up the roof of their house, which had been left with a slight sag by the force of the explosion, and things went more or less back to normal for them. Except that now their house was completely cut off from the new highway by the snarl of reinforcing rods in the abandoned section of the old road. So Thomas got rid of almost his whole stock of worms and turned for a livelihood to turtle-trapping and fishing.

In time he and his wife became accustomed to their isolation. Their life was somewhat lonely, but they were content with it and with each other. They got their food from the river, their fuel from the timber, and the occasional sale of a turtle or fish supplied the little cash they needed. They bothered no one and no one bothered them.

Their days had a careful pattern and they depended upon each other to see that this pattern was not disturbed. They arose, they worked, they ate, and they slept. They made do with their lives and they were happy enough.

When his wife died Thomas considered burying her in the river but decided against that because of the gar and the turtles. He did not take her to town and the cemetery because he could not afford to bury her there. He finally decided on a site beside the house.

He took a mattock and dug a grave for her in the center of the enclosure made by the rusting metal sheets of the old tank. He was not a young man and it took him some time to finish and when he did and had buried his wife he sat down in the chair by the tank and rested. He smoked a pipeful and then, after a time, he got up and went to the river and set the snag-line he put out every evening. When he came back to the house he went to bed.

A snag-line is a series of hooks on soft lead leaders suspended from a line. You set it up across a quiet place in the river and hope that catfish will come feeding that way. The blue channel cat feeds with an up-and-down motion as it moves along. If it runs into a hook on your line, it will give a flounce and then usually it is snagged by three or four other hooks as well. A snag-line is a fine thing if you tend it frequently enough to prevent the turtles and gar from getting to your fish. It is quite reliable.

The dry summer was very hard on the Southwest. There was no rain in some areas for as much as eighty days, and it was very hot. Around De Valls Bluff the rice-farmers were sitting tight hoping. Their hope was that their wells would carry them through, the dire possibility being that they might not.

This feeling of apprehension was shared by the goldfish-farmers in the area. They raised crops of goldfish for the market just as the other farmers raised rice—with plenty of water. And water was hard to come by that summer.

Unfortunately, it was that summer in which the telephone company brought to fruition three years of planning for a coaxial cable between Memphis and Little Rock: through the conduits of Memphis, underground across Arkansas, and into the conduits of Little Rock. It was a big project and the telephone company had spent much money and hundreds of man hours preparing for it. They did not look kindly upon the dry summer; it interfered with their operations.

The telephone company's right-of-way agents were sent out in the early spring to obtain easements. These right-of-way agents were fine fellows. If we cross your front lawn, they told you, we put down a canvas and take up the sod in rolls and put the dirt on the canvas very neatly and when we're done, every particle of dirt goes back in its proper place. Sod too.

The cable-laying itself was done by a plowtrain led by an over-size tractor upon which was mounted a giant share, two smaller caterpillars ahead on either side, pulling. The share on the big tractor ditched out an opening slightly less than a foot wide and about five feet deep. The coaxial cable was reeled out into this ditch and then the ditch was covered over by other cats and dozers. Under ordinary conditions the plowtrain was a marvel of efficiency and speed.

The other side of Forrest City the plowtrain ran into trouble. Twice it became mired for a day at a time, once in a rice field and once in a field of goldfish. And one sweltering day the share on the big tractor broke and that stalled the train for another five days. The most serious delay given the train, however, was the day-to-day obstinacy of the rice-farmers. This was what proved to be the most unfortunate consequence of the telephone company's bringing their plans to fruition that dry summer.

More than once it happened that the plowtrain, in going through a field, lost almost all the field's water. Word of these local disasters spread quickly ahead of the train along its intended route and then, in spite of the fact that easements had long before been obtained by the right-of-way agents, it was not uncommon for the telephone company to be met at a fence by a farmer with a shotgun cradled across his arms.

In some cases these gun-bearing farmers had to have it explained to them many times over that the men from whom they rented the land had already legally granted the company the right to cross over the field and that therefore the train had a legal right in the field. And most of the time, in spite of these repeated explanations, the farmers would not budge out of the way.

Because it is difficult to assess the amount of damage done to a field of rice by the loss of its water in mid-summer, even if that loss is only for a day, the telephone company faced with some reluctance the prospect of a multitude of claims against itself at harvest time. As a result, the plowtrain slowed to what for it was a crawl, taking extreme care of the dikes in each field that it was allowed to enter.

Nevertheless, some farmers remained obstinate, refusing to let the train pass in spite of renewed assurances from the right-of-way agents that all would be well cared for. And so the train was forced to skip from point to point along its route, trenching where it could. One week it would be outside Forrest City, the next on this side of Brinkley, the next on the other side of the Bluff. Finally it was stopped altogether to await developments.

For several weeks the cats and dozers sat in a fallow rice field watching with mechanical indifference the herons in the next field feasting upon goldfish and frogs. The splicers behind the train were almost out of work and the General Manager in the telephone company's area headquarters in Kansas City had begun to hope for rain almost as fervently as the farmers.

When the train came to a halt the only ditching going forward on the Memphis to Little Rock coaxial anywhere was just outside of De Valls Bluff in the timber next to the White River. There it was too thickly wooded, overgrown with scrub, and too uneven for the plowtrain to maneuver, and the ditching had to be let to a private contractor who worked with a dragline. So when the plowtrain was halted and its equipment left in the fallow field, the train's crew was sent to help the private contractor.

Cable had been laid across the White River, on top of the Engineers' mat, and it was the contractor's job to join this White River section with the section paralleling the new highway, which had also been placed. The contractor had to work through the snarl of the old highway as well as the underbrush and the timber and it was slow going.

The crew from the plowtrain helped as much as they could, clearing away underbrush and making themselves generally useful, but their hearts were not in their work. They considered it beneath them since they were all skilled tractor operators. Their foreman had brought one bulldozer to the bottoms and every morning the members of the crew quarreled over the privilege of running this machine; they wished to avoid the ignominy of working dismounted. Keeping the morale of his crew at an efficient level grew to be a burden for the telephone company's foreman.

The private contractor had his trench almost completed after three weeks' work—all but a stretch of about sixty feet, part of which was up and over the swell of ground on which Thomas had built his house. The contractor had worked his dragline without haste and dug a deep and a wide ditch. Deeper and wider than was necessary. He had worked slowly. At his own pace, that is, until the day that the management group from the General Manager's office in Kansas City came to the Bluff to look into the reasons for delay there and everywhere else.

When the group from Kansas City arrived, the private contractor—a citizen of De Valls Bluff—proceeded even more slowly than before, because he wanted no mistake made: He considered himself his own man, and the only operator between Little Rock and Memphis who would risk his equipment in the White River bottoms, even in a dry year.

But the arrival of the management men from the General Manager's office in Kansas City did produce a flurry of activity among the train crew. They wished, naturally enough, to make a good impression upon representatives from the front office. Preceding their accelerated work tempo there was, of course, a great shaking of hands when management met labor the first morning of the visit. Management in the telephone company—as perhaps elsewhere—operates on the theory that they are part of a great team. The team theory holds that the lowliest switchboard operator in the smallest exchange in the country is no less important than is the president of the entire system himself. Management has a saying which is often repeated in its offices to the effect that One Doesn't Meet Finer People Than Those Who Work for the Telephone Company. Since Management seldom meets any telephone people other than those from its offices, Management considers it an important part of any field-trip task to Meet and Make Friends with the Men. Thus, the shaking of hands.

Particularly was this spirit of camaraderie shown by the senior member of the group from Kansas City, Mr. Stanton, a tall, well-built gentleman of around forty-five, head of the area's Personnel department but being groomed for an even more responsible position in the White Plains main offices. Mr. Stanton made a special point of being friendly and cordial to members of the train crew, even going so far as to pitch several spadesful of earth upon one occasion.

Before leaving Kansas City, Mr. Stanton had taken the trouble to have it ascertained for him who, among the train crew, owned stock in the company. At the river site, when the opportunity presented itself, he let it drop, man-to-man, that he also owned a few shares of stock and wasn't this delay a dirty shame. "We're all in the same boat, aren't we," he said. "Have to watch our dividends next year if we're not careful"—this last, with a confidential low-throated chuckle.

The men from Kansas City had made their field trip to determine at first hand the causes of delay in placing the cable. They had talked with the splicer foreman along the route, looked at maps and reports, and were concluding their investigation with a two-day stay at the White River site. By noon of their first day there, the private contractor's dragline had reached the bank of the swell on which Thomas had his cabin.

Thomas had observed the approach of the dragline with interest. He had pulled his chair to a place in front of the old tank at the side of his cabin and he would sit there smoking his pipe and watching in front of and below him the huge claw of the dragline gouging away roots and dirt. He was reminded of his work for the Army Engineers during the Depression.

After lunch of the first day that the group from Kansas City was on the site, the dragline operator began to trench up the bank of the swell upon which Thomas' cabin was situated. By two o'clock he was up the barranca and there he was forced to stop. Thomas was in his chair, quietly smoking, and directly in the path of the dragline. The group from the General Manager's office was standing to one side of the cab of the dragline in conference with the foreman of the train crew. The operator called to them and pointed at Thomas. The senior member of the group, Mr.

Stanton, understood the operator's gesture and clambered up the bank.

Leaning against the cabin was the faded sign from worm-selling days, BUS'S PLASE, and the senior member glanced at it as he smiled and extended his hand. "How are you, Bus?" he said. "My name's Stanton. I work for the telephone company."

Thomas shook the hand and nodded, not rising from his chair in front of the abandoned tank. The dampness of the bottoms had worked upon him so that he looked and moved as if he were older and more decrepit than he actually was.

"Guess you'll have to shove over if we're going through," Mr. Stanton went on in a friendly and ingratiating tone. "Comes pretty close to your shack, I guess." He indicated the path of the ditch. "But we'll have it back-filled in no time." He waited but Thomas made no sign that he had heard.

After a silence of a minute or so, Mr. Stanton bent forward at the waist and said in a louder voice, "I guess you'll have to move, Bus. We don't want that dragline taking a chunk out of you." He laughed and slapped the elderly man on the shoulder.

Thomas looked up at him. He said, "Can't you go 'round?"

The question apparently surprised Stanton because he replied somewhat sharply. He said, "We've got an easement through here. That cable can't go around, the trench has to go through. *Right here.*" He pointed down the center of the enclosure behind Thomas' chair.

Neither spoke for several moments then, and finally Stanton turned and went back down the bank to where the AT&T foreman stood. Two of the train crew had returned from the riverbank where they had been re-piling rip-rap over the strip where the cable had gone into the river. They were perspiring and hot and the foreman was lighting a cigarette for one of them when Stanton came up. He related his conversation with Thomas and the foreman replied, "Well, I guess we shoot the old man and tell God he drowned."

This statement seemed to puzzle Mr. Stanton, so after a moment's further consideration the foreman volunteered that the cabin was on government land and that Thomas was, in fact, only a squatter. After making certain that his foreman knew what he was talking about, Stanton climbed back up the bank and again approached Thomas.

"Listen, Bus," he said, "we've got to go through here. You'll have to move, that's all. We're not going to hurt your cabin, just get out of the way."

But as before he received no answer. Thomas had refilled his pipe and sat smoking, relaxed, and looking levelly ahead at the dragline.

"Did you hear me?" Stanton said. "We're going through. We've been held up long enough as it is."

At this Thomas looked up and said, "If you don't mind, you'll have to go 'round." He seemed now somewhat concerned by the insistence of the man who stood over him.

Stanton turned and looked down at the foreman and the men from the train crew. He no longer tried to conceal his anger. "Couple of you men get up here and move this old buzzard," he said. "And pull out this." He pointed to the old signs which formed the enclosure that had been used for worms.

The private contractor shut off his dragline's engine and climbed down from the cab to smoke a cigarette and stretch while he waited for Thomas to move. When the foreman and the two men from the train crew started up the bank, he followed them. The other representatives from the General Manager's office in Kansas City stayed below. They were studying a chart of the White River.

When the foreman and the two crew members and the operator had gathered around Thomas, Stanton repeated his instructions. There was then a brief period of uneasy silence because the two men from the train crew did not seem to comprehend their instructions. At last their foreman stepped forward. He grabbed Thomas by the arm. Thomas stood up slowly then, but he did not move from in front of his chair. It was clear that any man there could have moved him easily. Still, he stood there, not aggressively, but seemingly worried now.

Stanton attempted to reason with him once more, but when he received no reply he gave up and motioned to the foreman. It was then that the dragline operator intervened. The dragline operator spoke quite slowly but he kept his eyes fixed upon Stanton's face as he spoke. He said that it was almost three o'clock. He reminded Stanton that in an hour they would be quitting for the day, anyhow, and he said they might as well quit now. He said that living alone for so long had not been good for the old man, and that in the morning, if they let him alone for now, he would probably be ready to move of his own accord. He said he did not believe in man-handling the elderly; it didn't look right. He suggested that they drop it for the time being, go into town, and give it a fresh start in the morning.

Mr. Stanton attempted to interrupt the dragline operator several times, and he grumbled at the suggestion that they go into town before quitting time, but in the end he gave in. Not, however, before vowing to bring the sheriff with them in the morning.

Thomas remained standing where he was until they were all out of sight. Then he went into the cabin and returned carrying his mattock, moving as if he were very weary.

When the train crew and the dragline operator and the group from Kansas City and the Sheriff arrived at the site of operations the next morning, Thomas was gone. The sheriff made a short search but could not find him.

Around the enclosure next to his cabin, on the side opposite the cabin, they found a newly dug trench, about two feet deep. It started where the dragline operator had stopped his ditching the day before, skirted at right angles the rusted metal signs which formed the front of the enclosure, paralleled the side of the old tank, made another right angle turn at the rear of the tank, and picked up the original path of the ditch with another right angle.

The discovery of this trench was greeted with laughter. Then Stanton told the foreman to get going before the old man showed up again. The train crew pulled up the rusted metal sheets of the tank and the dragline operator began his day's work. In an hour he had trenched across the swell of ground upon which the cabin stood.

The Little Rock to Memphis cable was completed in time to handle part of the heavy Christmas traffic that year. But today—

many years later—there are men of the telephone company who still speak of the difficulties they encountered that dry summer.

Mr. Stanton did get the more responsible position in White Plains, where he often related some of the many exasperating incidents which took place during the laying of the Little Rock-to-Memphis. He usually brought in, somewhere, the story of the detour ditch dug by the squatter. As if, as he said many times, you can bend coaxial cable at right angles.

Sometimes he injected still more humor into his narrative by quoting, drawl and all as best he could, the crew member who said of the ditch that if a snake were to urinate in it he would float away.

But Mr. Stanton's many new responsibilities did not often leave him time for such tales.

In De Valls Bluff they still talk of the dry summer. And still brag about the fishing on the White River, although the year after the dry summer an eight foot, one-hundred-and-ninety-pound gar was caught at Stuttgart. This gar still holds the record for size, and Stuttgart is not even on the White River.

Sometimes in the Bluff, when the dry summer is brought up, someone will mention the cable-laying that year. Whenever this is touched upon the talk comes finally to the digging up of the woman's body next to Thomas' cabin. One who spoke to someone who was there has it for a fact that the claw sheared her in two just at the chest. They agree in the Bluff that it was a terrible thing.

But since Thomas hasn't been seen by residents of the Bluff since the afternoon of the day he stalled the dragline, indignation is usually short-lived. To change the subject there is always the latest fishing innovation. Some of the natives go out at night now with a flashlight fastened to their boat. The goggle-eyes, in jumping at the light, flop right into the boat.

Henry Bromell is twenty-five and a graduate of Amherst College. He is presently living in Greece where he is at work on a novel.

PHOTOGRAPHS

1

The island was attached to the mainland by a long stretch of sand. Slowly it was civilized, first by Indians, who came to fish in the summers, and then by white men, who built mansions among the trees and brought their families out from the city. The women, planting flowers, discovered arrowheads. The reeds were cleared until each house had a beach. Yachts, moored offshore, revolved on their anchor lines, brass fittings winking in the sunlight. A tomahawk was found in the graveyard. Elizabeth, Matthew Duy's oldest daughter, married Quentin, Kenneth Richardson's oldest son, and a new house was built on the tip of the island, facing south. Because the house was exposed to the wind, it was very cold in the winter. Elizabeth planted roses and hung wicker bird-cages from the trees. Quentin raised golden retrievers and won trophies, hunted duck, quail, and pheasant. By the time Samuel was born, the civilizing was over. Twenty-four mansions lined the single road that ran down the middle of the island. Men hired from the village nearby kept the oak trees and apple trees and elms and evergreens pruned, the lawns and hedges trimmed, the leaves raked, the windows polished. Gardeners continued to find arrowheads in the soil, some of which they kept, some of which they turned over to their employers. Samuel, Quentin and Eliza-beth's only son, explored the island. He built model boats, air-planes, and cars, followed the pheasants and squirrels back and forth across the lawn, and listened to "Captain Midnight" on the radio. The stretch of sand connecting the island to the mainland became a public beach. The nearby village became a resort. But in the autumn, after the vacationers had left and before the snow had fallen, the island looked much the way it had when the Indians first came to fish. The sand was clean and white, the water sparkled like a handful of gold coins, and the houses were very quiet behind the trees, as if no one lived in them. Sitting outside one afternoon, watching a squirrel chase a walnut, Samuel smelled the smoke of the next-door neighbor's burning leaves and knew that someday he would have to go. The smoke, the small white cloud rising through the trees, seemed a signal. His mother was on the terrace, watering flowers. Out on the water a single sailboat slid through the sunlight.

II

There were two hurricanes—the first in 1938, when Samuel was in high school, the second in 1944, when Samuel was home from college for Christmas vacation. It was as he and his father were standing at the window, watching the wind tear and claw at the old oak trees outside, that Samuel took out his pipe and lit it. He heard his mother, sitting on the couch behind them, gasp. His father simply turned, stared for a moment, and then calmly looked back out the window, smiling.

III

Samuel's son, Scobie, two years old, watched his grandmother crochet an afghan of reds and greens. Her small hands plucked and soothed the yarn. She showed him her collection of spoons and a three-legged squirrel. Her rings, green, flashed as she stood by the window, pointing: "There, see him?" Scobie discovered the island—at first alone, then with his little brother, Matthew. His grandfather swallowed Oreos with one hand and pulled them out of his ear with the other hand. When Scobie's family moved to Greece, his grandmother came to visit, adding the Eiffel Tower

and the Parthenon to her collection of spoons. His grandfather
would not come, because the airplane hurt his ears. One morning
Scobie told his grandmother, "Fish is my hatest." She never forgot, reminding him even as he grew older that fish was his hatest.
He called her Nana, his grandfather Pa.

IV

At one time there were men on the lawns and women in hats.
Curtains fluttered as the breeze, smelling of salt and mowed grass,
came in through the windows overlooking the sea. Nana kept the
arrowheads she found in a little box on her bureau. Pa had an
owl stuffed in the city; it hung, green and blazing, on the wall of
his den. The island moved, shifted. Some of the beaches grew
longer, some shrank. Here and there the reeds reappeared. When
the entire family gathered for holidays, Nana would say, "It's
just like a dream. I can't believe it's happening." The men played
golf and the women croquet. A fact was mentioned, calmly, between strokes: "We found this country, built her up from nothing,
made her what she is today. Certain unnamed peoples wish to
destroy everything we have labored to create and it is our responsibility to stop them." Scobie imagined his father, forty-five
years old and a diplomat, hesitating halfway across an Egyptian
courtyard, reminded of something by the cooing doves and trickling fountain. "All the birds have gone for the winter," Nana
would write. "But they'll be back in the spring."

The island shifted another inch, stretching the sand. Scobie remembered the summer he discovered an arrowhead, the summer
he and Matthew went to the circus. There was a third hurricane,
in the autumn of 1960, which destroyed one of the oaks and covered the beach with oil.

V

The view from the front window was cluttered with boats. The
bay was dredged, and refuse poured in until the water turned
brown and the beaches gray. In the attic Scobie found a Civil War

sword, a photograph album, and a pair of lace-up shoes. One summer, he attended débutante parties in the mansions along the tree-lined road, dressed in a suit Nana purchased for the occasion. She told him, "You look so much like your father," and "You can be proud to be a Richardson."

VI

In the photograph album, Nana was an eighteen-year-old bride, with a small, delicate chin and defiant eyes. She sat on a beach, a large sun hat at her side, smiling into the camera. She was squinting against the sun, her hand raised to shade her eyes. The gesture gave her a startled look, as if she had just seen something unexpected off to the left of the photographer. On the next page, Pa was standing in a field with Scobie's father. They were both dressed in Abercrombie trenchcoats and business hats. Pa cradled a shotgun in his arms. Looking closely, Scobie saw that his grandfather was on the verge of laughing aloud, and that, in the distance, golden retrievers paced impatiently. It looked cold—a gray day in late autumn.

VII

Scobie came home from a Christmas party one night and found Pa on a stool before the fireplace, burning a boxful of letters and photographs. The paper wavered for a second on the uppermost log, then suddenly caught and curled at the edges, an ashy blackness slowly obliterating the faces and addresses.

VIII

In the spring of his junior year in college, Scobie went to visit his grandparents. They were waiting for him at the station. He watched from the upper level as they approached—Pa edging through the crowd like a boxer, shoulders tucked, feet shuffling, and Nana following at his side, tugging his sleeve, waving, point-

ing, waving again. The loudspeaker called "Philadelphia" and a
time, and then she was there, squinting, waving, patting her hair,
her dress, her hair, reaching up and pulling him down to her
cheek—a touch and smell so familiar he quickly shook hands with
his grandfather.

Outside, as they waited for Pa to return with the car, Nana
tugged at the hair on his shoulders and asked, "Don't you want
to get this cut?"

A taxi blared by. "Not particularly," he said.

She tightened her mouth, a quick, pouting lift of the lips. "For
me?" Fine silver bracelets rattled on her wrists.

Scobie looked off toward the parking lot. An airplane flew overhead, red and blue tail-lights blinking in the dark.

IX

Pa drove the silver-blue Chevrolet cautiously, in the right lane,
eyes narrowed by the oncoming headlights. Following the curve of
the coast, they approached the island. The car hit the bump that
had been at the beginning of the road for as long as Scobie could
remember. The headlights swung across the trees, picking out the
mailboxes and name-plaques. Gravel crunched as they pulled up
the driveway. Scobie stepped out into the sound of crickets and
pine branches. Nana climbed out behind him. "Well," she said.
"Here we are. Home." The old Greek cowbell swayed and rattled
as Pa opened the front door. The hallway smelled of lavender
and dust. In the kitchen, the refrigerator clicked. Squirrels ran
across the roof.

When Scobie was in bed, Nana came into his room, leaned forward once again, down toward his face in the darkness, and whispered, "Please, cut your hair. Tomorrow. For me."

X

The gravel driveway linking the house to the rest of the island
twisted in small, sectioned curves toward the mailboxes. The oaks

and evergreens and heavy apple trees uncurled in the bright
morning air. The leaves were wet and spongy, hissing gently as
they dried. Behind Nana and Pa's house was an older house, one
of the first built on the island. Now it was empty, but not too long
ago two aunts had lived there, two laughing ladies who would sit
at a table on the lawn, eyes shaded with sun hats, and knead wet
clay into ashtrays and cups. The mailboxes at the end of the driveway always contained more newspapers and advertisements and
bills than letters. In the hallway, next to the potted palm, there
was a mother-of-pearl cigarette box from Jerusalem. Looking up
through the complex net of branches toward the sky, Scobie could
see two knots of rope on the largest oak tree—all that remained
of the swing Pa had given him ten years earlier.

XI

Another photograph showed Nana and Pa standing together on
the deck of their yacht. They were holding hands, smiling. The
yacht was moored in front of their beach. Over their shoulders
Scobie could see the house, the large front window through which,
looking up, he now saw his grandfather walking across the lawn
with an armful of dead branches.

XII

At the end of the lawn was a tool shed—a damp, dark room that
reeked of kerosene and wet dogs. Two lawnmowers filled the
floor. Rakes and shovels hung from the walls. In the corner near
the door was a summer life preserver, a plastic, deflated horse.
Behind the croquet set was an old black flipper. No dogs slipped
through the hatch that led to the kennel. An airplane passed low
overhead, the drone slowly fading into the distance. Below the
tool shed, on the beach, was a well that squirted fresh water into
the reeds, and the skeleton of a duck boat buried in the sand. A
single buoy bounced on the waves. Near the only boulder on the
beach, hidden beneath the sand, was the fort Scobie and Matthew

had built as boys—six fist-size stones neatly lined in a double row.

XIII

In the kitchen, Nana would point to the sink and say, "Don't you think the way the light comes in there should be a painting?"

"A what?" Pa would ask.

"Painting."

"It's just a sink, that's all."

"Oh, but dear, look at the light. It's so beautiful this time of day."

Later, after Pa had left, she would say to Scobie or Matthew or her son, Samuel, "You have to try and understand him. He doesn't mean what he says."

Through conversation Scobie learned that she had taught him how to walk and that once, in the twenties, she had danced with a prince in the Bahamas. But when he asked her why she didn't paint anymore, she just shook her head and sighed. "You're right. I should. But I just can't sit still long enough." Or she said, "I don't have the materials anymore. I gave them to your father."

XIV

The island never had a newspaper of its own, but the nearby-village paper occasionally carried articles on the comings and goings of its neighbors. In a copy of Nana's Bible Scobie found a clipping that showed his entire family standing on a dock. The side of a huge ocean liner rose behind them. Nana wore a skirt that reached way below her knees and a wide hat with a veil. Scobie and Matthew were looking at each other, not the camera. Their father had his hands on their shoulders. Pa looked very proud.

XV

A week after Scobie graduated from college and two days before he left for a summer in Europe, Nana touched his knee and said, "It's so nice to have you home."

"What are you going to do now that you've graduated?" Pa asked.

"I don't know."

"What are you going to live on? Air?"

"I'll be all right."

"More potatoes, dear?" she interrupted.

"No thanks. Pa, what happened to your boat?"

"Stolen."

"Oh, I'm sorry."

"Why would anyone do a thing like that?" Nana sighed.

"Money," Pa said. "Same reason they do anything."

"I just think it's so *mean* for someone to do a thing like that," she said. "What plate do you have, dear?"

Scobie looked. "The train."

"Your favorite."

"Yes."

"How you loved that when you were a little boy."

Later, she came to the bedroom and stood in the doorway, plucking her sweater, peering. "You should go to bed, dear."

"Yes."

She moved closer. "Are you writing?"

"Yes."

"What?"

"A letter."

"Oh."

She turned down the bed, smoothed the sheets. "Don't forget," she whispered. "He doesn't mean what he says."

"That's all right."

"You'll get your hair cut? Tomorrow?"

"Sure."

"Good night, dear."

"Good night."

Scobie undressed, climbed into bed, and turned off the light. He was in the darkness, a part of the darkness, for a long time. He heard his grandfather shuffle up the stairs, snapping a light switch at the far end of the hallway. Pipes rattled and cleared themselves in some lower region of the house.

XVI

She died in the middle of the night, suddenly, without warning. She simply stopped breathing. Pa crumpled too, not dead but tired. She was burned. She wished her ashes to be spread across the water. Scobie and Matthew sat beside the bedroom window with their father and grandfather, watching snow cover the apple tree. A squirrel high-stepped through the snow. The refrigerator clicked in the kitchen.

"In the twenties, she was a flapper," Scobie said.

"No," his father said. "She just dressed like one."

It was very cold in the bedroom, so they built a fire in the fireplace and boiled water for tea.

"I knew she'd died," Scobie said. "I felt it."

Pa turned the pages of *National Geographic* and cleared his throat.

They had dinner downstairs with the rest of the family, aunts and cousins taking her place in the kitchen.

Scobie asked his father, "Do you think it's possible that I could have known?"

His father shrugged. "Yes, I think it's possible," he said.

Matthew sat on the bed, staring into the fire. Their father found an unfinished airplane model in the closet.

The next morning, they ate a big breakfast—hot cereal and bacon and eggs and coffee. Then Scobie and Matthew and their father went down to the beach and climbed into the rowboat.

"We have to believe in something," their father said. He stood at the bow. The wind lifted his hair, the collar of his coat. Scobie and Matthew looked across the bay at the houses. Their father tipped the urn over the water. It was so cold he was breathing clouds.

Shirley Sikes was born in Manhattan, Kansas, and graduated from Kansas State University there. She now lives in Leonardville, Kansas. Miss Sikes has published stories in *Denver Quarterly, Transatlantic Review, Four Quarters, Literary Review, Kansas Quarterly* and other magazines. She is at work on several novels, one of which deals with the family in the following story.

THE DEATH OF COUSIN STANLEY

Before my second cousin Stanley finally died from a disease of the nerves, he came home to my grandmother's and my great Aunt Edwina's to spend his last days. At the time I was only a girl of fifteen, and it did not seem strange to me that he should leave his wife (whom I remember as a fat, complaining woman, a shrew, who nevertheless made me feel very sorry for her) and return to the security, the tightly knit confines of the "sisters' home," as it was spoken of by the townspeople. Now that I look back on it, I can see there was something peculiar in the strands of affection my mother's family sent forth; none of them (there were originally two other great aunts who lived with my grandmother, pale creatures I vaguely remember sitting in lawn chairs in the summertime, sipping pink lemonade my grandmother was forever concocting), not even my mother, who returned to the fold, along with me, following the death of my father, ever seemed to become quite independent from the group. Some of them made attempts; my cousin got married (I remember my mother telling of the grim face my grandmother presented at both her and Cousin Stanley's weddings), and one of the family narratives, rendered as usual, by my grandmother, concerned the feeble attempt of my great Aunt Rachel to go out into the world and make a name for

herself. Evidently Aunt Rachel hoped to study corsetry, an ambition I am at a loss to understand, unless it was the only one she
could think of, but she soon returned, "broken by the world," as
my grandmother, in sepulchral tones, described it, adding she was
a "repentant prodigal." Aunt Rachel also returned with my cousin
Stanley, a baby she purported to have adopted in California—the
most wicked state in the union according to my grandmother—this
tale being accepted, at least on the surface, by the townspeople,
though Stanley bore a remarkable resemblance to my great Aunt
Rachel. Grandmother, I gather, never averse to sticking her neck
out, and no doubt possessed of a fierce notion that whatever
she set her mind to, she could succeed in cramming down the
throats of others, was given to remarking on the resemblance and
to saying they tried to match the babies to those who adopted
them and that she thought they had done a particularly good job
with Aunt Rachel. Whatever Cousin Stanley's origins, he was a
member of the family, hence fell under its influence, because it
was the same with all of them: sooner or later the family ties
strengthened and they all came back.

I think now that my Cousin Stanley, like my mother, married
from pure defiance, the state of matrimony being repugnant to
my grandmother—as, indeed, most close relationships were, not-
withstanding the fact she had been married herself and had borne
a child. As soon as she had completed what she considered, at
that time, a "woman's duty" to procreate, she dispassionately divorced her husband, an action which would have caused consider-
able scandal in those days but for the inventiveness of my grandmother, who told everyone her husband had died and wore
mourning clothes for months. This secret was so carefully guarded
that it was not until I was ready for college that I discovered the
truth about my grandfather: that he had not died, possibly even
then was living, and the idea of his suddenly coming back upon
the scene and claiming the affections of my grandmother offered
me many moments of romantic fantasies. That my grandmother
had persuaded her husband simply to disappear and offered his
decease as an explanation to the world, was only one of many
examples of her power over people. It also illustrates a **very odd**

family trait, one which was weakened in my mother and Cousin Stanley, but nonetheless there: a complete disregard for reality. If my grandmother did not want to believe something, she simply ignored it, refusing to admit its existence. Cousin Stanley must have wanted to die while under her influence.

When he came, there was a great deal of bustle, which was typical of my mother and the sisters, who always seemed to be carrying some secret between them and hence had to speak in whispers and half sentences, my memories of entering a room where the conversation suddenly lurched to a halt being particularly acute. All the preparations for his stay, which was never to be thought of as final, were undertaken in an attitude of mystery and disguise, with a sort of anxious complicity, as though the sisters had made some awful pact with one of the dark powers. The family dealt in euphemies; not once did either of the sisters or my mother hint to me that my cousin was fatally ill, that the disease was rare and incurable, progressively worsening. The only way I grasped it was from the manner in which they looked at him, full of pity and love, and the way they spoke of him, almost as a third person already nonexistent.

Great Aunt Edwina, tall and slender, ethereal, dressing always in pale print frocks that rustled through the darkness of the home as though she belonged to the spirit world, once absentmindedly confessed to me that he was very ill. "He has something, some *sick*ness, you know," and she winked, an habitual gesture which seemed anachronistic, relating her to a reality to which she did not seem to belong. "He's most ill." No sooner had she told me this than she put her fingers to her lips in a gesture of fright and rolled her eyes in the direction of my grandmother's room, as much as to say, "Don't tell her I told you, Clarissa," though she did not speak. She merely rustled away from me, faded from sight down the corridor and disappeared into the kitchen, where she spent most of her time preparing casseroles, chiffon pies, for all of us. Her escape was typical: she had almost grasped the situation for a moment, then, acquiescing in the attitude of my family, had denied it and darted away. If I had asked her again about my cousin, I am sure she would have blandly denied telling me anything and would have said it was owing to my childish imagination.

Whether it was due to the same kind of attitude in my cousin, as I feel it was, he seemed very cheerful when he came, though I remember how gaunt he was and what a change this was from my former image of him, when I was about eight. Then he had been husky and tanned; his manner had been rough and unpolished and he used to frighten me. This last time he seemed much quieter, more self-contained, as though he had made some kind of peace with himself, had become objective from a grander point of view. At the same time, he had a rather abstracted, puzzled air, as if he could not now comprehend ordinary life.

My Grandmother Stella promptly took the matter of my cousin's illness firmly in hand; when she heard he was ill (a letter from his wife informed her), she packed her bags, planted herself on the first bus that went to Stanley's hometown, and returned with Stanley in tow several days later, entrenching him in her home, over the protests of his wife, as I later learned. Though I was not consulted of course, I gathered from the unopened letters postmarked from Stanley's home, written in a coarse, sprawling script, and from the phone calls during which my grandmother firmly and unequivocally pushed the receiver down on the strident voice emanating from the other end of the wire, that the sisters and the wife were not in agreement as to the disposition of my Cousin Stanley. It was definitely a strategical error on the part of Mollie, Stanley's wife, to have allowed him to go. Though it seemed queer to me that Stanley made no protests, did not try to speak to Mollie, I think it was again part of the unrealistic outlook of the family. He no doubt foolishly hoped it would all work out if he simply ignored it.

However much Stanley depended on my grandmother, it was my mother whom he most admired. Something of her delicacy, of her kind nature, must have appealed to him, and when he was the sickest (I remember nights when I heard voices in the hall and the door to my cousin's room opening and closing, could hear him moaning, for at times he was in pain), he wanted her by him and would smile when he saw she was there. I remember my grandmother saying, in her stentorian, irrevocable tones, that if it had not been for my mother's devotion to Stanley when he first came, he would not have lasted as long as he did. She also added—this, while not looking at me, as she did when she said things she apparently hoped I would ignore, another quirk of duplicity in her character in which she said a thing while refusing to admit its implications, that "that woman," an oblique reference to Mollie, "would have killed him." She had, of course, no basis for this remark; like everything else she did, it suited her to make it. It was the last statement she ever did make about Mollie, and, as my grandfather had before her, Mollie simply ceased to exist. It is with a kind of sympathetic horror now that I realize how frustrating it must have been to Mollie to have been so completely denied existence. Perhaps the philosopher was right when he proposed we exist only insofar as we are perceived and recognized by others, though I think I would have amended this then to read only insofar as my grandmother perceived us.

I could never understand at the time my cousin came why he would want to live with the sisters. To me, their home was dark and forbidding, bare of any of the frivolities I like, which my mother liked too, though she was cowed when she was with them and did not express herself. It seemed to propose the maxim that harshness was godliness, for my grandmother was religious (at least, in a way she was—she had made God in her image, rather than vice versa, and she invoked His blessings and curses on the rest of us without hesitation). Aunt Edwina struggled toward faith, but her heart and mind simply did not seem to be in it, she merely bent her will in the direction of the rest of the family. Some of my other great aunts must also have been religious because I remember hearing my mother say her Aunt Rhoda had once professed to have "visions." I remember too that this had caused my grandmother no little irritation. She felt that, as the head of the family, God should have revealed Himself to her, and, as the story goes, she absolutely forbade Rhoda to have any more visions. Whether her injunction put an end to the heavenly visits or not, I cannot say.

I wonder now if the atmosphere of the sisters' home was nearly

as oppressive as I then imagined it. I was guilty of exaggeration
and misunderstanding of their attitudes, and I am sure I took it all
much too seriously, another family trait which I seem to have inherited. But, like everything else in our family, it was a mystery
into which I had to be initiated in order to understand. Sometimes
I think that if someone had just burst out laughing when we were
all bustling about, the illusion of our solidarity would have been
broken, and we might all have benefited. But our family traits
were like a current, and, once sucked in, we hardly possessed the
objectivity to see ourselves as we really were.

The sisters' home was large. It stood on a sloping hill at the
end of town, overlooking the whole of the city, and its aspect to
one approaching from the depths was one of forbearing contempt.
Like the sisters, it seemed to have withdrawn from reality, and,
with superior complacency, regarded the world with aloofness. It
was once the residence of the wealthiest man in the town, a veri-
table Scrooge, so I am told, whose life was ended by a pistol shot
through an open window one summer evening as he was dining in
the large, dark, dining room. To make the story even more exciting to me, it was said he had fallen over the table, placing a
bright red spot on the white linen tablecloth, a pool of blood which
then sank through to the wood of the table and was witnessed to
reappear on the anniversary of the shooting. Though I scrutinized
the table for years, I never saw the spot. But the story gave the old
mansion a sinister reputation, and, when I first moved in, I
brought all my friends to see it, elaborating on the violent thing
that had taken place there.

Inside, however, the house did not seem so expansive, for the
furniture was oversized and the decoration heavy and massive,
with great potted plants jutting ominously out from dark corners,
so that the effect was one of a crowded home. It was austere with
Victorian walnut paneling and sudden, angular shapes of dark furniture. Pillows were disdained, and the visitor rested uneasily
against the harsh contours of the chairs and sofa. Religious pictures—Daniel in the lion's den and Moses procuring the Ten
Commandments—stared back from the walls, their brown sepia
faded from the years but their messages intact, while the lamps

hideously shaded with tassels and fringes, the only concession to frills, vainly struggled to throw arcs of light against the high, tan ceilings. Even with all the lamps burning, there were inaccessible corners and angles where blackness sank like a weight, where the dense thickets of plants sprouted long, entangling foliage, suggesting a kind of evil absorbency. After evening dinner, while my grandmother and great Aunt Edwina stood Cousin Stanley and my mother at auction bridge (a game they played incessantly as long as Stanley was able), I would explore these corners until finally, tremendously bored, I would settle in one of the Victorian rockers and pretend to absorb myself with the stereoptic, intently peering at the Grecian temples and Roman aqueducts that made up my grandmother's collection of pictures. Devoting myself to their perusal with an intensity I did not feel, I would hear, in the background, the furious voice of my grandmother berating Aunt Edwina for a wrong play she had made, her voice the only interruption in the otherwise constant slap, slap of the cards and the sudden rushing sound of their being shuffled together. Sometimes there would be a shout of glee, a sign that my grandmother had trumped someone's ace, for, outside of managing everything and everybody, that was the thing she liked to do best. As I looked at the pictures, I would sometimes come across a faded photo of my dead great aunts, occasionally pictured alone, or with Aunt Edwina and my grandmother. There was Aunt Rachel, small and dark, whose eyes seemed to suggest some repressed vitality, which came out I guess, only once, when she endeavored to be a saleswoman and came home instead with Stanley; Aunt Rhoda of the heavenly visions; Aunt Edwina, posed between these two in another frilly dress, which seemed to be blowing in a faint breeze, for it clung to her slightly, her being seeming porous so that you imagined her mind as hollow corridors down which shadowy ideas stalked; and, last, there was Grandmother Stella in a high-necked dark dress, looking sullenly and self-consciously into the camera. A barely perceptible line of sadness showed around my grandmother's mouth, as though the responsibilities she bore were almost too heavy for her to bear, a look I think I can compare, without being unduly sacrilegious, to Christ's, as though they were both weary of all the sins and cares of the world and would have liked to tell their troubles to someone else for a change. An indefinable loneliness stared back out of that tight face, and, I think now, of all of them to be sorry for, surely my grandmother deserved the most pity.

All the sisters looked strange to me then as I studied them through the lenses of the stereoptic; they were younger, with only the hint of future philosophies revealed in their faces, and, as is usual with children, I could not really imagine them youthful since my images of them were always of them when they were older. There was a single picture of Stanley—with his arm around a buxom young woman I did not know, who had once been, I discovered when I finally asked Grandmother Stella about her (my grandmother being the curator of family history also) a beau of Stanley's, a woman of whom the sisters had sternly and unequivocally disapproved. "She was too pretty," my grandmother told me, as though that were the deadliest of sins. "Stanley was a little wild in those days," she added, not looking at me again. "You know men. They have to get it out of their system." She did not tell me what it was they had to get out, nor did she allude again to it or to his later marriage to Mollie, so that the explanation left me with the feeling for a time that there was something faintly unsavory about my Cousin Stanley's past.

It was obvious from the beginning that the family was happy to have Stanley back in the fold again. Grandmother and Aunt Edwina seemed to compete with each other for his attention, though I did not then recognize it as competition—they only appeared strangely silly to me when they raced to straighten his pillow if he leaned forward in the rocker in which he usually sat or when they outdid themselves trying to be amusing. Our diet for Sunday dinner was changed too. Always Aunt Edwina had prepared fried chicken, and it was a meal to which I looked forward all week. When Cousin Stanley came, Sunday dinner suddenly became composed of roast, mashed potatoes and gravy, and when I furiously inquired as to the change of menu, Aunt Edwina met my protests with a martyr's smile. "Cousin Stanley does not like fried chicken," she told me. I thought I could never forgive him for that.

It was not long after Cousin Stanley came that my aunts hit upon the idea of a faith healer, having seen a surreptitious ad in the paper. The doctor's prognosis for Stanley was, of course, hopeless, and, in typical family tradition, all of them refused to face it. I don't know if Stanley was actually aware of the futility of his condition, if, in the atmosphere of unrealistic outlooks he felt secure, but he did not seem averse to the idea of a religious healer, and, in due time, the healer came, surrounded with all the pomp and mystery with which affairs took place in my grandmother's home. I wonder now how much faith the family really placed in miraculous healing; was it a kind of wishful thinking on their part, another example of their inherent euphemy? It seemed to me even then a kind of superstitious rite, like the person who thinks he can change reality by taking thought, though even the Bible professes this foolish.

The family claimed faith, but I think now it was only because of an inherited tendency toward positive feelings; severe doubts may have lurked beneath their stolid exteriors, as, for example, when my mother questioned me about my beliefs in an afterlife. She was quite serious, and the fact that she was interested in my judgment, that of a child, made me think she was unsure. I know she wanted me to say yes, that I did believe in an afterlife, but I had too much of the sturdy logic of my father to place my faith in a resurrection. Besides, I was young, and it did not matter to me. I told her I did not.

It worried her; she and Grandmother and Aunt Edwina had a picture of heaven in which the whole family would be united, Grandmother Stella sorting out our relatives at the Pearly Gates was a part of it I'm sure, but, true Christians, they did not believe one got there by denying the Son of God. I did not develop for her my beliefs on the matter. It had always seemed to me that Christ, who told His followers to turn the other cheek, to love those who persecuted them, could not reverse His maxim and turn His back on those who did not believe in Him. How could He, a God, expect his weaker fellow men to adhere to a belief to which He Himself did not subscribe? And could the Son of God really reject a human being who, though believing in no reward, still tried to live a worthy life? I did not think He could, but even if He existed, I had ignored Him so long that I would have thought it ungracious to ask Him for anything.

So I was of no help in the prayer sessions which were led for my Cousin Stanley. The faith healer, much to my surprise, was a woman; somehow I had never thought of women preaching and following the religious life—nuns, yes, but ministers? She was short, fat, had straggly hair and false teeth. When she spoke, her dentures sometimes rattled so much that the effect, under less trying conditions, would have been ludicrous. She wore an attitude of intense forbearance and leaned forward slightly, as though bent by a burden as heavy as Christ's. She made all of us gather in the dark living room, Stanley in a chair in the corner and my grandmother and Aunt Edwina and Mother surrounding him, while I was placed a little to one side as though she sensed an unbeliever in me and separated my negative influence from the others. Then she called upon God to throw out Stanley's sin in a voice so wrathful and full of vengeance that I felt sorry for Stanley and was immensely glad that it was not I who was receiving treatment. I believe I expected to see some malignant Devil twine himself out of Stanley's body and throw himself at the healer's feet, beseeching mercy. At any rate, the healer told Stanley, "As a man thinketh, so is he. Rejoice, believe in Him, and you will be saved." I looked once at the family; Aunt Edwina and my mother were a little shocked by the procedure, I think, but Grandmother had a look of divine rapture on her face, as though the theatrics of the healer were worthy of her admiration and as if even she could not have done better. Then the healer placed her hand on my Cousin Stanley's spine (for the trouble proceeded from there), traveling up and down quickly as if zipping health in. "The first treatment has been successful," she said.

All this had the effect of making me a temporarily firm, if tardy believer. Stanley actually seemed to feel better (he did not complain, so I don't know to what extent the nervous ailment now caused him pain), and for awhile it looked as if the treatment *had* been successful. My mother began to cheer up, Grandmother and Aunt Edwina cheered up, and the house once again took on its customary atmosphere of blank disregard for all that was distasteful in life. It seems to me now that the family had made a circle of security against hardships; no wonder they clung together, for, united, they drew strength from each other, could place an unquestioning front of complacency against a harsh world. In any other atmosphere, the ridiculous performance of the faith healer, the blandishments, the false hopes would have seemed unnatural; there, the very furniture—the heavy drapes, the carpet, even the plants, seemed to soak up the unrealistic outlook, so that it was expelled constantly into the very air. I had the impression even then that a drought of wind, a flinging aside of the massive figured drapes would have resulted in a collapsing of the house, that it would cave in, as though the termites of reality were not to be denied and had steadily and irrevocably eaten away the timbers of the building.

As long as Stanley was alive, the family remained the same.

In the afternoons, my Cousin Stanley liked to sit in his rocker by the bay window in the living room (he was now unable to walk), and look out at the passersby. Sometimes when it was nice, Aunt Edwina would pin the curtains back so that he could see better, but she never made an effort to open the sash. I used to wonder what he could possibly find to amuse himself for hours on end, for, as I read a book or went once again through the faded pictures of the stereoptic, I would surreptitiously peek at him, studying his gaunt profile as it stayed immobile in an attitude of concentration. His was a craggy kind of face, rough and with a large, beaked nose, and dark tufts of eyebrows almost pulled together above his face so that the effect of his head on top of his thin body was out-of-proportion and slightly foolish. Yet for all this there was a feminine look about his face, perhaps in the eyes, brooding and deep, but with the same suggestion of vitality as Aunt Rachel's eyes had held, in photos of her.

He would sit, silently smoking, and I would stare as his long, bony fingers snubbed out one cigarette, reached for another in his shirt pocket, tapped it briefly on the rocker arm, then placed it in his mouth, rolling it around momentarily. The other hand would cup up with a match and there would be the brief, acrid odor of sulphur, then smoke would ooze out his nostrils. He would sigh and I would watch, fascinated, as his cheeks sucked in and then smoke was expelled. The whole procedure seemed imbued with some kind of dignity, though whether it was because I knew he would die and hence attributed romantic feelings to this ritual, I can't say. Sometimes he would turn and look at me, smiling, and then I would become suddenly embarrassed, as though I had pried into the inner recesses of his being. Death had not much reality to me, for I did not deny it as the sisters did, and the very act of denying often makes a fetish of the thing denied. I was curious, ashamed of my curiosity, yet I felt vaguely he wanted me to reassure him, to make some contact with him, as though it is only identification which keeps the puny human being able to bear his mortality. I did not know how to do this, so, for the first time I realized the essential loneliness of all of us, the irrefutable fact that in the great acts of life each of us is alone. Not even the family euphemy could dispel that.

Only once did Cousin Stanley ask about his wife. "Where's Mollie?" he asked Aunt Edwina at the dinner table one night, as though he had just remembered she existed.

Grandmother and Edwina exchanged glances. My mother seemed pained, as though she did not approve of their shutting Mollie out, but Grandmother drew herself up in hauteur and prepared to explain. To my surprise, Aunt Edwina interrupted what would ordinarily have been Grandmother Stella's speech, and, with an unprecedented insubordination, began in her abstracted way, "We thought it best she not be with you, Stanley . . . ," her voice suddenly subsiding into silence.

My cousin absorbed this for a moment, then seemed almost imperceptibly to shrug. "I hope she's all right," he said finally.

I wondered later if he would have preferred her boorishness, her basic animality, to the cool dignity of the family.

Not long after this, Stanley suffered a relapse. The sisters took turns taking care of him, as did my mother, and all night long his door was opening, shutting, sounds of discomfort coming forth, soft voices seeping into the coolness of the corridors. His voice, affected by the disease, sounded sluggish and slurring, yet it was like a shaft of sunlight in the dark corners of the house; it was not to be denied. It *was*.

The strain of sitting up nights with Stanley gradually began to tell and my mother looked tired and worried. Even Aunt Edwina lost her usual vacant cheerfulness and it was only through her sadness that I realized Stanley was nearly gone. About this time a heart complication set in, and, next, his lungs began to fill with fluid, his body protestant, but collapsing. The faith healer was summoned briefly, but could do no good and soon a doctor came and administered what help he could. It was quiet usually, except for brief whispers, discussions held by the women of the family, conferences in which Stanley's fate falsely seemed to hang.

But they could not forestall his dying, and, in the middle of one night, Stanley finally succumbed. All the family were gathered around his bedside, and he had asked that I be there too. I had expected a dying person to cling to the living, and I supposed that my grandmother would be holding his hand. But he did not seem to need this contact any more, as though the hardest part was the admission and the rest was easy. He lay in bed, a shriveled figure, the sheet sharply angled where his bones jutted out, his skin pulled taut across his face so that the underlying structure seemed to threaten imminent penetration, he alone seeming to possess a final, triumphant attitude. I was aware of the pitiful immaturity on the part of the rest of us, as though we do not see clearly until it is too late for it be of value to us. As Aunt Edwina stifled a cry, I went to my mother, took her hand, and led her out of the room.

After that, the closed circle of unreality that my grandmother and her sister had drawn was no longer intact. Stanley was buried, and the house settled back into its former existence, the daily ritual of living that was held before Stanley came, endless little routines presupposing a security that was not there. For there was a change: my grandmother was no longer domineering and she seemed like a faded shadow walking through the maze of furniture in the house; Edwina devoted herself to the preparation of meals and became sharply irritable with me if I tried to talk with her, until finally, always on the verge of too much introspection, she quietly became senile. My mother alone seemed to have profited from the experience, for she took me away to the East, sub-sequently sending me to college there, and we returned only once, briefly, for a Christmas visit. I can still remember how small and pinched the house seemed to me, and, when I went to inspect the plants that had once sulked in the gloomy corners of the house, I saw they were dead, that they had withered until they were only yellow husks in dusty earth.

Randall Reid was born in Paso Robles, California, in 1931. He received his A.B. from San Francisco State College and his M.A. and Ph.D. from Stanford University. He has taught at San Diego State College and the University of Chicago. Mr. Reid is currently Director and Dean of Deep Springs College in California and is working on a novel, a collection of shorter pieces (of which "Detritus" is one), and a critical work which focuses on Melville's *Pierre* and Fitzgerald's *Tender Is the Night*.

DETRITUS

I suppose I'm bored. That is an affectation, of course. And as a way to begin it is as banal as *Once upon a time*. But it doesn't matter, I don't aspire to novelty. Just memory and malice. And vanity. Portrait of a man alone with a mirror, making faces in the glass.

What next?

Wives are the best. Their purity has already gone to market, and they need not guard it anymore.

"But my husband, my children, my responsibilities—"

"You are too good for all that."

Secretly, at least, she will of course agree. And security palls. You appeal to her sense of freedom, her desire to be rid of it all. A little flattery, a little wicked titillation, and then the unanswerable question: "Why not?"

Well, why not?

•

Stopped for cigarettes at a newsstand and found myself staring at a magazine nude tacked to the wall. Another commodity. They have rouged and retouched her skin until it looks made of orange fudge. Enticing, of course—and her breasts are magnificent, or at least huge. But her groin is just another armpit, shaven and scented and sexless. Our modern mermaid, the girl with no way in. All her cleavage is above the belt.

I gathered my change. Her nipples watched me like fleshy pink eyes, her eyes saw nothing but the camera.

•

P.M.: Philip was here, talking of betrayal and heedlessness in his tormented voice. I tried to calm him. Useless. He is right, of course, but it doesn't matter.

•

I fell in love with Laura because her shoes did not fit. They made her totter when she walked, and her huge round eyes had a terror in them, as if she were always about to fall. It was comic in its way. There she was, with arms like thighs and breasts the size of cabbages. She could have given birth to an army and scarcely felt the pain. Yet she reminded me of a child. I pitied her, I wanted to touch her and tell her not to be afraid of the dark.

My sympathy made her cry. And tears made her helpless. She thought it very good of me to console her, in my way.

Treat a big woman as if she were very frail. Usually she is.

•

When Harriet left, I lived with two girls named Anne and Suzanne whom I fucked endlessly, separately and together, until they became for me a composite body with mouths everywhere, and too many nipples, and soft, superfluous thighs. They proposed a "real" orgy. I should do everything possible to each of them, and they would do everything to each other, and we would all watch. We did. And it excited me, even profoundly excited me. All those tongues and thighs and breasts, endlessly duplicated by the mirrors and our eyes. But at last something seemed to get stuck. Images repeated themselves: mouths sucking, hands grasping, orifices being plugged. It went on and on, like some dreadful labor we were condemned eternally to perform.

The next day I received a letter with an invitation—an old

friend had purchased a house with forty acres of woods and meadow. I went into the country for the sake of my health and the good of my soul.

Curiously enough, it worked. My senses blossomed, I discovered smells that were not recognizably female—oak leaves, hot dust at the edge of the road, the sweet, boggy smell of horses and meadow grass. Very trite, of course, but very pleasant. And my friend turned out better than I expected. The years had worn away his illusions without damaging his heart; he was that rare creature, a nice man who was not a fool. It pleased me to pat his dogs, admire his view, compliment his wife. I even acquired a remote and sentimental love for his daughter, home from her first year at college. She was such a little thing. Her clear gray eyes grew wide whenever you spoke to her, and she smelled as clean and pink as a new eraser. I felt strangely protective; it was a pleasure not to touch her, to leave her fragile and intact beside me.

We rode together sometimes, or drove into town for the papers and stopped for a picnic on the way home. Once we found a quiet place near the river, a grove of trees where a path led down to a pasture and a little spring. The day was still, hot. We ate our sandwiches in the shade and shared our silence. I had a pleasant regret to nurse, born of my approaching departure. Later, she wandered down to the spring and I went back to the car for cigarettes. I returned to find her stretched naked on a beach towel, asleep. There was no breeze, only the pure and soundless heat; her firm young buttocks glowed in the sun. I touched her, and her lips came apart. She whispered something I could not hear. But her arms reached for me, and we rolled together on the grass. Again and again, until the sweat stung my eyes. At last she slept, while I sat dazed and trembling in the sun.

That was ecstasy, if you like. Of course the sequel was not so pretty—tears, confessions, my friend compelled to act the outraged father, but too aware of his comic position and too confused in his outrage to be impressive. Instead of indignation, it produced only confused shame, as if we had all dirtied ourselves publicly. I left amid mutually averted eyes.

I saw Shriver today. He looked dried up, made of dandruff and parchment. Still very dapper, of course, but his eyes are fever-ridden. Those spiderish lusts of his. He loves delirium, fantasy, orgy—in his dreams, convent girls squirm in perpetual coition with monks and Great Danes.

I despise all voyeurs of the forbidden.

And the gourmet of handsome flesh, too. You know the type; he is found wherever luxury can be purchased—a fat, balding man with the mouth of a carp. To him, the flesh of young girls is a sensuous pleasure, like cigars and vintage wines, and a material solace, like money.

I am a seducer, not a satanist. A semiretired roué.

•

Dreams again, that drastic vaporous light. The sea is made of glass and the beach is patrolled by aging fairies with orange hair and purplish tans.

•

I seem to have settled at last. Here, on my unfashionable hill, with a view of freeway loops and a glimpse of the bridge, I sit like some bit of debris beached by the tide.

I do no work, but I have an income—now, like other things, rather drastically reduced. My career? Thirty years a lover—until one night I humped MacGregor's wife on a borrowed bed, and caught a chill.

Blue veins and congealed fat. Pubic hair like dead moss. And an awful, sourceless cold like an emanation. The sheets smelled of it—snot-cold, fog-cold. She tried so hard to feel some pleasure. And I pumped and stared at that flat face, stupid with effort, until the spasm came. Then nothing. A seeping cold that made me shiver in her arms. She cried a little. When I withdrew, I saw it hanging there, weak and cold and small, like a shriveled teat. And the cold has proved ineradicable.

But I see a question quivering on your tongue.

"Are you still . . . I mean, can you?"

The answer, madam, is yes—yes to the question as you meant

it, though perhaps I should say no. When the moment of revelation came, I was not visited by a penitential impotence. No, the machinery still works, obeying some law of its own. It works in spite of me. My orgasm is like a gun going off in another room; I scarcely hear the report.

●

Banal idea: Every desire breeds its opposite. To love is to hate, to hate is to love, ambivalence is the law of life, et cetera. And it doesn't stop there. Pleasure calls for pain. To desire success is to lust after failure. If freedom lures us, so does slavery—not just also, but *because:* desiring freedom makes us desire slavery. Hence vacillation, frustration, despair. A man cannot act without betraying a part of himself.

Antitheses are like sexes that blindly seek to couple and complete themselves—the secret love of vice for virtue and of virtue for vice.

●

Mara was not pretty, but she had a certain sluttish elegance. Her shoulders were always bare and round and buttery soft, cut by two little straps. When she bent down, her breasts would spill like water over the top of her dress.

Those were the days when every girl had a mouth like a whore's. Lipstick so red and thick you could see it shine. She had a whore's laugh, too. I hated her laugh.

It excited me.

●

I was a pale and delicate child. My school picture would amuse you—I sit like a little seraph amidst the grosser substance of my classmates. Beware the delicate child. Beware anyone who wears his sensitivity like a suit of clothes.

●

Women should always dress so that they can be gracefully undressed. The process, not the mere result of nakedness, is what matters; it is an art to be performed and prolonged.

And suspense is its soul. To be almost seduced, with the final act imminent but still unperformed, is to be deliciously helpless with anticipation. So I always let the final garment stay for a moment. I kiss her throat and breasts, brush my lips against the muscles of her spine, until at last my hands slide beneath the elastic and begin to draw her panties down. But slowly, slowly, so that she feels herself being exposed. Voluptuous sensation! The gliding silk against her skin, my eyes and hands caressing her—even the air whispers her nakedness. A little hesitation to savor it. Then down, all the way down, and that lovely mound is revealed, so warm and swollen, so exquisitely wet with her surrender.

And so it goes. Memories, little pictures from the past. Sometimes only the nerves remember. Whoever she was, she remains nameless. I am aware only of her freckled shoulders, the special flavor of her mouth.

They seem to be increasing, these phantoms of the senses. And all mixed up with the women are smells of forgotten rooms, the taste of some breakfast food I had as a child. Symptomatic, I suppose, the efflorescence of decay.

•

Things wear out, but not quite. Something is left, something meaningless, but sufficient. I am quite safe.

•

Philip accused me of his mother's death. She is dead, I said, what does it matter? Take the guilt if you want it, mine or hers. And of course he has. You can see death in him. He has that terrible bodiless rage—white face, pinched nostrils, a screaming horror in the voice. It is a convulsion of the nerves, with no flesh or bone to sustain it.

•

In one of those treacherously serene states which follows a debauch, I found myself paired at a dinner party with a girl who said she knew of me through friends. She was small, very plain, past thirty—one of those colorless little virgins who can be found aging in every library, every school. She bored me, but I didn't mind. In such a mood, to be bored seems virtuous, both charitable and ascetic. Some whim of gallantry even made me offer to see her home.

Whatever we talked about, it must have charmed her. She invited me in for coffee. I was inattentive; caresses were a reflex, and so were words.

But not for her. Soon she was half-undressed and quivering beneath me on the couch.

Her eyes were so helpless. I felt a qualm, or something, and I did a strange thing—I stopped. A pretty scene. There she was, with her skirt up and her dignity down, and I began to talk. I moralized, apologized, stalled. And every moment her bare loins grew more ugly in my eyes and in hers. The moment prolonged itself unbearably. She could not move, could not even cover herself. She just shriveled up until there was not enough left of her to cry.

There was destruction for you, admirably thorough. I leave it to those who have a taste for it.

•

I am troubled by dreams. Amuse yourselves with this one. A woman with no mouth and huge breasts—mottled, sausage-colored breasts. Often I squeeze them, they pop like boils.

•

Conventional bric-a-brac. Roués exude triteness, even in their dreams.

•

"But don't you really believe a married woman should be chaste?"

"No." My denial was as abrupt and titillating as a slap in the face. She found it irresistible.

Radical ideas induce tumescence of the brain.

•

I write by fits and starts, flirting with subjects as promiscuously as if they were women.

Scriptus interruptus.

•

Women are attractive only when they are frightened or aroused. Left to themselves, they run to teacups and little hats and fat—not woman fat, but steer fat: sluggish, neutered flesh. One torments them out of love and pity; one cannot bear to see them be so dull.

•

Carolyn was rich. And cultured and passionate and sensitive— one of those women whose appetites are insatiable but exquisitely refined. We had to make love to Mozart, or watch the evening darken while a flute sang in another room. Very pure it was, and very pretty, and it made me ill.

I despise serious music; it is ashamed to let its vulgarity show. Give me drums that pound and saxophones that wallow in their own ooze. Or moonlight and sweet dreams—lies too old and artless to conceal the truth.

•

The truth, indeed, as if I could tell it.

I try to speak, but my tongue misquotes me, my hands gesture blandly of themselves. I have the mannerisms of a veteran sales- man or a veteran whore.

•

Rain today, cold and damp. I sit and watch the blue flames of my stove, huddled close, with memories wrapped like a shawl around me.

And I have been rereading what I have written. I do not like it; it smells as withered and faintly rotten as an old apple. It is false, too; memories are only retrospective fantasies, not to be trusted. And why tell them? To write one's memoirs is only a complicated form of self-abuse.

I have begun to leak aphorisms. Onanism and morality. In his old age, Don Juan becomes just another sententiously nasty old man.

My dotage: I shall acquire kidney stones and prostate trouble, affect a cane and wear a flower in my lapel. Perhaps I shall even find a wife—a middle-aged practical nurse who believes in laxatives and the power of prayer, or one of those dowagers whose bosoms emit little geysers of lavender scent at every breath.

No, those dowagers no longer exist. Grandma wears stretch pants and rubber breasts and an orange wig.

●

An aphorism on aphorisms: they are the mark of a promiscuous mind. An aphorist avoids philosophy as a roué avoids marriage; he is afraid to commit himself.

●

Certain lies speak to us more powerfully than any truth. Therefore they are the truth. About us.

●

I became a seducer because I could not bear to lie. So flattery, betrayal, the violation of all my anguished candor. On principle. Like the gratuitous cruelty of the tenderhearted, with the vicious little pleasure such a violation always brings.

. . . Another lie.

●

Now every magazine has its flawless nudes. They are worse than travel posters, those assertions of ideal flesh. Like visions of Rhine valleys and castles and happy picturesque folk. Somewhere that never was.

It isn't just the magazines. Ideals are nasty things no matter where they come from. All that dirty Greek marble—petrified daydreams, the destroyers of life.

●

That little white-haired man was in the papers again, still cackling out pronouncements at ninety. He is a living reproach, I suppose. Rationality, the strenuous pleasures of the mind, *mens sana in corpore sano,* the public self—one of those who strut around in the light of reason like sun-worshipers at a beach.

Well, reason *is* a light. And like any light it blinds while it illuminates. Stay in the sun too long and you can't see in the dark at all.

•

You cannot make love with your eyes; close them. Our loves should be as private as our dreams.

•

I could feel her presence beside me in the bus. A curious intimacy: the night heavy with sleep and motion, two strangers traveling together in the dark. I knew nothing about her except the smell of her hair and skin, the texture of her dress, the whisper of her stockings as she crossed her legs. And I wanted her. The aura which enclosed us was as palpable as any touch.

We romanticize our urgency and make it the measure of our desire, and that is nonsense. I have never been less urgent, and I have never desired anyone more. The soft pressure of her thigh stirred me. I wanted to touch it—not possess it or violate it, just touch it—the way one touches animals or smooth stones.

She accepted a cigarette. Her hand touched mine, and in the flaring match I saw her eyes and knew. So we spoke, kissed. Whispering a little, we made what love we could.

As we neared San Francisco, the lights came on and we were confronted by the absurdity of other people. She withdrew, straightening her skirt. I put my lips against her ear. "Get off with me," I said. "Here."

She nodded at last, not looking at me. "I must make a call."

The depot was full of that peculiar smell that public places have—rest rooms, buses, lunch counters—a smell composed of too many strangenesses mingled and cancelled.

She made her call and we found a room two blocks from Market. The fading prints of elastic at her waist and thighs were like the marks left by fetters. I smoothed them with my lips.

And then for once I forgot myself and her, and made nothing but love. The dark was full of it.

I woke at noon and found her curled in sleep against me. Against my chest, the faint suspiration of her breath—a rhythm I could enter. My thrust was as deep and slow and effortless as her sleep.

In that long tranquillity of desire, there is ease, not frenzy—a perfect closeness in which sensations flow back and forth like tides.

Then sleep again. At last I dressed, went down to the cafeteria on the corner, and brought back coffee in lidded paper cups.

She had put on my discarded shirt and was sitting up in bed. The shirt queerly accented her femininity. In that mannish collar, her neck looked frail and bare, and the dark circles of her nipples showed against the cloth. We sipped the coffee and did not talk. Outside: streetcar bells, traffic, the vague noises of the street. They were better than bird songs.

Soon it was time. I watched her resume the constrictions of bra and girdle, bend to the mirror and redraw her mask. When she had gathered herself about her, she touched my lips and eyes and disappeared. Where? To the depot, I suppose, and another bus, something which would carry her back to whatever she had left.

The ring she wore proclaimed that she was married. And there were signs of children—faint stretch marks on the abdomen, nipples that looked as if they had given suck. But I did not ask. We shared an intimacy that only the anonymous can ever know. Without identities, we could be ourselves.

•

I have spoiled it. It smells of my aphoristic smut. Yet I remember that time with pleasure, and there are not many such times.

Real abandonment is rare. Our selves, our moralities, our constraints seldom slip away. Instead, we nerve ourselves to violate them, and the result is hysteria, not release.

It is like sleep, the ability to slip quietly into another self and be restored. But few can do it. Most are like insomniacs, our waking dead. I have heard them cry out in their pleasure as they cry out in their sleep.

•

Never mind all that. What about the smut?

Excuse me, I have neglected a duty. Certain things are expected when a roué tells all.

Anatomical secrets: Chinese girls are crosswise. If niggers don't get it twice a day, their glands swell up and they go crazy. I knew a girl in New Jersey who could pick up pennies with her pussy.

Novelty: French ticklers. The sixty-nine secret positions of a Tibetan goatherd. Do it under water if you really want a thrill.

Satisfied?

No, tell me more.

They are all lies. All the novelty there is lurks hidden in the familiar gesture, the customary act.

Novelty is a pimp's invention, a fraud.

Forbidden glimpses. Dreams. They are made for the solitary one, the little masturbator in his soiled sheets. Alone, with flushed cheeks and furtive hand, he pursues his phantoms: black stockings, the pale gleam of flesh swollen around a garter; a nighttime world where nipples glow and wink like neon lights. His pleasure ends in the smell of his own semen, cold as snot against the skin.

And what about you, buddy? You and the wife read any good dirty books lately? The bedside shelf, Marriage Manuals and Erotic Classics. How-to-do-it books. Before long, someone will be selling blueprints for orgies, and the guests can fit themselves together like prefabricated pieces in the latest erector set.

•

Philip again, looking worse. A hemophiliac, he is forced quite literally to live on the blood of others, and he would rather die. So he wears that look of ghastly suffering, like a vampire Christ.

•

Pills seem to stick in the throat even after swallowing. They
have a taste, too, no matter what they're made of. Bitter, chalky
things. They made me take them every morning as a child.

Enemas, syringes, syrups, pills. The smell of rubber sheets and
vaseline. All those implements they use. Cold, passionless fingers
that probe into you, proud of their indifference. There is no
violation worse than that impersonal touch.

●

They told me witches were not real, but I knew they were; I
had seen them. I had seen Hansel, too, and Gretel, and that
sweet hideous house. It tasted like the candy flowers on birthday
cakes. . . .

Hand in hand the lost boy and girl stand together in the darkness. The house lures them, frightens them. It is forbidden, they
know, all sweetness is. They taste, and the vision of sweetness turns to stale confectionary sugar on the tongue. And then
the witch's voice, with its unspeakable invitation.

●

On the day before my seventh birthday, I found a mouse fresh
caught in a trap. It was squeezed flat in the middle, like a pinched
sack full of something soft, but it was still alive. And it would not
die. The mouth gaped and closed, gaped and closed, until I
screamed and old Maria came and smashed its head with a
bookend.

Then she dried my tears. "You are a very tenderhearted boy,"
she said. "But why don't you ever cry for yourself?"

●

My first love was the sun-warmed trunk of a dead eucalyptus
tree. It lay in a tangle of morning glories and mallow weeds
behind the garage—a narrow, forgotten place where no one ever
went. I used to crawl in there and lie hidden in the sun. Hidden
and naked. I liked to stretch on my belly, feeling the sun on
my back and the warm smooth wood against my loins. And I

would begin to rock, gently. I thought of nothing—only the warmth and the smell of weeds and hot tar paper roofs, and the pleasure of my secret flesh.

I never told anyone and no one ever found me, so I felt no shame.

When I was nine, she came to live in the duplex on the corner. Her name was Lucille, though I never called her that. I never spoke her name, except to myself. She was young, married but still childless, a thin girl with pale cheeks and long white hands. She let me sit in her kitchen and talk to her while she worked. Her white hands looked cool and soft, and when she bent over me, I could see the little shadow between her breasts. I wanted to put my lips there.

I was teased, of course—by parents and playmates. But it did not matter. Each evening I watched her come out on the step to greet her husband, lifting her lips and her pale hands to his face. A beautiful gesture. If I was jealous, I do not remember it. I simply wanted her; it did not occur to me to want her all to myself.

She kissed me once, laughing, while I stood like a stricken fool beneath the Christmas mistletoe. I could only look at her until she saw my eyes and something in them made her laughter stop.

And then she was gone. They moved away and had a baby and I did not see her again.

•

Childhood memories are all lies. We condescend to them, we posture, we affect to be amused, we formulate official autobiographies which we tell ourselves and others—and all to forget the wounds that never heal. We cannot forgive ourselves for having suffered; it is a weakness and we despise it. We like to pretend that the child grew up.

•

Recess. A numbed girl with pimples and breasts sleepwalks through the corridors. Her eyes, behind the rimless glasses, are watery and pale, and her flesh tries to shrink up and conceal itself within her clothes. Whispers buzz like flies around her. Jackal laughter—all the bastards snicker and rub themselves through their pants.

●

It was her husband's idea, the portrait. He was young and rather stupid, therefore impressed by me. I knew books, could sketch a little—a man of many talents, all of them small.

But my pencil lied as easily as my tongue, so the portrait pleased her. I suggested a nude. She blushed, looked vaguely frightened. No, she couldn't do that.

"But you have a lovely body."

We settled on another portrait, this time in oils. She would sit for it in my apartment where the light was right.

And all the time she sat I talked quite shamelessly about myself and women, sometimes adding praises of her eyes and the voluptuous curve of her neck. She was fascinated, of course. To a virtuous woman, nothing is more exciting than the attentions of a roué.

I asked her to sleep with me, and she refused. A day or two later, I asked again. No. When I took her in my arms and kissed her hair and eyes, she trembled, went rigid, then broke away. Her speech was what you might expect. She said I had made her trust me and tried to take advantage of it. She said she loved her husband. She was not the sort. I had no right.

I agreed, apologized, and promised not to bother her again. Her disappointment was visible. Within a few days she called me and virtually begged me to resume my siege. And I did, with predictable results—despite her tears, fears, and equivocations.

But why laugh? She wanted intensely to remain chaste and she wanted intensely to succumb. What was she to do? The little drama I had launched was very exciting—it aroused both of her desires—but dramas, like syllogisms, require conclusions. There must be a final act.

And then what? The drama is over, but life isn't. One must

somehow fabricate another play, one in which there is something precious to be lost, something alluring to be gained. . . .

•

A curious point. Have you ever noticed that a seducer always ends his triumph by intimating that it wasn't a triumph at all? All he did was offer a pretext; his victim, he suggests, was really dying to fall.

The rapist: I made her do what I wanted her to.

The seducer: I made her do what *she* wanted to.

A true gentleman, the rapist exonerates the lady and takes full responsibility for his act. Not exactly. There is sovereign contempt in him, but no courtesy. He would no more grant her the right to say yes than to say no. He is the conqueror, the violator, the bloody lord.

The seducer, however, persuades the lady to violate herself.

The bully versus the cad, eternal opposites. They were all together in the Garden: the lordly rapist, the seductive serpent, the woman—and Adam, your eternal husband, placid, steady, dull, cheated.

It was Paradise, ruled by the inventor and sole proprietor, Old Omnipotence himself. Adam and Eve were his prize serfs. They didn't know they were naked, but God did. His little joke. Made for his pleasure, they were as innocent as animals, and as easily used.

But Paradise can never last, even for God. The serpent coils and waits. He has already had his encounter with Omnipotence— and is its victim, doomed and knowing it, a weakling who cannot fight but will not fawn. God, the lordly bully, strides the Garden as if it were a manor or a playground. Adam tugs his forelock, Eve spreads her thighs obediently at God's approach.

The serpent feels the tremor of those heavy boots. Sounds reach him: Eve's little shudder, the smack of flesh on flesh, that dreadful thrust. At last the lordly one is done. Sated, he rises and buttons his pants, while she lies disregarded in the dust.

The footsteps fade. In the streaming sun, she lies dazed and helpless, soiled. The serpent glides nearer. Her eyes wound him. He too has known what it means to squirm for God.

Goddess, he calls her, immortal beauty, adored by all creation. He positively seethes with desire—and with love, that unclean thing, born of his wounds. Caressing her, he takes pity upon himself.

Eve feels his words like a touch. His eyes, too, and the radiance of that supple insinuating form, so perilously erect.

In all those glittering scales, the same image is reflected, clothed in opalescent shimmers and nothing else. She has always been beautiful, but now she knows it. She is inflamed with visions: her mouth, her pomegranate breasts, her soft, dissolving thighs. Surrender is triumph, the consummation of herself.

So in exquisite apprehension she reaches for the apple.

The usual ecstasy. But as usual it subsides. Forbidden fruit, once eaten, tastes like everything else.

Yet something is ominously different. Though the visions fade, sight doesn't. She is still aware of herself. And the self she sees is not a goddess but a woman, a woman exposed, vulgar and vulgarly betrayed. By what? That limp little thing in the dust, the worm in the apple. It lies there, too spent even to wriggle, with nothing but malice left in its eyes.

And everybody knows. The serpent sees to that. It is his revenge for having betrayed himself to Eve. The final humiliation is his—the moment when she understands his impotence, that having seduced her he doesn't know what to do with her now.

Now she must endure Adam's stupid tears. And God isn't even jealous. He simply discards her—a trivial plaything that someone else has soiled.

She is no longer pretty. Her face is dull and her body feels heavy and unclean. She spends her days in hating—herself, the serpent for what he has done to her, Adam for what she has done to him. It is of course the rapist she really desires. If only God cared a little, or if only Adam would stand up to God.

But God doesn't want her. And Adam will submit to anything—his God, his fate, his wife. Numb shock followed by helpless self-pity—that is his only response. Then stupid submission, ac-

ceptance. Even of her beauty. He does not understand it, just as
he does not understand the motive for her shame. To live with
him, she must become as dull as he is, breeding and suffering with
stupid equanimity. That is her final lot. After violation and
betrayal, she must mutilate herself. She performs it. She lets
everything go—her looks, her desires, her dreams. She becomes
at last Adam's wife.

A happy ending, as stories go.

Ladies, I give you your choice: the rapist, the seducer, or the
eternal husband? That's all there is, in or out of Eden.

•

And where did he come from, that poor fool on the cross? He
was the serpent's brother, a younger son.

•

Philip on crutches, flanked by his fiancée, her eyes aglow with
the trivial fanaticism of sacrifice. A lovely pair.

But it didn't work. I could see hatred growing in him, and she,
sweet stupid girl, she didn't understand. She tried to be even more
devoted. He called her a smothering bitch and left her crying in
my rooms.

"But I love him. What can I do?"

"Get sick," I said. "Go blind or lose a leg. Let him immolate
himself for you."

She didn't, of course. And so it ended, as it should. We want
no heirs.

•

At Bilstein's house, I turned from the bar and saw Harriet
looking at me. Her eyes glazed quickly, but it was too late, I had
seen. I crossed the room like a man walking toward a cliff. And
I asked her to dance. While our bodies touched, we did not have
to look at each other.

I have always been afraid of eyes. They ask too much, betray
too much. They embarrass me like the nakedness of a woman I
do not desire. But there are moments, of course. Eyes look at us,

and we glimpse something incurable in them, something which is also incurable in us.

●

If I could have met her in the night, always in the night, with no face to look at, no face of my own to be seen.

This arranging of faces, this smoothing of hair, this conversation at breakfast when every word makes it more impossible to talk. We soon despise each other.

●

In the twilight of that summer, Harriet sits in the porch swing, watching the sky fade and darken. Her bare legs glow in a patch of light. They are classic legs: full thighs, long slender calves, thin ankles with the bone white against the skin. But now they are marred with dark sores, mosquito bites which she scratches until the blood comes, then scratches again, tearing at the scabs that form.

●

Harriet betrayed me and lied about it. And I understood why she betrayed me and why she lied.

Definition of a pervert: the rabbit who empathized with the dog who ate him.

Destroy sympathy. It is a disease. Cruelty and indifference are better.

●

With that tremor of the eyelids, that faint crouch of the body, Harriet seemed always to be trying to shrink, as if every touch were painful. Yet her most disquieting tendency was a total absence of reserve. She would tell anything: her morbidities, fears, humiliations—the time a teacher yelled at her and she wet herself in front of the class. And these same things would make her writhe in anguish. So she fascinated the vulgar souls, those who were flattered or titillated by so much intimacy. But it was not trust and it was not perverse self-advertisement. For her, confession was a desperate strategy. She reminded me of those sea creatures who eviscerate themselves when threatened, leaving their guts to fascinate the pursuer while they escape and grow new ones.

•

We had beer and cold crab and tacos, and we danced all that afternoon. Something came alive in her eyes, something I had not seen before. She arched her back and stuck her butt out in a proud little strut; her skirt whipped and swirled about her thighs. While the song sustained her, she was not afraid of anything, even herself.

•

Stillbirth: ominously appropriate. The next day I found her dressed and sitting in the corridor, making perfectly audible comments on the nurses as they passed. Then it stopped; her face went dead as suddenly as if someone had blown out the light. I led her in silence back to her room. No tears—she just sat there, her breasts swollen, the useless milk staining her blouse.

A year later there was Philip.

•

Real love is terrifying, unflattering, ugly. It is a violation. To be loved is to have your nakedness exposed, to the lover's eyes and to your own. Unbearable. To be seduced is to be given a flattering version of yourself, cosmetically clothed and unreal, incapable of being hurt.

•

And now a document:

Dear Joe,

I tried not to write because I knew you'd despise me for begging, and you're right, but here I am.

I want you to come back, Joe. I always knew I'd lose you and now I have, only come back to me please. I did that thing so you'd hate me, because I hated me and you should too. That makes no sense but that's why I did it. When you first came to me, I didn't believe it, it was too good, you made me so happy, and I wouldn't show how I felt because I didn't dare, because if they know how you're happy they know how to hurt you.

So I wrecked it, but please. It's not your fault, but I'm no good alone, I don't know what to do or think and I get frightened. Joe, Joe, I'm so mixed up. This baby, too, it cries and I can't help it. I'm no good at loving, I never was.

Oh God, Joe. I'll be whatever you want if you want me. Please come.

Harriet

●

Perhaps betrayal is the most intimate of all acts, the one in which complicity is most secret and most shared.

●

She stands brushing her hair while I lie in bed beside her. Her face is averted, her bare thighs an inch or two from my lips. And all the curving lines of belly and thigh converge on that little mound, there where her flesh opens in folds as smooth and intricate as the involutions of a shell.

I am married to that, even now.

I do not believe in divorce. I do not believe it is possible.

●

The fire began in her apartment they said. A careless cigarette, probably—something which smouldered in the couch and then burst and ran up the walls. It happened in the middle of the day and she was home, but she gave no alarm. When someone above noticed the smoke, the stairway was already in flames.

They said she must have been drunk or doped, but I know she wasn't. She was just afraid—afraid to sound the alarm because they would know the fire was her fault and blame her. It was easier to die.

So she burned. And so did the others who lived in that house—

a widow, a retired couple, three children who were home alone
because their mother worked.

She lived alone, said the newspapers. Her one child, Philip,
had resided with his grandmother in San Jose since the separation
of his parents.

•

My son who looks like a ghoul, who bleeds if you touch him.

•

And so it happens. A new love—as sudden as an apparition.
My neighbor, she says, she had "noticed" me before. Perhaps
"recognized" says it better. And whatever the signs were, they
must have been unmistakable. They brought her to my door,
with perfect confidence, at two in the afternoon.

She has all the equipment of youth—firm breasts, firm thighs,
a blue-white milky skin. But her eyes are the color of a bruise,
her mouth limp and stretched like old elastic.

Please God, her name is Sharon.

•

I don't want her. I didn't want any of them. I wanted to be
alone and quiet, and I never was.

•

Love affairs: a dismally expressive phrase, self-cancelling.
Words soon couple and exhaust themselves. Caresses turn into
gestures. Whatever it was becomes a charade, a game, a dance.

And the alternatives? Hysteria or habit. Blow your mind, as
they say—and a lovely saying it is: cerebral self-fellatio, the
beatific transport of the young. Or take the sanative fucking of
the decently married, who void their lusts as they void their stools.
Or take nothing at all.

I am tired of it. The flavor of lies and cleverness, epigrams.

•

My little Sharon again, as regular as any fate. But why? She
does not talk. If irritation makes me speak, she smiles and

murmurs something. When I mention my age, she says she prefers an older man.

She has a peculiar voice. It is echoless, unresonantly empty.

•

Now Sharon comes every day and fixes lunch. Her own idea. She is very efficient, too, even garnishing the plates with little sprays of carrot curl and parsley.

When the meal is done, she sits beside me. The afternoon wanes. There being nothing else to do, I pull down the blinds and we lie together on my couch. Her thighs part with the ease of many accommodations, her mouth releases little pleasure sounds. Yet even then that mild, dead voice never quickens. It is vibrationless, spent.

And that is our love. Perhaps we shall marry. She could accommodate herself to that.

•

Sat in the park among the pigeon-feeders. As usual, I watched the women—mothers, mostly, out with the tots for an airing. In front of me, a dark-haired girl with a blurred mouth lay dozing on the grass. She had that slack, stupid look. But her skirt twisted as she rolled over, and I saw plump white thighs, a curve of buttocks swelling out of her panties. It made me hot and faint. Walking home, I was actually trembling with desire, but when Sharon came, it vanished, and I was cold again.

•

A.M.: Dreamed about the woman in the park.

•

Went to see Philip at the County Hospital. He has been there a week, it seems, but I was not informed until today. Acute internal hemorrhages, prognosis reserved.

I have my own prognosis. His face has begun to collapse, and his arms have great yellow-green bruises from intravenous feeding. There was nothing to say. He lay in that ward and stared at me as if I were part of the wall.

I decided to walk back. The morning was appropriately gray, cold, and oppressive. Coming up the hill, I crossed the street to avoid a little tableau—a man and woman in sullen confrontation against the wall. He held her wrist in one hand and had the other raised as if to strike her, but he never did. Perhaps he enjoyed the suspense of that threatening hand. He cursed her, too, methodically. She stood with her head down, limp, as if she did not care enough even to cringe. A trivial scene. But as I passed, I felt a novel chill. It looked like Sharon.

Was it? I don't know. If it was, she did not see me, and I did not look back. Let secrets remain secrets. I don't want to know them.

●

Can one graph a recurring point in all the spiral wanderings of the self? Perhaps. And that recurring point, of course, would be the stake to which one is tethered, and one's spiritual voyages then would be the futile dashes and retreats of a dog on a chain.

I do not know what a recurring zero is, but I like the taste of the phrase. It is descriptive.

●

Sharon was here. She was as willing as ever, but afterwards, as she stooped and washed herself, she looked at me with her clotted eyes. "It's not much fun," she said. "Is it?"

●

At Grencher's party, we all stood around in the den, surveying our host's collection of trivial pornography. Someone gave me a little peep show telescope and told me to look into it. They said I would see something very special, and I did. I saw my own eye, hideously distorted and magnified by the mirror in the tube. It stared back at me, fat, with a fried-egg look, obscene. My face betrayed something, I suppose—enough to detonate their laughter. I excused myself and went outside to be sick on my host's lawn.

●

There is a child in the yard next door—a pale child with pale hair and bloated flesh. His eyes look like bits of celluloid left too long in the sun.

●

Philip falling on the steps, cutting his chin. He bled like some dreadful fountain.

●

Every animal suffers, we are told, the post-coital blues. But what about that peculiar desolation and resentment, that sense of irrelevance? We don't like to admit it. Instead, we claim the weariness of too much bliss. And we graceful lovers cover our retreat with kisses and endearments, withdrawal poetry. We lie our way out as we lie our way in.

I know all about exhaustion, the sag of spirits with the flesh, and I say it doesn't matter. The point is: something is not exhausted, something has been tricked.

Ladies, after all our ecstasies, I have but one honest thing to say: "I'm sorry. That isn't what I meant."

●

A.M.: Services for Philip.

●

Fog now, many days of fog. You can smell it in the curtains and the rug. I have not seen Sharon for more than a week. I should inquire, I suppose, but I prefer not to know where she has gone. I am alone again, and that is enough—an old man, a liar still, with no self but my own to betray.

MAGAZINES CONSULTED

Ann Arbor Review—115 Allen Drive, Ann Arbor, Mich. 48103
Antaeus—G.P.O. 3121, New York, N.Y. 10001
Antioch Review—212 Xenia Avenue, Yellow Springs, Ohio 45387
Aphra—Box 3551, Springtown, Pa. 18081
Ararat—Armenian General Benevolent Union of America, 109
    East 40th Street, New York, N.Y. 10016
Arizona Quarterly—University of Arizona, Tucson, Ariz. 85721
The Atlantic Monthly—8 Arlington Street, Boston, Mass. 02116
Audience—241½ 32nd St., New York, N.Y. 10016
Ave Maria—National Catholic Weekly, Congregation of Holy
    Cross, Notre Dame, Ind. 46556
Black Review—William Morrow & Co., Inc., 105 Madison Ave-
    nue, New York, N.Y. 10016
The Canadian Fiction Magazine—4248 Weisbrod Street, Prince
    George, B.C.
Carleton Miscellany—Carleton College, Northfield, Minn. 55057
Carolina Quarterly—Box 1117, Chapel Hill, N.C. 27515
Chelsea—Box 242, Old Chelsea Station, New York, N.Y. 10011
Chicago Review—University of Chicago, Chicago, Ill. 60637
Colorado Quarterly—Hellums 118, University of Colorado, Boul-
    der, Colo. 80304
The Colorado State Review—360 Liberal Arts, Colorado State
    University, Fort Collins, Colo. 80521
Commentary—165 East 56th Street, New York, N.Y. 10022
Contempora—P. O. Box 673, Atlanta, Georgia 30301
Cosmopolitan—1775 Broadway, New York, N.Y. 10019
December—P. O. Box 274, Western Springs, Ill. 60558
The Denver Quarterly—Denver, Colo. 80210
Descant—Dept. of English, TCU Station, Fort Worth, Tex. 76129
Epoch—159 Goldwin Smith Hall, Cornell University, Ithaca,
    N.Y. 14850
Esprit—University of Scranton, Scranton, Pa. 18510
Esquire—488 Madison Avenue, New York, N.Y. 10022

Event—Douglas College, P. O. Box 2503, New Westminster, B.C.

Evergreen Review—64 University Place, New York, N.Y. 10003

Fantasy and Science Fiction—347 East 53rd Street, New York, N.Y. 10022

Fiction—513 East 13th Street, New York, N.Y. 10009

The Fiddlehead—Dept. of English, Univ. of New Brunswick, Fredericton, N.B., Canada

Forum—Ball State University, Muncie, Ind. 47306

Four Quarters—La Salle College, Philadelphia, Pa. 19141

Generation, the Inter-arts Magazine—University of Michigan, 420 Maynard, Ann Arbor, Mich. 48103

Georgia Review—University of Georgia, Athens, Ga. 30601

Good Housekeeping—959 Eighth Avenue, New York, N.Y. 10019

Green River Review—Box 594, Owensboro, Ky. 43201

The Greensboro Review—University of North Carolina, Greensboro, N.C. 27412

Handsel—P. O. Box 558, Lexington, Ky. 40501

Harper's—2 Park Ave, New York, N.Y. 10016

Hudson Review—65 East 55th Street, New York, N.Y. 10022

Intro—Bantam Books, Inc., 271 Madison Avenue, New York, N.Y. 10016

The Iowa Review—EPB 453, University of Iowa, Iowa City, Iowa 52240

Kansas Quarterly—Dept. of English, Kansas State University, Manhattan, Kans. 66502

Ladies' Home Journal—641 Lexington Avenue, New York, N.Y. 10022

The Laurel Review—West Virginia Wesleyan College, Buckhannon, W. Va. 26201

The Literary Review—Fairleigh Dickinson University, Teaneck, N.J. 07666

The Little Magazine—P. O. Box 207, Cathedral Station, New York, N.Y. 10025

Mademoiselle—420 Lexington Avenue, New York, N.Y. 10022

Malahat Review—University of Victoria, British Columbia, Canada

The Massachusetts Review—University of Massachusetts, Amherst, Mass. 01003

McCall's—230 Park Avenue, New York, N.Y. 10017

The Mediterranean Review—Orient, N.Y. 11957

Midstream—515 Park Avenue, New York, N.Y. 10022

The Minnesota Review—New Rivers Press, P. O. Box 578, Cathedral Station, New York, N.Y. 10025

Mundus Artium—Dept. of English, Ellis Hall, Box 89, Ohio University, Athens, Ohio 45701

New American Review—Simon & Schuster, 630 Fifth Ave., New York, N.Y. 10026

New Letters—University of Missouri-Kansas City, Kansas City, Mo. 64110

The New Mexico Quarterly—University of New Mexico Press, Marron Hall, Albuquerque, N. Mex. 87106

The New Renaissance—9 Heath Road, Arlington, Mass. 02174

The New Yorker—25 West 43rd Street, New York, N.Y. 10036

North American Review—University of Northern Iowa, Cedar Falls, Iowa 50613

Northwest Review—129 French Hall, University of Oregon, Eugene, Ore. 97403

Ohio Review—Ellis Hall, Ohio University, Athens, Ohio 45701

Panache—P. O. Box 89, Princeton, N.J. 08540

The Paris Review—45-39, 171 Place, Flushing, N.Y. 11358

Partisan Review—Rutgers University, New Brunswick, N.J. 08903

Perspective—Washington University, St. Louis, Mo. 63105

Phylon—223 Chestnut Street, S.W., Atlanta, Ga. 30314

Playboy—232 East Ohio Street, Chicago, Ill. 60611

Prairie Schooner—Andrews Hall, University of Nebraska, Lincoln, Nebr. 68508

Prism International—Dept. of Creative Writing, University of British Columbia, Vancouver 8, B.C.

Quarterly Review of Literature—26 Haslet Avenue, Princeton, N.J. 08540

Quartet—186 Ridge Road, Utica, N.Y. 13501

Ramparts—1182 Chestnut Street, Menlo Park, Calif. 94027

Redbook—230 Park Avenue, New York, N.Y. 10017

Red Clay Reader—6366 Sharon Hills Road, Charlotte, N.C. 28210

Seneca Review—Box 115, Hobart & William Smith Colleges, Geneva, N.Y. 14456

Shenandoah—Box 722, Lexington, Va. 24450

The Sewanee Review—University of the South, Sewanee, Tenn. 37375

The South Carolina Review—Dept. of English, Box 28661, Furman University, Greenville, S.C. 29613

The South Dakota Review—Box 111, University Exchange, Vermillion, S.D. 57069

Southern Review—Drawer D, University Station, Baton Rouge, La. 70803

Southwest Review—Southern Methodist University Press, Dallas, Tex. 75222

The Tamarack Review—Box 159, Postal Station K, Toronto, Ontario, Canada

The Texas Quarterly—Box 7527, University of Texas, Austin, Tex. 78712

Transatlantic Review—Box 3348, Grand Central P.O., New York, N.Y. 10017

Tri-Quarterly—University Hall 101, Northwestern University, Evanston, Ill. 60201

Vagabond—P. O. Box 2114, Redwood City, Calif. 94064

The Virginia Quarterly Review—University of Virginia, 1 West Range, Charlottesville, Va. 22903

Vogue—420 Lexington Avenue, New York, N.Y. 10017

Voyages—Box 4862, Washington, D.C. 20008

Washington Square Review—New York University, 737 East Bldg., New York, N.Y. 10003

West Coast Review—Simon Fraser University, Vancouver, B.C.

Western Humanities Review—Bldg. 41, University of Utah, Salt Lake City, Utah 84112

Wind—RFD Route 1, Box 810, Pikeville, Ky. 41501

Woman's Day—67 West 44th Street, New York, N.Y. 10036

Works—A.M.S., 56 East 13th Street, New York, N.Y. 10016

Yale Review—26 Hillhouse Avenue, New Haven, Conn. 06520